Blaze

Blaze

A World of Mirias Novel

ELLEN MULLIGAN

GREEN PLACE BOOKS *Brattleboro, Vermont*

Printed in the United States

10 9 8 7 6 5 4 3 2 1

Green Writers Press is a Vermont-based publisher whose mission
is to spread a message of hope and renewal through the words and
images we publish. Throughout we will adhere to our commitment to
preserving and protecting the natural resources of the earth. To that
end, a percentage of our proceeds will be donated to environmental
activist groups and social justice organizations. Green Writers Press
gratefully acknowledges support from individual donors, friends, and
readers to help support the environment and our publishing initiative.
Green Place Books curates books that tell literary and compelling
stories with a focus on writing about place—these books are more
personal stories, memoir, and biographies.

GREEN
PLACE
BOOKS

GReen
wrʈʈers
press

Giving Voice to Writers & Artists Who Will Make the World a Better Place
Green Writers Press | Brattleboro, Vermont
www.greenwriterspress.com

ISBN: 978-1-950584-82-6
COVER ILLUSTRATION BY THOMAS DREW.

The paper used in this publication is produced by mills committed
to responsible and sustainable forestry practices.

To my parents, Margaret and William, who were more than generous with my carefree childhood where I embraced a lifelong outlet to nurture my overactive imagination.

Blaze

STORYTELLER

I T WAS CLOSE TO MIDAFTERNOON that Skelly arrived to tell his tale. He knew that the men would want to listen even if they didn't admit it openly. "Protection for their wives," they would say. Skelly chuckled. There was always one who had a wife who would more likely be the brute force, but she usually allowed her husband to think the other was true. Through the orb, called a Dragon's Eye, he watched them. The large gathering quietly waited, but with his keen insight into people, he knew they were anxiously waiting for him to arrive and get this show on the road. Skelly smiled, as he wrapped the Dragon's Eye in a Pyrrin silk, protecting the glass from breakage. The show was nothing more than him sitting down with children small and large positioned near his knee as he told stories that he was blessed to receive. He dropped the silken-covered orb in his pouch and headed to the commons.

Skelly wore typical attire for those in Timeria: a woven cloth tunic over breeches, leather boots, and a long cloak that billowed behind him. Upon arriving at the commons, the storyteller noticed a little boy all alone. Skelly reached down and asked him if he cared to hear a story. The boy looked up at the storyteller with wide eyes of wonder and hope. He took the boy's hand and walked him to where the other children sat. The standing adults opened up a path for the storyteller, recognizing him almost immediately from their own youth. He had not changed in all these years; he still held the same gentle smile and ocean-blue eyes that stared out from a tousle of dark-blond curls. He led the boy to the stump that would be his perch while he was in town and guided the boy to sit next to him, trumping the wealthier observers in attendance. Skelly glanced at the boy, his black hair a mass of unkempt snarls and his clothes in desperate need of cleaning. Yet the storyteller treated him as he would any of those in attendance from royalty to commoner. In Skelly's eyes, there was no distinction.

He had come prepared with one of the greatest tales of all. Skelly raised his hands, and those gathered hushed to silence. The storyteller glanced side-to-side and winked at the boy sitting on his feet. The boy wiggled closer, and Skelly inhaled, taking a deep breath before beginning his tale.

"Long ago, a great mage traveled the world. No one knew from whence he came. Perhaps he was born on a moon above or, as some say, the distant western mountains. Yet others call him a gift from the gods, dropped fully formed to aid the peoples of Mirias. And aid the people he did, everywhere he roamed. For in those days, there was much danger and strife. Dragons reigned the air, striking and killing wantonly. No one was safe from their savagery. Until the great mage, Ballard, knocked the terrors from the sky.

"Traveling eastward, Ballard challenged the vilest scourges to combat. One-to-one, two-to-one, three-to-one: none could overcome Ballard's mighty power. Victoriously, he left lands free and secure wherever he passed. But . . . these battles grew tedious and tiresome, even for one so great. Ballard yearned for somewhere to call home, yet none spoke to him. That is until he came to a place of a million lakes, shrouded in mist and wonder.

"Ballard looked with awe at the enchantment before him. In this land, the paths changed as he watched, and time seemed to stop as magic blew on the breeze, both whimsical and great. Intrepidly, Ballard stepped onto the shifting path, trusting his magic to guide him. Long he wandered, seeing deep pools filled with strange creatures that dove below as he drew near. There were glowing, ghostly horses that ran freely within the groves, only to disappear into the mists. Gone in an instant. People dwelled there as well, a peaceful solitary folk who were just as hesitant as the creatures. And yes, even here there were dragons disrupting not only the peace but the very magic of the land. After wandering for many a spring and summer, Ballard emerged on the eastern side in the kingdom of Ceretheena, over which reigned King Malin. The king and people greeted the great Ballard with wonder, for never had any stranger crossed the land of misty springs and lakes. A great feast lasting many days was prepared and Ballard was seated at the right hand of the king. Music and entertainment filled the nights while the days were time for history and lore, and even here, dragons stormed the barrier around the castle, trying to carry away those who sought safety within.

"Ballard fell in love with the land and wished to help the kingdom. This was a place that could be home. So he spoke to the king, offering a magnificent spell the likes of which the world had never seen—he would ban all dragons from the land forever after. Now King Malin, as you may guess, was doubtful that such a spell could exist and made a proposition of his own. 'Master Ballard,' the king said, 'you make a grand offer, but it is no longer within my power to grant you such a boon. This small forest is all that remains of my kingdom. The true power lies to the north. You must convince the greater king, King Essan, who dwells in Venesial castle among the fiefdoms of the North, to accept your proposal. No longer are we the two kingdoms of elven Ceretheena and human Venesialia, but one nation: Timeria. That king wields the true power. Go and seek his counsel.'

"So with the next day's dawning, the great Ballard set off, leaving the misty, magical forests behind him. The way was a mere dirt track stretching northward winding through mundane woodlands and meadows. A day's long ride and the land opened out before him into a great expanse of grassland. Dragons kited on the winds: Red, Green, Stone, Black, and Silver. Suddenly, one would drop down only to rise again with a wild bull or elk grasped in its claws. Ballard watched the aerial ballet, skillfully calming his mount, until the light dimmed as if a storm approached. Yet it was no storm! Death on wing dropped from the sky as a tremendous Red Dragon thundered down, tearing into those above the plain. Dragons screamed in pain and terror under its murderous assault. The stench of blood and death wafted on the wind, leaving carnage in its wake as the Red behemoth arose, soaring westward, trailing blood from its empty talons. Seven dragons lay still on the field. More were ravaged, crying in pain as they tried to drag themselves from the battlefield.

"Why, you may ask, did Ballard watch from afar? If he was so great, why didn't he destroy the dragons as soon as he saw the gathering? Well . . . that is a sign of greatness. Ballard knew that there is a place for all creatures. This was a place without humans or elves where the dragons harmed none but their own kind. Thus, he was right to let them be, and so he continued his journey northward.

"Days and nights passed as the trail meandered through woods and fields. Vast manors and farms lined the way, marking the fiefdoms of the North. The trail became a path and then a busy road. Finally, Ballard arrived before a majestic, soaring palace. Raising his hands, he summoned rolling thunder and iridescent lightning, proclaiming his arrival. Sentries shook in their posts. The commander of the king's royal guard rushed to the main balcony, confronting the mage. 'Wizard,' she demanded, 'what business do you have here? Speak truly or you shall be struck down where you stand!' Ballard bowed and said, 'I have come to propose a great boon to your king.' He tossed a sealed message into the air which glided magically up, dropping into the commander's hands. 'An introduction,' Ballard declared, 'from the Ceretheenian King to his most eminent kinsman,' and he bowed yet again. The commander closely examined the seal, handing it off to someone behind her. The whole courtyard remained frozen as the sun moved across the sky, broken, finally, by the commander ordering the sentries to escort the mage inside.

"Ballard gazed at the opulence of the audience hall, so vast that the enormous, marauding Red Dragon could easily spread his wings without brushing the sides. Above arced the ceiling, like the great dome of a midsummer sky, made of interlocking panels of translucent sapphire with wafer-thin white marble clouds. The floor shimmered in all the greens of a grassy meadow, interspersed with jewel-toned pops of wildflowers. A sapphire and marble path reminiscent of a bubbling stream lead to the raised dais upon which sat the young king on his intricately carved, gilded, honeyberry-wood throne. Ballard strode confidently forward until he stood before the throne. Blue-tinged shadows obscured King Essan's face as he sat as still and frozen as a statue. Ballard stood, waiting, feeling the king's smoldering ire as time crept slowly onward. As the shadows lengthened, the king finally hollered, 'SPEAK.' The one word reverberated through the hall, carrying all the king's power.

"Ballard began: 'Dragons hunt unchecked in the lands where Ceretheena meets Venesialia, as I am sure you know. I witnessed an immense Red Dragon dropped from the sky and slaughtered a multitude of those hunting dragons, many that nearly matched it in size. Given the devastation, I am sure that this was not an isolated incident. I propose an end to this. No dragons will soar through your skies, wreaking havoc on your people, provided you grant my simple request.' The king remained silent. Ballard, not to be gainsaid, continued without hesitation. 'I will cast a spell of protection about the entire nation, for one small price—grant me land for an estate where your two lands meet, the very same place over which the dragons battled, that I may dwell and continue to develop new magics.' Ballard bowed elegantly before standing proudly erect once more. Once he had finished, the young king waited, thinking through Ballard's promise. After some time, King Essan spoke with wisdom beyond his years.

"'Many have made such grand promises before you, and not one has been fulfilled,' King Essan, unmoved, responded. 'Why should we believe yours? You must prove yourself! Our fiefdoms of Reymont and Havartan in the northwest corner of our kingdom are besieged by a rogue Umber Dragon, poisoning the land, and carrying off our people. Bring us the head and tail of this dragon. Go now. Show us your power, Mage!' King Essan snapped his fingers and a servant emerged from behind the royal throne, a map case in her hands. Bowing to her king, she presented Ballard with the map and escorted him out of the castle.

"And so, the magnificent Ballard found himself on the Great Western Highway, headed toward the fiefdoms of Reymont and Havartan. The highway dipped and climbed through the hills of Venesialia. Great woodlands gave way to fertile farmland where little villages were happy to aid the great mage on his quest. It was a pleasant journey until the Great Western Highway met the Southern Highway. After this, the road became less traveled as it wandered to the northwest. The land became hillier, with rich farms nestled around walled villages in every valley and hillsides crowned with woodlands. After leaving one such village, surrounded by its bountiful crops with plump sheep and cattle grazing on the hillsides, Ballard entered yet another woodland. This one was denser than the last with trees so vast that they twined together, obscuring the light. Suddenly the ground crumbled beneath his horse's feet as the entire hillside slid away. Great trees and boulders flew into the air as if in a massive flood. Ballard quickly caught himself, levitating his mount above the churning earth until the dust settled. A vast wasteland spread across the horizon, filled with lifeless tree trunks, withered grasses, and expanses of burnt soil, all drained to a putrid gray and reeking with a sickening, poisonous stench. With a few magical phrases and a flourish of one hand, Ballard encased his horse's hooves in leather booties before gently lowering them both to the ground below. A path—of sorts—lead northwestward. Only the muffled sound of hoofbeats broke the ominous silence in this land devoid of life.

"After many hours, Ballard arrived, according to the map, at Havartan fief. The stone castle huddled within its outer walls as if it could remove itself from the encroaching devastation. As he neared the castle, a figure emerged from a charred postern door. The knight wore sooty, tarnished mail under a mahogany sur-coat, scorched at the shoulders and more patched than whole. A cyan-blue winged sword over a gleaming white leaping destrier was emblazoned on the front, a symbol of the Vassyric Order of Knights, faithfully cared for despite the wear. 'Well met, stranger,' she said as she took the horse's bridle and slipped the door into the wall, creating an opening wide enough for a riderless horse to pass. Ballard strode ahead of them into a crowd of makeshift shel-ters and bedraggled people, who stared at him with a frail glim-mer of hope in their eyes. One took the horse from the knight and led him away. The knight assured Ballard that they would see to the horse's needs while Ballard met with Lady Havartan, and they brought him by a winding path to the castle's great hall. Gone were the tables and benches. The floor was strewn with beds and bundles on which the retainers rested or prepared their weapons for the next attack. An ancient mage and his appren-tices huddled whispering in the corner. Ballard could feel their magic weakly washing forth to protect the castle. Desolation and exhaustion filled the air. Against this scourge, no one could pre-vail. Ahead, tapestries had been turned into screens at the far end of the hall, close to the once-grand fireplace, where a few small logs smoldered feebly, giving little light and even less warmth. They rounded the edge of the screened partition and Ballard beheld a beautiful maiden; her long, burnished, brown hair hung in two plaits on each side of her pale face. Determination gleamed in her tawny eyes and mail glinted at the cuffs of her fitted sleeves. 'Greetings, stranger. I am Lady Havartan. You surely have been blessed by the Twins to arrive here safely in these times. What brings you to my cursed, forgotten land?'

"Ballard gave her his most elegant bow. 'I am called Ballard and you have not been forgotten. King Essan sent me to free you from your plight with my magic. Please, tell me all you know about this dragon.'

"Lady Havartan met his eyes, weighing his words and his soul, before gesturing for him to join her at the table. 'It all began six, nay, nine months ago. To our north lies Reymont fief, which borders the higher western hills. Now until about nine months ago, hill-people were their greatest threat, as they would rush down from their camps in the hills to raid the outlying farms and villages. The dragons were more of a nuisance than a scourge, more of a problem with loss of livestock than loss of human life. Lord Reymont had no problem dealing with those things. Then the shepherds started noticing a strange, gray blight spreading across a ridgeline.

Reymont's foresters investigated and found the partial remains of a hill-people raiding party and land fouled as you have seen here. No one knew what to make of it, and Lord Reymont sent word to me seeking counsel. All was normal here. Then the dragon struck. He soared over the ridge, blotting out the sun and belching fire that incinerated the very ground, so large he could carry away an ox in each clawed limb. His umber scales glistened in the sun while each wingbeat created a gale, flattening forest and farm alike. Whole villages were consumed by the beast, and then the magic started. The dragon seemed to whisper above the gale and the land died, turning gray and withered. The waters were poisoned until, like here, the only safe haven was the castle. Reymont sent out his best dragon slayers and mages, to no avail. The dragon destroyed more and more territory each day until it passed into Havartan, where the pattern has repeated itself. My knights have been slain save one, of whom you have already met. My guard has been devastated, and it is all my mages can do to shield this castle. My entire fiefdom shelters within these walls. Reymont and I sent to the king three months ago and you are the first word we have had. We are running out of supplies and only the water in the castle's well is safe to drink. The beast could attack at any time, perpetually from the west out of the ridges and so high in the sky that there is no warning until he swoops like a falcon upon his prey.'

"'Fear not, my lady. The next time shall be his last, this I vow in Cerenth's name!' Ballard declared, his hand to his heart.

"Then they waited. Days went by with no sign of the dragon. Tempers flared and bellies rumbled from the short rations. Goddess Iolanthe's healers worked continuously to care for the weakest among the refugees. Archer apprentices foraged outside for the prized arrows made of silvestryne, that enchanted metal strong enough to pierce a dragon's metallic scales. Sentries paired with the mage's apprentices scanned the skies from the battlements ready to give the first alarm. In the end, the dragon just appeared above the castle, screaming his rage and blood lust. Ballard's keen senses detected the dragon's approach, he teleported to the sky hovering as the dragon appeared, leaving those below to gape in shock and awe before dashing for shelter.

"Ballard launched into a fierce round of spells, which burst into rainbow-hued smoke as they struck the beast's snout and wings. It shook its long head and glared at the one who had the temerity to attack it. Baring its fangs, the dragon snapped at the great mage as it whispered its spell of destruction. Ballard, with a grand wave of his arm, deflected the blast away from both himself and the castle below as negligently as one would shoo an annoying fly. With lightening and fireballs, he drove it farther and farther away over the plain, teleporting as soon as one spell was cast, driving the dragon into a blind rage. White fire blasts liquefied the soil and scarred the distant castle walls. The air shimmered with the poisoned, life-sucking spells the dragon hurled. Yet Ballard eluded each one as if in an effortlessly graceful, airborne dance to the music of the wind.

As the dragon tired, Ballard struck. The dragon reared back as Ballard loosed a mage's lance of silver light to hurtle at the dragon's breast. The lance ruptured the dragon's body as it continued in flight uninterrupted. The dragon plummeted, dripping blood, and implanted itself into the ground. The eyes, as big as cart wheels, dulled to gray, signaling its death. With its passing, a clean breeze blew over the land, clearing the poison. Everywhere the breeze touched, the color returned to the land, leaving sun-bleached golds and browns behind. Into this reawakened landscape, a procession emerged from the castle, with Lady Havartan and her knight mounted at the head. While they approached, Ballard raised the dragon out of the crater and spread the body out alongside it. The crater was over ten feet deep; in places, bare bedrock shimmered, buffed by the dragon's scales. A spring bubbled up from the head-shaped depression, gurgling as the water streamed down the neck to eventually fill the entire dragon-shaped basin.

"Lady Havartan bowed from her horse as she arrived at Ballard's side. 'You have done it, my lord mage. Your powers are beyond compare! Forever will we sing your praises! How may I repay you for this great gift? Are you injured? Healers come forward!'

"'No need, my lady,' Ballard replied, beaming as he gestured to halt the healers' approach. 'I am well. Your fiefdom's health and happiness are all the reward I need. However, the king does require this dragon's head and tail, so with your leave, I will remove them. What do you wish to be done with the rest of the carcass, my lady?'

"'Fulfill the king's request, Lord Mage,' the lady replied. 'When you are done, please eliminate the body before it draws something to the feast.'

"Ballard bowed and turned his attention back to the remains. Whispering arcane words of a spell, Ballard produced two huge guillotines of the same silver energy as the lance over the neck and base of the tail. With a flourish of his hand, the blades dropped, neatly cleaving the head and tail. Whispering again in the guarded language of the mages, Ballard raised a clenched fist and seemed to throw black flames over the torso. They leapt and crackled and yet emitted neither smoke nor heat. Just as suddenly as they appeared, they vanished, leaving only depressed grasses behind. Next, Ballard called forth webbing to wrap his prizes, and when that was done, he opened his pouch wide. He raised his right hand, pointing in turn at the head and tail and commanding them inside the bag, which he casually refastened to his belt. The gathered crowd gasped in awe at his magnificence. Before they could say a word, he vanished, as did his steed from the stables, never to be seen again in those parts, and yet honored there still.

"That very same day, Ballard arrived at the main gate of Venesial castle, where he was ushered straight to the glowing blue audience chamber where King Essan was holding court. An attendant whispered in the king's ear. The king dismissed everyone from the hall, except for Ballard and his escort, and the royal guard. Ballard approached and bowed deeply.

"'Your majesty, with your permission, I wish to present you with a gift,' Ballard said as he met the king's eyes boldly. King Essan tipped his head forward in acquiescence. Nodding in return, Ballard turned, placing his open pouch carefully beneath the apex of the dome at the center of the vast hall, before returning to stand next to the king. Extending his arms before him, palms cupped upwards, he slowly raised them high. The web-wrapped parcel hovered in the air before the king, ever so slowly rotating. The webbing spun off, evaporating into a cascade of glittering golden sparks. When the last of the sparks dispersed, the head drifted to the floor, facing the king, while the tail arced behind. 'The Umber Dragon of Havartan, as you requested, Your Majesty.'

"As before, the king remained silent, his guard rigidly attentive, flanking the throne. Long moments passed as the light softened toward dusk. Finally, King Essan spoke: 'You may go and cast your spell, wizard, uniting Malin's kingdom and mine by encircling our unified perimeters. If it proves successful, you may build an estate in the great central meadow adjoined with Wyssa's Wood where Venesialia meets Ceretheena.' The king addressed Ballard's escort: 'See that he has all the supplies he needs for his journey. Now go, Mage Ballard; we assume you have much to do.'

"Ballard was led through the back halls of the palace until they reached the storehouse, where an official ordered travel rations and a pack horse to be brought to the gate. Within the hour, all was arranged to Ballard's liking and, mounting his steed, he rode off through the north gate. The way was smooth and well traveled. Ballard trotted past many slow-moving merchant caravans winding their way northward to Doralis. Many a night he joined this one or that for an evening of camaraderie and entertainment, as he knew that soon the journey would be lonesome, and trackless. Reaching the northern border, he turned east. The king's map would be his only guide as he built his spell into the very ground. Days passed as he marked his magical line over land and water. Eventually, he emerged from the forest to the edge of the great woods. Here he would be exposed to both the dragons of these high, open hills, and to the dangers of the western Wild Wood. For many a moonset, Ballard skirted this desolate, windswept upland. The packhorse was often fractious, with white-rimmed, panicked eyes no matter where they were. Many a monster attacked, only to be obliterated by Ballard's magnificent spell craft. One day, when the horse was especially frightened, Ballard looked up to see three peaks covered in a flock of Black dragons, silently watching. None took to the sky, so he let them be, continuing into the night until they were lost from his sight.

"The land began to change again. The hills were no longer so steep, and woodlands were becoming forests. According to the map, Ballard saw he would soon cross over into Ceretheena. One quarter of the journey was complete. Anticipating an easier route, he increased his pace, hoping to loop the southern tip and arrive at the Spring District within the next month or two.

"One dark night, when the moons were all in crescents, deep in the forest of Ceretheena, a ghostly steed rushed past, terrifying his pack horse and Ballard's normally unflappable mount. It galloped, screaming in rage down the trail. A hushed spell froze the two animals in place and allowed Ballard the freedom to pursue the phantom. Running full out, he almost missed the sounds of an intense battle. Slowing, he stopped before the clearing ahead. The horse screamed again above the sounds of snarls and ring of steel on bone. One of the famed Dragon Knights battled five bugbears, whirling around them in a deadly dance that left them bloody while the Dragon Knight remained unscathed. The horse drove two more of the monsters out into the open from where they had attempted to ambush the knight. Blood matted their coats from the steed's sharp hooves. Huge by bugbear standards, each stood fifteen feet on its hind legs. Talons gleamed on each paw. The mottled brown, gray, and green fur on their backs seemed to absorb the light. A silver light flashed off the knight's sword and the bugbears collapsed on the ground with their brethren. Then the knight turned to Ballard. Armor the color of hematite with an ornate helm completely obscured his face, and he moved fluidly, without a sound.

"'You are the mage casting a spell along the border?' he asked, his voice reverberating as if from a great distance. 'Be wary of what you seek to do. There is more to this land than the folks you serve.'

"'I only seek to make Timeria safer for all,' Ballard replied calmly to the knight's implied threat. 'I promise you that all will benefit from this boon. All I seek is a place to dwell in peace. In fact, any of those other folk of which you speak may find asylum within my walls for as long as they need. Tell them this.' Ballard clasped hands with the Dragon Knight, who then disappeared into the night.

"Moons passed, and now the Spring District lay before them. Here the border was even less defined as time and space seemed to stretch and bend. Boldly Ballard blazed onward. Before he knew it, the supplies were nearly gone. Remembering where he had been, he magicked in replacements. Still the path wandered through mist and springs of the purest water, guarded by sprites. Ballard requested permission before quenching his thirst. The journey was as pleasant as it was long; however, all such interludes must end, and Ballard emerged into a mundane wood. Now the way was easy to follow, and soon he arrived in a familiar landscape. Here, the Umber Dragon had ravaged the countryside. He recognized the rock ridge's distinctive silhouette. Yet, he beheld a land transformed such that it could only have taken place after years of rebirth. Ballard realized that time had passed without his knowledge.

Fields bloomed and wooly sheep grazed peacefully on the hillsides under the watchful eyes of the shepherds. As he climbed a ridge, Ballard saw Havartan Castle glowing rosily in the afternoon sun. In the foreground, a dragon-shaped pond reflected the sky, a lasting reminder of the dragon's demise. A bright-sailed windmill turned gently on the bank, and snug stone cottages and barns stretched through the distance beyond. Unable to stray from his spell building, Ballard moved ahead until he was finally back on the Doralian Highway. Leaving the packhorse at a guard station along the way, Ballard was able to race south to the land of his dreams. Dragons still hunted above the plain. They would need to go before he could begin, and he needed to prepare for his most prodigious work.

"When the moons reached the proper alignment, Ballard stood in the center of the plain. Raising his arms, he pushed the dragons across the border. With their banishment, the great spell began. For a night and day, Ballard chanted as eldritch fire danced over his hands, which were lifted to the sky. As darkness fell once more, strands of fire in every hue streamed from his outstretched arms in all directions. As the night passed, he slowly and carefully wove the strands into a mesh, never faltering in his chant. As dawn's golden glow rimmed the eastern sky, Ballard shoved his glowing web up into the sky where it shimmered like an aurora until he spoke three words of command. For mere moments, its opalescence gleamed as a solid dome covering all of Timeria before vanishing into the morning sun. It was done and the spell complete.

"After a long, peaceful rest, Ballard returned to the palace. King Essan greeted the mage with surprise and wonder. 'Welcome,

Ballard, master among mages! You have kept your lofty promise and earned your reward. We feared you had perished. Seven long years have passed since you last stood before us, and no news had we heard until our guard returned our horse. Tonight, we feast in your honor. A room has been prepared, awaiting your arrival.'

"Ballard was accompanied to a luxurious suite where he could refresh himself until the evening. There, an attendant prepared a fragrant bath in the attached bathing room before turning back the covers on the soft feather bed. The mage felt clean and refreshed after partaking of both. When he arose, his eye caught a nearby stand, which held a rich, velvet tunic with soft suede breeches dyed to match. A belt and burnished boots completed the gift. Impressed, Ballard donned the raiment before joining the feast. There, seated beside the king, he was presented with the most glorious culinary delights, course after course, accompanied by the finest imported honeyberry wine and varied entertainments. A bard performed her most famous ballad, 'Death of the Dragon,' which recounted the great mage's fight at Havartan. Once the banquet was cleared, the dancing began, lasting until morning's first song. It was a celebration fit for a king.

"Renewed, Ballard left to claim his boon. On arrival, he levitated high above the grasslands where now the wild cattle and elk grazed undisturbed. Picturing the manor of his dreams, his hands moved to sketch the vision in the air as he began to chant in words older than time. As he reached the crescendo, Ballard thrust out his hands, grabbing and pulling his creation from the turf below. The mighty edifice soared seven stories above and many more below the surface of the field. Crafted of seamless, cream-colored granite, it was crowned with delicate arches. The polished surface gave back the colors of the landscape. Grasping and smoothing, the great mage added paved courtyards, ornate gardens, and all the outbuildings a fortress would require. Lastly, he ringed it with towering walls of native stone broken only once by an arched gate, flanked by two turrets. Everything was as he wished inside and out.

"Ballard's fame spread far and wide. Soon folks flocked to his side, offering their skills to serve him. Those who only wished to be near one so great built homes and farms outside the walls. Many more came to seek his wisdom. Seeing a need, one intrepid young lass built an inn along the new King's Highway. Thus, Ballardton was born, and the people prospered. That is, until a rival mage grew jealous of Ballard's power and fame. But that is a tale for another time . . ."

Skelly trailed off. The group sat mystified and in awe. The child at his knee had stayed awake, his attention never ebbing. Skelly placed down a hood and cowl in front of him, tossing in a coin or two to model the intended action. Most walked away. Some approached, thanking Skelly and congratulating him on a story well told, tossing coppies, ebons, and silvers into the hood and cowl.

The little one moved forward to see what people had thrown, and his eyes blazed with interest in the coins. Skelly reached in and pulled out a coppie, gifting it to the boy, who clutched the coin and ran away toward the fountain on the northeastern side of Ballardton. Skelly collected his hood, looping the coins in securely. He knew he would be back, but today was done. He hurried toward the east, disappearing into the shadows.

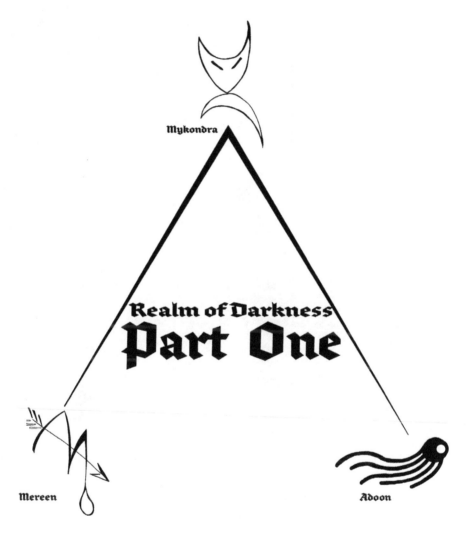

Mykondra

Realm of Darkness
Part One

Mereen

Adoon

CHAPTER I

BIRTH DAY

TODAY WAS THE DAY. Blaze inhaled the stagnant air in the area of Ballardton that he made his home. It filled him with joy and excitement.

Duties done, freedom lay before him. He would return to the guild laden with treasure. Master would present him with a pie and a wink. The pie was for his birth day and the wink acknowledged that Blaze had been born here. It was his eighth turn-year, which marked one milestone to another. He took pride in that knowledge. The others came from other places, but he was born to this life as a prince is born to his.

He inhaled again but coughed away the air. It was heavy today with the smells of boiling horse flesh, fat, and bones from the knacker yard. The smell was familiar to the boy, and he knew that the knackerman was boiling the tallow. A weathered pine clapboard building housed the knackerman and his sons, and today it emitted a malodorous stench from the incinerator's charred remains that burned Blaze's eyes until they teared. Many times, Blaze had seen a knacker cart driving along this very road with the head of a dead horse draped over the side of the cart and spilling out its raw, open guts onto the road. He always felt for the horse and he wished he could have done something to help it survive. Blaze knew why the knackerman was needed, but it didn't stop his empathy for the animals. Blaze noticed patches of manure along the road and he avoided them. There was no stopping him; nothing was going to get in his way. He had a plan. He had scrounged and begged for enough coin to buy his own stew at Two Realms Inn, the only inn that catered to all peoples, even someone of his class. His pouch was full of coppies, round bits of metal that were the smallest currency in Timeria. Ballardton was a mecca for travelers during the summer months as people of all races brought their wares, crafts, and foods for a grand festival. The kingdom of Timeria, ruled by King Kiril, was a merged kingdom of elves, sprites, and humans. Most Timerians were some kind of blend of the three different peoples making it quite common to meet peoples of all types along the highway.

Blaze continued his walk down the dust-filled road, passing a dirty, foul-smelling fountain while making his way toward the King's Highway. He noticed there wasn't much activity on the highway, so pickings wouldn't be so good, but then again, he wasn't interested in the travelers or even the locals today. His one desire was that stew and the hefty chunks of meat inside it. His mouth watered as he remembered the stew last year when Mason had returned to Ballardton to surprise Blaze with the special meal. Today, he was buying it for himself. Gathering the money was difficult as was keeping it safe from the other thieves at the guild. He even caught Pigeon nearly stealing it all away. He clutched his pouch in his hand, fearful that it wasn't even safe dangling from his belt.

Blaze found himself walking past the marketplace. He smelled the sweet allure of pies from the pieman's stall. He waved to the pieman's wife, whom he had spoken to at length yesterday about today's intended activities. As he walked along the highway, the sun rose over the horizon. A bright, directed light momentarily blinded the boy. He rubbed his eyes, wiping away tears from the burning light. He removed his hands from his eyes to find a woman crouching in front of him inches from his face. She was an old, wrinkled, gray-haired woman, who completely startled him. He had heard no footsteps of her approach, no rustle from her skirts. She just simply appeared. The inn was within his sight, but the road was barren of any activity on this brisk autumn day. He held his pouch closer to his chest with worried eyes as he stared intently at the grinning woman.

"Sonny, can I ask you a question?" Blaze looked down at his pouch, hoping someone else would appear to take on the responsibility of answering the woman. Unfortunately, no one else arrived and all of Ballardton seemed to have disappeared. "Good. I'm lost and I want help finding my way home. Will you help me?"

"Isn't there someone else you could ask? I was going to go to Two Realms," Blaze replied nervously. Being a child, Blaze was invisible to most people, which made the woman's attention unusual. One of Blaze's favorite activities during the annual Ballardton International Festival was listening to the storyteller. Many stories were of old beggars looking to test an unwitting traveler, and the tale would warn the listeners that these tests were often doled out by the gods themselves. To deny a request could result in being cursed for life. Nonetheless, Blaze posed the question, despite the impending doom; his stomach growled for the stew.

"Does it look like there might be someone else? Ballardton is nearly deserted today, and such a strong lad as yourself will surely manage to wait a bit longer," she replied with a smile, showing brown, decaying, and crooked teeth.

"All right, where do you live?"

"Oh, it's not that far, dearie."

"I thought you said you were lost?" The old hag started walking, then grabbed Blaze's arm to keep him moving on. "Um, where do you live? How do you know that you're heading in the right direction? Do you have a map?"

Blaze stopped walking and stood fast with his arms crossed. He mounted the pouch onto his belt and carefully secured it, so it was harder to lose.

"I sort of know the way, but I really would like to get some help. The gods arranged for us to meet. I might have a map somewhere here." Blaze's eyes widened with fearful knowledge. The woman again grabbed his arm and pulled him along.

"What's your name, sweetheart?"

"What's yours?"

"I call myself Amoria. What is your name?"

"Blaze, Blaze of Ballardton."

"Well, Blaze of Ballardton, I am glad that our paths crossed today." Blaze felt uncomfortable, but he continued walking with Amoria anyway. "Where do you go to school?"

"School?" Blaze laughed. "I don't go to school."

"No? I thought all children went to school these days. Ah well, are you at least apprenticed?"

"Kind of." Blaze's face reddened; Amoria stopped prying and the two walked in silence.

As aged and disabled as Amoria seemed to be, she never complained nor lessened her pace.

Trees opened up to a small grove and a series of paths that ran deep into the wildwood. Blaze hesitated. He realized that this was farther than he had ever traveled, and he sensed he was quite a distance from Ballardton, yet they hadn't walked that far.

"Um . . . Amoria?"

"Yes, child?" Her voice was light and inviting.

"Can you find your way from here?" Blaze turned to her.

"No!" Blaze jumped at the harshness of her response. "Ah . . . no, sweetie." Her voice returned to the previous sweetness. Blaze squinted his eyes, straining to see down the paths, but to no avail. Each was overgrown, and the trees loomed menacingly, attacking each traveler. Blaze's instincts were to run, but Amoria looped her arm around his and encouraged him to continue on.

"This way, Blaze of Ballardton." Amoria smiled, but there was an underlying deception that Blaze couldn't put his finger entirely on. Maybe it was the way she used his entire identity, as if she was pinpointing him for some distinction that he had no desire of receiving. Amoria guided him into the darkest path toward the left. Somehow, he knew that this was the path that Amoria would choose.

"Um . . . my lady . . . I want to turn around and go back to Ballardton . . . I forgot that today is . . ."

"Your birthday? I know; that is the reason for you to accompany me. Oh, dear! I've said too much already." Her words didn't fit her expression. She continued to smile, revealing yellow-brown teeth.

His stomach turned. "Amoria," he said, disregarding his previous attempt at respect, "didn't you tell me before that you were lost?"

"But now I am found!"

Blaze pulled back, glaring at the old woman with skepticism. "You are found? I'm confused—I thought you had said that you needed help finding your way home, right? But now you're telling me this is about my birth day. Wait a minute. . . . How'd you know about that? I didn't tell you."

"The others told me. It is a surprise. Surprise!"

"What?" Blaze's eyes narrowed, and he pulled away from Amoria. Now he knew that this was a trap. He stood, evaluating the rumpled creature that stood before him while his mind raced with questions.

"Easy, dear. We don't want any trouble."

"We?" His muscles tightened, and his jaw clenched shut. He spoke through his teeth, using a voice that was unfamiliar to his ears.

"Yes, *we*." It was then that he saw them. Emerging from the darkened forest in rows like a red-coated army, Blaze saw the small monsters coming forward with eyes glowing a burning yellow. One, who Blaze immediately thought was their leader, carried a flaming spear, and all were afire. All in all, there were more than a hundred pairs of eyes deep in the forest. Before he could react to the fire creatures, he caught sight of Amoria's ring. It was the symbol of Queen Mykondra intertwined with the symbol of Lady Mereen. Amoria and those with her were followers of the Dark Goddess, and what had come out of the forest was the stuff of nightmares. He couldn't fathom the understanding of how the hoard of devlins—little magical fire demons that traveled the night in search of prey—worked into the Goddess' plan. A thought crossed his mind: *Is Amoria the Goddess in disguise?*

The devlins continued their approach, but as enflamed as they were, the forest remained untouched. They soon surrounded Blaze. He could smell their sulfuric, bitterly pungent aroma wafting on the autumn breeze.

"By Eldon's crown!" Blaze shook with fear, and he cried while looking to the sky for a higher power, "Oh, Goddess, I apologize for anything that I have done against you!" Fear unlocked his body, and he fell to his knees with tears streaming down his face. Amoria cackled with amusement.

"Who? Oh, I see you noticed my ring, did you? No, I am not Her, nor Her follower. I am Amoria, Queen of the Devlins. These around you are in my keep as my friends and family. They do my bidding and in exchange for that . . . well you don't need to know any more, do you?" Blaze shook his head violently. "Stand up, boy. When I saw you, Blaze of Ballardton, I knew that you were perfect."

"Perfect for what? Oh, by the Gods, you're going to eat me!"

"No, no. . . ." Amoria laughed at Blaze's absurd thought. "Perfect, dear, to take my place."

"Your place?"

"Yes. Are you not able to hear well? That might be a problem..." Amoria muttered to herself until she finally made herself audible again. Blaze tried to hear what she was saying, but his pulse pounded in his ears. "Oh, no. . . . You can hear—you are just somewhat simple and didn't understand exactly what I meant. Is that right?"

"I am not simple."

"When I said place, I simply meant as Queen of the Devlins—well, we could change that to. . . let me see . . . Prince of the Devlins. You are much too small to be a king right now.

What are you, about eight, nine years old?"

Amoria continued to speak, but Blaze stood there, processing Amoria's request, trying not to stare at the glowing eyes that still kept watch on him. Why would she need an heir? Did she plan to die? Why him? What did she give them that was worth their loyalty? The smell of the devlins reached his nose, causing him to try to hack away the charred taste that lingered in the back of his throat. The devlins screeched, snarled, and hissed at their new prince. Amoria turned, clapped her hands, and stared at Blaze of Ballardton.

"Sit, Blaze of Ballardton. I have a tale to tell you of a day much like this one. The only difference is that, in my tale, you are me and I am my dear beloved, Wiltonia. She was the previous Queen of the Devlins, and she sought me out. Like you, Blaze of Ballardton, I was a street rat who hoped to find my next meal on the most recent traveler. I was young, maybe too young, but on my birthday, I met Wiltonia. She came up to me and wished me well when no one else cared. I didn't know how she knew, but she did.

"Wiltonia was beautiful. She had swirling, white hair that was tipped with red hues. Her face was angelic and young, although I thought her old. She asked me if I liked my life or if I wanted to become immortal like the elves.

"What do you think I chose? Of course I wanted to live forever; after all, I was always jealous of those stinking, high and mighty Nashiran elves with their long noses and pointed ears, and . . ." Amoria looked up and noticed the bewildered look on Blaze's face. He pulled on his own ears, hoping that she didn't see their points. "Um . . . anyway, I chose immortality. What an amazing gift! Don't you think?" Blaze blinked blankly at her, so she continued. "Ah, well, I was human after all—still am. But *you*, Blaze of Ballardton, can free me by becoming my successor. And I offer you the same gift that Wiltonia offered me: immortality!" At the end of Amoria's sentence, one devlin carrying the fire-tipped metal fire spear approached Blaze. It snarled as it scurried up to Amoria and it lit the brush with its approach. The devlin sniffed at Blaze, who was surprisingly not frightened any longer, and Amoria reached up and slid her hand over its head. She pushed Blaze to do the same; he simply reached up and patted it a couple of times. His hand burned at the touch, but he didn't pull away, afraid of Amoria's reaction to his rejection. Its body was hot and clammy, and its skin felt like rubber over plastic. The devlin hissed and clicked, which Blaze took to be a pleasurable sound. He looked into its face. He had never been so close to a monster before, and it was difficult not to explore its unique face.

The devlin's face was aflame, as was its entire body. It tilted its head, mimicking the tilt of Blaze's own. Its eyes entranced him; where there should have been eyeballs there were glowing yellow holes, which seemed to squint and move with the devlin's eye movements. Across the bottom of its face was a line of sharp razors that extended from one side to the other. Horns protruded from both sides of its head. It had hair, if one could call the roaring blaze that sat atop its head *hair*. But it was those glowing, yellow eyes that caught most of Blaze's attention. They were filled with sorrow, desperation, and regret; though perhaps Blaze imagined what he saw.

Blaze looked around at the devlins and into Amoria's face, considering everything that she had said. He was disgusted by Amoria's loyalty to the little monsters that surrounded her. He longed for his home and his pie that he had anticipated early this morning. He breathed hard, coughing away the smoke of the burning vegetation. He looked at the devlin, and it grinned back. Blaze turned away out of fear that the devlin would make him cry and he'd feel like a fool. It was then that he realized his hand was burnt beyond recognition. With this realization, he became fiercely aware of the pain but held back his cries, which was his nature. Amoria broke the silence.

"Well, do you accept our offer?"

Blaze stared at his hand and thought about the offer set before him.

"No, never! I want to grow up like any Timerian; and if I was supposed to be immortal, Gods know, I would've been born that way." Amoria drew in a great breath. Her face contorted. The nearest devlin wrapped its arrow-tipped tail around Blaze's shoulders, but Blaze wiggled free of its grasp.

The next thing Blaze felt were multiple burning shocks and jabs of fire from the devlin's flame spear. It directed Blaze's movements. The spear caused precision burn holes that melted through his tunic and cut off his belt, which dropped his pouch. It pierced into deep muscle, touching bone in some places. Blaze quickly learned to maneuver out of the spear's way only to discover that he was trapped amongst the sea of red devlins. He towered over them even at his young age, but every way he looked he met their menacing grins as they approached closer to him. He had nowhere to run until the Queen of the Devlins parted the sea of her followers.

"Stop! Do him no harm . . . yet." She smiled at Blaze. The color had washed from his face, and dark circles deepened his eyes under his black hair. His pouch and stew were the furthest from his mind now. His plan had changed to one of survival. "I want, no, need you . . . to meet Wiltonia, Blaze of Ballardton." Blaze looked past the devlins, trying to find the woman who Amoria had spoken of in her tale.

"I don't see . . ." His voice trailed off. He could feel the spear wounds suppurating. He was becoming dizzy with fever, and he thought he heard the chomping and slurping of hungry jaws.

Amoria broke his thoughts.

"Oh, no. She is right in front of you. She is my dearest devlin."

"Devlin? I thought she was a person." Blaze's mind fogged, but he tried not to show it.

"Yes, Blaze of Ballardton, how else did you think one would become immortal? We become one of our beloved creatures."

"Creatures? Monsters or demons, is more like it. I'm going to have nightmares for centuries about devlins. . . ."

"*If* you live that long. Right now, you have been pierced as a newcomer. When you looked into Wiltonia's devlin eyes, what did you see, Blaze of Ballardton? Your life and what it could be like?"

"No. I saw only despair and regret in its—er, *her* eyes."

"What? No, you're supposed to see what it will be like as Queen of the Devlins. Wiltonia, why didn't he see that? And don't tell me it is because he's a boy, you said that didn't matter, remember?" The devlin blinked and chortled, which seemed to infuriate Amoria. "NO! I did not choose wrong! He was the one, the *only* one in Ballardton, who came out when I used the spell to call the

successor. I did everything you said. You said to use this spell—"
Amoria pulled out a piece of parchment, and she shook it for
emphasis,"—and the one who appears is the chosen one to lead
and carry on. THAT ONE APPEARED!" Blaze felt his fever rise;
the devlins swirled around him as his eyes rolled in his head. He
was able to straighten himself out when he heard Amoria speak
again."Okay, fine! Just eat him then, and see if I care!" Blaze looked
down at Wiltonia, and she snapped her mouth at him. He noticed
behind Amoria that the path was still clear; unexpectedly, he
jumped over Wiltonia, knocking her to the ground, and pushed
Amoria into some of the other devlins. With a burst of adrenaline,
he sprinted out of the hoard at top speed, staggering somewhat as
he did. The devlins, slow to react, waited for Amoria's order. Once
she righted herself, she called out to them as she fanned her arms in
the air."HE IS YOURS: DEVOUR AND DESTROY!"

Blaze could hear the devlins springing into immediate action—
slurping, clicking, and snarling. The devlins scurried behind him.
Blaze glanced over his shoulder. The red fire blur moved as a single
unit. Behind the sea of red, Amoria ran, waving her walking stick
with her cloak and dress flying about her. The devlins appeared
closer, and Blaze started sprinting again after catching his breath. A
couple of the devlins jumped into the trees and swung along them
jumping from tree to tree. Blaze could smell the burning char, and
he was surprised by their speed.

The devlin closest to him sprang down on him. He rolled on
the ground, trying to get its small body off of him. His shoulder
burned. He floundered back and forth, knocking the devlin unconscious, until it died and lost its flame. Another devlin jumped on
him as he tried to stand. It chomped at his knee, and Blaze kicked
it away, sending it flying. He searched the area, knowing that the
others were still in pursuit. He moved his hand to his shoulder,
pressing against the pain. As the devlins closed in, Blaze thought
desperately that there had to be a way out of this. He picked up the
dead devlin and raised it in the air. Amoria and the devlins stopped
in their tracks with their eyes wider, their mouths dropped, and
their flames turning from yellow and orange to a dark brick red.

"No! Wiltonia!" Amoria cried out.

Blaze threw the dead devlin as far from him as he could. Then he
continued to stagger through the wood. He looked back as Amoria
and her followers searched the forest for Wiltonia's body, giving

up on their prey and mourning their loss. As he continued to push forward, every part of his body ached. Ballardton was unreachable; Blaze knew he had to find somewhere closer. He ran until consciousness was a luxury and his body betrayed him collapsing into leaf litter.

CHAPTER 2

HAVEN

"OH . . . ADOON'S POISON! By Eldon's throne…" Blaze swore when he awoke, still in physical pain.

"There will be none of that, young man. I don't allow that kind of language in MY house." Blaze squinted toward the source of the scolding voice. *Was it Amoria? Or someone else? What happened?* The last thing Blaze remembered was being chased by devlins.

"DEVLINS!" Blaze sprang up in bed.

"Easy, love. Lay back down. Don't you worry; there are no devlins here." The voice's face appeared smiling over Blaze. She was pretty, with long black hair, fair brown skin, and blue-gray eyes that seemed to smile on their own. Her clothing suggested she was neither wealthy nor impoverished. He thought she must've been strikingly beautiful in her youth. "You've been talking about devlins since Neid found you in the wood. You must be awful scared of those creatures. What's your name? Neid and me, we couldn't find anything about who you could be except that mark of Luminessa's half phase on your wrist there."

His eyes followed her around the room. She stoked the fire in the fireplace. It lit the room, casting dark shadows that created hiding places for the creatures of the night. He looked at his wrist and reexamined the crescent-shaped birthmark. *Why did she notice it?* Most people disregarded it as having any importance at all, even Blaze himself. He recalled trying to wash it off when he was first aware of it. The door flung open, making both occupants jump.

A man stood in the doorway holding an armful of freshly split logs. The woman ran to the man and kissed him squarely on the lips, causing him to drop the wood. Blaze turned up his nose and glanced away, giving the couple a moment of privacy.

"Nan, be careful of the wood! How's our little charge today?" Neid, Blaze surmised from the woman's reaction, didn't look in Blaze's direction; rather, he went directly to the wood trough and dropped the wood.

"Oh, he's okay. He finally woke up, and he spoke to me. You know, he is quite obsessed with those rotten devlin creatures. Oh, and Neid, he swears. Nearly every word is about the sacred ones and never about our sacred twins. May Cerenth and Rhiun protect us all!" She lifted a pendant with the symbols of the twins to her lips and kissed it.

"Well, Nan, consider where the lad must come from—he is not as well off as us." Nan held Neid's arm, and together they surveyed the fire-lit room as though it were a great castle.

"Praise to the Twins of Light!" Nan raised her hands upward. "We are so fortunate, are we not?" Nan leaned into Neid, her head on his shoulder.

"We are, Nan, no doubt. The Gods have blessed us in so many ways." Nan nodded while hugging Neid's arm. The fire light reflected in their tear-filled eyes. The two stood locked in the moment. A knock on the door behind the couple turned their heads. Neid opened it.

"Oh, sergeant of the guard! Is anything wrong, sir?" A man, in his thirtieth turn-years, entered the light-filled room. He carried a sword at his side and wore a surcoat with an embroidered emblem.

"No, Neid, nothing is wrong and we are not calling you to arms. Lord Gresham calls after the boy that you found. Is he well? Do you need anything for your farm? Lady Gresham sends her regards and at Nan's earliest convenience would like her to look after the castle's supplies in the apothecary." Neid nodded, and gestured his welcomed entrance to the sergeant.

"Please come and see him for yourself. He is faring much better thanks to the sacred twins and our lord's protection. Nan has been caring well for the lad. See for yourself." The man walked up to Blaze and stared at the boy, who hid his face under a sheet. Nan approached the small bed. She wrapped her arms about Blaze's head pulling the sheet out from his hands and away from his face.

She kissed Blaze's head, who glared at her and pulled away from her loving gesture.

"As you can see, sir, he is far better than he was when he first arrived. I believe he will need some more time before he can tell us anything about his travels and what happened to him. And, I will most definitely check on the apothecary's supplies. Is there anything that is needed immediately, by Lady Gresham?" Nan smiled at the sergeant awaiting his response.

"Nothing at the moment, Nan. Oh, except for maybe some of your special ointment. Riding with the guard is hard on our lord's back these days." Nan excused herself to see to the ointment at the sink on the far side of the room. She filled a jar with the ointment, wrapped it in a muslin cloth, and handed it to the visitor. The sergeant bowed to Nan and he turned to leave.

"Neid, a word outside." Neid exited the house with the sergeant. Blaze struggled to sit up. With Blaze's movements, Nan rushed back to the boy's side.

"Oh, no! You mustn't get up yet! The salve hasn't set yet. Those were some nasty lesions, you know. They might scar."

Blaze smirked and his eyes danced with glee. "Do you really think so? That would be amazing! I'd be really happy, if they did." Blaze excitedly questioned Nan, while she struggled to keep him laying down.

"Why in all of Mirias that is good, would you possibly want scars? You need to calm down, child." Neid reentered the house while Nan struggled with Blaze. He picked up a pipe and lit it. Small perfect puffs of clouds rose toward the ceiling and they caught Blaze's attention. "I think he may need a more experienced healer— perhaps one from the Cleric's Hall." The last part was directed at Neid, but Blaze answered returning his attention to Nan.

"No! No healer!" Fear crossed his face.

"Nan, he's our guest. We want him to be comfortable. Your herbs will heal his burns and they should leave no mark. Your prayers will save him from that." Neid hugged her shoulders reassuringly then walked closer to the bed.

"Well, how do you do, sir? I'm Neid of Gresham-fief. This here is my wife, Nan. I was out with the sheep, looking for a stray, when I crossed upon you face down in the wildwood. From the look of it, you must've had some trouble. You've been here for over a week while Nan here has been praying for you to the Goddess Iolanthe and covering your wounds with salve that she makes."

"Wait! A fief? This is a fief?"

"Oh, no!" Neid chuckled. "We are on the fiefdom's land, and we obey and honor our lord. In exchange for his protection, we share our livestock and tend his land, and Nan works as healer at the castle. So, what's your name, lad?" Blaze wasn't sure if he should give his name to Neid—after all, look where it had gotten him with Amoria. Nan was standing to his right and Neid to his left. Their brows rose in question.

"Um . . . my name . . . my name is . . . er, rather . . . I'm called . . . Rhatt's son."

"Ratson? That's a strange name. I've never heard it's like."

"You're telling me! But yes, that's what I'm called—Rhatt's son."

"Well Ratson, it is very nice to meet you. How did you come to be in the wildwood?"

"I thought maybe he had been attacked by a devlin, given the types of burns," Nan interjected. "His hands were burned so severely. May Goddess Iolanthe relieve this child of his wounds! Great Goddess of Healing, we ask for your favor to heal him in your gentle name! Please keep him safe from any more run-ins with devlins, if this is your wish. We thank you, Goddess."

Nan raised her hands in the air and then laid them down on Blaze's hands where he had petted the devlin's head. Neid had bowed his head while holding a hand to his heart in union with his wife. Blaze pulled his hands away but Nan held them in place. Blaze grimaced from the raw pain.

"Devlins . . . yeah, I met a devlin or two." Blaze's voice shook under Nan's hold. Neid, aghast, jumped on Blaze's words.

"This is serious. If the devlins are that close to Ceretheena, I must alert Lord Gresham, so he can take counsel with King Kiril! I will return." On his final word, Neid hurriedly flung on his cloak's hood and exited the house with his cloak trailing after him. Nan rose to follow Neid to the door. Blaze glanced at his hands, which were wrapped in white cloth that hid the wounds and which now throbbed in response to his awareness of them and Nan's touch.

"Ratson, are you hungry?" asked Nan. Blaze's stomach growled as if it had a mind and voice of its own. Blaze blushed and nodded his head. Nan lifted him up to the table, which she had set with a spoon on the right.

"Do not touch anything until I tell you to. Do you understand?"

He nodded and followed her with his eyes. From the cupboard, Nan retrieved a bowl, then went to the stewpot and ladled stew into the bowl. Blaze's mouth watered as the aroma found its way across the room. He licked his lips. She made her way back to him with careful steps, clearly afraid of spilling any. She placed it in front of him. He turned around and his eyes pleadingly waited for her okay. She gestured with her head for him to begin. He reached over the bowl and gingerly grabbed the spoon.

"Oh, you're left-handed like me." She had a smile in her voice. He began eating, amazed at the amount of meat.

After enjoying Nan's stew, Blaze slept. Nan stared at the boy. He reminded her of someone, but Nan couldn't pinpoint whom. She pulled back his hair stroking his forehead. His black hair stood up in all directions. She smiled lovingly at him, dreaming of the child she hoped to bear. The door swung open and Neid entered. Nan hushed him.

"What are you doing? Is he getting worse?"

"No, I was just thinking."

"About what?"

"Our child."

"Nan, we have no children. You know the clerics have prayed to Goddess Iolanthe, and said that we probably wouldn't have any. We've made offerings to Lady Marnie and the Goddess Solana, only to stay barren." Nan looked away; tears welled in her eyes. Neid's words were harsh, but truthful.

"I know, but I thought." Nan's voice trailed off. "Well, maybe Ratson, could be the one Lady Marnie sent to us. Neid, he is even left-handed, like me." Neid sympathized with his wife.

"No. I have been instructed by Lord Gresham to bring him to the capital. His devlin accounts worry our lord. Together, Lord Gresham and I are to journey to take counsel with King Kiril. He is not ours to have, Nan, you know this." He averted his eyes, understanding his wife's pain and sorrow, and gently escorted her from Blaze's bedside. It was Neid's turn to really look at the boy.

His hair was disheveled from Nan stroking his head. His face was thin and drawn, but there was a familiarity about it. His lips were slightly parted in his slumber. The boy turned on his side, revealing a slightly pointed ear that was not uncommon in Timeria, where elves, humans, and sprites dwelled in peace until the two main kingdoms, elves of Ceretheena and humans of Veneselia, melted into the unique people of Timeria. Neid was not a Timerian. He had traveled to Gresham-fief carrying supplies from Bevisson but stayed when he was offered some land in the fiefdom after he met, fell in love with, and married Nan.

The boy curled his hands up to his face. Neid counted ten small fingers that peeked out from under their bandages and examined them with his own farm-calloused hands. Then, Neid touched the boy's birthmark, the crescent moon. Nan had been so taken by it that Neid believed it had importance. Perhaps when King Kiril saw it, he'd understand the meaning. It would be wonderful to have a boy such as this; for a moment, Neid dreamed of fatherhood, too, but then Nan arrived at the bed and moved his hand to shake the boy awake, breaking his trance.

"Come on! Wake up! Ratson, we mustn't make Lord Gresham wait." Blaze woke with a sudden jerk. His hair stuck up around his head, making Neid laugh.

"I guess you could do with a bath and maybe some new clothes." Neid picked the lanky boy up and set him on his feet. Blaze stood there, blinking away the necessity of being awake. He wore one of Neid's white sleeping gowns, which extended far beyond his height and arms' length. Using the left sleeve, Blaze rubbed his eye.

"Ha, ha! Aren't you just the sight?" Nan reached for the boy, hugged him, and guided his half-awake body to a table. She lifted him into the chair, and placed a plate of eggs in front of him, and he instinctively ate.

Neid suppressed a joyous laugh and told Nan, "I'll be back."

"Where are you going?"

"Well, he can't go to court in my nightgown, can he?"

"Oh, no. I completely forgot about what to have him wear. I tried to save his tunic and breeches, but they were just falling to pieces."

"I think our lord's mother has some old shifts that would be appropriate for Ratson wear to meet the king and she did offer any help that we needed for Ratson." Blaze choked on his eggs. He was going to meet *who*? He coughed away any extra eggs that remained in his mouth.

"Did you say, 'meet the king?'"

"Yes, Ratson. We—you and I—are traveling to the capital, Venesial, to meet the king so that you can explain your run-in with the devlins," Neid said, very matter-of-factly."Now I must find you some clothing for high court. I'll be right back."

Neid left with Blaze following him until the boy tripped on the oversized nightgown. He struggled to unwrap his feet, pooling the extra material on his lap. He sat on the floor, defeated. *Soon, I'll be on my way to meet . . . the king,* Blaze thought, and he swallowed hard, entirely unaware that Nan was filling a tub with soap and water. He wondered, *How could my birth day have gone so awry?*

Lord Gresham sat high upon his charger. The gray steed stood over twenty hands tall, causing the fief-lord to tower over his subjects. Neid walked his horse up to Lord Gresham's flank. Sitting behind Neid, Blaze felt small as he glanced up at the lord, though he thought the lord's superior position made him an easy target. He worried that the horse would falter with his legs dangling against the horse's flanks, but Nan put him on the horse back at the castle.

"Ratson, I am the lord of Gresham-fief, you need to tell me more about the devlins." His voice bolstered a false authoritative tone as though he was only playing at being the lord. He wore a huge signet ring carved with his crest.

"Um, there was a Queen of the Devlins, and she, Amoria, had . . ." His voice trailed off as he tried to retell the events of his encounter. Neid and Lord Gresham looked at him expectantly, holding on to every word. Their stares caused Blaze to feel embarrassed.

"It's okay, Ratson. Lord Gresham is on *your* side... *I'm* on *your* side." Neid smiled over his shoulder at the boy sitting behind him in the saddle. It didn't help Blaze's confidence any.

"All right Ratson," said Lord Gresham."I know it is hard for a flotsam to speak with someone of my stature. I truly understand."

He understands? Blaze slumped as he rode behind Neid. He looked down at the fine threads of the tunic he was wearing and the black leather breeches and boots Neid had found for him. He unthinkingly rubbed the tunic's fabric between his fingers. Nan had even trimmed a"few" strands of his hair, shaping it into a presentable state. He felt like he was losing himself. Blaze glanced at the pompous lord. He let his left hand fall to the pouch and eating knife that Nan placed lovingly on his belt, making sure it sat within easy reach. She had kissed his forehead and then lifted him up behind Neid on the horse.

To Lord Gresham, Blaze was nothing, even though Neid and Nan treated him like family.

"Ratson, are you okay?" Neid sounded concerned, and he genuinely was. Blaze didn't respond. He leaned forward momentarily. He wished that Nan and Neid were his parents and that it was not uncommon to visit with the king.

Riding with his head resting on Neid's back, Blaze remembered his reality. He was a thief—not a great one, but a thief, nonetheless. He had been born to two thieves, Rhatt and Jade, who were neither married nor handfasted. Blaze had been a mistake—something Jade, his mother, had told him frequently until she left for Cadmaria. Rhatt was now dead. Blaze was unsure of the circumstances that surrounded his death, but Master Locke had reassured him that Rhatt had really loved him and would do anything for him. Blaze doubted it in his mind and heart, but still, to the other thieves he bragged about his lofty place at the guild. Secretly, he hated who he was. Likewise, he despised the constables, the clerics, the Cadmarians, and just about everyone.

He was self-reliant, but he knew he lacked talent for anything else. He had overheard Master Locke and some of the older thieves, most of whom had since left the guild, discussing in detail the fact that Blaze was bad luck and a menace. He hadn't stayed long enough to hear Locke's counter. As he remembered the past, hardened tears blurred his vision. He knew he would be nothing more than what Rhatt had been: it was his destiny. He sighed. The time had come to finish the charade of being part of Nan's and Neid's family once and for all.

Blaze scanned the area. The open fields of Gresham-fief had turned into a worn, tree-lined path with large ferns and brush. Innumerable trees cluttered the forest, keeping that which dwelt inside a secret. A rainstorm had left puddles along the pathway, which the wheels of the carts sprayed up at the individual riders. He could feel Neid breathing as he held his head to the man's back. After all, he had a place where he belonged, where a pie and a wink waited, he hoped, even after this long break from his normal activities. Blaze lifted his head off of Neid's back, but still grasped the man's tunic. Blaze had some riding experience of his own thanks to Rhatt, who had set up the lessons prior to his death.

"Rhatt had insight, which helped to provide you with what you need," Mason, one of the thieves, had assured him at the time.

Of everyone in Blaze's life, Mason was the one person who Blaze trusted most at the guild and who he wished to emulate. He was his confidant; the one he could gripe to when life was unjust and Master unfair. A tear ran down Blaze's cheek. He knew he couldn't travel to the capital to speak with the king. It wasn't something that someone like him ever could do – he was nothing in comparison.

They'll probably imprison me for pretending to be someone else. After all, the king knows all. Blaze believed this wholeheartedly. The Gresham caravan snaked out in front of and behind Blaze. Glancing behind him, he noticed a possible escape. He and Neid rode just in front of the food cart and its horse, which plodded along with great difficulty. The horse was limping slightly, and Blaze wondered if it had thrown its shoe with no one the wiser. He hatched his plan based on the position of the food cart and the horse's disability.

Neid felt the boy fall backwards off the horse.

"RATSON!"

Neid feared the racing hooves would trample the boy. The food cart driver turned his horse toward the wood on the side of the pathway. The sudden movement tipped the cart over. Blaze was nearly crushed, but he rolled away. Lord Gresham turned his horse around only to see the onslaught of disaster.

When the cart tipped, it smashed to pieces. Food spilled out and lay on the road. The horse also flipped, catching itself in its harness snapping its neck in the process. Neid turned his horse, avoiding the destruction, and attempted to control his startled mount. The domino effect continued down the caravan. The confusion spilled out of control—guards injured, horses spooked. Thankfully, the coach carrying Lady Gresham and her children was untouched aside from being pulled off the road.

"Ratson! Ratson!" Blaze could hear Neid calling over the other voices. Blaze fell into a puddle, muddying up his tunic. He removed his cloak and flung it to the side. He quickly covered the rest of his body with the mud. He grabbed some of the ferns as he ran up to higher ground. He grabbed more ferns and small sticks on his way to a hiding place. Blaze discovered a thicket of brambles, which scratched his bare back as he entered its center, the thorny branches intertwining to create a makeshift dwelling. He grabbed some of the small sticks and stuck them into his hair. He used his boot's sole to unearth the dirt below his feet. He dragged his hands through the dirt and darkened his face. He hid amongst the bushes bare from the waist up. Bugs bit his flesh, but he ignored them, focusing his attention on silence. He had strategically tossed the tunic using it as a decoy. Blaze longed for its softness, but some sacrifices were worth the loss. His ears pulsed with his heartbeat, and he worried that it would give away his hiding place.

A guard and Neid searched Blaze's side of the wood. As planned, Neid found Blaze's tunic. He searched deeper, only to pass Blaze several times without seeing him. Blaze had a clear view of the entire party's movements, and he watched as the other guards assisted with the tipped cart and dead horse. One guard pointed at the horse's hoof and indicated that it had indeed lost its shoe, causing all this chaos. They unhitched the horse from the harness and dragged it just off the roadway and into the wood, leaving it for the wildlife that lived within the boundaries of Timeria.

Neid called for Ratson over and over with tears welling and worry clearly readable on his face. Blaze hunkered down further amongst the brambles. Neid's foot caught a vine and he thundered hard onto the ground. Blaze felt badly for causing all of this harm. It was never his intention. Neid lay on the ground, regaining his bearings and breath after his fall had knocked the wind out of him. The man was mere inches from Blaze. Blaze huddled in, trying desperately not to move and holding his breath so as not to give away his position. He was sure Neid would find him. All Neid had to do was look to his left and see his muddy face. Instead Neid picked himself up and searched to his right. He moved through brush, seeming more and more frantic. He pushed aside brambles, which tore into his skin. Blaze knew he was caught.

"Please, Eldon. Please, Eldon. Please, Eldon." He prayed with his whole being.

"Ratson! Where are you, lad? By the gods, please bring him back safely. Poor, poor lad. He's all alone in the world, like I was until I came to Gresham. Gods, please save him. Ratson! Ratson!" Neid lamented.

Blaze was moved by Neid's love, concern, and desperation. He was reconsidering going back to the safety of Nan and Neid's protection when Lord Gresham called out to Neid. Neid turned toward his lord.

"Let's go, Neid. He is either dead or doesn't want to be found. Sometimes that's the way of those guttersnipes. Take my advice, Neid, and forget him. He's not worth your trouble. Someone should dispose of those types; they are using up the food supply of those of us who are worth something. It's such a waste of Timeria's resources." Blaze's anger boiled.

"Adoon's curse!" Blaze whispered under his breath, careful not to alert Neid who was hovering nearby in one last-ditch effort to find the boy. He watched as the caravan reassembled with the salvaged food stashed inside the coach with Lady Gresham. Reluctantly, Neid returned to the caravan and mounted his horse. He continually kept vigil, searching the wood with his eyes. He just *had* to find the boy—but there was no movement. Blaze watched the caravan and Neid stagger along the path, continuing onward to Venesial. He stared after them until night settled over the area.

A soft rain trickled down on to the foliage. Blaze stayed dry in his hideaway. The silence and the constant hush of rain in the forest overtook Blaze and lulled the boy to sleep.

CHAPTER 3
CHALLENGE

BALLARDTON GREETED BLAZE with a fall wind that carried the scent of baking pies. He had spent several days trying to find his way back to town. His stomach growled in protest and his mouth watered. He shivered, but he pressed on.

Once again, King's Highway was deserted. He looked around; autumn had grabbed hold of Ballardton. The trees had turned to hues of red, brown, and yellow. Blaze felt excitement arise inside him; this was his favorite time of the year. A throwing dagger flew by his head without fazing him.

"Blaze!"

"Hey, Dellanie." The brown-haired girl stood with another dagger poised for flight. Blaze raised his eyes, annoyed that she found him before he could get a tunic.

"Everybody's been looking for you. I think Master Locke was worried about you." She gave Blaze a sly smile.

"Yeah, right. I don't believe it for a minute. It was probably just gas." Dellanie smirked at Blaze realizing that Blaze continually downed any favor that master gave him. She glanced at the ground where the dagger had fallen. Her smirk turned to a frown when the dagger didn't land neatly in the ground pommel up as she had hoped. Blaze had a love-hate relationship with Master Locke, Dellanie assumed it had something to do with an event in the past. She sized Blaze up and down, noting his bare, bug-bitten chest with scratch marks that reddened his skin.

"What happened to your tunic? Or is this some new fashion that you're starting? I don't think it'll catch on." She pressed her dagger into his stomach, but it didn't puncture.

"Hey! Cut that out!" Blaze regretted the words even as he said them.

"If you want me to. . . ." Dellanie grinned, her eyes sparkling with enthusiasm. He suddenly felt uncomfortable, so he walked away from her. She turned, sheathed her dagger in her sleeve, and shrugged. He glanced back only to notice her retreat.

"Where're you going?"

"I have more important things to do than bother with you. Oh, and by the way, if you need a new tunic, there's one hanging on the line behind the constabulary. It should fit okay."

"The constabulary? Really?"

"That's what I said. See you!" Dellanie disappeared from Blaze's sight. He was jealous of her keen abilities, but then again, she was just a girl. He realized that she was right about needing a new tunic though, especially before going back into the guild house.

Blaze crept around Ballardton, hoping not to see his colleagues—especially his best friend, Venom. Venom, he knew, would tease him mercilessly. He detoured from his journey to the constables' barracks and headed toward the marketplace. As he had expected, both piemen were busy at work. Nearby, Gavin slept on top of an empty pie tray, his face smeared with pie filling. Blaze schemed to scare the sleeping pie thief. Gavin had mousy-brown hair with ordinary brown eyes. His looks were perfect for thievery because nothing made him stand out. Blaze thought he wasted his time stealing pies when he could steal coins and then buy the pies from the reputable pieman, Nerapi. At least then he'd know that they weren't poisoned. Blaze shook his head at Gavin. It was obvious to Blaze that the pies he had eaten caused him to pass out into a stupor. Blaze considered stealing Gavin's clothes, but after examining the younger thief's tunic, he decided against it. Blaze smirked when he thought up an ingenious and devious plan that involved the sleeping thief.

Carefully, Blaze lifted Gavin over his shoulder. Gavin's limbs lay limp and his head drooped across Blaze's back. Blaze teetered under Gavin's weight, but he quickly shifted and regained his position. He knew he had to be quick; otherwise, he would lose his strength and nerve.

Blaze ran between the empty market carts, passing by the Duke's manor house, until he reached the constabulary. With his energy nearly spent, he stopped to catch his breath. He felt something wet drip down his back. He made a face when he realized Gavin drooled in his sleep. Blaze readjusted Gavin's position as he rounded to the side of the barracks. There, as expected, was the hitching post for the horses and their drinking trough. With one quick movement, Blaze dropped Gavin into the trough.

The constables emerged immediately from the door, carrying mugs of ale. They stopped when they discovered a surprised boy sitting upright in the trough. Their laughter rose, and Gavin eventually joined in.

Blaze entered the thieves' guild still cinching his tunic closed. It was wider than anticipated, but Dellanie had given him the challenge.

"Blaze, you're back!" a dark-blond-haired boy with olive skin exclaimed. He ran up to

Blaze and playfully punched him in the side. Blaze smiled at him. This was Venom.

"Easy, Venom. I just got these." Venom stepped back to examine Blaze's new attire.

"Hm, not bad—but I did better. Don't you think?" Venom twirled around, spreading his arms so Blaze could admire his clothes.

"No." Blaze pushed him, and Venom fell to the ground in laughter.

"So, where've you been?" Venom asked as Blaze helped him up from the floor.

"Around." Blaze didn't meet his friend's gaze.

"Where?"

"Just around."

"Not in Ballardton 'around.'"

"True." Blaze walked to Master Locke's office door with Venom following him. Blaze knocked, and the door creaked from the pressure.

"So where?"

"Don't worry, Venom. I won't tell you." Blaze put his hand on Venom's shoulder to reassure Venom of their friendship. The door opened.

"Okay, great! So where?" Blaze entered Master Locke's office, closing the door on his best friend as he glanced back at Locke with a sly grin.

"Hey!" Venom cried out as the door swung closed.

Locke sat at his desk, which took up the entire room.

"Welcome back, Blaze."

On the shelves behind Locke were books, maps, and scrolls, all unknown to Blaze as they were kept clandestine by the master thief. Locke was perusing a book, which he closed when Blaze approached. Blaze felt slighted by Locke's secrecy, but he made eye contact with the master. When he reached the desk, he removed the signet ring from his pouch. He picked at the black wax that was embedded in the grooves of the emblem. Locke watched him curiously. *I don't want to give it up, but what am I going to do with this huge ring? Master will give me something for it, I know. Look how big it is!*

Blaze smiled, delighted, glancing up at Locke, who tried to see what the boy concealed in his young hands. Blaze tossed the ring onto the desktop, and it skipped across the veneer and clinked to a stop just in front of Locke. Blaze stared at Locke questioningly.

"How much?"

Locke picked up the ring and twisted it between his thumb and forefinger. Out of his desk drawer, he removed a jeweler's loop. He examined each stone, which encrusted a fiefdom's crest. Blaze sighed with impatience although he was pleased with Locke's careful analysis. "Yeah, so how much?"

"I'll have to—" Locke's words drifted into his own thoughts. Blaze banged on the desk, returning Locke's voice. "—Three ebons."

"No. One silver; it's from a fiefdom, and I know it's worth more than three ebons."

Locke was momentarily taken back by Blaze's sudden shrewdness and the appearance of this particular ring.

"Four ebons and a hollowed-out coppie."

"Nine ebons."

"Five, Blaze. That's my final offer."

"Eight and we'll be straight." Blaze smirked, pleased to use a rhyme he had heard Rhatt declare many times. Blaze really loved clichés; his absolute favorite was, "One day, you'll be skewered." He had told this to nearly everyone in the guild.

"All right, Blaze, you win. Eight it is." Pride surfaced in Locke's eyes, but it went unnoticed by Blaze. Blaze held out his hand for the ebony coins. Locke reached into his own pouch and counted out the eight coins. He handed them to the young thief, who put them away in his pouch. "Nice tunic, Blaze."

"Yeah, it is." Blaze straightened out his tunic until he matched Locke's gaze. "I don't like small talk, Master. You know that."

"I'm not trying to make small talk, Blaze. I was commenting on your clothes in the hopes that you'd tell me where you've been these past few weeks."

"Hm." Blaze considered and shook his head, denying Locke the information. However, Locke had a relatively good idea given the ring. Locke's mind swirled with questions. *How in the world did he get to Gresham-fief and get this ring that never leaves the castle? Does he know?* Locke glanced up at Blaze, nodded, and then reengaged the boy.

"Okay, Blaze, then I guess we're done here, and I have other business to attend to." Locke waved Blaze out of his office. As Blaze turned to leave, Locke opened his book and watched the boy exit. Locke sighed. "Blazey, what am I going to do with you?" He shook his head in exasperation.

Blaze reentered the bustling common room. Venom stood next to Locke's door waiting for Blaze, but he spent his time watching Nightshade. Blaze followed Venom's eyes. With both boys staring in her direction, Nightshade felt their intrusion.

"What? Can't you leave a tender girl alone?" Nightshade stretched out her arms and leaned in angrily at them. Venom and Blaze nearly split their sides with laughter.

"I don't see a 'tender girl' anywhere near here. Do you, Venom?" Blaze smirked, wiping tears away, and his eyes danced with mischief.

"Nah, me neither. What I see is . . ." Laughter took control of Venom so he couldn't speak again.

". . . a mule's end?" Blaze grinned wider, bursting into uncontainable laughter. Nightshade dashed toward them with fury in her eyes. She grabbed Venom's hair first and then Blaze's.

Blaze wrestled his hair free, tearing some out of his head as he did. Nightshade kept a firmer hold on Venom, who decided that trying to kiss her would be a better counterattack. The two struck the door and the hinges gave way from the strain. They scurried to the side before Master Locke appeared. There was a pulling on the door until the whole door came completely off its frame. Locke stood in the doorway holding the knob and the now horizontal door. His eyes showed the parental annoyance that rose inside him.

"Who?" Locke asked menacingly.

A small, female voice said Blaze's name.

Blaze furrowed his brow and mouthed,"Me?"

Locke apparently didn't care."All right, I want to see Blaze and Venom in my office. Nightshade, I'll talk to you later. Boys, in here, right now! And I expect *someone* to fix this door." Locke threw the door into the common room, careful that it did no harm. Dorken and Pip picked it up and carried it out of the guild house.

Blaze and Venom reluctantly entered Locke's office. They sighed in unison. Venom was the first to speak in his defense. Blaze stood quietly, unable to speak for fear that Master might ask him about his month away from the guild again.

"Master Locke, I didn't do anything! Actually it was . . ." Venom quickly glanced at Blaze. He had assumed that Venom would blame Nightshade, but instead he said,"Blaze." Blaze stared at Venom, mouth agape with incredulity.

"Is that so? Blaze, what do you have to say on your behalf?" Locke questioned. Blaze said nothing, anger raging inside him. *I can't believe this; I just got back! Oh, I'll get him for this!* He fumed and his anger locked his tongue to silence. His silence suggested his answer to Locke.

"Okay then. Boys, I believe you're both responsible for what happened to the door. I'm tiring of this. I am going to have you both . . ."

"Hi, Master Locke!" Aldric stood in the doorway with an impish grin across his face, spinning the timepiece that hung from a string on his neck. Blaze wanted to wipe that smile off Aldric's face forever. Aldric looked around the doorframe."I think you are missing a door."

Blaze sneered at Aldric, curled his lip and snorted with disgust. *Why does he have to be here? Get out of here!* Aldric had sun-bleached, blond hair and smiling blue eyes. He was nearly a head shorter than Blaze and had an enormously annoying habit of being overly cheerful.

"I have to show you what I got today!" He pushed in front of Blaze and Venom. Venom was pleased with the distraction and stealthily started to slip away. Blaze was annoyed at Aldric's showboating but followed Venom's lead.

"Wait here, boys," Locke said sternly. Both boys stopped in their tracks, keeping their stances of retreat."Aldric, can't you see that I am speaking to Blaze and Venom?"

"Ah, yes, but I'd like to cash out my lot, which, I think, is my best this week. I've got five necklaces, some bracelets, but they could be anklets especially if you had really large ankles—who is judging? They're multipurpose then. I've got another medallion, and I think it's bigger than the last one. I also found some ebons just lying on the ground, but I don't need to trade those. And I've got this ring. I think it's a ladies ring because it fits my thumb." Aldric grinned proudly. Master Locke sighed, knowing that he couldn't just ignore the intruding thief. Aldric just wouldn't let him.

"All right. Boys, just wait to the side. This will only take a moment. Go ahead, Aldric. Let me see it." Aldric reached inside his pouch and withdrew a handful of jewelry that outshined Blaze's single ring. The quality of the jewels was fair at best, but to Blaze staring at the sheer number of items in comparison to his find, they were unparalleled.

"Those are the ebons I found. I'll keep them. Oh, and here's the ring." Aldric popped the ring off of his thumb. It was tiny, probably a young noble's ring, but given that Aldric didn't seem to know, Blaze surmised that he must have found it on the ground with the ebons. Still, Blaze's face reddened and his blood boiled. Blaze tightened his fist and narrowed his eyes, feeling once again that he was lesser in his ability to succeed. This was not the first time Aldric had stolen Blaze's moment. At the tourneys during Ballardton's annual festival, Aldric typically beat out Blaze in most of the games. The majority of their peers didn't feel the need to be validated in their abilities, but then, nobody had Blaze's track record of failure. Blaze read Locke this time. He could tell that Aldric captivated Locke. The master's attention became Aldric's and Aldric's alone—Locke's face showed nothing but pride. Blaze bit down on his bottom lip and dug in his teeth. The taste of his own blood made him stop. Blaze watched red-faced while Locke calculated the total lot's value.

"I think a fair amount is two ebons and four coppies. What do you say, Aldric?"

"Sure, Master Locke. That's what I thought, too." Aldric leaned on Locke's desk hands folded grinning brightly. "And with the three ebons that I found, I made out pretty good. Don't you think, Blaze?" A disgusted look wrinkled Blaze's nose when Aldric mentioned him by name, and he momentarily turned away. Locke used a key to open his top right drawer and with both hands, he removed a small chest and placed it on his desk. Aldric seemed uninterested, whereas Blaze and Venom watched with great curiosity, even straining their necks to get a better glance. Locke clicked another key into the chest and the top sprung open. An interior, unnatural light illuminated the contents. The entire chest was over-filled with coins of all types. As Locke searched for the right coins, some spilled onto the desk. Blaze was sure he noticed a platinum, a few golds, silvers, ebons, and lots of coppies, and he could swear he even saw some dracoins, which were worth a king's ransom. His eyes drank in the sight of that little chest. Locke placed two ebony coins and four small copper coins in a scalloped dish on his desk. He relocked and replaced the chest in the drawer. Then he locked the drawer before returning his attention back to Aldric. Blaze followed Locke's hand as he secured the key in his pouch. A sly, knowing smile appeared on Blaze's face.

"Here you go, Aldric."

"Thanks, Master Locke! This is great, don't you think?" He turned toward Blaze and Venom. "It's so easy too." Blaze scowled, mocking the boy, and Venom smiled greedily. Venom agreed with Aldric because he just realized how he could pay for the broken door. Aldric picked up the small dish and poured its contents into his pouch. All the while he grinned at the two boys like a mouse stealing the cheese. Blaze wanted to jump him and wipe that cheeky grin off his face.

"All right, Aldric. That's enough. Now, go wash up." Locke's eyes tracked Aldric to the door where he waved a cheerful good-bye. Locke smiled and shook his head at the engaging little thief. The boy had talent, that much was obvious. *He probably charmed the jewelry right off of their owners' necks*, Locke thought. It was too bad that some of the others weren't as talented. Locke shook his head. *Thievery isn't for everyone.*

"Um, Master Locke, when do you want the money for the door?" Venom asked nonchalantly, bringing Locke to deal once again with the matter at hand.

"After Pip and Dorken return. Venom, you're free to leave for now. Blaze, you stay." Venom raised his eyebrows at Blaze and left. Blaze wondered what plan Venom had devised. He had known Venom for some time and the two became friends almost immediately, but it was a relationship that had consequences. Awkward silence filled Locke's room after Venom left.

"Blaze, you need to use your head more."

Annoyance, anger, and shame turned Blaze's eyes upward. It was a common manifestation that Locke had seen as Blaze grew.

"Let's get to the point, Master.".

"Blaze, I . . . I . . . ," Locke started, but there was an awkwardness between him and Blaze that he just couldn't correct.

"By Eldon's crown, what? Are you blaming me for the door? It wasn't really either of us, it was Nightshade. She pushed us. I'm not saying that I didn't fall into the door, I just feel that I needed to explain. If Venom and I have to pay for the door then we will, but it isn't fair. Getting it fixed is not very much, right?" Blaze spoke quickly and he spit out his words, trying his hardest to stay focused and composed.

He had wanted to blurt out,"I was attacked by devlins. I never got my wink. I never got my pie. All I got was horrible burns and you just don't care, Master! *Why?*" Instead, he demonstrated frustration with Locke, trying to show that he was strong and capable when all he felt was small and useless. Blaze banged his hands on the desk, drawing the outer room's attention. Locke closed his eyes and kept his anger in check.

"Blaze, you are going to Ceretheena when spring arrives; I've already worked out the details." Locke opened his eyes to Blaze glaring intently at him with the lights catching the tears in his hazel eyes."You'll be working at Duke Flynn's castle in Ceretheena. You'll be a servant there." Blaze stood motionless."It will be quiet there, for as you already know, the duke and duchess and their children departed the castle years ago. Therefore, there is no one to actually work for except for the house staff and the guardsmen. I have made arrangements for you to meet with Mistress Ree. She is fair and doesn't take kindly to nonsense." Again, Blaze said nothing, so Locke continued. He reached back on the shelf behind him and handed a scroll to Blaze, who refused to accept it."This will confirm your new position, the duties we've agreed to, and the duration."

Locked placed the scroll in front of Blaze on the desk. Tears welled up in the boy's eyes and they teetered on the edge of falling. His lip began to tremble. *Was he planning this all along? Even while I was gone?* A tear rolled down his cheek. Blaze finally broke his silence with his voice quivering.

"How long, Master?" Using his sleeve, he cleaned his face.

"Now, Blaze, remember it won't start until the spring, and it's fall now. Actually, come to think of it, you left on your special day." Blaze leaned forward, sniffling away the tears, anticipating the recognition of his turn-year."Hm, seems like that was forever ago now." Master took a deep breath and then continued on."I'll hold on to the scroll, and before we put an expiration date on this, perhaps you should see what this is like first. It will be good for you."

"How long?" Blaze slammed his palms on the desk, bending forward into Locke's personal space.

"At least . . . until your next turn-year."

"A full turn-year? That's so long."

"It's not that long, Blaze. After all, you are a Timerian and not a Bevisson human. Time is nearly irrelevant."

"Why do you have to send me away again? When I was a kitchen boy at Lords and Ladies Inn, you promised you'd never send me to a place like that again. I'm not going! Please, Master."

"It's not going to be like that. These are Timerians—not Cadmarians. You're going and that is my final word as master."

"No! It's going to be the same as last time." Blaze stamped his foot and banged the desk.

"Blaze, this is not up for debate. Rhatt wanted you to try other things." Blaze sputtered to silence.

"You always say that when you want me to do something that I don't want to do. Stop bringing up Rhatt. I'm going to get better, Master, I promise!" Blaze pleaded. Locke could still see the Little that he was."I got the ring, didn't I? I know it wasn't a lot, but it was clearer than Aldric's finds. Besides, I am Rhatt's son, and he was a great thief. Everyone says it, even Mason. But you keep sending me away because of that—I don't think Rhatt wanted me to leave. He called this my destiny. You know, I've heard what you've said to Mason about Rhatt and Jade. And I know that Pip and the others think I'm just a bothersome brat. I'm not. I am not going, and you can't make me."

As if on cue, Pip and Dorken returned with a door.

"Master, this new door cost *only* seven silvers and eight ebons, and the carpenter assured us that it won't break like the last one; that's why the high price. Check out all the details! It tells the story of how Ballard saved Timeria! Look, there he is in the middle of the door, smack-dab center! We both liked it and thought you would too." Locke shut his eyes, shook his head ruefully.

"Pip, Dorken, why didn't you just get the other door fixed?" Pip moved forward to answer, pushing Blaze to the side.

"Well, Master, the carpenter said that the other door wasn't worth its weight in gold or anything—not even coppies. Then he showed us this door and I just fell in love with it. When we saw this door, our hearts just knew this belonged in the guild. Look, it's identical on both sides! We were so lucky to be able to get it. He's charging the guild, you'll get the invoice by courier in the next day or two. It's a win. We can tell the Littles the story of the mighty wizard Ballard during the winter months and it doesn't cost anyone anything because the guild will pay for it! Win-win!" Locke drooped his eyes tiredly, knowing he'd have to deal with the pair spending the coin that would be needed over the winter for food. What they didn't know was that there would be two more mouths to feed this winter as well as all of the extra Littles that needed refuge. Locke exhaled exasperatedly.

"Thank you, Dorken, Pip. I'll expect the invoice then. Please hang it so there will at least be a door on the frame. Also, I expect a rousing story of the wizard Ballard this winter from you both."

Pip squealed with delight. Dorken glanced at Blaze; in response, Blaze curled his lip into a disgusted snarl. Pip laughed, catching Dorken's expression. Blaze overheard whispers from Pip and Dorken that bore his name as they worked on installing the door in its new home. He pursed his lips and sneered in their direction.

"We spent all that time looking for the bratty Little. Has Master asked him where he was? It would have been the first words out of my mouth," Pip whispered to Dorken.

"Don't worry, Pip, I'm sure that Master has his reasons and will talk to the scamp as soon as the door is closed under Ballard's watchful eye."

When the door was hung, the two thieves started to leave, but Pip offered an extra piece of advice. "Everything is done, Master. Be good, Blaze—Ballard is watching." Dorken placed his hand on Pip's shoulder as the two finally exited.

"Ballard isn't watching, so don't worry," Master Locke told Blaze. "He is long dead and his manor has become our dungeon. Now I'll hold the scroll until you leave in the spring, and Blaze, about the door . . ." Locke rethought the punishment for the door, as its detailed relief would be enough to remind the younger thieves to be wary of roughhousing. He was ready to talk to Blaze about the boy's whereabouts for the past weeks, but Blaze cut him off, fully aware that the wizard Ballard would be witness to the negotiations.

"Wait, let me stop you. Here's the money for the door." *I don't want to owe you anything.*

Locke raised his eyebrows, wondering what new reasoning Blaze would attempt this time. Locke knew Blaze was right about the feelings of the older thieves.

"I don't have to go until the spring though, right?"

"That's correct, Blaze. They have enough staff for now and asked for a boy starting in the spring. I chose you to go—"

"Because Rhatt wanted me to try other things. I heard you the first time. You'll all ways say what you think Rhatt would say because he's not here. If I wasn't born here, you might not be able to use what Rhatt wanted against me to do your bidding." Master sighed again. *Rhatt, your son needs you.*

"Okay, I'll take only some of your coins, Blaze, for the door. I just want you and Venom to think about your surroundings more. I'll hold onto the scroll for now. It's right here on this shelf. I am not going to address your comments. You are the right age for this move."

"I'll go, but I don't have to be happy about it."

Locke slid half of the coins back into Blaze's pile. Blaze took them and turned to leave.

"Also, Blaze, you'll need to leave your lock-picking kit with me here. You don't have to leave it right now, but you do before you go to Ceretheena." Blaze glared hard at Locke while holding onto the kit's pouch. It had been his father's before it was his. Leaving the kit would have to be one of the hardest things for Blaze to release, especially to Locke. He nodded. Then he turned around, looked at Locke, and smiled smugly.

"I'm telling them," he said as he thumbed the door, "that I've got a mission." Blaze inhaled, stood up straighter, and opened the door, struggling under the weight of it. "Boy, that's a heavy door. The guild will fall before it ever does."

Locke shook his head. "You're probably right about the door, and what you tell the others is up to you." He spoke only to himself, sighed, then unrolled the maps.

"Can someone send Nightshade in?" Locke yelled out to the ensemble that he was sure still listened near the door.

CHAPTER 4

WINTER

OORS, MISSIONS, and the Queen of the Devlins became distant memories as the guild made repairs in preparation for the harsh winter weather. Master Locke stockpiled wood and bartered for a new guild roof.

"Hullo, everyone! It's cold out there! I think it might end up being a blizzard. It is early this year, but don't you worry none. Denalisa will make sure that you are all filled with the best stew you've ever eaten." The woman spoke of herself in the third person, and she called to the ensemble as she walked into the guild carrying a basket with vegetables. Blaze grimaced at Denalisa's entrance, her irritating voice wrinkling his nose. Denalisa was wife to a fifth-level spy called Barden. Barden was working on taking his master test. He had once lived under the safety of the guild's roof; now, he and his wife lived in the vacant room that once belonged to Jade and Rhatt, where Blaze had been born.

The pair had come to the guild not more than a month ago. His wife was a nanny on a farm before they married, so she was excited to work with the boys and girls of the guild. Barden was so excited as he introduced her to the guild, and he was impressed that the guild hadn't really changed, except for the faces. It was notable that the new door to Master's office had given a refreshed macabre air to the whole of the guild, which made Barden laugh with child-ish delight upon hearing of the door's installation as he heard the actions of his friends, Dorken and Pip. Barden's arrival at the guild came just days after Pip and Dorken were sent on a mission, which would keep them away for many years. Many thought they were being punished for purchasing such a garish door for the inflated price of a few silvers.

Barden had made an extra effort when he met Blaze again. Blaze played the exchange over in his mind.

"Oh sweet Denalisa, I'd like you to meet Blazey. He was born here. He's Rhatt's son, but Rhatt died, and now this little guy is a ward of the guild. His mother is Jade, but who knows where the wind took her. Back when I was young, we'd play fun nasty tricks on him, but he knew it was all in good fun. Right, Blazey?" A laugh appeared in Barden's introduction, and he rustled Blaze's hair. Blaze tried to fix his hair as Denalisa bent slightly to meet Blaze's eyes. She reached down and hugged him as though he was a favorite doll of hers. Humiliation reddened his face and he backed away from her. After Blaze left, Barden whispered, "He's also Master's nephew, but no one ever mentions it. He gets away with murder, so beware."

The anguish of the meeting set Blaze off again when the tall woman entered the guild so cheerfully. Blaze had to admit that the food had tasted better since Denalisa started preparing the dinners at the guild. Littles climbed on her like goats on top of a shared mountain. They would push each other off of her, but all Denalisa would do in response was to help the Littles back up. The worst part about Denalisa was her insistence on manners, language, and cleanliness. Venom enjoyed the lady's attention as she inspected him for lice. He was clean of nits, but just being near her made him swoon with adoration. She gave him an herbal sashay, which would help him to bring out "just how handsome a lad he really was." Venom immediately wore the sashay, and Blaze informed him that he smelt like a rotting flower on a hot sweaty day. Venom ignored Blaze's taunts and returned to Denalisa, wholeheartedly enjoying her attention and conversation. Nightshade had found Denalisa intriguing, and she began educating Denalisa about each of her charges. Denalisa had asked specific questions about Blaze. The more the two spoke, the larger the tales Nightshade told began to explode. Giggling and glancing towards Blaze and Venom, Nightshade and Denalisa whispered to each other covering their mouths. Blaze let the two talk until he could no longer listen without intervening.

"Just . . . stop! I've had enough! I'm nothing like that!" Blaze turned to Denalisa. "And how could you listen to her? She lies . . . always!" Blaze's protests confirmed Nightshade's stories and Denalisa reacted by laughing in his face. Blaze was irritated beyond words and he stormed out of the guild. Nightshade stared after, happily knowing she had irritated him.

"He's so cute," Denalisa said. "He reminds me of this little boy I took care of when I was working on a farm. He was just as angry. His anger was a mask for what he was really feeling, so I won't take Blaze's anger at me to heart. It's so good to see him speak up for himself."

Nightshade looked at Denalisa and smiled sweetly. "Hey, we could do each other's hair! I bet you know a lot of different kinds of braids."

Denalisa laughed, agreeing with Nightshade's assumption.

"Yes Nightshade, I do! I used to braid my horse's mane and tail all the time when I was a girl, and then I had children to take care of with hair as beautiful as yours." Denalisa picked up her brush and started the task. Nightshade was surprisingly agreeable and let her work hair-braiding magic.

Outside of the guild, Blaze was still fuming. His heart pounded hard in his chest, and he placed his hand against it, hoping to calm it.

"Hey, Blazey! What's wrong? You look like you saw a hoard of devlins!" Barden said as he came upon the young thief. Blaze tightened his jaw, glared at Barden, and moved his arm to rest at his side.

"I have, but I don't think you are talking about real devlins, right?" Barden looked at him, puzzled. "Oh, never mind. It's her!" A laugh erupted from Barden, making Blaze jump.

"Oh, don't worry about Denalisa. She means no harm. She's just very caring and I love her for that. Blazey, when you have the love of a woman like Denalisa, everything is right in the world."

Blaze scowled. Barden looked up to the sky where he was a million miles away in love. Blaze looked to the sky to see what Barden was looking at but found nothing except for cloudy, snow-filled skies. He left Barden in his dreamy love-struck state. As he walked away from the guild, he realized that he didn't really have any place to go. Flurries of snow began to fall, and Blaze clutched his cloak closer to his body. Its warmth was a welcome comfort.

After some time, Blaze found himself walking to Spider's camp, which was hidden to the north of Ballardton inside a small cave. The flurries were accompanied by a blustery wind, which whipped aside the poplin cloth of Spider's door.

"Spider, you home?" Blaze called out, even though he knew that the boy would be inside.

A small voice spoke that could barely be heard over the wind that passed Blaze's ears. Blaze threw back the opening flap. Spider was covered in blankets from head to toe. The only part of him uncovered was his eyes. Those eyes were a spectacular blue with a ring of long full black eyelashes that blinked at Blaze.

"You okay?"

Spider nodded under the blankets. Blaze leaned down, resting his hands on his knees to talk to Spider.

"Are you cold?" Again, he nodded.

"Where's my big brother? Is he coming?" Blaze shook his head.

"No, um, I don't think Venom is." Spider frowned.

"Did he send you, then?" Blaze looked around the permanent camp that was Spider's home. It was clean for the most part. The ground was covered by a wool rug, which surprised Blaze as it really did prevent the cold from coming up through the ground. The camp was a shallow cave that could very easily have hidden a small Copper Dragon back before the barrier was erected by Lord Ballard. Two baskets that were usually filled with fruits and vegetables were mostly empty. As Blaze walked around the living area, Spider followed him with his eyes. In the corner of the cave sat a small table and a large rock.

"I sit there . . . to eat."

Blaze turned his torso toward the blanket-covered lump. He reexamined the baskets.

"Spider, do you want to come back to the guild? Get some food? Get warm by the fire?" The blankets moved in agreement. "Do you need anything to bring back?"

Spider uncovered his face, revealing a bed-head mass of black, loose curls. Spider searched through the blankets and pulled out a softie that he carried with him when he left the shelter. It was a sea dragon. The once blue-green scales of its body were now threadbare and full of bald spots. To Blaze, it looked like it should be thrown into the fire because it had lost all of its value. Blaze laughed quietly to himself that the younger boy still carried such a ridiculous trinket. Blaze gathered up a blanket and a pillow. Spider stood up in the pile of remaining blankets waiting for Blaze. He clutched the sea dragon in his thin arms.

"I'm ready! I don't need anything except my softie. His name is Lennowen. Lennowen, this is Blaze!" Blaze turned around to look at Spider. He snickered at the uselessness of the toy and Spider's choice of important things. "Say 'hello' to Lennowen, Blaze, or else he'll cry." Blaze groaned to himself. With an exasperated look and annoyed gesture, Blaze went over to the softie and shook its delicate paw, much to Spider's enjoyment. Lennowen's scales shook off with every movement, but Spider was pleased that Blaze had accommodated him.

Leaving Spider's cave, Blaze cursed now that the flurries had taken on large white puffs that gracefully stuck to the ground. Even in the short time he was in the cave, the storm had dropped a thin, white blanket that covered the trees, rocks, grass, and the path back to the road. The wind swirled the snow around Blaze's and Spider's feet. Spider laughed as the snow tickled his nose. He opened his mouth and waited for a snowflake to land.

"Your breath is too warm. You can't catch a snowflake. They melt before they reach your mouth." Blaze watched Spider waiting for him to be moved by Blaze's sage knowledge.

The younger boy shrugged and kept his mouth open as he started to walk in front of Blaze, nearly tripping him.

Walking back to the guild was quiet even though Spider had attempted to start a conversation every so often. When the fountain started to come into view through the snow, Blaze sighed with relief just as the snow began to uptick to a more aggressive storm. The wind itself was pushing and pulling the two boys as they rounded the corner of the fountain. Spider dropped back to Blaze, and he clung tightly to his brother's friend.

"It's been snowing longer here, Spider." Blaze trudged through the snowdrifts. "Come on up, I'll carry you." Spider sprang into Blaze's arms, and they began their journey down the street to the small, white building that was home for so many. The knackerman was out in his yard and upon seeing the two boys, he gestured for them to turn and take refuge. He ran to meet them at the end of his property, and Blaze quickened his pace. He was unsure what the knackerman would do if they went to his yard. He envisioned being placed in a cart and entering the fire. It was a recurring childish nightmare. He swallowed hard, running as fast as he could under

Spider's weight. The knackerman grabbed for him and caught his cloak. Blaze released Spider as he fell. He yelled for Spider to run to the guild and get help. Spider held onto Lennowen and ran as fast as he could.

"Venom! Venom!" he called as the winter wind deadened his calls and made his voice almost silent. Blaze rapidly worked to release the clasp on his cloak as the knackerman reeled him in closer. Just as the knackerman fished him out of the street, Blaze's clasp released and he sprinted back down the street empty-handed and without his cloak, fear and adrenaline carrying him to the guild.

Barden emerged from the guild's guest entrance and stood on the stoop, gesturing for Blaze to enter. The knackerman was closing in on him, arms outstretched, reaching for the young thief. Blaze didn't dare look behind him. He ran straight for Barden, tripped up three steps, and clung to the older spy. Barden laughed to see Blaze so frightened.

"You're safe now, Blazey. Don't worry about the big bad knackerman. He only disposes of horses, donkeys, mules, farm animals, and other unwanted things, and last I looked you're not a horse or even a horse-sprite." Blaze breathed hard, leaning against Barden. The knackerman kept coming. Blaze moved behind Barden, but Barden held him in place to face the knackerman. "Hello, sir. Is all well tonight?"

The knackerman stopped, breathing heavy, when he reached the railing of the guest entrance.

"No, not entirely. I had hoped these young ones would have helped me find my little pup. It ran off when the wind started to rock the shutters."

"Well, sir, it seems you may have given the lads quite a fright. Taken years off their lives. If we see it, we'll let you know. Animals are usually pretty resourceful in storms."

Blaze sneered at the knackerman, who bent down and whispered to Blaze just out of earshot of Barden. The man's breath was warm, rancid from chewing tobacco and liquor.

"I should have caught you, Boy. You walking in the road was what made me lose that pup. It was heading into the fire. Now I think you should go in." Blaze turned ghostly pale. The man's teeth were reminiscent of Amoria's. Blaze squeezed his eyes shut tighter than he had ever done before, all the while feeling enormous comfort from Barden's embrace. However, Barden didn't feel the same

for the boy and turned him to face the knackerman, holding Blaze
by his shoulders.

"Blazey, you should apologize." Blaze looked up at Barden
pleadingly. *I am not apologizing—didn't you hear what he wants to
do?* "As Denalisa says, manners are important. Go on, now." Barden
shook Blaze's shoulders to encourage Blaze's compliance.

"Sorry," Blaze muttered under his breath while his eyes never
made contact with the knackerman.

"Like you mean it." Barden was feeling very much like a father
figure.

"Sorry," Blaze said, grimacing, and then under his breath he
whispered, " . . . that I had to say that." Blaze stomped on Barden's
foot, releasing his grasp, and he ran inside, slamming the door
behind him. He entered the receiving area for guests who wished
to do business with Master Locke. The area was well painted
and maintained with a bench against a burgundy wall. Blaze had
never really spent much time upstairs. The previous master hadn't
allowed it, even handing down punishment for entering the sacred
space. A stairway hidden behind a fake wall led down into the main
quarters. Blaze descended the staircase at a clip.

"Oh, thank the Gods! You are okay. Where's Barden?" Denalisa
caught Blaze in her arms and hugged him. He pulled away. Had
it been before his turn-year, Blaze felt that he would have freely
accepted the affection; instead, he pulled away from her and gestured toward the stairs. He ran over to Venom and huddled with
him and Spider.

"You're as cold as an iceberg on the sea, Blaze." Venom pushed
him away.

"Lennowen was so scared. He cried." Spider rocked the softie
back and forth in front of Blaze's face.

Venom leaned over and whispered to Blaze, "So did Spider."

"I think Lennowen wants a kiss, Blaze." Blaze knocked the toy
away and joined the Littles at the hearth of the fire. His hands were
red and he tried to warm them with the fire's heat. Littles moved
away from him, acknowledging their lowly place at the guild. He
carried the outdoors with him on his clothes and body. He was
so cold that he felt that the only way to get warm was to climb in
the fire, but that was what the knackerman had wanted in the first
place. He backed away from it, grabbing a blanket that lay on the
floor unattended.

Denalisa waited expectantly at the bottom of the stairs for Barden. Aldric leaned into her and was deeply explaining how a pocket watch that he carried about his neck worked—or at least how he suspected it worked.

"It's magic! You turn this little thing and then it works! It has something here written in a different language. It was my mum's before she died." Denalisa was barely listening to him; however, she wrapped her arm around him and squeezed a comforting reassurance. Blaze smiled slightly, noticing that Aldric wasn't getting the attention that he wanted. Barden sauntered down the stairs and stopped just before reaching Denalisa.

"Oh, there you are, Barden. Is everything all right?"

"Yes, everything is fine. Just seems that the two boys jumped to conclusions. I'd think Blazey would have known better. Aldric, what's that you got?"

Aldric stood up proudly and began to explain again about his pocket watch. Barden descended the final step and then the two listened intently, providing Aldric with the attention that he had wanted from the beginning. Blaze scowled.

"Well, Aldric, it is definitely something to cherish and keep safe. Remember, this is a room full of thieves—you never know who you should trust," Barden joked as he slipped the watch of off Aldric's neck, only to return it to the surprised youngling.

"I know. I keep it safe all the time," Aldric agreed, smiling at Barden nervously. "Well, every time except this one."

Blaze looked around the room. Most of the company was close to the fire, trying to keep warm, but Blaze noticed that over in a corner away from everyone and in the coldest part of the guild house, Shadow and Gavin were quietly playing a sparse game of marbles on the floor. Blaze wrapped the blanket tightly around him and glided over to bother the two younglings.

Gavin was winning the game, but one more flick of the shooter and Shadow removed the last two marbles and won. The two weren't playing for keepsies as they split the marbles equally between them. As usual, Shadow was still hidden under his hood; no matter what the weather, hot or cold, Shadow kept his hood and cloak on. Today, Blaze could understand why he had it on, but he still attempted to uncloak the younger boy. It was a game to Blaze, but he had never seen the boy's face or even his hair color. Blaze believed that he must have a disfigurement that made him hideous because even Master allowed him to keep covered. Blaze reached over the two boys while they set up another round and tugged on Shadow's hood. It didn't come off, which was normal for this game. Blaze moved closer, holding on to the top of the hood, and grabbed it with two hands. He pulled with all his might while the blanket floated like liquid silver and pooled on the floor.

"Get off of him, stupid cloak." Blaze fussed and struggled against the younger boy. Then the fabric gave way to Blaze's grasp. Feeling a major win, he held up the small cloak only to discover another identical cloak still covered Shadow. Gavin snickered. Blaze looked contemptuously at the cloak. "How is that even possible?" He shrugged and tossed it back at Shadow, who quietly put it back on.

"Hey, Blaze. Please stop that. I'm trying to win some marbles." Blaze bent down to see the marbles that Gavin had next to him. His stench was not the same as the knackerman. Blaze couldn't place it. The reeking odor oozed out from his pores and his breath. Blaze held his nose and backed away while grabbing Gavin's shooter marble. He eyed it, twisting and twirling it and trying to find the pattern in the smooth cold stone.

"Give that back!" Gavin started to grab for it, then he thought better of it. Blaze saw the look of hurt in his eyes before Gavin dropped his head. ". . . Please." Blaze sighed.

"It's cold over here in this end of the guild house and you stink like onions and something else." Gavin glanced up at Blaze, grinning.

"Bananas!" Gavin exclaimed. "They were in the pies I had earlier before the snow started."

"Together?"

"Yes, why?"

"That's disgusting. I think the pieman is trying to kill you." Blaze knelt down to see eye-to-eye with the marbles inside the circular playing field. He flicked Gavin's shooter with accuracy, ease, and strength, knocking out five marbles. "Nice shooter, now go get your marbles."

"Thanks, but I could've done it and the pies actually tasted good. Borintak knows how to put flavors together." Blaze fanned the air in front of his face, drawing a cool breeze that chilled him. He reached down grabbed the blanket and pulled it up closer to his ears.

"Just don't talk to anyone with that mouth, or breathe. Yeah, don't breathe," Blaze commented as he stepped back over Shadow and dragged the blanket over the smaller, younger boy. Shadow glanced up at Blaze, the light catching his blue eyes.

Littles were continually revolving in and out, one after another. Getting to know their names or monikers was impossible, and if one did try to know them, they'd be gone the next day. Blaze had abandoned the task years ago. Of course, there were some like Gavin and Shadow who simply appeared one day and never left. Those were the ones you could try to remember. These two clung to each other like glue. Blaze had initially called Shadow 'Ghost,' but it didn't stick. The name made some of the older thieves and Littles nervous to think that a ghost was amongst them. Some of the thieves thought the very word would bring them about. Master had found the name Shadow to be a good reflection of the Little, and with his final word, it was so. Gavin had never been given another name. Venom had tried to call him Pieluster though absolutely no one else would call him that.

Blaze walked back toward the fire when he felt chilled. He passed Aldric and pushed him out of the way. Instead of reacting to fight, Aldric waved a happy greeting. Blaze ignored him and continued on across the quarters. He sat next to the woodbin that leaned against the wall. The spot was away from the fire but was still warm, nestled between master's office and the woodbin. His blanket kept his back warm. He could hear the wailing wind outside that whipped and rattled against the guild house. He froze when Denalisa walked up to the fire and stirred the pot, which emitted the fragrant smells of vegetables, browned meat, and boiled starchy potatoes. Blaze's mouth watered. From his vantage point, he could see Nightshade talking with Jewels and Dellanie. Everyone was back in the guild and there was nothing to do. Blaze wished Mason had been there.

Mason had a great way about him. He wouldn't have made Blaze apologize to the knackerman for not wanting to go into the death fire. He would have held the knackerman to a higher standard. Blaze wondered where Mason was now. He was always off on missions, but when he returned, he would tell of his run-in with some new love, for whom he fell hard but was unable to be with for some reason or another, or he would tell tales of when he and Master were on missions together. The mission tales were such extraordinary adventures and magnificent fights that they made for good pastime stories, even if Mason exaggerated them to heroic proportions.

Denalisa glanced over and saw Blaze nearly asleep. She thought it would be good if she gave him a job to help with his disposition. She clapped her hands and he snapped awake.

"Good, you're awake, Blazey." He didn't want her calling him that. That wasn't his name any longer.

"Don't call me that . . . please." He struggled to add the please, but he remembered Barden's words when talking to the knacker-man outside and he wasn't ready for another fight today. It just wasn't a word that was used openly or freely at the guild. There was a dominance that was needed and to use the word 'please' took that away.

"But that's what Barden calls you."

"I know, but I don't like it." Denalisa inhaled a breath.

"All right then. I need your help Blaze." Blaze got up, recognizing that he wasn't going to be able to get out of helping her. "Here, bring these dishes of stew to everyone in the room."

"Why not just have them come to you? That's how it has always been done." Denalisa didn't appreciate being corrected, especially by her subordinate. She turned toward him with her hands on her hips and ladle in her right hand.

"Good boys don't question their elders. When I used to take care of little boys, they knew not to question me. You'll learn the same! Now, bring these dishes of stew to everyone in the room." Denalisa repeated herself with authority. Blaze got up and took bowls of stew to each person in the room, starting with the Littles that were closest to him. Everything was going well until Blaze stumbled on Lennowen and spilled stew all over Lace, who was sitting down reading a map. The stew sprayed in all directions: on the map, in Lace's hair, down her tunic and breeches, and into her underclothing.

"By Mereen's vengeance, I swear you are going to pay for this!" Her outburst and her flabbergasted expression were too much for the gathering to resist, especially as she jumped up to rid herself of the flowing liquid. The thieves burst into laughter. Barden covered his face and Denalisa angrily sneered at Blaze who was still holding the bowl while he coughed out a laugh and hid behind the up-tipped bowl. Lace lunged at Blaze and knocked him off his feet, where he landed hard on the floor. She kicked him in the stomach as he curled to protect his face. Barden ran to stop the fight by grabbing Lace from behind, but Lace turned around and started pulling his hair, kicking and scratching at Barden to set her free.

Blaze regained his footing and even though Lace was bound, he punched her in retaliation. Barden released Lace and she immediately went after Blaze. Barden let them at it, knowing it was the way of the guild. Denalisa was screaming for everyone to stop; however, her screams were ignored. Barden was laughing to see such sport that reminded him of his younger days at the guild. Denalisa told Barden to stop this.

"This, Denalisa, is our winter manners. This is how we get rid of our pent-up energy. We used to always chase after Blazey, especially Ruri, but it was much quieter and stealthier then. It was so much harmless fun. Don't worry, he won't get hurt too much. At least not enough to go to the healers—and I'm sure Lace can handle him."

Denalisa watched in horror as stew spilled out of previously delivered bowls while Blaze ran around the guild, trying to find a way to escape Lace's wrath.

"It's no way for a young lady to act, Barden. Here! Stop this immediately!" Denalisa clapped her hands expecting the children to do her bidding. Lace was a broad-shouldered, stocky girl with dark, brooding eyes, a stumpy nose that was upturned so both of her nostrils could be seen quite plainly, and straight, thin hair that hung like noodles around her head. She was older than Blaze by four turn-years. She arrived at the guild when she was about Blaze's current age, and she had a growing number of followers, who thought they could become more successful by being around her because she manipulated them into believing that she was quite successful through her carefully laid lies and cult-leader charm. Most members of the guild were now in full pursuit of Blaze, including Venom and Aldric. They cornered him and waited for Lace to get her revenge. On her way to him, Lace grabbed a bowl of stew. She insisted on the others to hold him down and pin him to the floor. Barden laughed, amused by the nostalgia of the game. Blaze kicked at her while trying to pull away from his captures. She poured the stew over his face, and when she had finished, she kicked him in the side again.

CHAPTER 5

LESSONS

AT THIS POINT, many felt that Blaze had been punished enough and released him from the floor. The game was over. Lace, however, was prepared to finish him off one way or another. On the door, Ballard's eyes lit up, slicing through the dimly lit room of the main quarters. The door rattled and then swung open in a mystical light, banging against the wall alongside it.

Master Locke stood in the doorway, backlit by the light of his office. Blaze, wiping the stew from his chin and cheeks, could just make out what was going on behind Lace, who stood in his line of sight. As the door swung open, Barden rushed to help Blaze to a sitting position in the last moment.

"Lace, go get cleaned up. Here, Blazey, are you all right?" Blaze leered at Barden, completely aware that the only reason he had come to his aid was their master's presence. Blaze batted Barden away from him.

"Don't call me Blazey!"

Master approached Blaze and kneeled down to talk to him. Locke clenched his teeth and glowered at Barden, then turned a soft gaze on Blaze.

"Are you all right?"

"Like *you* care, Master," Blaze scoffed, and glanced away. Locke lifted Blaze's tunic to see bruising. He examined his swollen skin, gently pushing to see if anything was broken.

"She got you just under your left rib. Does this hurt?" Blaze cringed inside but didn't show it to Master Locke.

"No, I'm fine. You should see to Lace. I got her good." Blaze smirked smugly.

Locke remembered a similar game from the master's logbook that Barden and company would play many turn-years ago. It was no way for someone looking to become a master thief to act. In the books, Locke had read how Blaze would be the target of a game of cat and mouse. If the searchers could find him, they earned a point. If they could find him and bring him back uninjured, that was two points. If they could find him and bring him back injured, three points. Extra points were given if Mason, Locke, or Rhatt were around and didn't find out about the game. There was a note quoting the game leader, Ruri, that it was all in good fun. Soon after, Ruri had left the guild. With his departure, Blaze had been treated poorly by Barden, Dorken, Pip, and the other thieves at the time. Some of those deep seeded sentiments still lingered today.

"Blaze, I have clean clothes for you. After Lace is done with the wash bin, go get cleaned up. It's getting worse outside now. We are sure to get a blizzard; if not today, then in the next few. I'll bring you some clothes." Locke was trying to keep his anger in check. His thoughts ran through his head in rapid succession. *How dare Barden encourage this behavior! Doesn't Blaze have enough racked against him by being born here? I cannot wait until the spring when Blaze is safe at Ceretheena. I only hope that he will do as he is told—he never listens to me; he is always contrary, but I know he doesn't mean it. Not to mention the spilled stew. I cannot even talk to Barden and his wife at this moment and yet, I must.*

Locke traipsed through the guild house into his office without saying a word, retrieving a fresh tunic and breeches for both Blaze and Lace. The cupboard was filled with clothes of all sorts and sizes. He checked for undergarments but only found sizes for Littles; the pair would have to keep on their stew-stained ones. To Denalisa, he handed Lace's new clothes. She ran off to attend to the girl. Barden anticipated being handed Blaze's clothes; instead, Master just pointed at him.

"I will speak with you later, Barden." Locke said through clenched teeth. Anger had risen inside of Locke, but he knew that any lashing here would not be a wise choice. He would speak to Barden and his wife later after he had some time to effectively choose his words with clarity. He inhaled deeply and turned from Barden to look for Blaze. Fully aware that he had to speak calmly, he unclenched his jaw and spoke to his young charge. Master found Blaze with Venom and Spider, who clung dearly to his softie. He was glad to see the Little was in the guild safely.

"Venom, I'm glad you brought Spider here. It's getting bad out there."

"I'm glad he's here too. Thank you, Master Locke."

Master nodded his approval. To Blaze, he held out the clothes. Blaze grabbed them, knowing it was a rare occurrence. As soon as he was able, he'd get his own and not be obligated to his master any longer. Master Locke looked around the guild and noticed that everyone was wearing their cloaks except for Blaze.

"Where's your cloak, Blaze?" Blaze wrinkled his nose and looked down at the floor.

"The knackerman has it." Spider's softly voiced reply was hushed by Blaze and Venom. "What did I say wrong? He does have it, right? He dragged you by it, Blaze. He did."

Locke rubbed his face in disgust at the actions of the knackerman.

"Blaze, why does the knackerman have your cloak?"

Blaze pursed his lips, trying to quickly think up a reasonable answer.

"Because I have a blanket." He nodded at his remarkable response and balled up the blanket in front of him. "It's warmer than a cloak, too." Master Locke lifted an exposed corner of the blanket. Master recognized it as one he had given out last year and noticed Nohan's name embroidered on its hem.

"So, what is Nohan using?"

Blaze scratched his head and shrugged.

"Nohan? I don't know, why?"

Blaze couldn't quickly locate Nohan in the room. As a matter of fact, he didn't remember seeing Nohan at all in the guild.

"Don't worry, Blaze. Get dressed and then get to sleep. It's going to get cold tonight. I suspect the snow will cover the windows by morning." Venom glanced at Blaze and vice-versa. The two boys cuddled against Spider.

"Blaze, you're soupy."

"Oh, yeah. Right." Blaze waited until Lace and Denalisa returned, and then he went to take his turn at the wash bin, but the water had been dumped and snow was melting in its place. He glanced back toward the main quarters, confused. He changed out of his clothes. A chill went through him, and he quickly got dressed into the new breeches and tunic. He stared at himself in the mirror. A reddened mark from his nose to his chin showed signs of first-degree burns from the stew. *This mark isn't much. It won't even scar,* he thought with disappointment. The wash bin was cold to the touch. He used it to cool his face, but he could only hold it there for a short while until his hands burned from the cold. He glanced back in the mirror, which was dirtied with a metallic aura at the edges and marred with spots. He felt his hair with his hands. The stew had plastered his hair to his neck, and small pieces of meat ran through it. He pulled them out and ate them. He had had worse before. He'd eaten garbage. He'd lied to Gavin—when you are hungry enough, you'll eat almost anything, including banana and onion pie, or garbage, or even vomit. Food is food after all. He worried that if they only had small pieces of meat at the start of the winter, he knew there wouldn't be much near the end unless that was Denalisa's doing. He washed as best he could in the snow. The only thing that he looked forward to was sitting with Venom and Spider snuggled together against the harsh cold wind that would eventually break through somewhere in the guild house.

When Blaze returned to the main quarters, Spider was cuddled on Venom's lap, resting his head on Venom's chest and sucking his thumb. Lennowen had fallen onto the floor and Venom was holding it. Blaze sat down next to Venom. Venom rubbed his face into Spider's hair and kissed the top of his head. Spider wiggled closer into Venom and softly whimpered. Venom hugged Spider.

"Are you okay, Blaze?"

"Yeah, I'm fine, just a little bruise and my face burns a little. It should all be good tomorrow."

"Maybe with a healer's help it will."

"What is with that ratty old thing you're holding?" Blaze asked. Venom moved Lennowen so he could see the softie more clearly over Spider's head.

"This is Lennowen. It was my mum's softie, but she never used to play with it. She gave it to me and then after Spider was born, he was crying one night and I gave it to him. He has never been without it since. When my mum told us to get into a dingy . . ." Blaze burst out laughing.

"That's a funny word."

Venom didn't really see the humor in it. It was what it was called.

"I never really thought about it as being funny. It's just a small boat. Anyway, as I was saying, when my mum told us to get into the dingy, she handed Spider Lennowen and told us to keep him close and safe. She kissed us and told me to keep Spider safe, too, and for Spider to remember his prayers and she'd see us when we hit land. She then lowered our dingy into the sea. I knew that my mum's ship was sinking, but I never thought that she would go down with it. She was always there—it never crossed my mind. But now, I know she didn't make it. She'd find us if she was still alive. Anyway, Lennowen has seen better days. He ended up getting wet when a big wave swept us ashore. He fell on the ground many times while we traveled up to Ballardton and when we were hiding from the hill-people in the Wild Wood. We left him under the flower berries that I picked and sold. Well, you remember the rest, right?"

Blaze acknowledged that he did. Venom and Spider came into Ballardton with loaded pouches. Venom, who was new at haggling, was scammed out of most of his coin for a generic sword that was polished to a sparkling silver. Spider had lost his pouch between King's Highway and the market. He was young enough to be easily distracted and one of the thieves picked his pouch. Blaze suspected it was Lace. Venom reported the theft to the constables, who were uninterested in helping two stray children from down south.

Venom and Spider found refuge in the cave that Spider still lived in. One day, Blaze found them and invited them back for food at the guild house. The two boys were there for a while together, and all seemed well until Spider disappeared one day. Venom was beside himself, searching everywhere. He finally found him in the cave in a fetal position, calling for his mum. Venom gave him Lennowen and he asked Spider what happened. Spider never spoke about it, making Venom realize that Spider couldn't stay in the guild. He was always worried about Spider, but Spider could see that Venom was better when he was around other people.

The little boy was so brave, and he did as his mother instructed to say his prayers every night alone in the dark. Venom learned to steal and even went back for the flower berries, which were called wyssanberries, to supply the cave with what Spider needed, including a protection spell from the Mage School. The loneliness of the cave never dampened Spider's spirit and he seemed quite happy to stay there. Venom would do anything to keep Spider from ever having to go through what he did that day, no matter who he had to go up against. Spider's safety and happiness had been Venom's primary goal ever since.

Blaze took the softie from Venom, smiled at it, and tucked it under Spider's limp, sleeping arm. Venom's description of the importance of Lennowen rationalized the toy a bit in Blaze's eyes. Blaze moved closer to Venom and leaned on him until Venom realized where the chill was coming from.

"Blaze! You're cold. Go over there. What did you bathe in? Ice?"

Blaze snorted a suppressed laugh.

"Yeah, sort of. Snow."

Venom sneered at him, his mouth curled and his nose wrinkled with disgust.

"Why would you do that?"

"It wasn't really planned," Blaze retorted, grabbing his blanket and moving away from Venom.

Barden held Denalisa's hand as the two stood in front of Master Locke's desk. An hour had passed and with it, Locke had calmed his temper and rethought his words with care. Barden was sure he knew what Locke was going to say and he waited to be treated like a child.

"Please sit. Thank you. I want to start by thanking you for coming to help with the guild although I know that wasn't your main objective. I know it isn't an easy task and the children are a handful at times. I believe that you will earn your master title from our guild within the next few months. I imagine that by the spring, you and Denalisa will move on and begin your journey to find your own guild."

"Thank you, Master. I am honored to be taking my test here, and I am pleased to share my journey with my beloved wife," Barden responded with sincere gratitude.

"However," Master Locke continued, "and let me be very clear here, Barden, I will have no more of your game of points that you and your past agemates played at the expense of Blaze or anyone else. He is a full member of the guild and will be treated as such. In addition, he and all of the children will be treated with equal respect, or you and Denalisa will be ejected from the guild, blizzard or no blizzard. You will have to find another guild to take your test, which in itself is no easy task. That game that Ruri, who has since been banished from the guild, established many years ago was meant to torture and humiliate his key pawn, which had been Blaze because he is Rhatt's son and my nephew. I don't believe Blaze is even aware of the latter fact and you will not mention it again, especially not on these premises. I treat each of the children as they would like to be treated. Do you understand so far?" Locke looked to each for understanding of the task and consequences that should arise if Barden and Denalisa failed to comply.

"Yes, Master. I understand. The point game was juvenile and is in the past—a fanciful game of chase to pass the time. Tonight was a misunderstanding between Blaze and Lace, nothing more." Barden squeezed his wife's hand harder when he spoke of the point game. Denalisa leaned forward on her chair.

"A complete misunderstanding, sir. Lace had every reason to be angry after having the hot stew fall on her. The chase was unacceptable, I see that now. I will definitely try to do better. I really do like the children. They are all so interesting and have such stories to tell—Aldric and that time piece. He's quite a hoot! He is enjoyable."

"Keep in mind, Denalisa, these stories are their stories and not some tall tale being told by the storyteller; do not undermine their existence."

"Oh, no, sir! I definitely do not do that. I used to raise children on a farm out west. I even got the fight out of a couple. There were a couple of boys that were quite angry, similarly to Blaze, and I knocked it right out of them. Gave them a position to feel good about themselves." Denalisa seemed pleased with making this decree.

"Please do not try to change these children. They need the fight to survive. Now, I want to speak about the stew." As she contemplated Locke's words, Denalisa rubbed her apron, finding comfort from her misdeed.

"Oh, yes, the stew. I am so sorry that so much got wasted. I picked up some vegetables from the market. They are in a basket in my room. I will add them to the stew tomorrow."

"That is very kind of you to contribute. A few things to mention with the stew's preparation and its need to fill so many bellies. First off, the meat cannot be in miniscule diced pieces. It must be cut into good solid chunks for all of the young empty stomachs that will need to be full until the end of the winter months. By spring, they'll be well prepared to be more active. Their nutrition is a concern for the guild during these times. You will also see Littles come that are not here now. Do not condemn them as not being here all the time. They learn that they will get a good meal and a warm place to sleep at the guild house. Secondly, many of the guildmembers did not get to eat because of poor service . . ."

"That was because of Blaze not serving them," Denalisa interrupted accusatorily.

"I will tell you something, Denalisa, Blaze has had the chore of serving the stew for many years, and everyone approaches the pot and the bowls are filled that way. One at a time. It has been the proven method of distribution, with the least number of spills. So from now on, I expect that you will follow these guidelines. Of all of the younglings, who do you wish to help you service the stew in the evening?"

"Oh, I do like all of them. Hmm, let me think. Um, I think I'd like to trust sweet Jewels. She doesn't say much, but she does have a very nice disposition. She reminds me of me as a child." Master nodded his agreement.

"Yes, Jewels would do nicely as your helper. She is always eager to please. Please remember to be kind. With that settled, I'd like to request some more information about Blaze's cloak and the knackerman, Barden."

Barden straightened in his chair. *Here we go.*

"The knackerman had lost his dog and he wanted help finding it from Blazey. It was just a misunderstanding with Blazey and the new Little. They didn't know. I smoothed things out with the knackerman. He's a really nice man; I bet he'd be a great supporter of the guild . . . maybe even supply the boys with jobs." Barden explained how the knackerman was overloaded with work and how he told Barden that he always needed extra hands in the yard. It was good to see that Barden and his wife were there to help with the guild, he had said. Locke raised his eyebrows, listening to Barden's explanation of how things were and how they should change given that Denalisa had so much experience with childcare and planned to become a mother. Barden continued to enlighten Locke on the trials he believed that Locke had faced by being split between his obligation as master of the guild and raising the young ones in his care. How the two were almost synonymous, and yet completely separate. When he became a guildmaster, Barden planned to hire a wonderful couple, not unlike himself and Denalisa, to oversee the children, leaving Barden, as master, to operate the guild house as efficiently as possible. Locke remained indifferent in expression and heard Barden out. He closed his eyes, summing up all that was revealed.

"I hear you, Barden. I understand the difficulties that the knackerman has endured—even throwing away his daughter, who you know as Lace. Sons only for the knackerman. He walks through life as neutral and a follower of King Eldon's, but some of his less-than-savory tactics could fall into the realm of darkness. As for your other suggestions, I will think on them and will either address them as I see fit or not at all. This arrangement that we have here is only temporary as I am sure that you will achieve your goal of master. In the meantime, you and your wife will abide by the rules and policies that have been established by my predecessor and myself. You will not subject any members of the guild to any undue punishments, and any punishments that you *do* see fit will be presented to me prior to implementation." Locke opened his desk drawer and pulled out the tiny chest of coin; from it he removed an ebon. "When this storm is complete, I wish for you or your wife to purchase Blaze a winter cloak with lining for your misjudgment of the knackerman. There is enough to also purchase a small lap blanket for Nohan as it has been revealed to me that his has holes were there shouldn't be any. You both are dismissed." Barden reached over the desk and picked up the coin, then put it in his pouch for safekeeping.

The storm raged on for four days as it stalled over the Spring District before finally moving north toward Venesial. Once it was gone, the guild was bustling with excitement for the possibilities that snow presented: snow pixies, snowball fights, snow globes for telling fortunes, and romping around in the whiteness. As everyone was leaving the guild to enjoy the winter wonderland, Nohan arrived. In his arms was a small girl, no bigger than a toddler, wrapped in the warmth of Nohan's cloak. She was asleep. Denalisa ran up to him and took the sleeping girl. She glanced at Nohan.

"You can't carry her like that. You have no hand."

Nohan looked at her straight-faced, surprised to hear her observation.

"What do you mean I have no hand?"

He lifted his hands and then feigned a scream of horror when he saw that his right hand was indeed missing. Denalisa jumped in surprise and tried to explain the reality to Nohan.

"You have no hand because you lost it when you were stealing from the king. That's why your name is Nohan—because you have 'no-hand.'" He laughed in her face.

"If that's what you want to believe, yeah, I stole from King Kiril and he chopped off my hand. Who told you that?"

"Nightshade."

"Oh, did she now?" He retrieved the sleeping child from Denalisa. "I'll take the Little. We have become good friends waiting out the storm together. I'm going to take her to see Master. Excuse me." Nohan carried the girl through the quarters, kicked at the door to knock, and entered to introduce the girl to Locke. Denalisa stood watching after him, mouth agape, and her finger to her lip. *Well, he does seem quite able, but so horrible that he wasn't imprisoned for stealing from a king, I guess I'll see more of that sort of thing as Barden's wife.*

After Barden consulted with Master Locke about the upcoming test, he approached Denalisa, handing her the ebon coin. She accepted it and knew what she must do: get a cloak and a lap blanket. Bundling up, Denalisa wrapped her long wool-lined cloak around herself and headed to the farms. Barden watched as she shimmied away, fully aware that he watched after her.

"What took you so long? Did they do something to you?" Barden greeted Denalisa with a kiss and questions. Exhausted from her experience at a farmhouse, Denalisa could barely talk. She lifted up her new acquired items: a red knitted blanket, a cloak, and a sack that visibly moved on its own from within. Barden opened the sack and out popped a fluffy, white, round-bellied puppy with a gray muzzle. It yipped and licked Barden's face. Barden couldn't help but smile.

"Why do you have a dog?" he asked.

Denalisa sighed exhaustedly.

"I saved it. I think it might be the pup that the knackerman was looking for. It cost me a whole ebon to stop it from being killed by the farmer; however, you can bring it over to the knackerman and get him to pay at least twice that. He's so cute, look at him. I am keeping that red blanket for our bed, Nohan can have our old threadbare one. I worked like a fool to get this blanket and I'm not going to give it to some child who stole from a goodly king. The cloak is not really a winter one, but who cares. It's a cloak, and that's all your master really wanted."

Barden agreed. "Okay, Denalisa. Just make sure the puppy stays quiet; Master Locke wouldn't like that we were harboring it." Denalisa opened the door to the guild house.

"Plans don't always go as prepared, my dear husband. I've just had a thought, and I'm going to do one better and *tell* him about this pup in our keeping. I think he'll be happy to know that I found it. He has a soft spot for little stray things, I think. If not, I'll just plead with him. Here, give me the blanket and the cloak. I'll swap the blankets first and then I'll go into your master's office. Rhiun, may you bring me luck." Barden pushed the puppy back down into the sack and gave everything to Denalisa.

The pup was a welcome addition to the guild, entertaining the children and allowing Denalisa to have some peace and quiet. She was pleased that Master Locke agreed to allow it to stay for the winter. It was a happy dog, and Barden didn't mind taking it out to do its business as Master required, even if he did have to shovel a space free of snow for it to run in. The pup loved the Littles and was always playing with or lying next to one or two of them.

One afternoon, Denalisa walked around the guild, picking up this and that—whatever was left on the floor. She noticed Nohan playing on the floor with the Littles, teaching them how to play "Lost Stone," which was a game from his home. The pup came over and Nohan allowed it to be petted and even mess up the gameboard. The Littles, after being distracted momentarily, returned to play the game. Using the charred end of the fire poker, Nohan redrew a large square on the floor. He then divided the square into nine smaller squares. Then he took out ten stones from his pouch that he had picked up earlier in the day. He started placing the stones in each of the smaller squares and then left one outside of the big square. He told the Littles to watch and listen. Denalisa watched intently, impressed by Nohan's knowledge.

"Okay, one. Say it with me, one." Nohan pointed at the first square with the first stone. Then he counted the second box and the second stone, calling it two. He continued in that same manner all the way until he reached the one stone that was outside of the big square and called it ten. "To play this game, you will all close your eyes and turn around. I will remove one of the stones. The first one to tell me which number is the Lost Stone wins. Ready. . . . Turn around!" The Littles did as they were told. Nohan removed the first stone. "Okay, you can open your eyes and turn back around. Now!"

"Three." "One." "Two." "Ten!" Nohan tickled the tummy of the Little who screamed ten.

"Good playing. Yes, Cups, you won that one. Okay, do you want to play again?" The children yelled in unison, "Yes!"

Nohan had the children turn around, he removed a stone, and then listened as they screamed out the number. Nohan was a natural teacher, and he rewarded the children with smiles and praise. Denalisa stood there thinking about the game and came up with an idea that she must tell to Barden right away.

Blaze, Venom, and their age-mates were asked to sit in a large group on the floor while Denalisa sat in a rocking chair. The children wondered why they were all seated together. Blaze had a strong feeling that something was coming. He knew it couldn't be good—why else would Denalisa keep them in such a stance? The pup was curled on Denalisa's lap as she stroked it. Blaze caught sight of the animal opening one eye and then closing it, as though it was sizing up each onlooker. It matched eyes with Blaze and Blaze felt a sudden twinge of the pup's thoughts, and not just by reading its body language. The pup, realizing that Blaze could sense his thoughts, jumped down from the woman's lap. It sauntered up to him, staring him down until Blaze looked away. The pup pawed at him, scratching his leg. Its paws were large, telling Blaze that this was no ordinary dog.

"Hey, Venom, do you see this?" Blaze whispered.

"Okay, listen up, everyone!" The pup startled when Denalisa clapped her hands, demanding everyone's attention. "I have chosen you from amongst the other children here to learn. Many places in the world, children go to school. School is, for the most part, a place to learn together. I, myself, went to school when I lived on a farm.

Thanks to Nohan . . ." Boos and snarled lips sneered at Nohan, who was as much in the dark as the children who scoffed at him.

"Oh, the dog? Yeah, he's a good boy," Venom whispered, grabbing the dog to place it on his lap. The dog accepted the short-term arrangement, seemingly annoyed at being treated this way.

". . . Thanks to Nohan, I have decided that I will teach you how to read. Barden agreed that learning to read is a skill that all of you should have, especially for your futures. I will take each of you one by one and have you read this book to me. It is a primer that I found on a shelf in my room." Someone threw a balled-up handkerchief at Nohan for his participation in this new initiative. He batted it away and shrugged.

"The pup isn't acting like a dog exactly. I don't think it's a dog." Venom scoffed at Blaze.

"Of course it is. Look at the way it is playing with Spider now." The pup rubbed against Spider while Spider placed Lennowen on its back to ride it. The dog glanced back at Blaze, who felt the dog's exasperation and saw it give a despairing headshake to indicate its feelings.

"I will start with the girls first—Jewels, then Dellanie, and then Nightshade. I'm sure you are all good readers." Denalisa triumphantly called out to the girls, clearly proud of their feminine solidarity. Rather than indulge Denalisa, Dellanie and Nightshade looked at each other with utter annoyance, which read across both of their faces. Together, they smiled sweetly back at Denalisa. Jewels had quickly moved a stool over next to Denalisa and picked up the primer. Realizing that he was going to have to recite the words to Denalisa, Blaze quickly forgot the dog and inched forward to listen, trying to memorize Jewels' words.

"Very good, Jewels. What a good reader you are. How long have you known how to read?" Denalisa saw Blaze move forward, and she was pleased with his interest.

"Before I came here, my mother and father taught me. My mother was a domestic in the duke's manor here in Ballardton, and my father was a smith." Denalisa shut the primer and rested her hands on her lap, listening to another story that she was eager to learn. She was sure to invite more conversation with Jewels about her parents and how it came that they left her to reside at the guild.

"Oh, dear, what happened to them?" Jewels hung her head and wrung her hands nervously.

"They died. I'd rather not talk about it."

Denalisa's heart sank for the girl, and she grabbed Jewels' arm and squeezed it. Jewels pulled away fiercely, not wanting Denalisa's comfort or pity.

"Dellanie, your turn," Denalisa hollered. Dellanie walked up to Denalisa, picked up the primer and read it as fast as she could. "Very good, Dellanie. Next time slow down a bit. You will be able to understand the words better if you can hear what you are reading clearly."

Dellanie tossed the book onto the stool. "Yeah, sure."

Nightshade sauntered up to Denalisa, tipped her head sideways, and excused herself. She had noticed Blaze and she moved the stool to sit with her back facing him. "Thank you, Denalisa. It is so good to remember how important it is that we know how to read. Oh! Yes, I remember this book from when I was younger." Nightshade read it as quietly as she could, and Denalisa strained to hear her. When she was finished, Nightshade gently handed the book back to the woman. "Do you want Nohan next?" Denalisa nodded.

"Nohan!" Nohan flashed a malicious smile and pulled a book out from underneath a floorboard before approaching Denalisa.

"I'd prefer to read from this one, if you don't mind, Mistress." Denalisa agreed that that was fine. Nohan began reading and once he had read a full page, he glanced at Denalisa, whose mouth was agape. "Yeah, I think we're finished here," he said. Nohan snapped the book closed and walked away.

Denalisa called up the rest of the children as she saw fit. Venom and Spider went up together.

"Denalisa, if you don't mind, I'll let Spider go first."

"Okay. Why are you called Spider?"

Spider looked to Venom, waiting for him to answer.

"Oh, I came up with it. When we were in the cave, there was a spider that was on his shoulder all day long. I had knocked it off, but by the end of the day it was back on him. That's how he got his name. My name came from myself because I couldn't think of something else that went nicely with Spider, and it fit me."

"Well, do you have another name? A real name?"

"Of course, we all do."

"Why don't you use your real name? Barden uses his own name."

"Because then no one has power over who we are really."

"Oh, I don't think that's really a thing, Venom. I bet your name is nice—you should use it."

Spider glanced at Venom, waiting to see how his brother would respond.

"I like you, Denalisa, but you have to let us have our names. Master always calls us by what we want to be called. He's master of the guild and he respects us, why can't you? Here, give me that book. Spider, you read it and then I'll read it." Spider picked up the book read the words, stumbling on one or two near the end. Venom helped him along. "I think that covers both of us even though you asked for me. I wanted to show off that Spider could read, too. Hey, Blaze, you're next."

Blaze froze with fear. He couldn't read. Rhatt, Locke, and Mason had all tried in the past, then gave up on him as a lost cause. Cautiously, and knowing Denalisa's eyes were on him, Blaze stood up to face the primer. He swallowed hard, hoping that something would take away everyone's attention. Every second felt like an hour, and he watched himself approach Denalisa as though he was bewitched and in slow motion. Frame by frame, he moved closer to the doom he knew he was about to face. Panic overtook his senses as he tried to recall the words that Jewels had read. *Something about a frog or a hog. . . . Was the frog and a hog on a log or was the frog in a bog fog? Or was it something about a jigsaw. . . . No, that's what Nohan read.* He bowed his head discouragingly. *I think. . . . I'll go with the froggy boggy fog.* He nodded to himself.

Denalisa's expression was expectant, and Blaze glanced around the room. The girls were gone, Spider played on the floor with the pup, Venom was whittling a stick, and Nohan was deeply involved in the book he read before while overseeing a Little's game of Lost Stones. In the south end of the guild quarters, the older thieves were playing a game of cards and Gavin was talking incessantly to Shadow and Aldric. He figured no one would know as long as everyone was engaged while he tried to read as quietly as he could.

"Please sit here, Blaze." Denalisa held out the primer for him as he sat. He looked so much younger than he was. Black hair streaked across his pale features with fearful hazel eyes that pleaded with her to not make him do this. He took the primer in his hands and could feel them shaking with anxiety. He opened it without looking afraid for what it would do or show him. "That is not how you hold a book; it's upside down. Here, like this." Denalisa grabbed the book and shoved it correctly back into Blaze's hands.

The whites of Blaze's eyes grew larger, as he knew that she wouldn't understand. He knew how to hold a book in general, but he opened it without glancing at it. He bowed his head, keeping his eyes closed as he was already waiting for what was to come. The stool felt harder under the weight of the task. He opened his eyes.

The words on the page magically twinkled and began their dance. It was a dance that his eyes couldn't track. The letters spread apart from each other. He identified an"a," following it up into the ceiling until it blew away into a sparkling of stardust. His eyes caught another word that wiggled across the page until it vanished out the door. His eyes tried to catch anything. Another"a"—or was that another letter that he never learned? He thought back to the time when Mason tried making normal things into letters, like rocks or a string, for him to identify. But when all the letters were assembled together, they danced, bounced, flew, evaporated right before his eyes. It made him different, the way he couldn't read the words, the same way he couldn't touch wyssanberry without it drying up, turning brown, and crumbling in his hands; the words would dry up and disappear, too.

"Go on, Blaze." Denalisa broke his concentration. He glared at the pictures, but the words were growing, blocking his sight. Before too long, the purple-black ink covered the images, making it impossible for him to even decipher what was in the primer from the pictures. He thought back quickly, struggling to remember what Jewels had read.

"A boggy froggy and a loggy hoggy." *Yes, that was it.* Oh, praise Eldon, he was right! It made perfect sense and he could hear it rhyme as he said it aloud. But when he looked at the primer again, the letters were hopping around, laughing at him. He tried to catch one to place it back on the page. It might have been that stupid frog—he'd keep it in that bog. Placing the primer on his lap, he caught the word and then hammered it flat against the book. *Nope, not staying still.* He closed the book. The letters and words dissolved. He caught sight of Denalisa's reaction to his unsightly treatment of the primer. He glanced down and the primer was torn where he hammered the frog into the bog. She tore the book from his hands, shaking her head with disbelief and irritation that he wouldn't comply.

"I see, you're trying to be funny. Let's see how funny you are at writing. Come here to the table." He sighed. Pen and ink did nothing more to improve his ability to read or write the letters. He knew he could make an"a" out of a blanket, but he didn't think she'd appreciate his skill. He sat down. On the table were parchment, pens, and an ink bottle. She handed him a pen, and he moved it to his left hand. She slapped his hand hard for his disobedience. She replaced it in his right."The darkness only uses their left hand. It is said that is how the God of Poison, Adoon, makes his potions so powerful. You will use your right hand." After she whispered the god's name she spit, removing the word from her mouth."You made me say that name."

Blaze frowned. She went to slap him but refrained. He was getting to her.

"Adoon isn't going come smite you because you said his name."

Denalisa slapped him across the face. Tears welled in his eyes as he gazed at her. She removed twine from her bodice and grabbed his left wrist unexpectedly. Her grip was tight as she pressed her nails into his skin out of pure anger. Her face was red and her jaw tensed. She bent down, tying his wrist to the table leg and making sure it was restricting his movement. She grasped another larger piece of twine, this one pulled from her bosom, and secured his arm to his body, making sure the knot was behind his back so he couldn't get to it. She knelt next to him.

"You little brat, the next time I hear you say the God's name, you will be punished. Now, write your letters on this parchment." His right hand didn't always listen when he tried to get it to do things that his left preferred. She leaned over him, taking his right hand in hers, inked the pen, and began making his letters for him. He closed his eyes before the written letters could sashay across the parchment. She grabbed his face when she noticed his eyes were closed."You cannot write if you cannot see. Stop being such a rude guttersnipe and do as you are told. Such disrespectful behavior!"

The entire assembly watched the incident unfurling. Shadow started to rise, only to have Gavin pull him back down to sit. They waited to see what Blaze would do. Nohan, feeling the situation escalating, removed the Littles from the main quarters to the outside quietly and efficiently. He called for Spider to join them. Blaze pulled away from Denalisa while working to pull the twine off his wrist. He twisted and turned the string that held his arm under the table, hoping that it would snap. His hand was turning a deep red from lack of circulation, but the twine refused to give way.

"Denalisa, I . . . I'll . . . try." He twirled his wrist in the opposite direction, releasing the pressure, and attempted the straightforward approach of pulling his wrist out. He lifted the pen and dipped it in the ink. He raised it to meet the parchment and scribbled what he hoped would be an "a." It wasn't. It looked more like a big ink splatter. Denalisa wasn't amused. She removed a needle from the shoulder of her dress and pricked Blaze's right hand with it. He made another attempt and another until he had tiny red dots all over the back of his hand. All the while, he tried to force his other hand out of its restraints. Finally, the rope gave way, shaking the table and causing the ink to spill over all of the precious parchment. Blaze stood up and faced Denalisa defiantly. "You can't make me."

She went to slap him, but Venom held her arm. She looked around the guild and the younger thieves were on their feet.

"I guess we are done for today." Denalisa began cleaning up the ink. "Oh, the cost for these papers. Barden won't be happy with me for wasting this coin." Denalisa threw the ink-filled parchment in the fire, praying that Barden wouldn't find out.

Spider and the puppy were becoming quite good friends with each other, and Venom enjoyed Spider's happiness. Things were turning back to normal, even though the weather hadn't turned warm yet. The piemen were still actively baking and the market was still alive with vendors and patrons. Venom insisted that Spider stay at the guild through winter and return to the cave when spring arrived. Spider agreed. Venom, Spider, and Blaze had walked up to the cave to grab a few more of Spider's things. The pup had followed along and was the first to rush through the snow to the entrance. The boys were laughing as they rounded the wood near Spider's domain. The pup yipped a warning and ran to the boys, specifically Blaze, and back the entrance. Blaze noticed the pup's ruff was sticking up and he pulled out his dagger. He held his arm out for the other boys to wait.

"Spider, stay here. There is something up ahead."

Venom held Spider close, making sure he was behind a tree. To Blaze, the entrance seemed untouched, but he glanced at the dog again, sure that there must be something amiss.

"What is it?" he asked the dog. With great caution, Blaze picked up a fallen stick and poked at the curtain. The cave remained still. He walked closer and slid the curtain open. The pup was at his heels; its yips became growls. "There's something in there, right? Is it a snake? Or is it something bigger?" The pup barked out a sentence and then it mouthed Blaze's cloak and pulled him back. Blaze pulled his cloak out of the pup's mouth. "I have to go in." Again, the pup reacted in the same way. Blaze kept moving forward, stick in one hand and dagger in the other, dragging the pup inward. Exasperated, the pup let go and followed after him, running between his legs and stopping in front of him. A strange musky stench permeated the cave and as Blaze closed in, he could see the outline of a small creature. The pup lunged forward, biting and snarling at the being. Blaze couldn't distinguish between pup and creature. He held up the stick and awaited the moment to strike, his eyes adjusting to the lack of light.

Finally he recognized that the creature, or rather monster, was a gnasher. They were sometimes mistaken for walking infants, but infants that had overly large mouths and pointed shark-like teeth. They were called gnashers because gnashing their teeth is how they attacked their opponents and prey. Blaze remembered hearing some guild members talk about gnashers after venturing into the dungeon. He struggled to remember what they said but couldn't think with all of the movement surrounding him. The pup was holding onto the gnasher by its neck. The gnasher pulled at the pup with its arms but failed to remove the dog. Blaze hit the gnasher's back with the stick, but instead of his intended action, he dislodged the pup from the creature's leg and sent it flying. The pup shook itself off and bit at the gnasher's leg. Voices came to the forefront of Blaze's mind: *A good gnasher is a dead gnasher. They'll kill you in a heartbeat. Hungry, they are.*

The gnasher leaned over the pup and opened its vicious teeth for a bite, but then Blaze raised the stick and conked it on its head. It fell limp immediately, and the pup yelped. Blood rushed from the monster's nose and it was unconscious, but its teeth were still stuck in the pup's back. Blaze got closer, striking the gnasher's torso with his dagger and hoping that he would strike its heart and put it out of its misery. It may be a dangerous creature, but it deserved a peaceful death, as did everybody. Blaze heard it takes its final breath.

As he got ready to roll the gnasher off the pup, Blaze felt a thump on his back. Another gnasher came from the front entrance, hurling small stones at Blaze. The pup was still stuck under the first gnasher. Blaze grabbed the first gnasher and pulled it off the pup. The pup yelped and whimpered. Blaze threw the dead gnasher at the second one, hoping that it would take its leave. Instead, the second gnasher dodged the other's body and charged at Blaze. When it was within reach, it hurled itself in Blaze's direction. Blaze moved just in time, but it landed on its feet and turned back to attack, the mouth gnashing. Blaze realized that it had to close its eyes when it chomped its teeth to make room for the physical ability of that large mouth and therefore was unable to see. He grabbed the stick again, ready to strike. Just as Blaze was beginning his attack, the pup made its own attack again, grabbing the gnasher's leg in its mouth. Momentum forcing him to change direction at a moment's notice, Blaze swung the stick back around and hit the gnasher in the head. The head dangled lifelessly to the side. It instantly dropped to the ground and stopped moving. Blaze reached down to the pup. It whimpered in pain. Blaze took off his cloak and wrapped it around the pup, careful not to touch the wound. But when Blaze turned to lift the pup up, it lunged, biting Blaze's left hand.

"Stupid dog!" He didn't really feel that way, but the dog's bite was painful, and he held his hand. When he examined it, he saw that the pup's small, immature teeth had punctured the skin and something white was stuck in his hand. He was just stunned, holding his wrist away from his body. He wanted to scream out in pain; he wanted to call out his hatred of the world. But instead, he sat there. Next to him, the pup slid itself closer to Blaze, leaning against his thigh. Blaze found comfort in the act. He leaned his head back and wondered if he should go back to the witch Denalisa for help. *Nah, I don't want her touching me. I'd rather die first.*

"Blaze, is everything okay?" Venom called into Spider's cave, interrupting Blaze's pondering. He noticed the pup was asleep, its chest moving up and down laboriously. He had wanted to touch it, pet it, give it some reassurance that he wasn't angry.

"Yeah. Everything is fine. There was a gnasher in here but it's dead now. Oh, two. Of course, they hunt in pairs. How could I forget that?" He palmed his face with his right hand, feeling imbecilic for not remembering such an important detail. Venom and Spider gingerly stepped through the cave. "Shhh! The pup's asleep. He's been hurt."

"Are you way back there in the dark?"

"Yeah, I'm past the table. I didn't know it went back this far. When Spider returns, we should make sure this end is closed off with rocks and stuff." He picked at his hand. The little white thing that he couldn't identify protruded out of his skin. He pinched it between the nail of his forefinger and thumbnail. "Oh, it's a tooth." After pulling out the tooth, his hand started to throb.

"I paid good money to make sure no monsters would get in here and yet, here they are!" Venom spewed. "I'm just glad they didn't come in when Spider was here by himself. Okay, I'll make a fire. That way, we can see what happened to the dog." Venom went straight to work with Spider. The two had the fire lit in no time. From the distance, the light shone a spectrum of reds, oranges, and yellows that warmed the cave though Blaze couldn't feel the heat. Venom and Spider walked down toward the back of the cave. "Where's your cloak? Oh, I see."

"Don't pick it up. The dog's hurt." Spider squatted next to the pup opposite of Blaze. Spider felt the need, and urge, to pet the dog. Blaze gently slapped his hand away. "It bit me when I tried to touch it."

"We need to get help. Are you all right?"

"Yeah, I'll be fine. It's young so it hasn't gotten its grown-up teeth. You can see by its tooth here." Blaze picked up the tooth from where it dropped on his tunic. "It doesn't feel much different than Denalisa's needle pricks from yesterday." Venom glanced at Blaze's hand. It was definitely different than his right, but knowing Blaze, he'd just wait it out.

"What is that smell?" Venom inhaled, as did Spider. Spider held his nose.

"That stinks," Spider remarked about the musky, rotting stench.

"It's the smell of gnashers . . . and death, I think. It'll get worse before it gets better. You've got to let the maggots do their job, but you could dispose of them away from here, Venom. We don't want to lure anything else into the cave, especially since your spell didn't work."

"I don't want to touch them, but I have to get rid of that smell. I can't stand it!" Venom pulled up his cowl and covered his mouth and nose. "Spider, stay with Blaze. See if you can find something to wrap around his hand." Spider scurried away, bringing back a small, burlap sack filled with linen scraps.

"I got these from the Bevisson fabric trader a while ago. I told her I was from Bevisson and then moved here. She gave these to me a day later. She was so kind. Do you think the pup will be okay?" Blaze wrapped the first strip of linen around his hand, pulling it tight with his right while holding the other end in his mouth. The pulsing pain ceased for a moment, and then as the linen became wet and red with blood, it started again. Spider tried to help with the bandages. His attempt was more twisting the ends together, which didn't hold. "I'm not good at knots like Venom. Mummy said so. She said I was made for something else." Blaze wrapped his arm around Spider, pulling him close to reassure him.

"What's going on here?" asked Venom. Blaze released Spider.

"Nothing. Spider was just telling me that you're really good at knots. How come you haven't entered the knot tourneys yet?" Venom reached over and forcibly grabbed Blaze's hand, bandaging it with tight knots over the wounds.

"Yecch, some of these ends are wet. Were they in your mouth?' Blaze confirmed Venom's guess. "I haven't done the tourneys because I couldn't get the killick hitch knot right to hold our dingy to the dock. I can try next time. Spider, go get some snow in your basin and bring it back inside and let it melt by the fire." Spider ran off to follow Venom's instructions. "I want to make something clear, Blaze—it is my dream for Spider and me to live in a real house and get all of the opportunities that he deserves instead of living like this." Blaze nodded in agreement. "And I will make sure that dream becomes a reality. I don't care who I hurt if they get in the way of that dream. Understand?" Blaze nodded again. He *did* hear, loud and clear. "Now, what do we do about this dog? I think I'll put it out of its misery and then I'll dump it with the gnashers."

"No, don't. I have a strange feeling that it's going to be okay. I've been noticing weird things about it since yesterday. Almost as if it's trying to talk to me. I've never seen one before, but I think it's a lupin or a wolf-sprite. And from what Mason has said, a sprite, no matter what kind—wolf, horse, bird, deer—will heal itself if they sleep it off."

Venom raised his eyebrows.

"So then, if it is in that deep of a sleep, we can move it closer to the fire. You need to get that hand looked at. It's swollen and might still be bleeding, even though I tied it tight enough so it should stop soon, if not already." Blaze stared at the pup. *No, I don't think we should move you.*

"Go back to the guild. I'll wait with the lupin pup until it wakes up. I don't want to move it. It lost a lot of flesh and blood. My hand will be fine. Besides, no one will miss me." Spider came back to the group, carrying the small basin of melted snow. Venom and Blaze smiled at him, giving him the impression that everything was perfectly fine.

"Okay, but I'm getting a blanket from Spider's stuff and giving it to you. The wind was picking up when I went outside with the gnashers." Venom found a blanket and placed it over Blaze and the pup. "Come on, Spider, let's get the other stuff that we came here for. Blaze is staying. Don't worry, he'll be fine." Venom guided Spider back to the entrance. He glanced back at Blaze. "I'll be back tomorrow to make sure the fire stays lit." Blaze raised his hand, acknowledging Venom's last statement. He leaned his head back against the wall.

After a long night in the cold, Blaze was famished. The fire had been out, and Venom had yet to return to check it. Blaze only moved from next to the lupin pup when he couldn't hold his bodily functions any longer. He propped the pup against the blanket and slowly slid away from it. Poking his head out of the entrance flap, he noticed another storm had blown in, and he and the pup were stuck in the cave until it passed. He hoped it would be over soon. He stood near the entrance and did what was needed, yellowing the snow opposite the door's opening. He walked around Spider's home and discovered a small amount of wood that could last maybe a few hours. The back area was actually not as cold as it was nearer the entrance. The large pile of blankets that Blaze had discovered Spider wrapped in were gone. *We did come for the blankets in the first place. But they could've left two of them.* Blaze rummaged through a chest that was hidden by a jutting rock. It was locked.

He pulled his lock-picking kit off of his belt. Scribbled words embossed the top flap. He rubbed his thumbs over the words. He couldn't read it, but he knew it spelled out "Rhatt." He never looked at it straight on because, like worms, the letters wiggled and crawled off the leather. He opened the kit and pulled out the smallest awl and paddle tools. The kit had served Rhatt well as it did Blaze now. He inserted the paddle into the lock, twisting until it found the prongs of the lock's interior. He closed his eyes as he concentrated, waiting to hear the familiar sounds of the prongs moving out of the way. When all of the prongs were separated, the chest opened with a joyful chink. Blaze opened his eyes, replaced the paddle, and carefully raised the lid. There was little in the chest: a parchment (useless) three coppies (who cared?), and four palm-sized paintings. Those were interesting. Blaze had never seen such small portraits. In one, there was a woman in pirate clothing, her dress hiked up to show off her shapely leg. Blaze surmised it was their mother. The woman had flowing, brown curls that ran down her back to her waist, and her eyes were shaped like Venom's. Spider, on the other hand, had his mother's nose. But the grin across her face was hers alone. Blaze took an immediate liking to her. For Venom's and Spider's sake, he wished her to still be alive.

The second portrait was Spider. He hadn't changed that much since the painting was done, but his smile brightened the canvas and was the whitest thing on the whole portrait. *I bet the painter started with his smile,* Blaze mused. The third, Blaze assumed, had to be Venom. In the portrait, Venom was not much younger than he was now, but his hair was curlier and flowing below his shoulders. He wore an ecru tunic with blousy sleeves that laced at the neck. Blaze pulled out the fourth painting. It was a portrait of a horse gleaming in the sun. A purple cast of light shimmered off its black mane. Blaze shrugged, placing all of the items back in the chest. He turned the locking mechanism's teeth to accept a rod that secured it closed. Then he placed it back where it had previously been, as if it had been left undisturbed. The tent flap blew open and Blaze wrapped his arms about himself while rubbing them for warmth. He put his kit back on his belt first and then headed to secure the flap.

He made a fire, and settled down on the rug to wait for the day to pass. He held his stomach, feeling the familiar pangs of hunger from his early childhood return. After lying down for some time, he fell asleep and the fire dwindled. He awoke suddenly, realizing that had he missed an important opportunity to keep the fire stoked. Blaze knew that the fire needed more air as well as another log. Before long, the fire ignited in a small steady flame. He was amazed that there was still enough wood to keep the fire going. The flap whipped in the wind and Blaze went and checked again on the pup. He carefully unwrapped his cloak that had been keeping the pup safe and warm. The wound was looking better already, and Blaze was positive that this was a lupin. He carefully picked up the lupin pup and moved it to the rug. It stretched out, whimpered, and continued in its slumber.

Through the rest of the day, Blaze kept vigil over both the pup and the fire until he had used up the last log. His injured hand was warm to the touch, and he realized that he probably had an infection, but there wasn't anything he could do given his current situation. Fear and anxious thoughts erupted as he worried that he would end up without his hand like Nohan. As the evening progressed, the fire dwindled to nothing. Even though he was cold, Blaze couldn't do anything to fix the lack of wood. To keep himself warm, he fell asleep snuggling with the lupin. A relationship that had not been forged before became tight throughout those days.

By the third day, Blaze was startled awake by a cascading, hollow echo. He felt for the small pup's body and it wasn't there. He sat up and searched the cave. No pup. He called it as he would a dog, as it was so keen on pretending to be. The flap was flying freely in the wind, and the snow was deeper than when Blaze and the pup had arrived days ago. As Blaze went to secure the flap, he noticed a large pile of fresh wood near the entrance.

"Venom," Blaze called out.

Instead, a boy similar in age entered the cave. Blaze grabbed for his dagger.

"Blaze, you can put that away. I'm not going to hurt you," the boy remarked with a deep accent. "I already bit you by accident. I won't do it again." A wide smile greeted Blaze. His light, buff-colored hair draped over one eye, concealing it from view. The other eye Blaze couldn't help but stare at because it was oddly tilted and square. His brow followed it, making it seem even more ethereal. His eye was green. He wore no clothes, yet he came from the cold. *Is this the form of Adoon?* Blaze wondered, realizing that he may have sealed his own doom when he mentioned earlier in the week that Adoon would not come to smite Denalisa. "Oh, I apologize for not introducing myself. I'm Traveraluchan." Blaze stood dumbfounded.

"What?"

The boy laughed.

"I'm Traveraluchan, but you can call me Lupi for short. I'm the pup you saved. I'm sorry I bit you, but you did touch the wound. It was a natural reaction." Blaze slowly nodded, glancing around and wondering if he was hallucinating. He hoped that something could verify his vision. "Don't worry. I got wood. You were so tired; I tried to wake you earlier."

"Trav-eleck-ian?"

Lupi roared with joyful laughter echoing through the cave.

"Good try! It's in my native tongue of Lupinish. Can you try it again? Tra-ver-a-lu-chan. If it is easier, you can just call me Lupi, most people do. Lupinish is a bunch of sounds that replicate growls and guttural sounds that are easier for us to make in wolf-sprite form." Lupi walked closer to Blaze. "Do you mind if I borrow the blanket? It's cold in . . . areas." Blaze hurriedly passed Lupi the blanket, glad that he covered up. Lupi wrapped the blanket around himself and sat down. "I grabbed some yarrow root, which is good for bites. My baby brother is always biting someone. He's such a snap pup. Ma always cures everything with yarrow root. It's hard to find, especially here in Ballardton, but if you sniff it out you can usually find it." Lupi held out his hand, waiting for Blaze to place his hurt hand in his own. The lupin untied all of the linen strips, clearly impressed by Venom's knots and the length of time it took to untie them. "Venom should have tied me up. I'd never have been able to get out of it." Blaze didn't appreciate Lupi's thoughts about being tied up by Venom or anyone. It just sounded wrong.

"Here, do this instead." Blaze took up his dagger and started to slide his blade between his wrist and the bandages. Lupi stopped him.

"We might still need them after, and I am really enjoying the challenge. I hope that's okay with you." Working at the knots, Lupi removed all of the bandages. Blaze's hand was swollen, red and punctured like a decorative pillow. "I'm sorry. I don't know why it should be this bad. I only bit once out of pain from . . ."

"The gnashers!" They spoke in unison.

Lupi grabbed the yarrow root and instructed Blaze to chew it, but not swallow. He started chewing; his mouth watered, and he found that he actually enjoyed the earthy taste of the yarrow root, though it could have been more that it was the first thing he had eaten at all for three days.

"The juice will mix with your spit and you'll swallow the spit. That's good. Don't eat the pulp because we are going to make a paste that will go on your hand. Make sure you chew it until it is a pasty green." Blaze mumbled inaudibly."What did you say?"

"How will I know? And why did you hide that you're a lupin? The guild accepts all." Blaze managed to articulate between chews.

"Oh, believe me, you will know when that is done. It's a pasty chalk that dries out your tongue by the end. I didn't tell anyone because I was afraid. I haven't been able to transform because of a spell."

"What were you afraid of, Lupi?"

"The knackerman. He tried to throw me into his fire, but I transformed and ran as far away as I could. He knows I'm a lupin. He had lured me to him when I was here with my Puppa—that's my father. Puppa is a diplomat from Dianthe, and this was my second time coming with him. The knackerman hid me in his yard. I tried to escape several times, but he kept bringing me back." Lupi bowed his head as he contemplated the reality of this discrimination."If I kept pretending to just be a dog, I thought I'd be okay. I slipped into a barn at a farm. The man thought I was after the chickens, which I was. He told me that he was going to deal with me later, tucking me in a sack by an old outhouse—he magicked it closed, else I'd have been on my way home. Stick out your tongue." Blaze stuck out his tongue, and it was coated by a slick, green pulp."Not ready yet. Keep chewing. When it's ready, it'll be a kind of green goop ball. I had tried several times to change back and I was surprised that I couldn't change until after we were attacked by the gnashers. I guess I should have slept in the first place." Blaze stuck his tongue out again. A big glob of gooey green was forming."Is your mouth dry yet?"

"Yes."

"I mean really dry, so you want to cough."

"I think so."

"It's not ready—you'll know, believe me. Keep chewing." Blaze kept at it, but it was like chewing on a leech and candlewax. Shortly thereafter, Blaze coughed and hacked."That's it—you sound like a feline with a hairball! Here, spit it out."

"Gladly." Blaze dropped the goop into his hand and handed it to Lupi, who pressed it into each puncture wound and smeared it around Blaze's whole hand."Do you really need to put it on all of it?" Lupi acknowledged him with a nod. Each individual tooth puncture felt as though acid was eating through his skin. He shook his hand, attempting to stop the sting.

"Keep it on there. I have to get one more medicinal flower."

Blaze sweated through the pain, rocking back and forth and tucking his hand between his thighs.

"You're still not wearing any clothes," Blaze snarled through gritted teeth.

"Oh, I'll be faster in my wolf form anyway." Lupi changed forms and was out the door before Blaze noticed.

By the time Lupi returned, Blaze's pain had subsided. He lay on the rug, replaying the events of the last few weeks in his head. The swelling still remained, but the puncture wounds had begun a rapid cell restoration. Lupi ran to him, afraid for him, and knelt down beside Blaze in his sprite form.

"Blanket!" Blaze screamed, startling Lupi, who laughed at Blaze's modesty. Grabbing the blanket with his left hand, he uncurled his right to reveal a green stem with five leaves that when in bloom had been a white bell flower that dangled in a droopy arc. The plant had many names and was found in mountainous areas as well as, surprisingly, the Spring District. Lupi called it cinderoot.

"Eat the leaves. They have a peppery, smokey taste, but they're not too bad." Blaze did as he was told. "Stay here. I'll be back."

Lupi transformed into pup form again and sprinted back to the guild house. When he found Barden, Lupi yipped to get his attention. The lupin ran to the man and then back toward King's Highway, eager to have the spy follow. Barden bent down to pick him up, but Lupi eluded him. The knackerman heard Lupi's yip and came running.

"That's my lu. . . . er, pup! Get 'im!"

The two ran after Lupi, who ran erratically through their legs, around the guild house, and down the street. He waited at the fountain for them to follow.

"Barden, get him for me, and I'll make that compromise." Barden agreed while he tiptoed to catch the wily lupin. Slowly, Barden closed in, but just as he lunged forward, Lupi dashed up the road, waiting about a hundred feet for Barden to catch up. They played the game until they reached the cave.

"Wait a minute! What have we got here?" Barden stopped and stared at the cave's entrance. Lupi sneezed exasperatedly. Barden was cautious as he started through the cave door. "Stay! Don't move," he scolded the lupin, still treating him like a dog. Entering the cave, Barden made his way in, scrutinizing every element as his training had taught him. A noise from the center of the cave halted Barden in his tracks. He kept to the shadows. Barden jumped when Blaze moved forward with his dagger drawn.

"Lupi, is that you? I'm feeling better."

Blaze moved with the natural fluidity of a Timerian noble; it was the first time Barden had noticed. Rhatt had a solid strut when he walked, but there was a silent subtleness about the boy.

"Blazey, what in all of Mirias are you doing in here? Is this where you have been this whole time? Master had me out looking for you these past three and a half days. He'll be pleased I found you." Blaze raised his hand where thankfully the swelling had receded. He opened and closed his hand. It still felt tight, but eating those leaves was the best thing he had ever done.

"This is Spider's place. It's a secret. Where's Lupi?"

"What are you jabbering on about?"

"The pup. Where's the pup, Barden?" Barden had almost forgot about the pup. He ran outside, and the pup was gone.

CHAPTER 6

CROSSING

AFTER A LONG, cold, snow-bound winter, things had started to return to normal at the guild. Barden had passed his test; he and Denalisa were on their way north to start their own guild. Blaze couldn't care less. He just worried about the task ahead of him. From the market, he had almost everything he needed for his trip to Ceretheena. He unrolled the scroll for the fortieth time that day. The words danced on the parchment. He blinked away their uselessness and examined the accompanying map. He located Ballardton and Ceretheena. With his finger, he traced the dotted line that showed his course. It would be a long journey. He didn't want to go, especially alone. Blaze's attempts to trick the other thieves into believing that he wasn't being sent away backfired, and they enjoyed the laugh instead of him. Their enjoyment at his expense pressed him to move forward with the journey to Ceretheena Castle.

Blaze looked around the market. He watched Gavin slip away from the piemen unseen while he carried three of the hand pies—one in each of his hands and one in his mouth. Blaze let out a scornful laugh.

He turned to his left and spied Dellanie walking up the road that led to what was known in Ballardton as "the dungeon." Blaze knew Dellanie loved to explore the ruins of the mage's manor, and he shivered when he remembered his own experiences within the dungeon. A subtle movement caught his attention, one that would have gone unnoticed by an untrained eye.

The movement was Shadow. The younger boy ghosted between carts and foliage. Blaze ignored Shadow's journey when he saw the people that he passed. Blaze couldn't believe his eyes. *They're here! They haven't forgotten me, even after the long winter.* A man and woman huddled together, appearing worried and distraught. The man stopped people on the street and conversed with them. The woman raised her left arm and indicated something on her wrist. The response from the people of Ballardton always was the same: a negative shake of their head before they continued on their way. The man and woman looked at each other and hung their heads in despair. Blaze knew the two and for whom they searched. Blaze examined his wrist and frowned. He felt compelled to run to them. His mind played the images. *He bounds up to them. They turn and embrace him. They call him "Ratson." He confesses his real name and his identity as a thief. They don't care. The trio walks hand in hand away from Ballardton into the sunset.*

"Hey, Blaze! I've been looking for you. What are doing?" Venom interrupted Blaze's dream.

"What do you think? I'm getting ready for my mission."

"Oh yeah. Your *mission*. You're still calling it that? You do know that everybody knows that you're being sent away by Master, right?" Venom bent over with laughter.

"Well, they're ALL wrong and so are you! Just cut it out!"

"Ouch, Blaze, what a way to stab me! Don't you remember that there was no door on master's office when he demanded you leave that day last autumn? It wasn't exactly hard to hear what he was saying."

"Yeah, well, what would you say if I told you that I wasn't going to Ceretheena after all and I was actually going to live on a fiefdom? Have anything and everything that I could possibly want, even Drisanian toys?"

Venom stared at Blaze wide-eyed terrified of being caught in another lie. "That's great! When are you leaving? I remember I had a Drisanian toy on my mom's ship! It used to poke little animals out of different windows. I'd watch it for hours. Can Spider and I come too? We wouldn't be any trouble—I promise." Venom's eyes were full of emotion, anticipation, and promise of a better life. Blaze closed his eyes and sighed. "I'll get Spider and my stuff! We'll be ready before the sun hits zenith. Wait for us here, Blaze." Venom was talking a mile a minute, his exuberance showing.

"No, Venom. I'm not . . ."

"This is going to be great! This is just what we've been waiting for. I knew one day this would happen!"

"Wait! Come back, Venom! I'm not going to a fiefdom! Adoon's blood, come back here and listen to me!" Venom ran from him toward the fairgrounds to find Spider. Blaze could hear Venom yelling as he ran away. "Spider, Spider, guess what? We're going to be a family again!" Blaze stared after him.

"Venom, wait! It's a . . ."

"Lie. Aww! Isn't that sweet! The three of you living in a fiefdom. Go stop them, Blaze. It would be the right thing to do." Blaze turned around, startled. It was Nightshade. She was leaning against an empty market stall with her arms crossed across her chest holding a small dagger in her right hand.

"What are you talking about, Nightshade?" Blaze glared at the girl and his mouth curled into a snarl.

"Let's see how many lies Blaze can tell in one day." Nightshade raised one finger. "Number one, you're still going on a 'mission.' Number two: you're going to 'live in some fiefdom and get whatever you want.' Let's face it, Blaze; you'll never get what you want."

"Oh really, Nightshade, and what is it that I want?" Nightshade smiled malevolently.

"Respect, Blaze. But you'll never get it, and I know why."

"What do you mean, 'you know why'?"

"Here, Blaze. Let me see your hand. No, the other one." Blaze rubbed his hand on his tunic and then laid his hand out in front of Nightshade. "Ah, yes, here it is."

"Since when were you a fortune teller, Nightshade?" Nightshade ignored his question.

"This line says that you're going to have a short life, and this line tells me that you'll never get what you desire. Oh, and this—this tells me that you, Blaze, fought a hoard of devlins and lived to tell about it back before the autumn snow." Nightshade had her finger pressed hard into Blaze's birthmark. Blaze pulled his hand away from her, but she kept a hold of his arm. "So . . . tell me, Blaze—or should I say Ratson? What's stopping me from ratting you out to those people? I spoke with them—Nan and Neid of Gresham-fief. They are giving a bounty to anyone who can locate you, dead or alive. They have been searching for you all winter long. Hmm, I wonder what their lord will do with you, stupid little thief." Blaze's

eyes were fearful. He pulled away from her, looking into her menacing grin. "I'm going to send you back to them, and dead is always
better than alive."

He ran away from Nightshade and out of Ballardton as fast as
he could. At his retreat, Nightshade laughed hard and her cackling
followed him down the road. *I'm sorry, Venom. I'll make this up to
you and Spider.* His mind replayed the past months of deception
over and over.

Nightshade was right: he *had* lied. He had lied about his name,
and about who and what he was. He recalled how he had jumped
off the back of Neid's horse and made his way to the side of the
food cart. How he had used all of his weight to topple it. Yes, he had
been nearly crushed, but he had made it back home to Ballardton
in one piece. *Home.* What a lie that was!

Locke didn't want him, and he had made a fool of himself by
bragging that he was going on a mission. Then there was the whole
debacle of Denalisa and Barden. How she made him try to read in
front of everyone—humiliating him when it wasn't his fault that
the words did all those crazy acrobatics. And the knackerman! And
Lupi who just up and disappeared after Barden arrived to take
Blaze back to the guild. Blaze yelled at himself, pounding his head
as he spoke. "Stupid! Liar! Stupid, stupid liar. Stupid me! Stupid,
stupid Blazey! Why am I always so stupid? I hate myself!"

Blaze walked on and on, passing through fields of greens and
streams, all the while imagining Venom and Spider waiting for
him back in Ballardton. He could see Spider's eyes sparkling when
Venom told him about the fiefdom and then both of their disappointment when he was no where to be found. In the pit of his
stomach, Blaze knew that Venom was seething. Blaze slept by the
side of the road and dreamed of devlins and Lupi. After waking and
traveling a short while, he arrived at the stone gate of Ceretheena
Castle. The gate was foreboding, with large twin turrets that rested
high above him atop the arch. He presented the gatekeeper with
the scroll Master Locke had given him. Blaze waited for what
seemed like hours. When the gatekeeper returned, he presented
Blaze with a new scroll. Blaze began to open it, but the gatekeeper
stopped him. He gestured for Blaze to go to another gate, which
allowed access into the castle.

At the second gate, a woman and man stood, apparently waiting for Blaze. The woman watched Blaze's movement. The boy had grace, that was certain, but he was so filthy that a bath would be necessary. The woman smiled. Her favorite part of her job was helping to get these children off the street, out of occupations such as thievery or a stint in the army. This boy would be saved.

"May I please have your scroll?" the woman requested as Blaze walked up to the pair. "You are a very fortunate young man. I am Ree, headmistress of the house staff. This is Reneth and he is in charge of the gate and outer staff. There will be times that you will report to either of us or possibly to both. What is your name, child?"

"I am Blaze of Ballardton." Blaze lowered his head as he spoke.

"Lift your head, child." Mistress Ree grabbed Blaze's face, squeezing his cheeks. "You should be proud of who you are now. Your master has given you a great gift. As a member of the house staff, Blaze, you will have specific duties, but you will learn those later." Ree turned his head from side to side, checking for lice, scratches, or signs of disease. She then examined the boy from head to toe and spun him around. Finally, convinced that the boy was free of any foul parasites, she lifted her head and prompted him with a "Follow me," and entered the castle. She held the door for Blaze. It was a courtesy to which he was unaccustomed. Blaze noticed that, although the duke and his family had fled the castle many turn-years ago, the staff continued to maintain their duties as though the royals were still present. The house staff's clothing was a slate gray. Blaze wondered if it was intended to make the staff blend into the castle walls. Ree stopped at a closed door that was located in the left wing of the castle and knocked; the door opened, seemingly by magic. Blaze was drawn inward before Ree entered. She frowned.

The room was filled with ornate fabrics from floor to ceiling. Tanned leather was piled underneath the only visible window in the room. Leather scraps lay in a heap near Blaze's feet. Humming reached his ears, and he started to investigate deeper, but Ree forcibly held his shoulders. He looked up at her. She shook her head and quietly whispered for him to wait.

"Is this the new boy, Mistress Ree?"

"Yes, Tailor Sito."

"Do you think the gray will suit him? Or rather, will he suit the gray?" Behind Blaze, Ree had no time for Sito's nonsense, especially since Sito had known that the boy was coming. Tailor Sito was quite a character and he asked her the same question with every new staffer, much to Mistress Ree's annoyance.

"Yes, he'll suit the gray . . . with training."

"Good."

A short, little man with untamed hair emerged from behind the wall of fabric. He carried a pouch full of his tailoring effects. He smiled broadly at the boy. "Mistress Ree, does he have a name?"

"Oh, please excuse me, Tailor Sito. Yes, his name is Blaze."

"That's a different name—did you give it to yourself or did you earn it?" Tailor Sito winked at Blaze and then nudged him.

"My father gave it to me when I was born!" Blaze's stance reflected his indignation. "I knew both of my parents!"

"All right, all right. I see, you're a little high-strung, child. Your father named you appropriately."

Ree frowned. For the first time, she was thankful that the royal family was not here. This child was going to be difficult, but she knew she was up to the challenge of curtailing his wild behavior and curt tongue.

Tailor Sito grabbed Blaze underneath his arms, making the boy jump. He ran his hands down Blaze's side to his feet. Then he laid his hands hard on the boy's shoulders, encircled his neck, and followed his arms to his wrists. Blaze felt uneasy.

"Blaze, your tunic is too big, but your breeches are the right fit, though travel worn. All right, Mistress Ree, you may take him. I will have his first set of clothes ready soon and then the rest by tomorrow evening. Oh, Blaze, leave your boots by the door."

"What?"

"Your boots—leave them by the door before you exit. I'll need to have custom-made boots and indoor shoes made for you."

"Yes, Tailor Sito. I will make sure the boy attends to your requests. Your time constraint is more than generous."

"You're welcome. Goodbye, Blaze, and good luck. See you around the castle!"

Blaze wasn't sure if Tailor Sito was welcoming him or sending him to his ultimate doom. He removed his boots and left them at the door. His heart fell as he left shoeless. So far everyone seemed nice—*too* nice actually—and if Blaze knew people as well as he thought he did, things were going to change for the worse.

"Come along, Blaze. I'll show you the children's quarters. Every child is paired with an older staffer. That staffer will teach you your responsibilities. I have to think who I will assign to you. For now, I will show you around." Ree turned around, hunched down, and spoke directly into Blaze's face. "Okay, Blaze, before we go any further, there are a few courtesy items that we need to address first. As a member of the house staff, you enter last, especially after the royal family when they return. Next, you need to tame that anger or else. Lastly, this *is* your home, Blaze. Your duties will include cleaning the chimneys, assisting the housekeepers, and any additional duties that are asked of you. Most of the staff will not address you by your name, but rather as boy or whatever your job is at the time—for example, 'chimney' or 'chimney sweep.' This is not an insult. Do you understand? Tell me you understand."

Blaze was taken aback by Mistress Ree's intrusion on his personal space. He confirmed that he did understand as he felt she would only be satisfied by that one answer. "There are many children that run through the jobs, so most staffers do not learn names. Do you understand, boy?"

"Yes." Blaze was still stuck on being called "boy" or "chimney." Blaze worried that he would lose his identity. Ree continued walking with a frowning Blaze following behind. Ree showed him the different areas of the castle and she ended the tour at Blaze's new home.

"This is the children's quarters. You will stay here. Find the bed with your new tunic on it; that will be your bed. Do you know how to bathe?"

"Yes, I used to bathe in the river behind the guild."

"A simple *yes* or *no* would suffice. I do not need to know the details of your previous life."

"Uh . . . yes."

"Hmm, not very convincing, but I'll accept it for now. Make sure you clean under your fingernails. Before you dress, one of the older staffers will attend to making sure that you are thoroughly clean. After that inspection, put on your new clothes. Someone will come by to fix your hair—it's shaggy. They will cut it so that it is neat and tied back. We always keep up a clean and neat appearance, understand?"

"Uh-huh."

"No, that is not how you respond, Blaze. A proper response to most women in general is 'yes ma'am.' As for myself, I expect you to address me with 'yes, Mistress Ree.' If you're addressing a man, you will say 'yes sir,' or if he is a staffer, 'yes Master,' and then his name.

Every adult staffer is either Mistress or Master except for Tailor Sito because he prefers to be called either Tailor or Tailor Sito. It is his preference; ergo, we honor him with his request. Understand?"

"Uh-huh . . . I mean, yes ma'am."

"How did I want you to address me?" She stared down her nose.

Blaze dropped his head, took a deep breath, and responded.

"Please accept my apologies, Mistress Ree."

Blaze bowed, mimicking behaviors of young noble visitors in Ballardton during its midsummer festival. Mistress Ree tilted her head back with an heir of superiority and a hint of surprise and looked down at Blaze. "Hmph. All right, then. I will leave you to your bath. Oh, and Blaze—don't disappoint me, or we will send you back to your old life where you can bathe in the river." Blaze half smiled, confirming his understanding.

"Yes, Mistress Ree."

Before he could finish her name, Mistress Ree had already fled down the hall, leaving Blaze to stare at the entrance to the children's quarters. Slowly, Blaze entered the wing. He half expected to see Venom and Dellanie angrily waiting for him. Instead, the area was surprisingly empty. There was a long hallway with doors on either side. He walked down the hall until he noticed an open door on the right. It was a simple, bland room with a bed, a wardrobe, and a desk. On the bed was set a towel, a water basin, soap, a slate gray tunic with matching breeches, ecru hose, and underclothes. Near the door, Blaze located soft kid-leather slippers that he imagined were the indoor shoes of which Tailor Sito had spoken.

Although the room was simple, Blaze felt as if he had just become a king. He picked up the items and remembered he had passed a water closet that was similar to one he had seen not that long ago in the rooms of an exclusive, humans-only inn back in Ballardton called Lords and Ladies, where he once was dispatched to work by Master Locke. He lay down on the bed, squashing the freshly pressed clothes, and allowed the basin, soap, and towel to fall to the floor. The bed was comfortable in comparison to the flat mats that they had at the guild, but it was hard compared to the beds at Lords and Ladies. *It's not too bad, I guess.* Blaze had not realized how comfortable the bed would be for sleeping, or even that he was tired. He fell asleep before too long.

"Hey, wake up!"

Blaze groggily opened his eyes and saw a preteen looming in the doorway. The boy leaned against the door and held a pair of boots in his hands. "Don't let Mistress Ree catch you sleeping on the job! She'll ring both of our necks!" The boy had neatly trimmed, dirty-blond hair that was tied back with a gray ribbon and a round face with a freckle on his right cheek. Looking at him, Blaze figured that would be his hairstyle soon. "I'm Calam. I've brought you your boots from Tailor Sito and I'm being assigned to show you around. Oh, and I don't do the clean body inspection. Just quickly wash up and get your staffer uniform on." Blaze quickly went to work, gathering up his uniform, towel, and the bowl. "I'm not one to know any better, but I'm sure you can get cleaner if you use soap." Blaze immediately realized what Calam meant. The soap had found its way under the bed. Blaze retrieved it and then ran into the water closet.

After washing up and changing his clothes, Blaze was shown where to hang up his tunic and breeches and where in the children's quarters dirty clothes went to be cleaned. Blaze wondered how anyone could tell the clothes apart from each other since they were all identical, but he refrained from asking. Calam started Blaze on a tour of the castle. He started in the children's quarters, introducing him to Mistress Eyres, who waved while hurrying away to help a Little.

"That's Mistress Eyres, she's assigned to us. You'll like her, most of us do. She is always attending to the youngest staffers as they need the most help. You're older, so I can help you get used to stuff. You'll be following me around for a couple months until you get the hang of things. You'll also have to work a month with Tailor Sito; everyone learns to sew. He's quite funny and he is a comfort to talk to because you can be open with your thoughts and feelings. He won't tell anyone your secrets except maybe his cat, which I have never seen and I've been here for many turn-years."

Blaze and Calam walked out into the main hallway. The rug felt like Blaze was walking on air. There were portraits and tapestries on the walls, armor in the hallways, doors that were taller than eight feet high. They walked to a landing that overlooked a grand foyer. There were floor-to-ceiling curtains that covered eight windows in a row. The floor reflected like glass and wooden bannisters ran along the whole staircase. Another staircase was behind them and it, too, was marvelously shiny.

"You cannot go up that staircase, it is forbidden," Calam whispered in Blaze's ear, giving a mysterious air to their explorations.

"Really, why not?"

"Because it is a down staircase." Calam laughed uncontrollably for a short while until he regained his composure. Blaze blushed embarrassed that he had fallen for the joke. "Yeah, whew, I've been waiting to tell that one for a while and you're the first one who would get the joke. Sorry." Calam took a deep breath and held his hands out to refocus himself. "Seriously, though, the up one is along that hallway to the left and up three steps through another door. This area is where the duke and duchess would receive guests. However, we have to clean it all to a sparkling shine as Mistress Sibby always says. You'll meet her later. She is very nice and treats us all with respect. You'll like her, everybody does. She is the royal nanny; however, she also oversees some of the housekeeping duties."

Calam walked Blaze through the rest of the castle, showing him all the different types of jobs that were required by staffers. There was dusting to do on a daily basis, drawing drapes even though there wasn't anyone who would notice or care, making beds, and keeping everything neat and tidy. Footsteps approached them and Calam pulled Blaze back against the wall. A guardswoman walked through the castle; she never glanced once at the boys. "When you hear someone approach like that, you must make yourself invisible. When the duke and duchess return, we will be here, but never seen. I know what I have shown you so far is a lot, and you're probably hungry. Let's head down to the kitchen and get some leftovers from Mistress Ree's and Master Reneth's plates. They eat the best and they are always served more than they will eat. If it's later in the day, like now, we can see if cook will make up a plate of our own. We'll have to eat it in the kitchen near the stove, but I don't think you'll mind. Come on!" The two boys walked swiftly through the castle, finding their way to the kitchen to eat. Blaze wondered what was to come tomorrow or the next day. Would he really become accustomed to this place? He instantly liked Calam, enjoyed his joke, and hoped that he would be his friend. *Being at Ceretheena Castle,* Blaze surmised, *might be the best place I've ever been. Maybe I will actually like it here.*

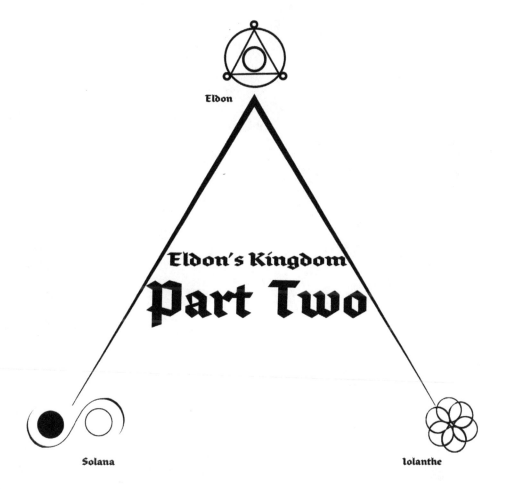

Eldon

Eldon's Kingdom
Part Two

Solana

Iolanthe

CHAPTER 7

GROWTH

YEARS PASSED. Blaze, now a young teenager, ran through the hallways of Ceretheena Castle. He felt a kinship within the hallways and a deepened understanding of his duties. Tailor Sito had even learned his name, as had Mistress Eyers. He and Calam had become closer, and the two spoke of their futures at the castle. He passed the royal suite, the royal nursery, and a royal portrait. He skidded to a halt at the portrait. Taking a moment, Blaze stood in front of it. Magnificent in its color and height, it was a favorite of his; its ominous presence had always intrigued him. When his duties were completed, Blaze would stand here and look into the faces of the royals that he believed were never coming back. He met Duke Flynn's gaze.

It was common knowledge that the duke and his family had fled, but the reason behind their leaving remained a mystery to the people of Timeria. Blaze felt a strange connection to the family. He bowed to the duke. Surrounding his painted visage were his wife, Duchess Reseda, his daughters, Princesses Valorie and Glenna, and his twin sons, Princes Derry and Tarn. The girls were young, still clinging to their dolls, and the boys were not much more than babies. The portrait was painted turn-years ago. The girls would now be older than Blaze; that is, if they were still alive. Everyone in the castle believed that the boys had probably perished since they were so young at their departure that they were still handled by their nanny and wet-nurse. But the words went unspoken, and to express those thoughts was treason to the crown.

"Boy! You there, boy!"

Blaze looked down the hallway and noticed the royal nanny, a jovial, warm-hearted, plump woman with graying hair, who never had an ill word for anyone in the castle and made the best-tasting, most mouth-watering cinnamon teacake. Blaze stood at attention as he had been trained.

"Yes, Mistress Sibby, what may I do for you?"

"There is a messenger coming from the northern territory. This sickness is escalating. Go meet the messenger at the inner gate and cover your mouth with your linen face covering at all times." Blaze bowed to her, raised the material about his neck, and followed orders. Mistress Sibby rubbed her hands together out of worry. Most of the older staffers had fallen ill. The most recent case was Mistress Ree, and she was worsening by the hour. Sibby knew what had to be done: she had taken control of the house staff. The messenger hopefully would bring word that the children and any nonessential staffers would be moved to King Kiril's castle before they, too, fell ill.

Sibby paced back and forth before the duke's portrait. She glanced at the royal family, bowed, and then continued her pacing. She felt a strange new understanding of the duchess and duke's decision.

"Excuse me, Mistress Sibby."

Sibby turned to see the boy accompanied by the king's messenger.

"Thank you. You may leave us." Blaze bowed and left, returning to run through the empty corridors. Exploring the working castle, the walls, and the surrounding grounds was Blaze's favorite pastime.

The castle had fulfilled every desire and need that Blaze had. He continued his trek across the castle to the children's quarters. It was there that Blaze discovered Calam leaning against the wall in the hallway. Calam was melancholy and pale, and seemingly anxious.

"Calam, you're not getting sick, are you? Should I get Mistress Eyres?"

"No, I'm fine. But I just overheard Master Reneth tell Tailor Sito that we are all going to go to the king's castle." Blaze pressed his lips together, acknowledging Calam's insight that aligned with the messenger's arrival.

"That makes sense, Calam. Everyone is getting sick. I just brought a messenger to Mistress Sibby and they were from the castle. If we go to the king's castle, won't they get sick, too?"

"That's just what Tailor Sito said, but he also said there are many protections we can take, including the linen face coverings that we wear when we are near anyone outside of the castle. And Master Reneth said that they didn't think that the sickness would spread any further north than here."

"How would they know? Back where I was from, our kind-of-healer, Mason, told us that sickness spreads usually from person to person. Wouldn't we bring it with us?"

"My thoughts exactly."

"Well, Calam, if the clerics in Venesial know of a way to keep everyone from getting the sickness, then why do you look like you're sick already?"

"It's the king's castle."

"What's wrong with it?"

"I've told you before, I came from there. . ."

"Yeah, so . . ."

"So, it's just not a good place for staffers who are currently unassigned like you and me. My mother is head of the house staff and . . . well, she's the one who told me that I should transfer down here."

"And?"

"And, it's just bad, that's all. I can't explain it."

"Well, it can't be as bad as my last home."

"Oh, yes, it can Blaze! I'm telling you, it is really bad. Everyone is always backstabbing each other. The king and queen are okay, but I've heard that the prince is an absolute nightmare. He screams all night long, and in the daytime he whines and cries. We'd be stuck having to entertain him. I don't want to go, but what other choices do we have? Take our chances at getting the sickness?" Calam slid down and slumped on the floor. Blaze sat next to him.

"I don't know, Calam. I'm sure your mother wouldn't make you do anything too unpleasant. She sent you here and that was good, right?" Calam coughed; Blaze eyed him closely, pulling up his face covering. "Are you sure you're not getting sick?"

"Yeah, I'm not. I just finished beating the entrance rugs and you know how dusty they get."

The two friends sat in silence, contemplating the impending journey and what unknown future awaited them both. Blaze's thoughts wandered to Ballardton and the guild. He wondered if anything had changed and if anybody missed him. A feeling of embarrassed dread overtook him.

"Blaze, are you getting sick? Your face is bright red."

Blaze grinned. "Naw, I'm fine. I was just thinking, Calam. That's all."

"Staffers! Attention, please!"

Mistress Eyres had entered the children's quarters and was clapping her hands to get their attention. "Boys, out of the hallway with you!" she scolded them both. The young staffers all stood in their doorways, and Blaze and Calam moved to Calam's door together. Mistress Eyres was a vibrant young woman who loved the children in her care. She had ivory skin, long light caramel hair and kind brown eyes. She took the time to listen to each staffer. Her kindness was contagious. "Thank you all for your quick reactions. Due to the sickness, we will be trekking from Ceretheena to the northern capital, Venesial. When we get there, Calam's mother, who is headmistress, will help us to settle in. Everyone knows Calam, right? Calam, raise your hand, please. Thank you. You won't have to worry; we will travel together. Retrieve your belongings and wait in the outer courtyard. We will leave after the sun goes down." Calam raised his hand, garnering Mistress Eyres attention. "Yes, Calam?"

"Why are we leaving so late?"

"Good question. I'm sure you're not the only one who has that same thought. Master Reneth believes that by traveling at night we will make better time, given the amount of travelers this time of the year."

"Isn't the Festival going on now in Ballardton?" Blaze asked quietly to Calam, but Mistress Eyres answered.

"Yes, Blaze, good observation. We will bypass Ballardton by going around it. Good question. Any more questions?" Mistress Eyres looked around. She noticed the concerned expressions on each of the children's faces. They said nothing more, and her heart reached out to them all. "All right, then. Now you will need all of your uniforms and any small personal effects. Do not worry about food. We are bringing along a small food cart with us. Now go and prepare."

Mistress Eyres went into the younger children's rooms to help them. As she passed Blaze and Calam, she placed her hand on Calam's shoulder and addressed the two older boys. "Don't worry, boys, things won't change that much in Venesial, and there will be other children your age. Actually, I think it will be a better, more social placement for you both. Also, Calam, you've grown since you

were helping at your mother's knee, and time changes all things."
She smiled at them and they reluctantly nodded their agreement.

As the troupe slept, Blaze sat awake. They were close enough to
Ballardton now that Blaze could hear the late-night bustle. He
pondered the day and wondered what tournaments would be held.
Suppressed memories of a time not long ago entered his mind and
he had no one to share them with. Tears welled in his eyes, but he
held them back.

His thoughts drifted to Rhatt, his father. In his mind's eye, Rhatt
was the most handsome man he had ever seen, and even the scars
on his face were heavenly. He assumed that he favored his father's
looks since he didn't resemble Jade much. Blaze had remembered
for the most part that Rhatt loved him unlike any other. It was a
love that was strong enough to live beyond death.

Thinking back to the guild, Blaze remembered the times he had
shared with Rhatt. The young staffer remembered his father as a
caring and doting man who taught him how to survive and live
in the moment. Scenes crossed his vision and he could see himself
and Rhatt from afar like a spectator: Rhatt scooping Blaze up in a
swinging motion that made the toddler giggle and beg for more of
the impromptu amusement; Rhatt celebrating Blaze's first theft in
front of the other guild members; Rhatt talking to Blaze about the
importance of his scars. Blaze had a sudden urgency to see the guild
one last time before he ran toward a new life of castles, princes, and
kings. He had to see the old one and see if it had changed since he
himself had changed.

He stealthily rose, careful not to wake Calam. Blaze grabbed his
tunic from his travel bag, put it on, and then tied his hair back in
typical Ceretheena fashion. He stuffed his bag back into position
to hide his disappearance as he snuck out of the camp. He needed
to see the guild—maybe it was the chance to show Master just
how much he had changed for the better, or maybe it was Mistress
Eyres' comments about time changing all things that compelled
him to return to Ballardton. As he walked, he could smell the fires
of the travelers that camped just outside of Ballardton's border.
Blaze walked in the warm summer stillness of a new day awaiting its sunrise. The sounds were familiar childhood sounds: the
murmur of different languages and the rhythm of songs that were

played for centuries amongst the travelers. Cook fires drifted in the soft warm summer air and his mouth watered. These were a few of the pleasant memories of his childhood and his heart sang with joy. The anticipation and excitement of the Festival rose inside him. He began to race through the city and take in the sights, sounds, and smells of days long gone.

He stopped at the crossroad of his former home and King's Highway. He turned down the side road and found the fountain that marked the way, home was only a stone's throw away. Its unclean water emitted an odor that was unique to itself. In the red moon's light, Blaze's uniform seemed to glow as he crept down the road. He could hear footsteps and muffled voices. He thought to go back to camp, but he had come all this way, and it was just a short distance more. He walked past the knackerman's yard. It was quiet, but the fire was still ablaze. He shivered when he saw the death fire's undying flame lighting the darkened grounds in a red, smoky hue. Blaze thought he could make out figures in the light. He stopped and listened, but he heard nothing and saw no visible movement. He glanced ahead of him to see the dark temple of the Goddess Mykondra. *Perhaps they're the priests or a follower,* he reasoned.

Turning to his left, the thieves' guild house stood smaller than Blaze had remembered it. He made his way around the back to the lower living quarters and quietly peered inside. Time had stood still while Blaze was away. The children slept in a pile while the fire still burned in the hearth. Blaze remembered tending the fire in his younger years. He turned his gaze aside, realizing that this was no longer his life and he was better for it. He was stupid to have come all this way to find something that was probably never there in the first place. He turned and leaned against the building, sliding down to sit on the ground for a moment.

"Wait until I tell Mistress Eyres that time doesn't change everything," Blaze whispered to himself. He shivered with the feeling of being watched, but he shrugged it off. Castle life had numbed his senses. He looked around and saw nothing and no one. He rose and started his trek back up the road. As he passed the yard, voices whispered in the firelit sky, and he thought he saw three figures emerging from the dark. He quickened his pace.

Once he was nearly to the top of the road, just shy of King's Highway, voices began to gain life. Happy, drunken voices like those from the tavern along the highway. He breathed a sigh of relief; it was nothing to fear. He passed by a couple of warehouse buildings on his right. Up ahead, he could see the fountain, and he knew he was almost to the crossroads. Behind him, he could hear muffled whispering. He slowed his footsteps, trying to get a better sense of the voices. He managed to reach the fountain when the voices became more distinct with recognizable names.

"You're only going to get one chance, Venom!" Lace was urging Venom to strike now.

"Now's the time!" Nightshade echoed her sentiment.

"He's finally back and he lied to you. He took away Spider's security. You need to make him pay!" Nightshade and Lace whispered in the night.

A slight movement of Venom's cloak caught Blaze's peripheral vision just as Venom pounced. Blaze braced himself for the attack holding his hands out toward Venom.

"Blaze! I am going to make you pay!" Blaze smelled the acrid, yeasty stink of alcohol on Venom's breath. As drunk as he seemed to be, Venom had complete control of his movements. His momentum knocked Blaze hard to the ground. The rock edge of the fountain was near inches from Blaze's head. Blaze turned over and faced a savagely enraged Venom, who was out of his mind and prepared to strike again. Blaze clawed at the stonework for any piece that might be cracked or loose, but there was none. In his struggle, he scraped his fingers and broke his nails.

"Venom . . . What are you doing? Stop this at once!" Blaze's language had changed since his days at the guild, which infuriated the older thief more.

"I'm going to kill you! I told you . . . I told you . . ." Venom's fist came down and hit Blaze in his gut knocking the wind out of him. Venom pulled the staffer to his feet, unsheathed his dagger, and held Blaze at knifepoint. Blaze was stunned."How could you?" Venom's knife slit Blaze's tunic and chest. Blaze jumped back just missing Venom's next knife thrust.

"How could I what? What are you talking about?"

Blaze took a blow to the head that knocked him to the ground again. Venom sat on top of Blaze, punching and stabbing him. Blaze cried out,"Stop!" but his words were unheard by the other boy.

Inside of Venom's mind were the words of the two girls. Earlier that night, Nightshade had led him out of the guild house by flirting with him. She brought beer and encouraged him to drink. By the fifth bottle, he was done in. It was then that Lace arrived. The world spun, and the more they whispered of Blaze's fateful misdeed of lying to Venom about the fiefdom, the more enraged Venom became. They told Venom to find Blaze and make him pay for all the humiliation that he caused so many years ago. Tears welled in Venom's eyes as he remembered the look on Spider's face when they ran back to find Blaze gone. Blaze knew—because Venom had told him many times—that he couldn't mess with Spider's happiness . . . or with his own.

"How could you leave me and Spider here? How could you do that to Spider?" Venom's anger festered, and the tears rolled down his face. He felt years of anger and regret as he remembered the sight of Spider's excited expression when he heard that Blaze was going to take them both to the warmth of a fief, that they were going to be a family again.

Finally, Blaze disarmed Venom's knife hand, but Venom grabbed Blaze's left hand. With all of his strength and fury, Venom broke Blaze's index and middle fingers. Blaze heard the snapping of bone along with the intensity of pain. Instinctively, he clutched his hand while involuntary tears streamed down his face. They fell with the knowledge that he had done something awful and that he deserved this payback. Venom retrieved his dagger from the ground. Blaze curled his hands closer to his chest. He tried to protect himself by resting against the fountain's base, keeping his back toward Venom.

"Venom, I never went to a fiefdom! I'll tell you the truth!" Blaze's words fell on deaf ears. There was only the madness that Venom carried in his mind. The disrespect from Blaze was more than Venom could handle—he had spent years meditating on vengeance fed by the two girls, and today was the day that Venom would have his justice.

"I'll make you pay!" Venom tried to stab Blaze in his back.

Blaze rolled away from the attack and sprang awkwardly to his feet. Then he attempted once again to disarm Venom. He reached his hands up to catch the blade as he had done hundreds of times against Dellanie. Blaze grabbed at the blade with his right hand. Either Blaze had lost his edge, was too hurt, or simply too slow, but Venom raked his blade into Blaze's palm. Venom had the advantage and Blaze truly did believe Venom indeed intended to kill him. Venom grabbed Blaze, turned him around and placed the blade to his neck.

"I'm sorry, Venom. I'm sorry. Please don't," Blaze pleaded, twisting to free himself from Venom's grasp. He kicked Venom's leg, knocking Venom off-balance. He tried to make his escape by going through the fountain, but Venom snagged the material of Blaze's uniform. Blaze cursed the fabric's strength. Venom regained his footing and jumped into the fountain after Blaze. Anger fueled Venom's need to fight, but he knew he couldn't kill Blaze—it wouldn't be enough to let him off without suffering for all those years.

It was then that he grabbed Blaze's left wrist, cutting off the circulation and causing Blaze's hand to open. Holding fast against Blaze, Venom dropped his dagger. He reached down and pulled out a hefty knife with a thick spine and a finely sharpened biting edge from a sheath buckled to his thigh. Venom jabbed his new blade against Blaze's ring finger, preparing to sever it. He had waited painstakingly for this day of retribution and had prepared this blade for just such a use. He slid the ultra-sharpened blade smoothly through both the ring finger and the pinkie. "There, that'll make you remember what you did to me and Spider! A finger for us both, so you'll remember of the hurt you caused."

Blaze's lost fingers fell into the fountain in a bloody, cloudy haze. Blaze's hand was bleeding uncontrollably; he clutched the wound with his right hand, attempting to stop the bleeding that oozed through his fingers and down his arm. He started to shake and his jaw quivered uncontrollably. He had a single thought in his head: *I won't drown. I have to get to the side.* With all the stamina he could muster, he fumbled through the water. He made it to the stone wall when he started to collapse. The blood lost, the dismemberment, and the shock of the attack caused Blaze to feel faint. As he fell, his head bounced against the stonework.

Venom uncaringly walked over Blaze's limp body. He reached deep into the fountain to retrieve his dagger and his battle trophies. He clutched the two severed fingers, and pulled Blaze the rest of the way out of the fountain.

"You can't get away with this that easy," Venom spit. He placed Blaze face up next to the fountain's base, vomiting next to Blaze's head while glancing back at what he had done.

"I've got to get Master Locke. I won't let you die, Blaze. You know why I had to do this." Venom staggered away toward the guild house. He wrapped the two swollen fingers in a handkerchief and placed them in his pouch. "Master will know what to do."

Lace watched Venom retreat back to the guild house. She exhaled disappointment, shaking her head at Venom's lack of follow through. When the street was clear, she approached Blaze. He looked so peaceful passed out and lying in the mud, his black hair pooling around his head where it had lost its hair band. She could admit the gray was a nice look for him. Now it was her turn to feel powerful and unlike Venom, her reasons were not as noble. She raked Blaze's face from nose to ear using four metal fingertip razors; she leaned down and whispered into his still face, "That'll teach you. Payback for the stew." She spat, bringing up a large amount of phlegm that clung to Blaze's cheek. Lace walked away as though nothing had transpired.

Blaze laid in a willow grove on top of a soft bed of ferns. The smell of green growth enveloped his senses. He breathed in its renewed life, deeply filling his lungs. His eyes fluttered open; blurred hues of green lit his skyward view. His head fell to his left. A shadowed figure sat next to him, but his eyes rolled in his head as he returned to the darkness of his subconscious mind.

The green hues had deepened in color while he fought his way back into consciousness. This time was not the airy drift that had been his previous attempt. Blaze's eyes remained closed, and he could feel every muscle, nerve, and touch. His face burned and cooled simultaneously. The fern against his body soothed his bare back. He moved his dominant hand only to discover intense throbbing pain. His reaction to the pain drew his hand to his chest. He clutched it with his right hand, extending his swollen thumb to touch the throbbing area of his left hand. The gentle pressure caused him to cringe in response. Tears streamed down his face, wetting a cloth bandage that stretched across his face and tied behind his head. He held back the tears, sniffling. Crying was not a sign of bravery. Blaze tried to emulate the teachings of his father, but he knew his father would be disappointed and angry about Blaze's great loss in his fight with Venom.

Blaze knew he hadn't fought hard enough; Venom should've been the victim, not him. Rational thoughts returned as he remembered why Venom attacked him. *The couple from the fief. . . What were their names? Ugh, Spider.* Blaze noticed, too, that his left index and middle fingers were splinted as well. *Broken . . . I remember and my other fingers, gone.* His face screwed to a grimace of pain as he pulled his hand closer to his body. As he continued to become aware of his injuries throughout his body, his hazel eyes fluttered open. He struggled to sit up, but his body showed its mortal limits, and the change of position made him light-headed and nauseous. He fell back into the ferns, which emitted a puff of air from the sudden impact. Blaze turned on his side, but quickly turned back. The sick feeling overtook him, causing him to sit up and disregard his previous fear.

"Adoon's sickness!" Blaze invoked the dark god as he retched, moving forward onto his right hand and knees. He clasped his stomach and wiped his mouth on his sleeve. In his current position on his knees, he got a better view of the grove and his bandages. *Who helped me?* was his only foggy thought. The grove was carefully kept with supplies of cloth, herbs, and a mortar and pestle. He leaned back, sitting on his legs while reaching for the mortar. The pestle fell, spilling salve onto the ground and Blaze. He considered all the people who could have helped him and came up with only two names: Calam and Mistress Eyres. *It must have been one of them.* He palmed his forehead, exasperated with the lack of intelligence he showed. *Of course, after noticing that I was missing, they came looking for me. They wouldn't just leave me behind.*

He sat there until he could no longer sit. His legs, numb with sleep, worked hard to help him stand. He staggered, and then fell. Again, he cursed. Finally, he stood with more control. Night had set upon the grove. Wearing just bandages and stiffened, blood-stained breeches that weren't meant for outdoors, he trudged away from the cozy woodland oasis into the dark unknown. He looked for his tunic, still struggling to think, and deserted the search when it wasn't in open sight. His journey was taking him toward the smell of food. His mouth watered as he closed in on the cook fires. Strange faces at the cook fires kept him away like a wild animal.

Somehow, on sheer instinct, Blaze made his way to the staffers' camp. To Blaze's immense disappointment, the camp was deserted. He bent over the ashes of the fire pit, placed his semi-good hand in its center only to discover it was cold to the touch. He stood up, spun around, and called out.

"Calam! Mistress Eyres!"

There was no response. The realization that the staffers had fled without Blaze barely hit him. He called for his friend, tripping on a branch. Instinctively, he braced his fall with his hands. The painful impact ran up Blaze's arms immobilizing the teen on the ground as blood seeped through his bandage on his left hand. Exhaustion and the loss of stamina caught up with Blaze. He slept in that spot for more than a day.

Waking in the deserted camp, Blaze had only one option. He would have to return to the thieves' guild and the life he had before leaving for Ceretheena Castle. He looked around the camp. There was still nothing for him to use and his clothes were a sure sign of his failure. He realized that just returning would be seen as failing, but he knew he had to walk in like he had never left. He could understand Venom's perspective for doing what he had done and never blamed Venom again, only himself.

The next day, Blaze tried to scale the lime-washed brick edifice of the Lords and Ladies Inn. The roughened points made for handholds that Blaze would normally scale with ease, but given that he couldn't use one hand, he was unable to and instead found another entrance underneath the inn. He located a large opening at the base of the foundation and slithered through it on his stomach. He noticed a word written in the common language with an arrow pointing to the way in; he turned away from it as the letters began their familiar dance. His head emerged from the opening into the wine cellar. There was no room to turn around, so his only way forward was to jump into the dark room. Rat feces covered the hole that he had wiggled through and had left stains on his clothing. He guessed that the rats must have crossed from the hole to the rafters, which therefore had to be the safest way for him to enter the cellar without falling headfirst onto the stone floor.

He reached across and grabbed the closest rafter, following the path of the rats. He pulled his body the rest of the way out of the hole with the aid of his feet and legs. Blaze rested the majority of his weight on his right hand, cringing as he dangled his left leg in midair. He swiftly changed his direction and stretched toward a wine cask nearby. The barrel was further than he thought, and when his toe touched it, he felt the pull in his groin. When he felt that he had a toehold, he followed with his other leg, all while still holding on to the rafter with his right hand. Suddenly, the barrel shifted away, and he fell down into the wine cellar. With the wind knocked out of him, he sat and held his leg that had taken the brunt of the fall. It throbbed and momentarily hurt more than his hand.

"Eldon, Eldon, Eld—" He swore through gritted teeth until the door opened. He slid on his stomach into the stack of barrels, hoping not to be detected, then crouched on his knees until he was as small as was physically possible. He could see the barkeep walking around to the hole from which Blaze had just escaped. Dirt and mud streaked down the wall from Blaze's entry, and Blaze was sure he was caught.

"Stupid rats. I told them about the creatures, but they said, 'Oh, no, we don't have no rats here, especially not in the cellar.' Here is my proof!" The barkeep picked up a small tray and collected the dirt. Blaze made his way quietly and stealthily out of the cellar. He hobbled up a stairway that was used by only servants, a stairway that he had used years ago when Master Locke had sent him away the first time under the pretense that it was Rhatt's wish. Blaze sighed. He knew that servants and staff would appear at any moment. A dinner cloak for a kitchen boy was draped over the handrail. He quickly put it on and walked into a hallway that connected the rooms of suites. *Third floor, wing seven,* Blaze whispered, reminding himself of the location of the newlywed suites. He had visited these rooms many times before, knowing that this wing wasn't for the visiting royals or anyone of any real importance. It was an ideal location for a thief. The guests might report missing items, but the innkeeper wouldn't acknowledge any thefts at their prestigious inn of Ballardton. In the past, Blaze had been careful not to take anything that would be of significant value; however, a shower and clothes would be suitable for today's take. A couple left their room as he approached. He bowed his head, concealing his face.

"Oh, I am so sorry. I forgot to leave the tray outside of the room to be removed." The woman unlocked the door. She held it open for Blaze. "We are done with it—you can just head in to get it. I'll leave the door unlocked. Just lock it when you leave." He said nothing to them, just bowed slightly to acknowledge their request.

The man embraced the woman, and the pair ran down the hallway like children.

Inside the suite, Blaze bathed, certain that he would not be disturbed. He ran his right hand across the cuts on his face and the puncture wounds on his chest. They were nearly healed, but sensitive, purple-black bruises darkened his skin. He frowned, realizing that none of it wouldn't scar. He wished that the scars would stay just like his father's battle marks. He checked his leg: it was bruised as well. He'd survive it. He kept his hands wrapped in the bandages. He knew they would get infected if the dirt got inside of the wound. He checked out the different soaps and fragrances, choosing carefully so as not to smell like a pungent flower. After his bath, he stood by a washbowl and mirror. A razor was ready for the young newlywed to shave what little beard he had tried to grow. Blaze left it untouched. He poured water into the washbowl from a large pitcher. He unwrapped his right hand. The scar had scabbed over, but he noticed that because of his falls and use, the scab was broken in some places. The cuts still bled in those spots, but they weren't enough of a bleed to worry about. It would scab again. Then he unwrapped his left hand.

He worried about the look of it. The first thing he saw was the discoloration of his hand. Then he focused on the remaining fingers. He turned his hand over, amazed at how long and slender it was. His eyes rested finally upon the empty space of the fingers that were not there. It was hard to process when his mind could still feel the two fingers touching his palm as he opened and closed his hand. *I see they're gone, but I feel them touching me.* It was mindboggling. He reached to stroke them with his thumb and examined the cut, which was clean. He stared at the wounds, and as his pulse in his chest increased, so did the rhythm of throbbing in his hand. His palm was squarer than he remembered.

Blaze decided that the only way he felt he could leave the inn and return to the life that he thought he had left was to find something that would conceal the injuries. He would have to be whole again, or else he wouldn't be able to enact the next part of his plan. He washed his hands for the first time since the attack. The soap burned, but he knew from the old adage that it was a good sign of healing. *If it doesn't hurt, it isn't working.* He patted his hands dry using a small, bleached hand towel with two golden embroidered crowns surrounding what must have been the words "Lords and

Ladies" in script. He couldn't look at the letters, but he knew what they must say.

Bathing done, he exited the bath and walked into the living quarters. A small table and two chairs were set for a meal. The dining cart that he was to have removed was in the middle of the room. He scrounged through it. The couple had eaten most of the cart, and the remnants they left were only suitable for beggars. A beggar he was, and he ate until he was full. A bed and a wardrobe were on the north wall of the room. He opened the wardrobe. The young mistress had neatly hung up all of their clothes. He perused the offerings of the young master. An amber linen tunic with soft, kid-leather breeches along with a matching belt and gloves were hung on the last peg. *Hmm, gloves. Yeah, I think that'll work.* With renewed enthusiasm, he grabbed the tunic, breeches, and belt out of the wardrobe, along with the gloves. He searched for underclothing and found them in the drawers below. He noticed the mistress' underthings and quickly closed that drawer. He tossed everything on the bed.

The bed had a beautiful, white, high loft quilt on it with a wedding ring motif. There was a pink ribbon on each cross point, and the pillows were puffed up for a newly married romp. He looked at the door, which he had locked when he first arrived, then smiled and belly flopped onto the bed. He landed with a pillowing puff of air and sank into its comfort. The bed was the nicest part of his whole day. He wished he could just sleep there, bare naked, in the center of the lofty feather bed; however, he had taken take his time in the bath and was unsure of the young couple's scheduled return. He quickly dressed. When finished, he returned to the bathing room. His hair was mostly dry, so he combed and brushed it, trying to straighten a wayward strand. He grabbed a ribbon and tied his hair back awkwardly. It would not be an easy task to learn how to do everything without those fingers. Finally, he carefully pulled both of his gloves on with his teeth. He grabbed a pair of boots from the young master and stepped into them. A bit large, but not overtly so. His final task was to return most things to normal. He straightened the bed, cleaned up the bathing room, and picked up his old clothes and boots, placing them under the cart to hide them from view. He stuffed the kitchen coat under a metal cloche on the tray. He opened the door, and saw that the hallway was bustling with servants. Blaze was taken aback. A servant ran up to him.

"I am so sorry, sir. Here I will take that for you. Is there any other service I may provide?"

Blaze stared at the young boy, who was about nine or ten turn-years old. Blaze raised his head and adjusted his posture, channeling Mistress Ree's demeanor.

"Yes, there are many things that need to be adjusted inside. Please see to it immediately." He emphasized the last word, as was a common habit of the headmistress. The young servant shook with nerves, and he entered the room and began cleaning for the newlyweds. Blaze walked out of Lords and Ladies unnoticed and unrecognized.

CHAPTER 8

BORN HERE

THE DINGY WHITE BUILDING that looked like a box stood before Blaze. He felt it luring him back, and as he stared at it, he felt the weight of its existence and the insignificance of his own life. There was no way that he would ever be free of this place. Its foreboding presence shadowed Blaze's future. His return home was another step in the series of misadventures that had been a common theme throughout his life. He breathed in deeply and trudged reluctantly through the upper door. From the upper level of the guild, he could tell that the house was unusually quiet. The hidden door slammed, drawing everyone's attention to the upper staircase. Blaze stood in the doorway, adjusting his vision to the change of lighting, then sauntered down the stairs. He recognized most of those present: Nohan, Gavin, Aldric, Jewels, Dorken, Pip, and Nightshade, among others. There were some faces he didn't recognize, but he didn't much care.

"Who is that?"

"Ugh, 'Mr. Born Here' is back," Dorken announced. "He's nobody important. It's just Blaze."

"Oh, Blaze, it is so good to see you back here!" Pip squealed overenthusiastically. To Dorken, he whispered, "Master won't be happy. I think he was happy to get rid of him."

"Yeah, I agree. I think we were all happy to get rid of him."

"Shh, he'll hear you."

"I don't care."

"Blaze! You're back!" Aldric bounded up to Blaze just as he descended the final step. He was smiling broadly, arms spread wide for a hug and nearly knocking Blaze over. Blaze pushed him to a halt, punching the younger boy in the chest. Pain struck Blaze's left hand, but he disguised it with an annoyed frown. Aldric laughed it off, grabbing Blaze in a bear hug.

"Get off me! You're . . . you're weird, Aldric."

Out of the crowd in the common room, Nightshade emerged.

"Well, well, well . . . it figures you'd be back, Blaze. You're like a cursed object: just when you're sure it's gone for good, it returns." Blaze glared while locking Nightshade's eyes in challenge. She didn't accept the unspoken contest; rather, she smiled coyly. "Nice gloves."

From behind Nightshade, Blaze caught sight of Venom, who moved forward toward Blaze. Blaze began to walk deeper into the room in an attempt to avoid Venom. However, Venom had a different idea, and he approached Blaze. Venom grabbed Blaze's right hand, pulling Blaze's chest into his own. He patted Blaze's back in friendship while he whispered in his ear. "I should've cut off your whole damn hand. I would've gotten more from the trader. Mess with me and my brother again, and I will kill you."

Blaze nodded. He felt sick with the knowledge.

"You sold my fingers? Who'd buy fingers?" Blaze whispered back.

"You'd be surprised. I actually had a trading war for them . . . very profitable, very," Venom whispered. Then he continued to speak, using a voice that could be heard throughout the common room. "We're back together. I'm glad you're back, Blaze."

"It's good to be back, Venom. Thanks." Blaze kept up the façade. He gave a half smile to Venom while approaching Master Locke's office. As he approached the master's door, the images of Ballard seemed to scold him, and he turned away from the garish images. The door was a reminder of his youth and the mess-ups that stared him in the face just like Ballard stared in disgust. Blaze knocked on Ballard's grave image out of spite.

"Come in, Blaze." Blaze momentarily backed away from the door. Had Ballard spoken to him? "Blaze, come in."

Blaze cautiously turned the knob that was a stark contrast to the ornamental door. The metal of the knob was dented, rough, and lackluster. He could feel the metal give under his grasp. "Well, that took you quite a while, Blaze."

"Um . . . Master Locke, I . . . uh . . . left." Blaze stumbled with his words.

"About a week ago, when the troupe camped just outside of Ballardton. I know." Blaze couldn't believe it—Master knew! *Of course he knew*, Blaze reasoned. *Did he send Venom after me? Did he buy my fingers? Does he buy things like that?* Blaze hid his hand behind him. "We've been looking for you. Your blood—a lot of it—was found in, on, and near the fountain. I'm glad to see that you are standing, but what happened?"

Blaze's eyes were wide, his face was ashen, and he felt dizzy.

"Blood? My blood? How did you know?"

Locke smiled at the boy. He had grown so much and reminded Locke more than ever before of his younger brother, Rhatt. Rhatt had the same smug demeanor that Blaze possessed, but there was something else that wasn't present in Blaze. His brother had an irresistible taste for the dark side—and women. Rhatt had worshipped at Adoon's temple, learned the art of poison, and had moved on up to Mereen's temple. His life had ended suddenly, leaving his son fatherless, confused, and angry. Blaze was still angry, but mostly toward Locke. Today was no different. Blaze slammed his gloved hands hard onto Locke's desk and pain ran up his arm. "Answer me!"

Blaze hadn't arrived at the guild angry, yet he yelled like a spoiled child at the master. Something about Locke always crept in to make Blaze feel resentment toward his master. This time was no different. *How did he know it was my blood? There was no way he'd know, unless he was there to see what happened.* The thoughts caught in Blaze's throat, and he felt sick.

"What? Oh, yes, Blaze, I'm sorry. It doesn't matter." Locke was distracted for the moment. The news that Blaze had been nearly killed had impacted him, but Blaze would never know.

"What's that supposed to mean? 'It doesn't matter.'" He paused for just a beat. "So you're not going to tell me. Fine. Then you already must know that I lost my fingers."

"We knew that you were seriously hurt."

"Did you buy them?" Blaze mumbled the question to his chest. Blaze rubbed his gloved hand thoughtfully, suddenly looking childlike. Master sympathized with Blaze. There was nothing he could do to reattach what was gone. Locke had heard the mumbled question, but thought he couldn't have heard that correctly.

"What did you say?" Locke asked with indignation.

"Nothing. It's not important." Blaze didn't really want to know anyway. Master sat back in his chair.

"What is important, Blaze, is that you are alive. Do you wish to continue on to Venesial with the rest of the staffers?" Blaze glanced up, his eyes glassy. *I can't let Calam see me like this. What would he say? How would I explain this or why I left?*

"No, I'm where I'm supposed to be." Blaze tilted his head back with street prowess. He turned to leave. The door was staring at him. He cringed when he met Ballard's eyes, and their gaze made him almost stop breathing.

"I can send word to the castle that you were detained. It would be a simple message and nobody would know."

Blaze contorted his face into a sneer.

"Nobody would know. *I* would know. As soon as they saw me, they would know. How can you say that?" Blaze turned his head side to side with disbelieving astonishment at his master's lack of understanding."Heh. 'Nobody would know.' Right." He was done. He turned back to leave. This time he didn't react to Ballard's façade. Master stood up.

"Wait, Blaze! You'll need these." Locke gestured to a small, tattered pouch with 'Rhatt' scratched into the flap, which Locke tossed on top of his desk. Blaze recognized it immediately.

"My kit. I'm surprised you didn't sell that, too."

"What are you talking about, Blaze? Why would I sell . . . oh, never mind." Locke flopped back into his chair. Blaze glanced sheepishly to the right.

"Yeah, I guess I will need that." Blaze took the pouch, removed his belt, slid the pouch on, and then refastened it. Blaze walked to the door and opened it.

"I can't believe you kept this creepy door. You could've at least covered it up. You've got a ton of maps in here," Blaze said, offering his opinion with a sneer as he walked out, shutting the door as he would at the castle. Master stared after him. Ballard seemed to grin at Locke knowingly.

Way too expensive and nothing will stay on it—not paint, not plaster, not a map, not a tapestry. Nothing, Master thought to himself. *I still see the plaster caught in your nostrils, Lord Ballard. It truly is ugly as sin.* Locke exhaled a sigh that equaled any of Blaze's, then went back to work.

Twice winter had passed and once again spring arrived in all of its floral-splendored glory. Blaze had settled back into the guild. Spending time with Venom was hard in those first months, but little by little he regained Venom's trust and friendship, squeezing his way into the guild's familiar patterns that he had left so many turn-years ago. Blaze accepted Venom's reaction to being lied to so many turn-years ago, realizing that losing his fingers was his burden to bear to be for returning to the guild. There were always consequences for one's actions. Disrespecting each other always carried a sentence—that was the way of the guild. Time did give way to some changes, but nothing worthy of Mistress Eyres' theory on change. His thoughts never wandered back to the castle. It was best forgotten, like a brief lapse in stasis.

A long spring rain teemed down on Ballardton, its roar deafening Blaze as he took shelter under a market cart. From his position, he could make out the blurred images of the piemen, their voices muffled and distorted. Leaning against the cart's wheel, Blaze closed his eyes. His mind drifted back to days embedded deep beyond conscious thought. A rainy, wet day similar to this one from long ago. . . .

***

"Blazey, be a good boy and stay right here. Okay, boy? Stay!"

Blaze nodded. Rhatt smiled at him, rubbed his head for luck, and left. Blaze was young, just before his third turn-year; his eyes still held a blue haze that covered their true color.

"Rhatt!" Blaze called out after only a few minutes. He hated to be alone. At the guild, he was never alone. There was always someone around to bother and entertain him. They showed him many games that included "find the box" and "take my pouch." Blaze had a natural talent for finding the charmed objects. "Rhatt! I want you!" he called again. He peeked his head out, but the market was wet and barren.

"Hullo, Blazey!" A woman with chestnut hair and ocean eyes, coaxed him out. Blaze knew her, but he recoiled from her. "Now, don't be like that. Rhatt sent me to find you."

"No! Go away! I hate you!"

"Now is that any way to treat your own mother, Blazey, especially since I've come all the way back from Cadmaria with presents just for you? There is even a toy from Drisana in there." Blaze glanced up."I have them right here, Blazey." The boy crept cautiously closer. Jade held a large sack open for Blaze to see inside. When Blaze reached the top opening, Jade trapped him in the empty sack, tying the strings closed. Blaze wiggled and kicked inside. She slammed the sack into the cart. Blaze slumped. Jade swung the sack over her back. The rain started up again.

"Damn! I hate the rain!" She looked around, making sure Rhatt was nowhere to be seen.

She slunk into the shadows until she stopped at an outside bistro table at Lords and Ladies.

She set the sack in her lap, and then she waited. A hostess came outside and approached Jade."Ma'am, wouldn't you rather come inside out of the rain?"

"Is there outside service today?" The woman looked back at the restaurant and motioned to a waiter who shooed the hostess back inside.

"May I help you?" The waiter approached Jade.

"Yes. I'll have today's special."

"Would you like it peppered for taste?"

"Yes, and I'd like to give a compliment to the chef."

"Of course. Maybe I could bring your compliment to him?"

"Certainly." Jade handed the waiter her sack. The waiter returned with a steak covered in parchment. Jade removed the parchment and placed it in her belt, concealing it from prying eyes. Sacrificing the brat to the traffickers would yield immense loyalty from the powerful traders that dwelt in Ballardton. Jade began to eat her steak, ignoring the young man hurrying up to her.

"Jade! Where's Blazey?"

"Who? Oh, the brat. I can't say I've seen him." With the final word, Jade ate another bite of steak.

"I want him back, Jade! Give me my son back!"

The rain broke to a trickle.

"*Our* son," Jade corrected, gesturing at Rhatt with her meat-filled fork.

"Where in Mirias is he?"

"Probably out, playing with the rats."

Rhatt pleaded with Jade that Blaze was all that he had. Jade chortled."All right, Rhatt. I'll whisper it to you." Rhatt cautiously approached Jade. He knew Jade was capable of almost anything; however, Jade kept her promise, whispering Blaze's probable whereabouts in his ear. With the information, Rhatt scurried away, anxious to get his son back.

Blaze returned to consciousness in the presence of strangers. His wrists and ankles were shackled. Around him were children of different ages in similar conditions. Blaze didn't recognize any of them. Most children were crying until a whip flew out over their heads, garnering their surprised attention. A man dressed in fine leathers examined each child; some other men accompanied him, but this one seemed to be in control. Blaze scrutinized the man as he approached him.

"So, this is the newest one?"

"Yeah, it's from Ballardton. Jade secured it. She'll be paid heftily for it."

"Good. Hey, check out these ears! Points always bring a good price."

"I know. And . . . and it's still a baby, so that'll bring a higher price—can't always get a Timerian baby these days. Their dams are always scooping them away just as we get close."

"Yeah. Teeth look good, too—pretty straight. It has a bump on its head; probably from its capture. Sometimes these things happen. We'll get the healer to fix it up. I can see a bidding war over this one. Can't wait to see what it fetches in Bevisson. Okay, move out!"

Blaze whimpered. He twisted his hands, trying to get out of the wrist shackles, but the more he twisted, the tighter they became. The wagon carrying the children began to move.

"Rhatt, I want you." Blaze whimpered quietly, looking around for his dad.

Rhatt could see the wagon. Jade hadn't lied, for once. They were headed toward him, but a single horse and rider approached. Rhatt waited.

"Whoa! The master mage approaches!" the leather-clad trader announced. The children cried out, and the whip snapped again. The mage was feeble as he walked. "You're late, mage."

"I know, I know. It's been harder getting away from the Mage School these days."

"I don't care about your problems, old man. Just do your thing and be gone." The mage nodded his head as he reached for a wand in his belt.

"Gladly." He moved to the back of the wagon. He looked into the forty or so eyes with pity. "I see there are more of them this time."

"Yeah, now get to work!"

"Is that a Timerian or Elvin baby?" The mage moved over to Blaze.

"Eh!" The trader grunted with a shrug. "Timerian. Its mother and father died, so it's going to the orphanage with us. Can we get on with this? We have a schedule to keep."

"Oh, ah, yes. Um, instead of the usual golds, can I have this one? I've never asked for one—please?"

The trader laughed.

"Are you kidding me? What is a worn-out old mage like you going to do with a Timerian brat? Look at you; you can barely take care of yourself. Maybe you could adopt it after we get it to Bevisson. We'll keep our original deal; that is, of course, if you do your job."

The mage reluctantly agreed. His robes were a muted blue that marked him for retirement, but he did not want to choose that new lonely life. He withdrew a spell book from his pouches and began to read, raising the wand high over the group of children.

A sparkling blue light shot from the wand. A spray of sparkles settled on top of the children. Blaze giggled with excitement as the spell was cast. He pulled the magic to him. The magic light became contained in a sparkling ball above his head. He reached for it with his shackled hands. The ball lowered into his lap, changing its color to scarlet. The mage stared, wide-eyed. The boy had amazing magical abilities, focus, and control. The trader snapped the whip again, regaining control of the children. Surprised by the sudden noise, Blaze squashed the ball, leaving only a pile of sparkling dust.

"What just happened? That's never happened before." The trader insisted on an explanation.

The mage's expression was full of pride at the discovery of a magical prodigy. He removed his glasses and cleaned them on his robes. "Amazing! This lad redirected my magic and then changed it to make it his own. It is a very advanced skill."

"So, you're telling me that this baby can do magic and is good at it too?"

"Yes. He should become a ward of the Mage School instead of being adopted."

The trader wasn't listening; he was envisioning the money that the boy would bring at auction. He realized the boy would have to be marketed at a special sale, bringing patrons from all nations. *What a find,* he thought gleefully.

Rhatt began his descent from his hiding spot. The traders seemed distracted, and he could easily overtake the old man. Withdrawing his dagger and sword, Rhatt raced toward the wagon. The old man watched Rhatt in horror, frozen in place.

"Leave *my son* alone!"

Rhatt wielded his weapons with ease.

The old mage, fearful of an encounter with Rhatt, cowered under the children-filled wagon and covered his head. Rhatt cut the mage's robes as he passed.

Rhatt stopped at the corner of the wagon. He examined his son's forehead before he lifted Blaze out. *It'll heal,* Rhatt thought relieved. Blaze's expression was joyful and thankful. Rhatt hugged the boy while balancing him on his hip. A crossbow bolt hit Rhatt's shoulder. Rhatt, still carrying Blaze, turned to face the leather-clad trader. The trader stood poised to shoot again. A smile rose to the trader's lips. He launched a bolt a second time, but the bolt exploded into a sparkling array of fireworks. Eyes wide, Rhatt took the opportunity to tip the wagon and make his escape, running until his legs could no longer carry him and Blaze.

The two hid amongst the brush of the forest. Rhatt set his now-sleeping son down, pain showing on his face. It was time to break Blaze's shackles and remove the crossbow bolt. Sweating as he fought against the pain in his shoulder, Rhatt removed a pouch that contained his lock-picking kit: tools of the trade. Using an awl, he probed the interior mechanism of the wristbands. Holding the awl in place, Rhatt picked up a paddle-like metal tool, replaced the awl with the paddle, and quickly released the locking device. He smiled. The second wristband was just as simple. But Rhatt glared when he removed the second wristband and discovered the metallic burn that wrapped around Blaze's wrist. He took a deep breath, held back the pain, and woke the sleeping child.

"Rhatt?"

"Yeah, Blazey, it's me. I'm here. I need you to do two things. One is to get these shackles off of you and the second is to get the bolt out of my shoulder. First, watch me. I'm going to show you how to open these shackles, okay?" Rhatt's voice was calm and he annunciated each word, trying not to alert Blaze to the distress that he felt. The boy nodded. Rhatt sat him on his lap while assisting Blaze's hands to maneuver the tools, and they opened the first ankle band. "Okay, now you try on your own."

Blaze looked up at Rhatt and smiled adoringly. Rhatt retuned the smile and kissed his head. Within a few minutes, Blaze released the inside mechanism. His reward was Rhatt's praise and the freedom of his ankle. Rhatt beamed. He held Blaze in his arms, tickling the child's tummy. Blaze giggled, curling his stomach away from Rhatt's moving hands. Rhatt cringed in pain from the excessive movement.

"Rhatt, you're hurt!" Blaze said matter-of-factly.

"Yep, I am. Are you ready to help me with the second thing, Blazey?" Blaze beamed, happy to be needed. Rhatt's voice was shallow and breathy, and sweat rested on his furrowed brow as he clenched his jaw to not show the pain he felt to his son. "In my right shoulder, there is a crossbow bolt. Okay? I need you to pull it out. Do you understand, Blazey?" Blaze walked around Rhatt to his back. "Right here, do you see it?" Rhatt gestured the location with his hand over his shoulder.

"Uh-huh." Blaze noticed the end of the bolt sticking out of Rhatt's back; blood soaked his father's tunic.

"Okay, Blaze. Grab it and pull!" Blaze did as he was told. The bolt slid out of Rhatt's flesh like a warm knife sliding through butter. Rhatt grunted and gasped until the bolt was removed. Holding the bolt in his tiny hands, Blaze showed it to Rhatt. "Good boy!"

"Rhatt, did you get skewered?"

"Yeah, but I'll live."

"Will it scar?" Blaze asked with enthusiastic glee.

"Definitely!" Blaze smiled and shook with excitement. Rhatt pushed Blaze's head playfully. "You are something else, Blazey." Rhatt ripped the bottom of his tunic with his dagger. He made a long bandage that he awkwardly wrapped across the wound. While Rhatt secured his bandage, Blaze played with Rhatt's kit. He made the tools into weapons, fighting invisible foes. Rhatt laughed, recollecting his own imaginary adventures as a child. "Okay, Blazey. Give me back my kit. Good boy!"

Blaze waited while Rhatt hid the kit. The light flickered across Rhatt's face, making shadowy tracks that made his scars more prominent. He stared into Rhatt's face, lifting his hand to trace the scars that cut deep into Rhatt's flesh. Rhatt smiled, letting the boy play, but after a while he caught Blaze's arm. Surprised, Blaze looked at Rhatt questioningly.

"These scars, Blazey, are a map. Follow them and they'll take you to the greatest treasure that you'll ever know. One day, sweet boy, you will wear the map also. Scars are important to us, Blazey. They show the world that we can handle anything and have successfully done so. Now this is the most important advice that I will ever give to you: you can only get a scar from someone else's blade. Otherwise, it's cheating. Remember that!"

Rhatt touched the center of Blaze's forehead. Looking eye to eye with Blaze, Rhatt spoke. "Let's follow my scar map to my treasure, okay?" Blaze nodded in agreement. His eyes sparkled with excited anticipation. "We have to go east toward the border." Rhatt pointed to the right and sighed. "It's time to go back to where I lived when I was about your age."

Death lived in Rhatt's childhood home. It was either stay and be killed or leave and live. Rhatt chose the latter of the two. Death had a name, and its name was Jaegon. Rhatt knew he just had to communicate with his own mother and father bypassing his oldest brother, his sister-in-law, and most importantly his nephew, Jaegon, who incidentally was Rhatt's senior. If he could do that, Blaze would be safe, cared for, and loved. Rhatt was hopeful.

The pair reached the castle at dusk. The endless walking tired the boy, so Rhatt carried him. The stone wall stretched as far as Rhatt's eye could see. The nimble thief located the crack in the wall's foundation. Thankful that it had remained open after all this time, Rhatt set Blaze down, laying his sleeping body against the wall. Rhatt entered the outer courtyard that surrounded his childhood home but then froze with fear. He began to turn back, afraid of the death inside. Then he thought of Blaze and the child's life as a thief. Rhatt wanted a better life for Blaze and he feared Jade's wrath even more than Jaegon's. Rhatt continued his journey around the courtyard. *I found it!* There, overlooking Mummy's garden on the second floor within the turret, was his mother's private chamber, her solar. Rhatt knew this was where his mother stayed all day and long into the night. Memories of him at her knee while she read to him or while she did her needlepoint filled his mind. It was a sanctuary from Jaegon's fury when his big brother, Callanan, was unable to help him. The solar was illuminated with a warm, orange-yellow glow that flickered soothingly in the wake of darkness. Rhatt remembered the long hours of comfort in that room. A smile rose across his face. *Mummy.*

"Halt, thief!" An armored knight jumped in front of Rhatt, wielding a broad sword. But Rhatt showed no surprise recognizing the knight's voice immediately.

"Hello, Jaegon. Still playing Knights and Knaves?" Jaegon raised his helmet to confront Rhatt directly.

"How do you know my name?"

"Because I'm your uncle, Arhatton. I need to see my mother and father at once." Rhatt ordered with the utmost authority.

"Arhatton's been dead for many turns of the season."

"Yes, Jaegon, I made it look that way. I killed a calf from one of the farms and I . . . well the details don't matter. I'm here to see my parents. Let me pass."

"Oh, I see, is that why you're sneaking around *my* castle? Why don't you send a message to *my* grandparents and I'll be sure to get it to them right off, Arhatton."

"I need to see my parents. Let me pass."

"Ask for a counsel."

"I'm asking, Jaegon."

"Well, obviously, you're not using the right avenues."

"I haven't the time for this or the right avenues. I need to see my parents. Let me pass."

"You died in their eyes."

"I know they'll talk to me. Let me pass!"

"Sorry, Arhatton, this is as far as you go." Rhatt glared at Jaegon, who was prepared to pierce Arhatton with his sword at any moment.

"Wait! I'll show you why I need to speak with them." Rhatt reluctantly ushered Jaegon to the sleeping boy. "My son . . . my son, Bl—Eren, needs to be cared for. His mother, Jade, is after us both, but if I could just leave him here . . . Please, Jaegon, it's not for me; it's for the boy." Jaegon stared down at the child. He poked the boy with his sword. Rhatt hesitated and didn't stop Jaegon, hoping he would understand and allow him audience with his parents. Jaegon bent down and examined Blaze's hair, ears, nose, clothes, hands, and boots. Upon reaching Blaze's boots, he removed the footwear and counted the child's toes.

"Well, he seems mostly intact. He's as homely as you, Arhatton. Why don't you just sell him to a Cadmarian trader? It'd be less work. I can't say that grandmum and grandda would like to see your face like this." Jaegon rose and gestured with his sword by drawing an invisible circle around Rhatt's scared face. "You look absolutely ghastly! Now take your little Bleren child and be gone! We don't want your kind here." Jaegon blocked Rhatt from returning through the cracked wall.

The only thing Rhatt could do was to go back to Ballardton and hide Blaze somewhere else, perhaps deep in the dungeon. Taking one last look at his childhood home, Rhatt picked up his son and ran back into the wood. Jaegon noticed the wound in Rhatt's shoulder, which had soaked through his tunic and cloak.

"Do you want me to pick him off, sir?" A mercenary man-at-arms stood just inside the wall and out of Rhatt's sight.

"I want you to follow them now. When the moment's right, kill Arhatton—he's injured anyway—and bring me the boy. He'll be a perfect dead ringer for Nairn, he looks exactly like him; nobody'd ever notice the replacement. I'll mold the boy to my liking and we'll kill Nairn. No one will stand in my way. Now *go*."

Jaegon watched his mercenary head out along the path Rhatt had taken. The mercenary was fully armed; there was no way Arhatton would outwit Jaegon this time.

As father and son arrived in Ballardton, Rhatt became aware of the mercenary's presence. The man was clearly waiting for the right opportunity. True hunters mimic their prey's footsteps so as not to be detected. Clearly, this mercenary was not an expert. Rhatt looked down at Blaze; the child's energy was nearly spent, but the relief of being in the familiar city was apparent on his small, delicate face.

"Blazey, listen carefully. I want you to run to the guild as fast as your little legs can carry you. Don't talk to anybody, especially Jade. Okay?" Blaze nodded and scampered away. Rhatt watched Blaze zigzag between people, running through a forest of legs. He lost sight of Blaze in the crowd and he hoped the child would make it to the guild house safely. Then, he turned to face the mercenary.

Running from Rhatt, Blazey didn't look behind him. He knew he had to do as he was told lest he be spanked for not obeying his father. Blazey ran in between the crowds of legs and carts on the road. He halted quickly when he saw hooves rearing up, the horse clearly startled by his unexpected appearance. The horseman yelled at him in another language, scaring him into running faster. He ran with single-mindedness. For a moment, dust rose up and he noticed the knackerman's loaded cart heading back toward his yard. Blaze followed behind it, knowing that it was near the guild. He glimpsed the fountain with its stonework and breathed a sigh of relief. He raced to it, sure that the fountain was as much a safety point as was the guild. He climbed up on the wall and balanced along the edge. He glanced up at a cloaked figure sitting on the wall. He tried to walk over the person, but they grabbed him. He struggled to get free. The hood fell off his captor's head revealing his worst nightmare: Jade.

Jade held her hand over Blaze's mouth to keep him from screaming. The last thing she wanted was for the entire guild to come running. She thought to break the boy's neck, but a live sacrifice to her Lady would bring more favor. Her eyes fell upon a scar just above the boy's right elbow. *Damn Locke and Mason for stopping me when I had that bone almost severed through*, she thought.

Blaze was amazingly still. He sought silent help from above. His thoughts were of Lady Marnie; perpetually a child herself, Lady Marnie was the protector of children. Blaze prayed to the young goddess. "Please, Marnie, help me." Blaze's plea reached Jade's ears. She cocked an eyebrow and snorted a chuckle.

"Little Marnie cannot help against the power of Queen Mykondra!"

Blaze cringed and covered his ears at the mere mention of the Queen of Darkness' name. As young as he was, Blaze knew of the dangers of Mykondra's rage.

Rhatt had engaged in a horrific battle against Jaegon's mercenary. The mercenary lay dead and Rhatt stood panting in the pool of blood that oozed out of the man's body. Though mortally wounded himself, he remained standing. Blood covered his face as it gushed from a skull-crushing hole. He prayed to the gods for strength to stop Jade and the god known as King Eldon granted Rhatt his request, guiding him toward Blaze and Jade.

The thief scuttled across town, following his intuition to Queen Mykondra's temple. Two priestesses had begun to prepare Blaze for the sacrifice. Blaze squirmed and clawed, trying anything to get away. One of the priestesses slapped him across his face and yelled at him to stay still. Blaze looked around, trying to figure out how to leave this place. He stopped wiggling when the high priestess brought out her wand, an infant's skeletal arm. He grabbed for it and she made it dance, calming him. She tried to build a rapport with him and garner his confidence and trust. It worked, and he began watching her quietly as she examined him more closely. She ran her finger down his face, feeling the soft and supple skin. He fought her as she pulled open his jaw. The priestess pressed her thumb and forefinger just behind his last teeth, forcing him to open his mouth and release the joint. Realizing that it was futile to fight against the pressure on his cheeks, he let her look into his mouth, which relaxed her grip on his face. When she reached in to check a tooth, he bit down with all of his might. She pulled her finger out of his mouth to discover a bite mark that drew blood and would result in bruising.

"You think you are so smart, you churlish little caitiff?" The priestess grabbed his hair forcefully and pulled his head back.

She then made him drink from an altar cup that was filled with a Silver Dragon's blood and the priestess' sacrificial mead. Blaze choked and coughed as he tried to resist swallowing, to no avail. He retched and vomited on the altar. His head spun. She raised the cup again and made him continue to drink. He fell against her chest. "-See, I wasn't deceiving you. Now I can do what I want. I don't take kindly to your stubborn and defiant behavior. If you weren't given so freely to me, I would have rejected you, you little cur."

The high priestess for the dark goddess laid the boy down on the altar. He drunkenly protested as she spread blessed ashes on his forehead, marking him for the goddess. Invoking Mykondra's blessings, the priestess cut his nails and then ripped hair out of his head. She placed them in a sacrificial container. Blaze whimpered. She disrobed him and tied him to Mykondra's altar of shredded human skin, which was tautly stretched across a menagerie of bones. She mixed more Silver Dragon's blood with his hair in a vessel. The priestess sliced Blaze's chest just above his heart, opening a wound that poured out blood. She added his blood to the bowl, then poured the concoction over the open wound. Blaze recoiled against the warm liquid. The altar held his arms in place. He whimpered and tears slid down his temples, wetting his hair. He shook his head, pleading with his eyes to let him go.

"He is ready, my queen." She spoke to the statue portraying the likeness of the goddess. The priestess picked up the wand of bone, circling it over Blaze while chanting a spell of sacrifice. His sacrificial wounds illuminated with an ominous glow. They burned and he cried harder.

Death magic filled the room, awakening the statue. Rhatt, arriving at the vestibule, froze in fear of the goddess' power. Jade was robed as one of Mykondra's priestesses and stood on the sidelines, idly watching her son's torture. Blaze screamed and Rhatt moved forward as it echoed in his mind. The priestesses pawed at Rhatt, hindering his movements while they tore at his clothes and raked him with their nails. He pulled away from them, as his desire to save his son was more powerful. One of the priestesses began an incantation and jumped in front of him. For a moment, he was under her spell, but his hands caught his sword at his side and he thrust it through her and the spell died with her. He wrenched the sword from her body and turned to face the other priestesses, who stepped back, giving him clear opportunity to reach Blaze. Sword and dagger drawn, Rhatt broke the altar and released Blaze from its grasp. Blaze jumped into Rhatt's arms, clinging to his father. Mykondra's statue stood in response to the disruption. She willed a sacrifice and would not leave Mirias without one.

"Blazey, run home to the guild! We both won't die this day! Marnie protect you in all ways!" Rhatt shoved the boy away while he pushed his dagger and pouch into the boy's empty hands. Blaze exited the temple, looking back in time to see Mykondra's statue ripping Rhatt's writhing body in two.

Blaze awoke with a start at the crack of thunder. His hand reached to his chest. The scar had faded over the years, barely visible unless Blaze looked hard for the change in skin color.

CHAPTER 9

BITTERSWEET

A FTER THE STORM, Blaze watched the emerging crowds from his hiding spot under the market cart. The metallic odor that followed a rain stung his nose. He breathed in deeply. A swift breeze wrapped in strong lilac cologne passed him. Blaze recognized its smell as the cologne given to royal guests at Lords and Ladies. He followed the breeze to a ruddy-faced man in Cadmarian attire. A large, swollen pouch rested just in front of the man's right hip. Blaze followed him from a short distance back. As he walked, the man's massive arm knocked into the pouch. The jingle-jangle of coins enticed Blaze. He decided to make his move.

"Hey, Blaze!" Venom yelled across the marketplace. Blaze stopped and watched the large man walk away. Blaze sighed, frustrated.

"Poison, be damned," Blaze uttered under his breath. Venom towed Spider with him. Spider ran up and hugged Blaze.

"Hey! Where are you going? Spider and I just came from getting stew at Lords and Ladies."

"Yeah, Blaze, I even had a popover. They're so-o-o-o good." Spider reached into a pocket in his cloak. "I saved one; would you like it?" Spider held the pastry up toward Blaze.

"No, Spider, you keep it." Blaze smiled at him and rubbed the little boy's head.

"Why are you still wearing those gloves?" Spider inquired innocently.

"So nobody can tell that I lost my fingers. It kind of makes me stand out, like I've got a sign over my head in blinking lights which says 'thief.' This way, I'm just like everybody else." Blaze opened and closed his hands over his head to approximate a blinking sign. Venom roared with laughter.

"Yeah, can't you see it? Boy, Blaze, that would be hilarious!" Venom laughed so hard that his eyes started to tear. Blaze raised his eyebrows at Venom as his face reddened.

"It wasn't that funny, Venom."

"Oh, yes it was, because that so would happen to you!" Blaze coughed out a laugh and nodded his reluctant agreement. "Hey, hey, did you see the tourney boxes get hit by lightning earlier? They caught on fire and some of the mages had to put it out with magical water. It was so cool! Well, not as cool as a blinking sign. I'd really like to see that." Venom had regained his composure until he turned the conversation back to the sign reference. Blaze just shook his head.

"So, Spider, were you with Venom when he saw the boxes get hit?" Blaze ignored Venom and focused his attention on Spider.

"Yeah, and Venom and me, we could see everything from Lords and Ladies until people came and stood in our way, but then it was okay because Venom was able to find the popovers. He told me to put them in my cloak—so I did."

"Uh-huh, everyone was distracted by the fire, but I *did* pay for our stew. So where were you, Blaze? Getting a sign . . ."

"Funny, Venom. Can't you ever let something go? I was in the market. I had a bad dream about my mother, but I don't really remember much about it except that it was bad, and she was in it. I hope it doesn't mean that she's coming back." Blaze looked forlornly at his feet. Just imagining Jade's return was troubling enough, and he hoped that the dream didn't mean that she was coming back to Ballardton.

"Why? You're so lucky to still have your mum. I know we'd love to see our mum again. She was a pirate with her own ship. We used to sail all over the world and dock in real exotic places. It was great until . . ." Venom looked down to see Spider crying. "Aw, it's okay, Spider. Don't cry; we'll find her again, I promise."

Blaze listened to the story that he had heard a thousand times before. It always brought Venom some comfort to think that his mother was still alive, even though every sign pointed to her demise. Blaze didn't like to see Spider sad any more than Venom did. The little boy was sweet and compassionate and because of those qualities he was hard not to like.

"Hey, Spider," Blaze began kneeling to Spider's height. "Do you remember the day you came to Ballardton? Because I do." Spider sniffled as he held in his tears. "You and Venom were walking down Kings Highway. Venom had a great big smile on his face, like he does now. Do you remember?" Spider's eyes turned from sorrow to glee. There was definitely something about Spider's smile that made you want to make him happy.

"Yes, Venom had coins in his pouch. Lots and lots of coin, Blaze!"

Blaze smiled with Spider, his own worries gone while he comforted the Little. Venom looked excitedly at Blaze, too, hanging on to Blaze's words for the next part of the story. *I wonder if this is what Skelly feels like when he's telling one of his tales*, Blaze thought.

"Yes, that's right. I did have lots of coin in my pouch from when I sold all those berry flower sprigs." Venom excitedly added his own perspective.

"From what you described, it was wyssanberry. It can give you quite a lot of coin, but it has to be cut right; at least that is what Mason always says," Blaze added.

"And Venom cut it right," Spider gleefully announced.

"Yeah, I guess. I never saw it, but based on the way Venom got all that coin, I guess so."

"Are you feeling better, Spider?" Venom asked agreeing with Blaze's assumption while he pulled out a copper coin.

"I think we need dessert after the stew and the popovers. What do you think, Spider? Are you up to going to get the pies? They are two pies for a coppie." Venom tossed the coin to Spider. "Get one for both of us." Venom winked at Spider, who dashed away quickly to retrieve the sweet pies.

"Sit down and tell me about your mother. I know you haven't seen her for a long time. She hasn't been here since Spider and me arrived," Venom said. They sat on barrels, moving another barrel over for Spider.

"Well, you know how I was born here Venom, right?"

"Yeah, that's old news. You've been saying that for as long as I've known you."

"Right. Well, Jade wasn't really the best mother. I've overheard Mason talking to Master Locke about her. Mason said that she'd just leave me on the floor or wherever she happened to be; she didn't really bother being a mother unless it was convenient for her. And then after Rhatt died, she just left me for good. She went to Cadmaria. She's master of the thieves' guild over there. At one point, she came back to take me with her, but Master Locke stood in her way, and instead he sent me to work in the kitchens of Lords and Ladies. This was way before you and Spider came to Ballardton.

"But before she left, she cut off all my hair. She said she needed it, but she never told me why. I think she was selling it." Blaze shrugged. "Master was really angry that she did that, but she's still my mother. Oh, here comes Spider." Spider ran excitedly back toward his brother. An enormous grin lit up his face. The older boys jumped down off the barrels to greet him.

"Look, look! They just *gave* me the pies! He said I looked hungry and that I must live on the streets. I nodded my head yes, and they gave me these pies! I still have the coppie in my pouch!" Spider opened his hands to show off his wondrous gifts, but Blaze and Venom immediately knocked the pies out of his hands. The pies fell to the ground and Spider cried at the loss of his generous gifts and the surprised reaction of his brother. Blaze and Venom stomped on the pies, making sure that Spider didn't attempt to eat them.

"Spider, I don't ever want you to get pies from that man again!" Horror and fear ran across Spider's face. "Borintak will poison you! Is that what you want—to be dead? He hates children, especially street ones. Understand?" Spider shook his head, disagreeing with Venom. Venom threw up his hands in despair. Blaze knelt down, resting his knee in the squished berry filling.

"Spider, there are two piemen: one good and one bad. The bad one's name is Borintak, and his cart is on the right. Nerapi is the good pieman and his cart is up further and on the left. Borintak wants children to steal his pies because he's deliberately poisoned them, which is why they're so easy to take. Do you understand what I'm saying?" Spider nodded his head in agreement. "Good. So you can understand why Venom and I knocked the pies out of your hand?" The boy shook his head no. Blaze dropped his head defeated. "Okay, why not?" Spider began to cry and tried to speak between sobs.

"Because . . . because I got these pies from the good pieman on the left!" The boy erupted into uncontrollable sobbing. Venom reached down and picked up a piece of squashed pie. He sniffed it then ate it.

"Yep, it's good. It's really good, m-m-m."

Blaze closed his eyes and tried to comfort Spider. Venom continued eating the ruined filling and crust from the ground.

"Sorry, Spider, we just assumed you went to Borintak. Venom! Stop eating that!" Blaze stood up, but he slipped on the pie filling that covered his entire boot's sole. He landed hard on his tailbone, spraying dirt and filling in all directions. His fall so delighted Spider that his tears turned to uncontainable laughter. Venom joined in, nearly choking on the half-eaten piecrust in his mouth. Blaze's face reddened. He got up and stomped carefully out of the marketplace.

Blaze sat next to the river, listening to the roar of the water. He had washed his tunic and breeches, which lay next to him on the river's bank. He realized that the berries from the pie filling had stained both pieces with purple-red spots. The most noticeable was the one on his tunic that covered his entire backside and another on his breeches that went under his crotch. The aggravation of having to acquire new clothes annoyed Blaze. He had hoped to wear these ones until winter set in, but clearly that wasn't going to happen. He could go and talk to Master Locke about needing new clothes, but that would mean admitting he'd failed even more drastically than normal. Locating clothes would be hard, but not impossible. His mind wandered to the oversized Cadmarian man with the large, inflated pouch. He knew where the man would be and he knew, based on the pouch and the cologne, approximately which wing of Lords and Ladies he was staying. He smirked while developing a scheme to acquire what he needed and desired. Blaze waited until his clothes were completely dry, then walked back to the guild house. He found Nohan's cloak on a hook and used that to cover the stain. The cloak had holes in it and smelled of mildew, but it was long enough to meet Blaze's need.

The grays of twilight shadowed his path as he traveled down King's Highway toward Lords and Ladies. Stealing from the inn was something that Blaze felt entitled to do because he hated the Cadmarian proprietors. A hatred deeply seeded from a time between his seventh and eighth turn-years when he was sent to work in the kitchens there.

The colossal man waited in the darkened suite. He fancied himself Lord Pickering of Cadmaria; however, he was just a wealthy merchant who acquired an abandoned castle in Cadmaria. Pickering walked to the window for the thousandth time since returning to the suites. He examined a looped rope that encircled the floor and then glanced out the window eagerly, awaiting someone's arrival. He opened the window wider, stuck his head out, and waved to passersby in the street, ensuring that he was seen. The lord was not a patient man under any circumstances. He looked across the room to his son, who held the other end of the rope that draped from the ceiling.

"I'm sure somebody noticed the copper-filled pouches. I made sure to shake the coins and show off the golds at the top. What is wrong with people these days?" Lord Pickering's son said nothing as he readjusted the rope in his hands. "I even poured that awful pungent cologne over my entire body just to show off my wealth! What is wrong with these children?" Pickering's son, Haxan, shrugged.

Pickering perused the suite in all its grandeur; he strutted around, grabbing a piece of fruit as he did. He scowled as he calculated the huge expense of this trip. The expenses would be justified if and only if the bait was taken.

During the day, Haxan had dropped back behind his father's stroll around town. The younger man had spotted three possible targets. The most noteworthy were a slim girl with a little upturned nose and a sly smile, a boy with bland features near the pie stands, and finally, the slightly older boy who seemed agile and who at, one point, Haxan had thought was ready to make his move. Then suddenly the boy had backed off, which stopped Haxan's spell casting. Still, any of the three would do. The prime location of Ballardton was worthy of its reputation. The targets, or as Lord Pickering preferred to call them, 'guests,' would be rewarded for their generous donations. Of course, it all depended on whether or not they actually decided to take the bait. Lord Pickering fumed.

Blaze entered the inn through the hallway window. It was not the quickest way in, but it would allow Blaze the luxury of time. He knew what he had to do: locate the rotund man, get in, grab the pouch and jewelry, then slip out without being noticed. Easy as pie; at least, that's what Blaze thought. He made his way down the hallway, his boots sinking into the lush purple and gold vair carpeting. A fleur-de-lis pattern decorated the walls, and vases of soft pale-peach irises sat systematically on small tabletops between the rooms, giving off a scent that gently filled the air. These were the royal suites, and the further down the hallway Blaze walked, the more extravagant the rooms became. Blaze sneezed, alerting those around that someone approached. He held his breath until he felt that no one stirred. He hoped that the wafting odors of Nohan's cloak would not reveal his intentions and class. He tightened his fist out of frustration.

As he stalked the empty hallway, he listened at each door, although nothing seemed out of the ordinary. Blaze had almost given up hope of finding the hefty Cadmarian when suddenly a door flung open, nearly hitting Blaze in the face. He hid against it. Haxan emerged with rope still in hand.

"Father, I give up. I don't think any of them are coming." Haxan released the rope, letting it fall back into the room.

"Wait a little longer. I know they'll come and they'll learn of my generosity. I want to give away the pouches to some unfortunate young Ballardtonian." Blaze listened intently, careful not to touch the door. He furrowed his brow out of confusion. *Giving away pouches? Who in the dark realm does that? This can't be true.* He realized that something was amiss—if someone *needs* money, they *want* money; if someone *has* money, they tend to keep it for themselves. Nobody gives anything away without wanting something in return, especially Cadmarians. He knew he was stupid to have come all this way for nothing. Another room, then. He turned to leave, mapping out his retreat through the room next door, but Nohan's cloak drifted through the space between the frame and the hinge of the open door.

Haxan spied the corner of the cloak. Typically, these waifs arrived through open windows, but not here in Ballardton. Apparently, these Ballardton tearaways were bold enough to approach the suite's door. Haxan silently gestured to Lord Pickering, who jiggled with glee and quietly clapped his hands. He grinned from ear to ear and danced with excitement while Haxan began reciting an immobility spell. Haxan gestured instructions to Pickering and the lord followed them by speaking loudly and dramatically about the need to be a generous soul and help the poor youths of Ballardton. He dripped false compassion. Blaze, caught unawares, gasped as he tried to leave and found himself unable to move. Haxan chanted the spell as Lord Pickering rounded the door and grabbed Blaze with his massive, swollen hands.

"Oh, it's you. The best specimen of the three, don't you think, Haxan?"

Haxan continued chanting the spell until the door was locked and the window sealed, and they were safely within the confines of the suite.

After being released from the spell, Blaze struggled to free himself from the lord's grasp. Blaze noticed the rope hanging, which made him work harder to free himself. *By Eldon's crown, they're going to hang me.* Lord Pickering pushed the boy onto a couch. The lord sat next to Blaze, nearly sitting on him and pinning his cloak underneath his enormously large rump. Blaze attempted to untie the cloak, but Haxan reached down and unhooked it for him. Then Haxan reached into Blaze's belt and removed all the tools that could be used as weapons. He checked Blaze's sleeves and his boots and reached around to see if he harbored a weapon behind his back. Then he unfastened Blaze's belt that carried all of these items and brought it to a small writing desk.

"Haxan, let the boy be; he is our guest, after all." Lord Pickering gestured to Haxan, and Haxan smiled. Blaze felt violated and he watched Haxan as he laid out everything that Blaze had been carrying onto the desk. Blaze noticed that Haxan took great care with each of the items, even shining the blades of every piece of metal."Now, you dear poor child, I have been hoping someone would come and join us today. And here you are! Oh, wonderful day! Are you hungry?"

"No. Give me back my stuff."

"Well, *I* am hungry. You'll join us for a bite. Then you'll get your stuff back. One can never be too careful with visitors." Pickering clapped again with joy."Haxan, call in-house dining! We will eat like kings tonight!" Haxan nodded and walked into an attached room. A loud bell sounded and Blaze knew its familiar sound from his days at the inn.

"Child, what is your name? I am Lord Pickering of Cadmaria and the young man who left to call the kitchen is my son, Haxan. I wander the world hoping to help unfortunate souls like you: those forgotten by the world—tossed out like insignificant refuse. How old are you, child?"

"What do you mean . . . help?"

"Not very trusting, are you? That's actually a good quality to have learned in life. You shouldn't trust just anyone. When I said help, I simply meant to make life a little easier for you." Haxan reentered the room carrying several pouches jingling with coins. "Ah, good Haxan; yes, these are just what I needed. Perfect timing, my son." Haxan placed the pouches in front of his father on a small sitting table. The round pouches kept Blaze's attention.

"Here, child, now you will not be so skeptical of me and my intentions." Pickering reached onto the table, grabbed one of the pouches, and tossed it toward Blaze's chest. Blaze instinctively caught the ball-shaped pouch with his left hand and gripped it with his three fingers. "Do you trust me now, child? I hope so. Now what is your name?" Blaze did not speak, but rather opened the pouch's strings to examine the contents. His expression flashed a show of unbelievable shock at the ebon, silver, and gold pieces inside the palm-sized pouch. He raised his head to look at Pickering and Haxan. *Who in their right mind would just hand me a pouch full of coin? What is that rope on the floor for anyway? Who are these people? I've got to get out of here.* Blaze tossed the pouch back onto the table.

"I want my stuff back. You can keep your coin." Blaze went to stand.

"What is all this on your backside?"

Blaze sat quickly back down, embarrassed.

"It looks smashingly good enough to eat. What is your name?"

"Names have power. I won't tell you mine."

"His pouch says R-H-A-T-T. I think it is pronounced 'Rut.' Names are different in Timeria, are they not?"

"Just give me my stuff and I'll leave—I won't even remember what you look like. I am very bad with names and faces. I just can't remember any. I think your name is Lee, and you're Leeson." The lie stuck in Blaze's throat.

"Oh, don't worry about anything, Rut, we already know you won't remember." Haxan stared at Blaze with a deadpan stare.

"When do we eat? Is he the right age, or is he too old? How old are you?" Pickering leaned over inches from Blaze's face. Blaze pulled away.

"Why do you have a rope? I'm just over thirteen turn-years."

"That is fine. So, Father, a turn-year, and please do correct me if I am wrong, is the year that you physically change, making you just thirteen turn-years. In Timeria, there is a long time between turn-years, whereas in Cadmaria, a turn-year is literally one physical year. It should be okay, because we've invited other Timerian guests and they had sprite blood as the country is a blend of mixed races. We should be all right," Haxan reassured Pickering.

"Indeed!" Pickering gleefully remarked. "I am looking at you, young man, and I have noticed that you have quite unique ears. In Cadmaria, we prefer ones that are perfectly round like Haxan's." Haxan pushed his hair away, showing off his perfectly rounded ear. "Yours are, I think, more pointed. Can I see your ear?" Blaze touched his ear and hid it from Pickering's view.

"Father, do not worry yourself with this information. It will all be revealed in due time. Rut is still at an age that'll suffice."

"Suffice?" Blaze's memory returned to Amoria.

"Oh, goody!" Pickering hopped in his seat. "This is going to be fun. Remember, we only help children, and you have to be less than sixteen turn-years old and unmarried in any terms. Understand?" Pickering was smiling broadly. Blaze was done. He was getting out of there now and he was going to make it out alive too.

"No, why are there restrictions?" A knock on the door indicated the kitchen boy's arrival. Haxan opened the door and the kitchen boy, whose gender seemed ambiguous regardless of their title, entered the room with a pencil and paper. They wore their strawberry-blonde hair in a tight braid and they were considerably shorter than Blaze. Their electric-blue eyes and fair skin were their best features. Their uniform indicated their position, which tended to be reserved for orphan boys. Blaze once held such a position here.

"What can I get you?" The youth smiled at Blaze and it lit up their whole face.

Blaze didn't respond to their smile, but he wondered if they, too, felt uncomfortable with these two royals. Lord Pickering stood up and walked up to a parchment on a stand that indicated the kitchen's menu. He pressed his finger to his mouth as he made his selections.

"Yes, bring us one of each entrée, a selection of your finest drinks, along with service for three. Oh, and I will also need a small burner and a pot of water."

"Excuse me, my lord, but burners are not allowed in the rooms any longer."

"I'm sure the manager will make an exception for me—I'm a Cadmarian lord, and I have given a lot of business to this establishment through my own connections. If the manager has a problem, please have him come see me. The burner is needed to brew my own special tea."

"Yes, my lord. Brewing tea is a necessity of our guests and you will find that there is a magical fire here in the pantry. It conforms to the local regulations of Timeria."

"Ah, well, Haxan, isn't that convenient? Please bring back our order and then explain how to use the fire to my son. Don't worry, girl, we tip very well." The youth bowed, though clearly anguished to be labeled. They retreated out the door. Lord Pickering turned around while smiling at Haxan. Everything was going swimmingly.

"Imagine that, a magical fire in our room! Isn't that perfect? This place just keeps getting better and better. Why did we wait so long to return to Timeria?" Haxan retreated into the pantry. Lord Pickering walked around the room, pulling down hangers that mounted the rope to the ceiling. He ended his stroll next to Blaze. He urged Blaze to stand, and Blaze's cloak gently slid off his shoulders onto the couch. The boy met the lord's eyes. Pickering was outraged and offended—in Cadmaria, the meeting of eyes was a true insult of one's position, and this boy had no position other than peasant thief. However, instead of an abysmal expression to match his true feelings, Pickering wore a mask of utmost love and concern. His face had a stumpy, bulbous nose with beady eyes, both of which were set between globular cheeks that wore the day's growth in stubble. The sight of that face repulsed Blaze, especially since its younger iteration stared eagerly from across the room. Blaze sighed. Pickering raised his stubby, massive arm and rested it heavily on Blaze's shoulders. Pickering caught Haxan's eye and Haxan nodded his agreement to the next activities.

"So, Rut of thirteen Cadmarian years, I'd like to honor you with being our 'king for a day.' It is a way for us to feel like we've helped someone who so obviously needs help. Okay?" Blaze's eyes narrowed and he quickly marked out a way to grab his kit, eating knife, dagger, and belt off the table, avoid the two men, and run out of the room. At this point, he didn't care who saw him in pie-stained breeches. *Prince of Devlins*, he thought as Pickering repeated the king for a day announcement, clearly waiting for a reaction.

Before Blaze could answer, someone rapped on the door. Blaze figured that when the kitchen boy came again, he'd put his plan into action, escaping the lord and his son. However, Lord Pickering put his arm around Blaze's shoulders, holding him in place while Haxan opened the door. It was indeed the same youth who wheeled a serving cart with multiple plates. As the server moved the cart deeper into the room, they bowed to show their devotion to a lord who the manager freely spoke of as a man with a generous nature, which led to scrubbed policies. The adolescent covered a table with fine Cadmarian linen and centered a candelabrum. Next, they placed three very delicate Pyrrin glass plates with matching stemware at equidistance from the edge of the table. Finally, the server added the entrées. The rich scents of seasoned meats rose from the table and tickled Blaze's nose. They returned him to his days working at Lords and Ladies when he helped in the preparation of food for the visiting human royals who took up residency at the inn during the Festival. Blaze shuddered from a chill that traveled up his spine. Pickering responded to his trembling and pulled the boy into his mountainous form. Blaze pulled away, but Pickering kept him close.

"My Lord Pickering, may I express the management's sincerest gratitude at having you as our beloved patron. Please accept these gifts of Cadmarian delicacies in addition to your order. The food you ordered will be charged to the room." The youth moved the cart close to Lord Pickering, revealing pastries, pies, and a vast assortment of other desserts. They bowed once more prior to their departure. Pickering smiled broadly. Still holding Blaze in his grasp, Pickering moved to the table. He manipulated Blaze to sit down.

"Hmm. This certainly smells delicious. This is quite a wonderful treat, don't you think, Rut?" Blaze nodded his head slowly, still trying to find a way to act on his plan. Blaze could feel Haxan breathing down his neck. "Good, now I'd like to present you with the honor of being our king for a day."

Haxan set a forged circlet on Blaze's head, moving the hair away from Blaze's ears, which confirmed Pickering's suspicions—they were indeed pointed. The circlet touched Blaze's ears and rested low on his forehead, wrapping itself around his temples. Blaze wanted to escape, but there was no easy way, especially now that the two men's attention was entirely centered on him. Pickering blocked the window, and Haxan held Blaze's shoulders.

"Your highness, King Rut, may I present you with studded wrist bands, rings, and anklets that are worthy of your stature." Blaze tried to wriggle free and resist the jewelry, but then his head began to spin and he briefly thought he was a king. Haxan placed the wristbands on his forearms and secured them at his wrists, then removed Blaze's gloves, clearly surprised that one hand was less than whole. Dirt spilled onto the floor, no longer filling out the glove.

"Father, you should see this."

Blaze was unaffected by Haxan's scrutiny; nothing seemed to matter. Pickering rose from his plate of food and examined Blaze's left hand.

"It's okay. The right fingers are appropriate for our needs and more divine. I believe three will more than suffice." Blaze blinked, trying to clear his mind, but a magical glamour bathing everything in illusion began to cloud his head. He could see Haxan in royal purple attire and Pickering in clothes that Blaze had seen King Kiril wear at the tourneys. *Is that King Kiril?* Blaze could see Haxan placing jeweled rings on his right thumb and two consecutive fingers. The jewels were larger than any he'd ever seen in his life. Finally, Haxan bent down, pulled off Blaze's boots, and placed multifaceted jeweled bands on his ankles. Blaze sat in the chair and blankly stared across the room—he felt the heavy weight of the wristlets and anklets keeping him still. He had no conscious thought or real awareness of what was truly happening. "I want his ears, too, for my collection. Perfect specimens. I have Nashiran, Kamarian, Doralian, and Drisanian tips…I don't think we have any Timerian yet, do I, Haxan?"

"No, these would be the first Timerian ones. It will be my pleasure to obtain them for your collection, Father." Pickering watched with delight as the solid metal rings shrunk around Blaze's fingers, cutting them from his hand. Blaze's blood dripped into an empty wine glass while Haxan harvested what he needed. Lord Pickering held Blaze's severed thumb carefully. He handed Haxan back the thumb and Haxan disappeared into the pantry. Soon, he emerged, carrying a plate of three meat sticks. Haxan presented them to Pickering. Pickering inhaled the aroma through his pug-like nose, then took his fork and pierced the thickest of the sticks. He tore into the flesh, devouring it around the bone. Then he dropped the bone into his wine. He did the same with the other two meat sticks.

Haxan waited. The wine glass was about half filled, which still was not enough. The younger Cadmarian grabbed a metal tool that was manufactured in his home country. It was an ingenious device, actually. It fit perfectly over the ear, allowing the elfin points to stick above the metal. A small lever attached to a sharp blade which permitted a precision cut of the ear. The ear would be perfectly rounded, as it should have been made in the womb. Haxan shifted the lever and cut into the cartilage; blood oozed out of the incision, wetting the device and dripping down Blaze's head. Haxan removed the severed cartilage ear and moved on to the second ear. As he moved around Blaze, he tossed the ear tip onto the plate sitting in front of Blaze. When he completed the second ear, Haxan tossed it with its twin. Blood dripped down the sides of Blaze's head onto his tunic. Haxan realized then that they should give the boy new clothes after they cleaned him up. He removed the ear device and delicately put it in its metal case. Dried blood decorated its interior, but Haxan didn't seem to care. He glanced down again at the wine glass; the blood had reached the rim.

Haxan lifted the glass and glanced through the opaque liquid. He waved his hand over the glass, channeling the goddess of dark magic's gifts. He cast the spell with Mereen's favor, then handed his father the glass of blood.

Lord Pickering accepted it with joy; actually he jiggled all over from his excitement. This was the only drink that ever quenched his thirst: the drink of immortality. He would live another one hundred years, and he was happy. Haxan knew what was to come. He, too, drank from the glass. As Blaze sat mindlessly unaware of his surroundings, Pickering hacked and coughed while he grabbed the glass from Haxan. He emptied the contents fully this time, his size rapidly decreasing, skin tightening, and wrinkles smoothing to youth. Haxan had contorted his face with the pain of reverse aging as he reached back down to his late adolescence. He still wished for his independence of adulthood, and those three small sips had granted him such. Pickering no longer felt the deep constant pain in his joints, his back straightened, and he sat higher in his chair as his posture returned to that of a man of thirty. Each change was painfully endured until all was resolved. The man who rose from the chair across from Blaze was no longer old or large. He looked at Haxan and smiled. He patted his chest and clasped his son, pulling him forward in a sport triumphant hug.

"You've done well, Haxan. Now we can pay him for his gifts." Haxan chuckled and followed his father's instructions to the letter. "Take the cloak and buy him clothes that will last him through the winter with some of the coins from the pouch. Make sure they are worthy of a noble. He will feel like a king when he awakens from the glamour!" Pickering walked over to Blaze and bent down in his expressionless face. "Thank you, lad, I will not forget your generosity. I never expected the ear tips, such an added bonus. Thank you for coming. You have fulfilled your destiny."

Haxan left with Nohan's cloak in his possession. Pickering moved to the table and devoured the food. Then he moved on to the cart. The desserts were delectable little delights. He tasted each one, determining the Cadmarian sweets as the best. He picked up an air cloud of maple resting on a candied flower, called a pixie twist, which was one of his favorites. He squished it between his fingers and shoved it into Blaze's mouth. "Enjoy, Rut." After enjoying his desserts, Pickering staggered to his chair and fell fast asleep.

The inn's door slammed shut, awakening the sleeping lord. Haxan had returned with clothes for Blaze. The pouch of coin that Blaze had tossed back on the table earlier rested on Haxan's hip somewhat smaller than its original size. Haxan held the clothes over his arm and in one hand he carried new boots. He moved toward the table and held the clothes up for Pickering's approval. The supple sable leather breeches were trimmed in fur and matched the tunic and cloak. The boots he carried were lined with sheep's wool. Another cloak, a rare and special one made from a magical cloth that could conceal any who were underneath its interior, was draped over his arm.

Haxan bathed, dressed, and released Blaze from the prison shackles that kept him in his control and tethered to the chair. Haxan carefully made sure that there was no evidence of his or his father's presence on the boy, in case the constables should care to investigate. The probability here in Ballardton was slim, but one must remain vigilant when such risks were present. Haxan lifted

Blaze over his shoulder and hid him from view under the second specialized cloak. He trudged down to the healers' abbey."Okay, you dirty little thief, a few final items and you will awaken from being king for a day. Here is Pickering's payment for your service to Cadmaria." Haxan attached two pouches to the boy's belt."Here are your gloves and your stupid little thieving tool kit with your name on it. You can fix them when you wake up. And you will remember gifts galore until you were attacked, which is how you lost your fingers and ear tips."

With his final word, Haxan removed the charmed circlet from Blaze's head; then with a twirl of the special cloak, Haxan disappeared from sight, leaving Blaze slumped on the steps of the center building of Iolanthe's healing abbey.

CHAPTER 10

DUMPED

SELMAN WALKED OUT of the clerics' abbey, wearing a pristine, white cleric robe with a golden sash that caught the wind. He pulled his robe close to his body as he began to descend the staircase. Watching his footing, Selman noticed a child who lay motionless in his path. Selman ran down the stairs to the child's side. He was relieved that the child still breathed, and judging by the clothes he wore, he was worthy of Selman's time. He noticed the two pouches that hung from the boy's waist. Selman glanced around, bending down and lifting the pouches. He felt the weight and size in his hand. A jubilant, satisfied smirk crossed his face as the healer picked Blaze up, carrying him into the abbey.

The inside of the abbey was composed of multiple cells that extended off the main hallway. The cell walls were bare other than the individual devotion stations to the goddess Iolanthe. A settee occupied most of the first cell, and this is where Selman positioned Blaze. Placing the boy on the settee, Selman could see his injured ear tips. This was not to be taken lightly. An injury of this nature needed to be alerted to the constabulary. The cleric walked out of the cell and hailed an apprentice to summon a constable immediately.

Upon reentering the cell, he saw that the child had awoken and was attempting to leave. Selman intercepted him. The boy reached for a dagger, but instead he found a fist-sized pouch filled with coin. The boy stopped and opened the pouch. Staring in utmost wonder, Blaze examined the contents. Most coins were coppies, but a few were ebons, a couple silvers, and when he spilled the coins onto the floor, he discovered a gold. Selman bent down, picking up the rolling golden coin. He placed it in his robe. Blaze's mouth dropped.

"A generous gift is always appreciated for our efforts, lad." Selman smiled at the boy."Now, let's take a look at those ears." Blaze reached up with his left hand. His ears pulsed and he was positive he could hear his own blood rushing through his veins. He closed his eyes, wishing he wasn't at the clerics. The children of Ballardton and the poor were anathema to the clerics.

The cleric pushed against Blaze, gently moving him back toward the settee. Blaze felt nauseous, but he refused to succumb to it. He allowed the cleric's will to overshadow his own while he momentarily held back the vomit rising in his throat. Blaze pawed at Selman with his right hand to get him to leave him alone. Red blood streaks stained the cleric's robe and Selman, upon noticing the marks, shot a repulsed look at the boy. Blaze leaned in and studied the red stain, then looked at his hand. He let out a blood-curdling scream that rocked the abbey. Shock overtook him and he felt lightheaded. Blaze laid on the settee with his head in the remainder of his hands. Tears ran down his face involuntarily.

Selman took hold of the boy's hand and examined the flesh, which appeared to have been severed through by mere pressure. Selman needed another opinion, and he was sure the boy's scream called all clerics to the cell. The cleric once again left the boy alone, though this time, he locked him in the room.

How did this happen? Blaze struggled to remember but as predicted there was no memory. Snippets of memory. *A man dancing. Was that King Kiril? A kitchen boy? A crown?* He regained his strength of will.

He examined the cell and noticed its lack of windows. He presumed it to be an interior room and assumed that the cell must have an offshoot, but after a thorough investigation, he discovered there was no door or any way out other than through the one the cleric had exited. He thought about rushing it, but just at the idea his ears began to throb again. The turning of a key in the lock made him rush to sit down.

Selman returned, towing another cleric after him. This woman looked down her aristocratic nose at Blaze. Blaze felt shameful, even though he wasn't sure why. Her abhorring stare reminded Blaze why he hated the clerics. After she scrutinized his ears and hands, she spoke, but not to Blaze.

"Cleric Selman, can this child pay for healing?"

"Yes, Cleric Lania. He has two full pouches, and his clothes are admirable. He must be a child from one of the outer fiefdoms. Poor thing came into some trouble." Selman smiled broadly, wealth dancing in his head. Lania smirked.

"Very well, child, we will heal your injuries. The constable will be here shortly." Blaze nearly jumped out of his skin, and Selman had to hold him down. Lania began her healing by running her finger over Blaze's ears. The air glimmered around her hands. Her rubbing irritated his skin, reopening the wound. She explained that the fresh open wound would heal better than one that had already begun the healing process. He felt a warmth of flesh meeting flesh under her touch, and within minutes, Lania had sealed the wound completely. She moved around him to his next ear. A knock on the door stopped Lania's healing.

A constable walked in, and Blaze immediately recognized him as Constable Sterling. The constable was well formed. Some had said that his inherited beauty gave passage into many circles that were typically tightly closed. It was how Sterling rose within the ranks of the constabulary, although Sterling's true desire was to work directly under the king's command. Blaze began to struggle under Selman's grasp, aware of the constable's opinion of him.

"Well, well, well, Blaze-the-Thief, is it? I wondered why I found this case with Rhatt's name on it near the stairs on my way in. I think I'll have to take this in for evidence." Constable Sterling frowned. Lania and Selman drew in a long gasp. "Got yourself into a bit of trouble?"

Blaze reached for his kit, trying to snap it out of Sterling's clutches. Sterling held it above his head. After several attempts, Blaze slouched, reluctantly giving in and knowing how this would play out. Sterling reached out and pulled on Blaze's ears, then grabbed the boy's hands. Blaze didn't pull away from Sterling, but he did cringe from the touch. "This is Blaze, son of Rhatt and Jade, both thieves as well. Rhatt got himself killed and dear mother Jade has left her mark on many men throughout Timeria. I hear she is giving favors to some Cadmarian these days. The son will end up just like his filthy old sire. Okay, thief, tell me what happened?"

"Nothing happened. Give me back my kit. It belongs to me."

"That's not going to happen; besides, I think I can figure this out just by looking at you."

Selman and Lania listened intently as Sterling began.

"You found yourself a nice bit of change, right? Thought you could use a bit of coin and some nice clothes, but you crossed the wrong people this time. Stop me when I'm wrong, Blaze." Blaze frowned and kept his eyes fixed on a small crack in the floor. "They grabbed you, held you down, and using a Cadmarian Ear Cutter, they cut off your ears. It serves you right, little thief. And since they were Cadmarian, they decided to cut off three of your fingers just for good measure. Ain't that right, boy? But what happened to the other ones on the other hand? They've been healed for a bit. Look at me when I'm talking to you!"

Sterling grabbed Blaze's hair and pulled his head upright. With his lips next to Blaze's shoulder, Sterling spoke just for Blaze's ears. "I really enjoyed your mother."

Blaze curled his left fingers and punched Sterling in the jaw with the heel of his left hand. Selman and Lania tried to subdue the thief, who began to fight harder against his captors. Sterling smirked as blood ran from his mouth. He grabbed Blaze's left arm and fettered the boy to the settee. "I knew it would be just a matter of time." Sterling cut the pouch strings from Blaze's belt and he tossed the pouches to the clerics. "This one will pay for his current wounds and this one will be for resisting, understand?" Selman and Lania nodded and they left the cell.

"I didn't do anything wrong, Constable. I don't think . . . I don't remember much. Just something about . . . something." Blaze scrunched his nose as he searched for a memory that was not there. Sterling lifted his gauntleted arm and backhanded Blaze, breaking his nose. Blaze held his nose catching blood as it pooled in his hand.

"He is uncooperative! I must subdue him." Sterling yelled toward the door. Blaze couldn't believe his ears; he wasn't moving at all just sitting on the couch as instructed. His nose swelling and turning black and blue. Sterling removed his dagger from his belt. "Fight me, boy!"

"No." Blaze's voice was nasaled.

"You will pay for your defiance!" Sterling raised his hand again, Blaze recoiled. Sterling smiled pleased with the boy's reaction. With Sterling's hesitation, Blaze spoke again.

"Constable, if you could just find the man. He was a really big man and he had a son. Oh, I remember, sort of! There was a kitchen boy, but not a boy, I think, and they saw me with them. Please, Constable, help me."

Sterling stood, prepared to attack.

It was then that the realization of what the constable's next intentions were hit Blaze. Tethered as he was, Blaze dodged Sterling's attack. The constable, under the authority of law, finally made contact with the boy's throat. He sliced Blaze's neck, but the wound did not falter the boy. Sterling was amazed at the boy's stamina and strength. Blaze moved the settee couch across the cell and using it as his only weapon, swung it at the constable. The dagger dropped to the ground, and Blaze kicked the constable in his groin. The constable fell to his knees. Blaze reached down, picked up the dagger, and began to lunge forward. Just then the door swung open, and Selman subdued the teen. Sterling, barely able to stand, stumbled to the boy and punched him in the gut. Blaze doubled over and his nose dripped with blood.

Lania entered the room and immediately assisted the constable. Her eyes threw daggers at the boy.

"Are you all right, Constable Sterling?"

"Yes, thanks to your wonderful abilities, my lady."

"Oh, how you do honor me, Constable." Lania giggled coquettishly.

"Healer Lania, heal the thief and then I'll take him back to the constabulary."

Sterling pulled Lania into him and then he passionately kissed her. She staggered backwards upon his release. Lania instructed Selman in healing Blaze. The male cleric was not as adept at healing as Lania, but his abilities would suffice. Returning the thief to full health was not important.

Constable Sterling dragged Blaze across the commons to the constabulary. The thief would have to explain to Sterling's superiors what had transpired, especially what he had done to the constable. Lania would back up anything as long as she got what she thought she wanted. Sterling worried about only one thing: the master of the thieves' guild. He hoped the master would be too busy to come to the aid of the boy or would be out of Ballardton on a mission. Master Locke (if that was his real name, and Sterling was sure it was not) would get the boy's release because Sterling's superiors had valuable history with the master. It was the reason that so many thieves ran amuck in his fair city. Sterling looked around for any of the guild members and saw none.

Shadow stood motionless in the tree's shade, hidden from most eyes, his cloak concealing his pale features. The boy's eyes followed the constable and his charge across the common. He noted every detail of the two figures. It was uncommon for a constable to walk openly through town in full armor; this alone had alerted Shadow earlier that something strange must be occurring. Shadow's quiet nature and fear of being recognized made him an excellent spy and helped him elude detection.

Blaze pulled away from Sterling, trying to make a scene. Sterling hushed the boy momentarily, but Blaze began again. Sterling turned to face him. The inaudible whisper reached Shadow's ears.

"Do you want me to make mincemeat of your face like I did to your father?"

Blaze blinked at Sterling, who sharply pulled the boy up to the constabulary. Shadow moved closer to investigate further; even Blaze didn't perceive his approach. Sterling dragged Blaze up the staircase and threw him through the constabulary's door. Sterling entered the constabulary and waited for acknowledgement from his chief.

Sitting at a desk, Chief Constable Tommik waited. The man had achieved a large girth that came from excessive sitting. He was a jovial man, but his size intimidated many criminals. Behind Tommik stood a shelf, which contained many items from all over the world. He was proud of that shelf and the tiny items that resided there.

"What have you got there, Constable Sterling?"

"A thief, sir."

"It looks like a little boy to me, Constable."

"This is Blaze-the-Thief, son of Thief Rhatt and Thief Jade. The boy has resisted and assaulted two of the clerics at their safe refuge while they were trying to help him." Blaze rose, hoping to get a chance to respond to Sterling's accusations. Tommik leaned forward and addressed Blaze directly.

"Son, what do you say to these charges?"

Blaze began to speak, but the words refused to be voiced. He raised his head to look at Tommik as he tried to force the words.

"See, Chief Constable, the boy doesn't deny the charges," Sterling interjected.

"I will tell you what I see, Constable. I see a boy who is too scared to speak. Place him in the holding until I can speak to his master. I believe the boy has suffered enough by looking at him. He's been barely healed by these two 'saintly' clerics." Sterling followed his orders and guided Blaze to the holding cell. Sterling opened the gate and then immediately closed it without letting Blaze inside. He then walked past the holding block and through the corridor of cells to solitary confinement. The door to solitary was a heavy iron vault door. Sterling shoved Blaze into the opening and then sealed it shut. Shadow watched the events unfold, appalled by the constable's behavior. He moved quickly back to the guild to alert Master Locke.

The darkness took hold of Blaze, and his eyes did not immediately adjust to the complete blackness. He worried that the vault had no air, and he began to panic. He banged on the inside of the door, but the noise echoed back, deafening him temporarily. He tried digging his fingers into the metal surface, but it did no good. Blaze curled up against the back wall, willing the door to open.

Alone with only his thoughts to keep him company, Blaze started to see things in the dark. In his mind's eye, glowing yellow eyes surrounded his space. They were on top of him, around him. He could imagine the smell of their sulfuric burn, could almost taste them, hear them chortling. Their foulness repulsed his senses. He batted them away, but they kept swarming around him. He screamed, but the scream remained loud only to him. Blaze could see her now—just beyond the darkness and to the right of the devlins' ghostly impression. It was Amoria. Her voice was muffled in his head as she shouted for him to join them. She reached out for him and he touched her hand. Together, they sat in the silent darkness of his nightmares.

Locke swiftly reached the constabulary. After listening to Shadow's account of the events with Sterling, Blaze, and the vault, Locke knew he would have to tread lightly to convince the chief constable of Blaze's location without tipping him off that he knew Blaze was in the vault the whole time. A piece of him wished that Shadow was wrong and that Blaze was safe. Solitary confinement was typically used for violent criminals, not for children. He opened the door to locate the chief constable, who was resting comfortably at his desk. Locke cleared his throat, but the constable didn't stir awake. He gently knocked on the desk and called the constable's name. Tommik awoke; surprised that Locke stood before him, the chief constable's eyebrows raised in question.

"Good day! What can I do for you, Master Locke?" The chief constable wiped his mouth free of the saliva that had collected there during his slumber.

"Tommik, where's Sterling? I'd like a word with him."

"I'm terribly sorry, Locke. Sterling has been issued a leave."

"Did he say where he was going, by chance?"

"No, he did not, though I believe he went home to Bevisson; something about his mother being ill. It was all very sudden." Tommik leaned forward, linking his hands on top of his desk.

"Thank you. Oh, and I'd like to see the boy that was taken in this morning."

"What boy?"

"The boy Sterling brought in before he left."

"Oh, he escaped from the holding cell."

"When?"

"*When?* Right after I told Sterling to put him in holding, he escaped."

"Have you checked the other cells?"

"Of course, I have checked the other cells. Do you think I'm incapable of doing my job?"

"Oh no, of course not. It's just he could've been misplaced."

"*Misplaced?* I have never misplaced anyone or anything in my trust. The child escaped. I'm glad, too, because he was pretty scared—especially after having his tips cut off."

"His tips?"

"Yes, he was at the clerics' abbey because he had been attacked and someone had cut off his tips. Sterling went to the abbey to question him, but he refused to speak. Actually, he fought Sterling. Sterling brought him here. He was Rhatt's son, right? The poor thing was scared to death. I sent him to the holding cell until we could reach you, but he escaped. In fact, I am pretty surprised to see you here. Oh yeah. You probably came for this." From his desk drawer, Tommik removed Blaze's kit. Locke received it and rubbed his thumb across Rhatt's name.

"He never came back. Frankly, no one has seen him and I'm rather worried. Would you humor me and check all the cells? The child has a talent for misadventure."

"Yes, we can check the cells together, if you want. I guess he truly is Rhatt's son."

Tommik escorted Locke through the constabulary. They passed the holding cell and Tommik showed him that the boy was not there. Next, the two walked through the corridor of cells. "As you can see, I have only two prisoners in here. They'd been making a fuss in the market; they're just here to cool off for a bit. See, the boy isn't here." Tommik gestured for Locke to move back into the main foyer of the constabulary.

"What about the vault? It would be just his luck to find himself trapped in there. Would you mind opening it?"

"Ha, ha, in the vault? I don't think we've used that thing in years, but sure, I'll need to get the key just in case its locked. Just wait here, okay?" Tommik left for the moment and when he returned, he seemed somewhat distraught. "Um, Locke, I don't know how to tell you this, but the key is missing."

"Of course," Locke sighed gustily. "I am sure he is in there now. It would be just his luck. Would you mind if I try unlocking it?"

"Well, let's first check to see if it really is closed. We try to leave it open when it's not in use." Tommik escorted Locke to the vault. "Well, apparently it's closed and locked, but it is charmed to stay locked until we use the key. I'll send someone to the mage's guild."

"All right then." Locke leaned back against the wall.

Tommik left to find someone to retrieve a mage to open the vault.

"I've sent Constable Avery. He's very thorough so he won't be distracted. I can't say that about most of my men, as you know." Tommik stood next to Locke. "I really hope the boy isn't in here. It can cause damage."

"Oh, he's in there. The sooner we get him out, the happier I'll be. He's seen too much not to be terrified in that hole. I can only image what nightmarish evil he is envisioning."

"That vault will bring out the demons inside your mind. I've seen full-grown men catatonic after a short time in the vault. It turned their hair white. Absolutely amazing! I kind of think someone cursed the thing, but that's my opinion and off the record. Oh good, here comes Avery now." Constable Avery arrived alone. "Where's the mage, Avery?"

"Not coming. They're in some sort of meditation or something."

"Great, just great. May I try now?" Locke's voice was calm but irritation was creeping in.

Tommik looked from the vault to Locke and back again.

"No. If this thing is cursed, it could possibly crush the boy to death. I wouldn't risk it; would you?"

"Then what do you propose? I'm positive he's in there. He cannot be left in there until the mages finish their annual time of solitude. If you fear it's cursed, why not send to Rhiun's or Cerenth's temple?" Tommik placed his hand on top of the vault's door.

"I fear the cost could not be justified to the lord mayor for just a looksee."

"Just send for someone. The guild will cover the cost. There will be no need to inconvenience the lord mayor." Tommik nodded. Avery left immediately to retrieve a priest from the twin's temple. Before long, the constable returned, towing a priest.

"Thank you so much for coming to our aid." Tommik greeted the priest with a handshake. "It seems that we have a child who may have accidently entered the vault. Off the record, I believe the thing to be cursed. You see, I've seen men turn white and fall to their knees."

Locke tightened his fist and looked to the ceiling. The priest ignored Tommik's ranting and began to examine the vault. After careful inspection, he lifted his head, acknowledging Locke and Tommik.

"I am Priest Keeson, and I am from Our God Cerenth's temple. I have examined this containment unit and I do believe it is cursed." He addressed Locke. "You have some skill at lock picking?" Locke nodded. "Good, I will need your assistance, if you please."

"Just tell me what you need and when to act."

Keeson smiled, nodding his approval.

"I believe the child within would not have accidently entered such darkness on his own. You can learn much from watching children—they are so much smarter than most people give them credit for. They have more sense than adults. What is your name, sir?" The priest addressed Locke, but Tommik spoke.

"I am Chief Constable Tommik, sir."

The priest inhaled, held his breath and smiled. "Thank you, Chief Constable. I am quite aware of who watches out for us here behind your desk. And what is your name, sir?" He addressed Locke directly.

"I'm called Locke, Your Grace." Locke removed his kit from his belt. He opened it, revealing a multitude of tools. After examining the vault's lock, Locke selected two tools.

"Well, that seems apropos. I can see why." Priest Keeson removed his outer robe. He placed it carefully on a chair. "Locke, when I tell you to, I need you to release the tumblers."

Locke moved into position standing at the ready with the lock just millimeters from his fingers. He watched Keeson intently. The priest began by touching the surface of the vault to find the one spot that breathed with life. Keeson's hand pulsed to the beat under the surface that only he could see and feel. He closed his eyes, swaying back and forth. Locke held his breath in anticipation. Keeson began his incantation, his words in rhythm to the magical pulse. Soon, he opened his eyes and with a thunderous voice he released the curse on the last chord of the incantation. In response, the vault shook from side to side.

"Now, Locke!"

The master thief lunged at the lock with his tools and with a few twists of his wrist, it opened. The door swung ajar.

Tommik fully opened the door and revealed Blaze's nightmarish state. His eyes were clenched shut, his face pale and pasty, and he was curled into a fetal position against the back wall mumbling incoherently to himself. Locke stepped inside and gently lifted Blaze's coiled form. The boy was rocked by violent shudders, which Locke's embrace did little to soothe. Locke whispered soothingly into Blaze's ear, trying to comfort him like he did when Blaze was a babe. With gratitude, Locke spoke to the other men.

"Thank you, Your Grace and Chief Constable. I'll take him home now, if you've no objection."

"None whatsoever, Locke. Thank you. Your skills are exceptional." Priest Keeson complimented.

Tommik cleared his throat and motioned with his head toward the priest.

"You honor your temple. Please take this with my gratitude." Four gold coins appeared between Locke's fingers. The priest nodded his agreement. Locke left the priest and Tommik standing at the vault.

"Hunh! I cannot believe he was in there. He must've crawled in there on his own and the door shut after him. You know how boys are, eh?"

Keeson stared, unbelieving, at the chief constable.

Blaze continued to shudder as Locke left the constabulary. Locke made soothing sounds as they walked back to the guild. He nodded to Shadow, who was hidden in the window well beneath the adjoining building. The light seemed to help more than Locke's comforting. Locke entered the guild through a secret back entrance. There was no reason that the others needed to see Blaze in this state. Locke set the boy down on his own bed, which was located in a secret chamber within the guild and removed Blaze's cloak. The intricately woven fabric of Blaze's clothes surprised Locke. They looked as if they were made specifically for the boy, but that was impossible.

Locke examined Blaze's ears. It was true; his points were gone. He loosened Blaze's belt and accidentally touched the boy's hand. It was then that Locke noticed Blaze was missing additional fingers. He was outraged, but he could do nothing until Blaze awoke from his inner demons. The constables treated the boy worse than any known criminal; Locke would wait, but he would eventually avenge Blaze's mistreatment.

CHAPTER 11

HEALING

THE RIVER RESTED behind the thieves' guild. Today it ran silent with a soothing trickle of current. The sun was after zenith and the day remained lazy. The gentle wind cooled Blaze's cheek and the sun warmed his body. His head lay on a pillow of hay. He wondered how long he had been there. Blaze had had many violent dreams, of which he remembered none. Voices had entered his head within the blackness of night. He feared the night now, but he didn't know why. He recollected some memories that were never whole. Vivid were the faces of Constable Sterling and the clerics. He shuddered while raising his hand to catch a falling leaf. He gasped; the hand was monstrously transformed, and his heart fell at its loss. Footsteps crunched the leaves behind him, and he remained silently still.

"He's still not awake. It's been over four months since everything happened. Poor thing, what he must've gone through. Master said to keep an eye on him. Why is he sitting here in the sun?"

"Let him be, Dorken. Blazey's been through enough, don't you think? Between losing more fingers and his ear tips and then getting locked in the constables' vault, poor thing hasn't woken up since. I have been boiling wyssanberry, but it hasn't been very effective, yet. If he doesn't wake from this . . ." The voice trailed off. Blaze recognized it as Mason and his heart leapt, but like any child he lay still, gathering intel.

There were many things that Mason had taught Blaze over the years. It was Mason who told Blaze to make sure he bathed in order to remain unseen, as odors good or ill allowed attention. Mason was the one to whom Blaze could complain about Locke or anyone at the guild; Mason in all ways could quiet Blaze's raw emotion.

Blaze's attention faltered as he watched the wisps of clouds against the azure sky of autumn. The clouds stretched quickly, giving an image of white dragons flying just above Ballardton. Blaze wondered what it must be like to see dragons flying in the open and free. *Someday,* he thought, he may just want to leave Ballardton, but he had no inclination at this moment. He felt as free as the cloud dragons until a splash of nearby water caught his attention.

He kept himself in the same position, listening.

"Mason?"

"Oh hello, Nohan! Or should I call you by your real name, Adan?" Mason's voice was melodic and always had a smile in every word.

"Please call me by my guild name, Nohan. I actually have kind of come to like it. But Mason, I'm worried."

"What about?"

"Well, I'm not sure how to say this." Nohan placed an empty bucket next to him and then he sat in front of Mason, rubbing his hand against his thigh. Mason looked puzzled at the youngster. If something worried Nohan, then it had to be serious.

"It's okay, Nohan, just say it. Dorken, leave us for the moment." Nohan was relieved. His conversation wasn't meant for the others' ears.

"Well, Mason, you know how I lost my right hand; everybody kind of knows that, don't they?" Mason nodded. "Um . . . I didn't get my hand cut off when I was stealing from someone. I was apprenticed to a woodcutter and we sort of triggered a magical spell in the forest. It left me without my hand and my master dead. I returned without my master, but everybody thought that I was bad luck and useless. That was when I left everything I had known and came here to Ballardton. I didn't really have any way of making any money, but then Master Locke found me and he took me here. I really owe him my life because I don't know what I would've done if he hadn't found me. I can make do . . . even without one hand. Actually, I try to do more than my share because it makes me feel valuable . . . and that's okay, because I want to." Nohan began fid-dling with the bucket.

"Nohan, what's bugging you? It's okay. And everyone appreci-ates what you do here, even though they may not tell you, especially Master." Nohan looked at Mason, emotions beginning to take hold of him. Blaze gave a wry smile and held back a laugh, snorting slightly. Both Mason and Nohan looked in Blaze's direction, but the boy seemed to still be asleep. After a short period of silence, Nohan began again.

"Um . . . Blaze . . . I want to talk to him, um . . . about . . ." Nohan trailed off and Blaze listened intently.

"His fingers?"

Nohan nodded.

"I thought I could talk to him and tell him that, you know, I, um, understand."

Mason smiled and patted Nohan on the back.

"I'm sure Blaze would like to hear that, and maybe you could even help him deal with it, too. It's good that you're here and want to help Blaze. Hopefully, the sun will help him. It's been months since Locke got him out of the constabulary. Nohan, can you check on the wyssanberry for me? See if it's boiling, okay?" Nohan rose, picked up the bucket, and nodded. Mason watched the boy leave back into the guild house.

"Blazey, I'm glad that you're awake." Blaze's eyes widened. "Ev-eryone was quite worried. We were about to send you to the cler-ics." Blaze bolted upright.

"*No healers!*"

Mason chuckled.

"Yeah, that's what I thought. Same old Blazey and I'm glad for that. You gave us all quite a scare. Lie back down." The change in position gave Blaze a headache, and he felt lightheaded. "Do you remember anything from what happened in the vault or prior?" Blaze held his fingers to his head and he rubbed them across his forehead, pressing his fingers against the pain.

"Mason, why do you still call me Blazey? It's kind of embarrass-ing, don't you think?"

"No, but if it makes you uncomfortable, I'll try to stop." Blaze thought for a moment.

"Um, you can call me Blazey, but only in private, okay?"

"Deal. So, do you remember anything, *Blazey?*" Mason teased.

"Um, I remember Constable Sterling and the healers, but every-thing seems fuzzy."

Nohan appeared through the door of the guild house carrying a pan filled with wyssanberry juice. Mason acknowledged the boy and took the pan. Nohan returned to the guild, briefly glancing at Blaze. Mason poured the berry juice into a cup and set it aside. Then, he took a rag and dipped it into the pan. The rag turned a rich purple and steam rose from it. Mason moved over to Blaze and gently pushed him back onto the hay. He placed the rag on Blaze's head. Purple turned to a brown paste, and Blaze started feel his headache fade—but his mind raced with chaotic, clipped images of days past.

"Here, Blazey." Mason lifted the boy's back and held the cup to his lips. Blaze nearly spewed the wyssanberry tea into Mason's face.

"Yuck, Mason. That's awful!"

"It doesn't taste that bad, Blaze. Keep drinking because it works!" A wide smile warmed Mason's face. "Here, finish it up." Blaze turned up his nose and curled his lips.

"Do I have to?"

"Yep."

"All right, but I can't help it if it comes back up. It tastes like drinking dirt." He held the cup and stared at the brown sludge he was being forced to drink. He never liked wyssanberry, but it was a main component of Mason's non-magical healing skills. "Why is it brown?"

"It's not—it's purple. Now drink up," Mason encouraged. *It looks brown to me.* Blaze brought the cup back to his lips and sipped it very slowly. The effects of the tea soon took hold, and he went back to sleep. Mason lifted him and carried him back into the thieves' guild. He placed Blaze on one of the mattresses in the common room. He looked threateningly at the audience of thieves and exited into Locke's office.

Mason shut the door behind him, leaving the main quarters for the quiet sanctuary. Beyond the office, Mason was privy to the interior where important documents that were related to the crown were stored. He knew of the other rooms and the underground tunnels that ran deep through Timeria. It was an information web, and Locke was an elite member. Mason was pleased that he did not have to worry about such important matters although he did take on many missions that supported and supplied the web. Mason walked around the rooms to find Locke in his study, poring over town records from years prior.

"There you are, Locke. I have to tell you Blaze was awake, but is now asleep again." Locke looked up from his ledger.

"What does that mean exactly, Mason?"

Mason grinned at Locke while pulling a chair up next to him.

"Wyssanberry. It's such a cure-all." Locke was taken back.

"Wyssanberry for Blaze? Really? It turns to slimy gray-brown sludge with him. You didn't make the poor kid drink that?" Mason reddened with embarrassment. "You did." Locke sat back in his chair, happy for the distraction and relishing in the good news, but his happiness soon turned to frustration. "I have leads out looking for Constable Sterling. I still cannot believe that Blazey was in that atrocious vault. I swear I will get that taken down one way or another." Locke slammed his fist down. He breathed in, pressed his lips together, and held his anger.

"Okay, Locke. Count with me. . . ."

"Don't patronize me, Mason. You weren't there. You didn't see him. He was so vulnerable, so little, and so hurt. I brought him in here and sang to him like we did when he was a Little. Mason, is he ever going to return to himself?"

Mason comforted Locke with a pat on his shoulder.

"I don't have the magical foresight to answer such a question. However, I can tell you that when he woke, he was listening to what everyone was saying. You know how he does that when he wants to find things out. I didn't notice until he gagged while swallowing a laugh when I was talking to Nohan. Laughing is a good sign, of course. On the other hand, he is still as pale as a ghost. He probably should be seen by a healer that isn't associated with the abbey. I know of one; she lives along Lillium River." Locke nodded his agreement thoughtfully. "What are you thinking about?"

"Did he talk to you at all about his fingers and his ears? Mason, I don't believe the constabulary or the healers considered the serious nature of what has been done here. Someone cut off his tips and threw him away like an old dead cat. Tip removal is a serious crime in Timeria, but because of him being a thief and part of the guild; no one cared that this happened."

Mason sighed. "You're right. All he said he remembered were the constables and the clerics. And regarding the constables—they only see what they want. Tommik is just complacent, as are the others.

It's easy pay to sit at that desk all day and ignore the real problems around here. And now with Blaze's hands the way they are—it'll mark him as a thief." Mason chuckled, thinking back to a time long ago. "Rhatt was always spouting off about his scars, saying they made him a 'real thief.' But it marked him as well. They could see him coming for miles; it's probably why he turned to the dark arts. I hope that doesn't happen to Blazey. Oh, he doesn't want to be called Blazey any longer. It's hard to let him grow up."

Locke had returned to reading the ledger; he glanced at Mason. "Did you know that the vault was last used back before Blaze was born? It's noted in here. According to the official records of Ballardton, the vault was used on a murderer. I cannot read the name. It's scribbled in here." Mason pulled the record to him and was unable to read it also. He shrugged. "Anyway, the person was placed in the vault overnight, and in the morning, they removed him. He wasn't breathing. Clerics called the death. It hadn't been used since, until Blaze." Locke was fuming again. *Tommik was so convinced that he wasn't in there. What if Shadow hadn't told me?*"- Mason, this is wrong. The vault needs to be dismantled, and Blaze needs all the help we can give him. Get the healer—is she that old girlfriend of yours? I'll pay whatever and do what you need, to help Blaze."

Mason rested on his arm, contemplating ways to get Blaze help and to reenergize him. First, he'd ride to the healer's cabin and bring her back to the guild.

Mason headed out after leaving Locke's room and checking on Blaze. Locke sat sentry in the main quarters that night, keeping an eye on the boy. The others stirred, and, upon seeing their master's gaze, went immediately back to sleep. Blaze did sleep, but he was still tormented by nightmares. Locke wished Mason would hurry, and when the nightmare became too much, Locke tried to soothe Blaze by rubbing his back. Instead of being comforted, the boy flailed his arms and fought off the unseen threat. Locke bowed his head and prayed to Goddess Rhiun for her guidance and for Blaze to find peace within his dreams.

Time had slowed down at the guild for Mason and Locke as they continued their care of Blaze. He had received healing without his knowledge and in the secrecy of Locke's quarters. For more than three months, Blaze never ventured outside for more than twenty minutes before returning to the guild house. Most of the other thieves kept their distance, though Gavin brought him pies and Venom brought him a root beer skin. He didn't touch either but stared vacantly at the gifts as though they were some foreign objects of which he had no understanding.

During the eight months that followed, each of his agemates tried to reach him. One afternoon, Dellanie threw a dagger at his head, and Blaze blinked at her from across the room. "Boring." She sighed, frowning as she retrieved her dagger. Another morning, Jewels stood up after trimming the last thread and brought him a tunic she had made for him. It was made of remnants of cotton fabric scraps that she had bought at the market. It was craftily sewn together with alternating panels of light and dark grays. For the lacing at the neck and sleeves, she had braided plaits; she had even recruited Nightshade to help. She handed Blaze the tunic, holding it up for him to see, but again he blankly stared through it. She hung her head in disappointment but dropped it into his lap. Locke saw this and claimed it, holding on to it for the day that Blaze had enough energy to want it back. One night, Shadow had found his gloves under the stairs at the abbey and left them at Blaze's feet. Blaze did pick those up in the middle of the night while everyone but Nohan was asleep. Nohan was trying to explain to Blaze that it isn't so bad to lose your fingers or your hand. Blaze turned his back on him. The moons changed phases as the days turned longer.

"Look what I found Blaze!" Aldric burst through the guild door, so exuberant at his find that he ran straight to Blaze to share it with him. "It a dead cat! We can swing it!"

Aldric was sure that Blaze would be interested in his great discovery. He started to remove the malodorous feline from its burlap sack. The older boy glanced around to see the others waiting for his reaction. Blaze grabbed the dead cat by its tail and he swung it across the guild where it fell apart in midair, dropping fur and flesh over the quarters. A howl erupted from all of the occupants.

"I just thought you'd want to get rid of warts. Hey, can I tell you about my timepiece? I wear it around my neck, and how it works is . . ." Aldric began telling him again about his pocket watch. Blaze pushed Aldric away, whose face fell, clearly heartbroken. Mason watched as all the children of the guild worked to include and engage Blaze in activities, to no avail. Eventually the children began to give up and allowed him to sulk and isolate, as it was his choice.

While Blaze sank into his own despair, the guild began to bustle with enthusiastic energy. The Ballardton festival was set to begin in only two weeks. The town prepared for the annual event in the normal manner with banners, trumpeters, and guardsmen strategically placed throughout the area. Blaze imagined the unfolding events as he stayed sequestered in the guild house. Locke was worried and wished for the boy to venture beyond the limits of the four walls, but Blaze refused to leave the guild, and no one could convince him otherwise. Nightly horrors continued and overtook him—so much so that he began sleeping during the day under the comfort of the sunlight.

The days passed quickly and the Festival preparations erupted into a jubilant day with bustle and found treasure galore as visitors from around Mirias descended on the town, bringing with them jewels and coin. Unable to stay asleep with all of the excitement surrounding the guild, Blaze kneeled on a bench, looking out of the single front window in the upper story. His heart ached—he was torn between his desire to be at the upcoming festival and his fear of the outside. He thought himself foolish, but he still couldn't physically venture out. There had been times when he felt lost in his fear, convinced that he was still in the vault and at the mercy of the clerics; and then there was something else, worse than the Goddess' temple. It was the dark sinister thing that took his fingers and ear tips, but there was never a face—just a thing that Master Locke called a Cadmarian Ear Cutter. Its name sent shivers down his spine and he knew it must have been painful, but he couldn't remember anything but fog.

Mason emerged from Locke's office and directed his attention entirely on Blaze, sitting next to him on the bench. Blaze inched away and although he felt compelled to leave his spot, he remained, wanting to see anything that trouped by that was associated with the faire. Mason noticed that Blaze wore the gloves that Shadow had given him, but he said nothing about it. He had been searching for the words that he hoped would comfort Blaze, just the right thing this one time, and had been racking his brain for weeks for the perfect words, the perfect lure. It had finally come to him today.

"Come with me, Blazey." Mason began to rise. Blaze rested his head on the windowsill in protest. "Come on Blazey, don't be that way. I want to show you something, okay?" Blaze quietly stayed in his position. "And . . . I brought you something back from my last mission, but I've been saving it. Interested?" Again, Blaze said nothing. "Well, I have it right here; do you want it?"

Blaze raised his head and Mason smiled, though the boy never turned to look at him. Mason reached into his pouch and removed a small metal dragon, its wings raised in flight and talons extended to rip its prey. "I saw them flying right overhead in Nashira. Do you want to hear the story? I know you like dragons." Blaze said nothing, but he took the dragon and held it curled in his left hand. Mason smiled again. "There's something I want to show you, but you have to come with me, okay?" Venom entered the guild and upon seeing Mason, bounded over to him, ignoring Blaze entirely. "Hello, Venom. I can't talk to you right now, I have to go with Blaze to show him something, okay?"

"He's leaving the guild? That's weird. Can I come with you, Mason?"

Mason wrinkled his forehead. Venom was smiling broadly, which not only annoyed the spy, but also angered him because he knew that Venom wanted to take his attention away from Blaze.

"No, Venom. Only Blaze today."

Blaze smirked, glancing at Venom to see his reaction, which was surprised disappointment. Venom shrugged and stomped away. Blaze thought there was nothing better than getting to go with Mason after Mason bluntly declined to let Venom accompany them. "Blaze, are you ready?"

Blaze rose, still clutching the tiny statuette. Fear stayed in his stomach, but a gentle pull from Mason encouraged him to exit the guild. He grabbed for his cloak and hooded his head and his disfigured, perfectly round ears against the sun.

Blaze walked quietly next to Mason. The adolescent's steps were as soft and light as any elf's, but his lack of confidence showed in his posture. He walked hunched over while his eyes moved to catch every movement. He searched for something in the shadows, and Mason doubted that he would find it. He flinched at every sound that alerted his attention. Night was far off, but the circles under Blaze's eyes confirmed that he was tired. Under the direction of Master Locke, Mason hoped to rouse Blaze back into the land of the living. It could still take many more months, but Mason had a good idea about how to help speed up Blaze's recovery.

Mason escorted Blaze onto the tournament grounds. A guard at the entrance to the grounds nodded to Mason, acknowledging the spy's reputation and earned respect. The two climbed up to the king's box that allowed a global view of the tourney. The seats were plush and luxurious. Mason sat in the queen's throne and, at Mason's encouragement, Blaze sat in the king's. The stench of cleaning oils stayed contained in that box, and Blaze wondered if the king hated the smells or if it dissipated before the king's arrival. He hoped for the king's sake that the latter was true. He opened his hand and examined the little dragon. It had tiny jewels for eyes and was sculpted with beautiful scale designs over its body. Blaze wished he didn't have his gloves on so he could feel the delicate features, but he could wait until he was back in the guild for that. He wasn't ready to show his disfigured hand to strangers.

"Blazey, what do you see?"

"A dragon."

Mason let out a belly laugh in response to Blaze stating the obvious, and Blaze smiled, still staring at the statuette.

"I see, but that's not what I meant. What do you see out there?"

"Where?" Blaze looked up, and the stadium was empty.

"Out there in the tourney grounds."

"Oh." Blaze moved forward and leaned nearly over the railing that protected the king and queen. "I guess I see nothing but a few benches, a couple of guards, and some cleaning staffers." *Staffers.* Only someone who had worked or lived within one of the Timerian Castles would know that word. Blaze made Mason proud, but Mason still needed to help him out of this rut.

"Yes, I imagine that is all there is to see with your eyes. But what I see, Blazey, is a chance for the *best* thief to show the world that he is the *best*."

"Oh, so you're going to compete Mason?" Mason laughed and Blaze's mood lightened. He looked adoringly at the spy.

"No, I'm not, but I will be watching the best thief when I watch you compete in two weeks." Blaze's shocked expression faded to humiliation. Mason patted him on the back.

"I'm not the best, Mason. Just look at me." Tears welled in his eyes. "I am the worst, and this shows it." Blaze lifted up his hands. "You know it, Master knows it—everybody knows it. And I *really* know it! I used to think that having a scar was really incredible and was what I wanted, but now I know that it just identifies me. My ears . . ."

"Make you look like me." Blaze looked confusedly at Mason. Mason moved his curls away from his ears, exposing perfectly round ears.

"I forgot your ears weren't pointed." Blaze's eyes widened in shock. "Are you a Cadmarian?"

"No, you know there are other places with round-eared citizens besides Cadmaria."

"I didn't know that. I guess I never thought of it. I just hate Cadmarians." Blaze contorted his face in thought. "And my fingers are . . ."

"Beautifully hidden under your gloves. That was a very smart move on your part and one that Rhatt never would've thought of, if he had lost his fingers." At Rhatt's name, Blaze took more of an interest in Mason's words. He hoped that Mason would talk more about Rhatt; he never tired of hearing the stories that involved his father. "Do you remember that I was there the day you were born?"

"Yeah, I remember you said that."

Mason fell silent, lost in memory of the day and the familiar uncomfortable urge that tugged on his soul when he thought of Blaze's birth. Blaze respected his silence. After a small lapse of time, Mason raised Blaze's chin to face him.

"Blaze, *you* are the best thing that both Jade and Rhatt ever did. Do you understand me?" Blaze shrugged; his face reddened from embarrassment. There was a glimpse of relief over his face, but it quickly faded as he looked down at the ground before him.

"Hey, Blazey, don't leave me here." Blaze looked at Mason confused.

"I'm not leaving, what do you mean?"

"I thought you were retreating back into your own thoughts."

"Oh, I see. I was."

"Blaze, do you remember how you used to outdo Aldric at the tourneys?" Blaze nodded, surprised that Mason would mention that fact from so long ago. "Well, I thought you might still want to outdo him. Am I right?" A guilty smile crossed Blaze's face. Finally, after a long silence, Blaze nodded. "Great, so this is what we're going to do. . . ." Mason described in detail his plans for training Blaze. Blaze was overjoyed but skeptical as to Mason's motivations—why would Mason want to help him beat Aldric?

"I can't do that, Mason. My fingers . . ."

"Yes, Blazey, they'll make it difficult, and you'll have to learn to adapt and change to meet what you can do. *Can't* isn't an option, so try to eliminate it from your mind. It will be difficult, but you *can* do it, as long as you're determined to succeed. I'll help you every step of the way. Are you willing to try? What do you say, Blazey? I believe in you."

"You're the only one."

"You'd be surprised to know just how many people believe in you—whether you expect them to or not."

"Yeah right." Blaze spurned Mason's words.

"Well, regardless of what you think, they still believe in you. But more importantly, do *you* believe in you?"

Blaze was speechless. He had no quick comeback or obnoxious remark. He considered what Mason said, then very quietly he spoke."No."

Mason sighed, then chose his next words with care while gazing out across the fields unseeingly."Blazey, for now you'll just have to have faith in us until you find faith in yourself again. Will you trust me?" Tears returned to Blaze's eyes, and he pushed them back. He didn't say a word while he followed Mason down from the king's box.

Two weeks later and Blaze found himself waiting in the galley of the tourneys. There were competitors from nearly every kingdom, and he began to worry again about his skill level. He was not the oldest, but he was definitely not the youngest, as Aldric clearly was. Blaze suddenly began to feel the fool—stupid and uneasy. He decided that the best thing was to leave, but there was no way he could maneuver through the throngs of competitors to exit the gate. He hoped his turn would come quickly because the waiting was starting to make him contemplate who he was deep down inside, and he wasn't coming up with any real positives. All he could do was trust Mason, who, Gods knew why, trusted him.

Aldric made his way over to Blaze."It's okay, Blaze, I'm here. I saw you looking nervous. You don't need to be nervous." Blaze raised his eyebrows annoyed that Aldric felt that he was taking care of him."Besides, Mason said that I should help you while you were down here." *Oh, I am so out of here*, Blaze thought just as the caller yelled out his number.

He stumbled out onto the grounds looking down at his feet. The caller cried out the first test at hand. Blaze was to climb a series of walls in a variety of heights. He looked up at the walls that snaked around the grounds and noticed that the tallest must reach to the height of the king's box. He was annoyed at the task, and then he heard someone in the audience holler, "*Hiss!*"

The bell chimed the start of the test. With great agility and skill, Blaze scaled the walls with ease. He stopped at the top of the tallest one, stood up, and looked directly into the king's eyes. He tilted his head back slightly, raised an eyebrow, and smirked, keeping eye contact with the king. His time mattered, but that was a moment he could not resist. It could have been seen as disrespect, but for that one brief moment he was an equal to the king of Timeria. Blaze glanced down. He could jump down and risk breaking his leg, but the risk was small, as he knew how to land correctly.

He did just that. He vaulted off the wall, and as the ground neared, Blaze tucked in for a somersault. He stood up, faltered a bit, then ran to the next wall. This one was no higher than the one around the duke's manor house in town. He easily climbed it. He leapt down with grace and continued his run over the other side of a box platform. A cross bolt thudded into a hollowed box, echoing his completion; his speed was decent. As he waited for the results, Blaze looked around at his competitors. He noticed Dellanie at the end of the line, looking disappointed. He whispered her name, but she didn't respond. He hoped she had seen him at the top of the wall. He realized then that he was still smirking and he tried desperately to remove his smile. That moment, his defying and defining moment of standing eye to eye with the king gave him strength, energy, and resolve.

He strutted across the grounds to receive his reward with his head high, surprised that he won the top spot, even without his fingers. The reward was more than merely what he was given by the proctor, but rather his renewed self-confidence. The crowd erupted in applause at his win. Locke and Mason sat in the stands. They glanced at each other. Mason stood up and joined in cheering while Locke nodded his approval knowing that he did the right thing when he called Mason home for Blaze. This was more than Locke could have asked for. *Good job, Blazey!*

Blaze raced past an old oak tree that spread its limbs out past the King's Highway. Had Blaze taken a moment, he would have noticed the figure dangling his legs over a high bough. But Blaze continued running; he had taken Mason's advice as he prepared for the next tournaments. Five years had passed, and Blaze waited all year for the Festival to come around again. His heart soared when he thought of another challenge and another win. At the city limits, he turned and ran back toward the center of town. He was sweaty, he breathed hard, and his eyes blurred. He tripped as he ran back over the overgrown roots.

"Hah, hah! That was so worth waiting for!" Blaze scowled and looked around to see who taunted him. "Are you looking for me? I'm up here!" the voice bellowed from above, its words slurred from intoxication. Blaze looked up into the tree. He could see the man now. He had a wiry build with hair the color of walnuts and had the dumbest-looking grin on his face.

"Oh, you're an elf. Have you come to the Festival? You're early, if you did." Blaze didn't really want an answer to his question, but the elf retorted.

"Yeah, I know. I came with my brother and sister. I hate it here. I'd rather be working on the Patrol." The elf jumped down. Blaze caught his breath and slapped the dirt off his knees while he prepared for the next leg. The elf tried to help Blaze fix his tunic, but Blaze quickly pulled his tunic down and turned to face the stranger. "Have you ever seen the Patrol?"

Blaze was disappointed and unimpressed by the sight of the inebriated elf. Blaze thought elves were above such mundane things.

"Oh, um, no. What's the Patrol?" Blaze asked as he turned to resume his training for the upcoming tourneys. The elf smiled.

"It's in Drisana and it's actually called the Border Patrol. We patrol against the Mahdurnians who are always attacking us. My sister and I are captains there." Blaze couldn't believe that this elf was a captain of anything, except maybe a bottle.

"So what are you doing here? Or are there other captains there now?"

"Yeah, there are. I'm here with my brother and sister."

"I know, you said that before." Blaze didn't care about anything this elf said.

"Uh, yeah, I guess I did. I'm 'Marn, which is short for Telmarn. My sister's name is Telmar, and we're twins."

"Oh, okay. Well, I've got to go. Training." Blaze began to rush out of the tree's shelter, but 'Marn caught his tunic.

"Really? What are you training for?" Blaze stopped and waited for the elf to let go of him.

"The tourneys; I compete every year." The elf nearly jumped out of his skin with excitement. Blaze pulled away in fear, releasing the elf's grip.

"I could help you train."

Blaze smiled nervously.

"Ah, that's okay. I don't need any help. I've won every year for the past five years, and I intend to win this year as well."

"Oh, okay. It would've been nice to help you. I just spend my days here, sitting up on that platform and waiting for the stupid festival to be over." The elf slumped and looked disappointedly at Blaze. Then suddenly, he perked up and made bird sounds over Blaze's head. Blaze took this opportunity to sneak away.

"Telmarn, I see you finally fell to the ground."

Another elf, not quite an exact copy of Telmarn, but close, jumped down from the branch above them. "You really need to join us at Two Realms Inn. Prince Delrik needs us both to prepare for the upcoming summit with the Timerians. You can't hide in the trees all day." Telmarn scowled at the young woman. He bowed his head and turned away from her.

"Telmar, I'm staying here! I like this tree. It's filled with magic, amongst other things." Telmarn rubbed the tree lovingly and kissed it.

"Hmm . . . the magic of honeyberry wine, no doubt. Now is neither the time nor the place for that, brother. It's disgraceful. Consider yourself on duty while you're here. Prince Delrik will not be pleased with your conduct." Telmarn sighed, clearly exasperated by his sister's attitude.

"Why do you keep calling our our brother by his title? And if he really felt that way, then he should've let me stay home!" 'Marn retorted with a glazed, pouty expression. Blaze slipped away, hoping the other elf would not notice him.

Blaze raced further down King's Highway. The traffic of arriving carts began to overflow onto the road. Blaze took these obstacles in stride and maneuvered around the pounding hoofs of the horses. Some horses spooked, but Blaze ignored them. He stopped at the fountain that led his way to the guild house. As he raised his arms and rested his hands on his head, he noticed a woman and a girl perched on the fountain's edge. The woman's dress was a deep red and her cloak a rich blue; the girl's clothes dripped in hues of gold, purple, and white. Blaze thought it was sort of strange that they had chosen to rest on the dirty fountain and in this area of Ballardton.

"Just a word of warning: you shouldn't be down this way. It's not safe. There are many people that would wish harm on you both," Blaze called to them. The woman kept her head down and covered by her oversized hood, and the girl looked up smugly. "Um, did you hear what I said? Mistress? It's not really safe here." The girl watched Blaze approach. He waved at her and directed the conversation to her this time. "Do you understand me? You shouldn't be in this area. It's not safe."

The girl had light, spiral-curled, red hair and her bangs stood up straight as though she styled them in that manner. Her green eyes sparkled with an unknown delight. Blaze stood between the girl and the woman. They were merchant class—Blaze could tell by their clothes—and merchants were strict with their coin.

"I can hear you. We're not leaving. We're waiting for my brother." The girl replied with a snotty tone that gushed with spoiled privilege.

"Here by the fountain?"

"Yes, Blazey."

The woman lifted her head as she spoke, and he immediately recognized her. *Jade!* The thought barely crossed his mind before she grabbed him. The girl followed suit. They were surprisingly strong. They dragged him behind a storage house and out of sight. Fear overtook him, and he struggled to escape their grasp. He swung his arm down and released the girl's grip. He tried to run back down King's Highway, but Jade held steadfast against him. He tugged to get her off of him and when he could feel her losing her grip, she called for the girl's aide.

"Tima, grab him!"

The girl reached for him and intercepted him, trapping him between Jade and the storage house. Together, they subdued him, pinning him against the building. Tima looped her leg around his ankle, toppling him to the ground. She kicked him until Jade pulled her away. Jade bent down and spoke gently to him. "Why, Blazey, aren't you happy to see your mother?"

He scowled.

"What do you want? Why are you back, Jade?" Blaze clenched

his teeth, grimacing with the agony of Jade's return."Who's the girl? Where did you pick her up from?"

"Blazey, Blazey, Blazey. Is that any way to talk to your mother? Especially as you haven't seen me in awhile?" Her expression was filled with disappointment. His thoughts wandered to his training. Her presence would put a damper on it, but he was still intent on winning the tourneys. He moved to sit up against the edifice. His face was smeared with dirt, anger, and humiliation. As he moved, he noticed that his arm hurt from Tima's attack.

"Don't call me Blazey. You don't have that right, *only Rhatt* can . . ." Blaze sneered. Suddenly,he realized that she hadn't seen his fingers but that if she was to pry, she'd learn the truth. He covered himself with his cloak, closing off anything that would show Jade any weakness.

"You cannot talk to my mother like that!" the girl yelled at Blaze, and then gazed adoringly at Jade,"And she's the *bestest mother in the whole world!*"

Blaze felt like gagging. *This girl. Where did she come from?* He wanted to hate the girl as much as his mother simply by association, but he felt a sadness there, even as she defended Jade. Blaze inhaled deeply.

"All right Jade, what do you want?" Blaze said, giving in and sounding much older than his years. She pulled Blaze up and held him by his collar at eye level.

"I see you've grown some, Blazey." She paused, then continued after noticing his ears."And lost some. Just like your pathetic father. How long until scars will land on your face?" Blaze said nothing, even though her words had wounded him.

"Yeah, just like your pathetic father!" the girl chimed in, and Jade gave her a stern look. She recoiled from her mother's gaze and then glared at Blaze, reminding her mother that her attention should be elsewhere. Blaze considered spitting into Jade's face, then thought better of it.

"All right, Jade, what is it that you want from me?"

Jade yanked him closer and clenched his injured arm. She jabbed her nails into his skin.

"That's a good boy. I guess you're not so simple, after all. Here's what you are going to do. Do you see my daughter Tima here? Well, you are going to help her find a sweet place at the guild, understand?" Blaze raised his eyebrows and looked away."Look at me when I'm talking to you, you little son of a cur!" He met her eyes. "You're going to protect her from the other thieves just like a real brother, got it?" Blaze nodded. "Excellent. Because if you don't, I'll come back and kill you myself."

Blaze swallowed hard. *She's not kidding.* Jade smiled, pulled Blaze close to her and kissed his cheek.

"Tima will send reports back to me and if I hear anything that I don't like . . . Well, you'll be feeling the pain tenfold, you miserable little wretch." Jade threw him down. He winced when his arm hit the ground and landed on a stone footing, but he ignored the snap of bone and leapt back to his feet. Jade grabbed the girl's arm just under her armpit, squeezed her to the point of leaving a handprint bruise under the girl's sleeve, and threw Tima into Blaze. "She's *your* responsibility now." She motioned a farewell to Tima and said her good-bye. "Be the worst you can, my sweet, and make sure you give dear Locke a run for his money, too. Mommy loves you!" Jade yelled over her shoulder. Blaze stared after her and glanced at Tima, only to discover the clear disappointment on the girl's face. He watched Jade retreat. She strutted away uncaringly, for while her daughter would sleep tonight in the guild, she would find herself lavished at Lords and Ladies Inn.

When the girl recovered her stance, she turned to face Blaze. She grinned smugly again, reflecting her mother's expression. Blaze blinked the similarity away. Tima scanned Blaze from head to foot, clearly judging every inch of him. She grabbed at his gloved hands; he pulled away and gave her a stern glare worthy of Master Locke.

"Why are you hiding your hands?" The girl leaned back and crossed her arms across her chest. Blaze hid his hands behind his back.

"I'm not."

"Are too!" she taunted.

"Listen, if you're going to stay here, I'm not going to call you Tima, that's a stupid Cadmarian name. I think we'll call you . . ."

"Hey, Blaze, who's the little snippet of a girl?" Blaze grinned at Venom, who approached towing Spider behind him.

"Snip! Her name is Snip! And unfortunately, she's my sister. Jade just dumped her here with me."

Spider glanced shyly around his brother and waved at the girl. The girl turned up her nose, although she glanced back and smiled at him. Spider decided that he and Snip were going to be fast friends just like Blaze and Venom. Blaze gestured to his friends."This is Venom and his little brother, Spider. I think you and Spider are about the same age; well, you're both about the same height at least."

"It's nice to meet you, Snip." Venom reached out to shake hands with Blaze's sister."I'm glad Blaze gets to know what a pain it is to have a little pest around." Venom mussed Spider's hair, and Spider's face reddened with embarrassment. He didn't understand why he felt sort of strange around Snip, but he did.

"Hi. Venom doesn't really mean that, Snip. It's really nice to meet you."

Venom intently gawked at Snip's bangs. After a moment, the girl began to gawk back with the same dumbfounded look as Venom. Blaze chuckled. *Maybe she's not so bad after all?*

"Um, why is the front of your hair kind of green?" asked Spider. Snip smiled.

"Oh, that's because I like to do this!"

The three friends encircled Snip while she sneezed out mucus, dragged her hand over her head, and ended by pulling on her bangs, which became wet and sticky. They burst out with roared laughter. Even as far as thieves go, nobody was that disgusting.

CHAPTER 12

DUTY

JADE WATCHED HER CHILDREN, knowing the purpose for which they were meant. She was happy to exploit them both to her liking. It was as it should be. Had anyone known exactly what she was capable of, neither of them would be standing there so innocently. That innocence brought Jade back to her beginnings when she was called Jadelyn. Everyone had always underestimated her power and thirst: Rhatt, Locke, Mason, her sister, her stepfather, even her own mother.

* * *

I know there is a way, Jade had mused, many years before, *to show Mother and him just how much better I am then her.* There was no denying that Amraelt, her younger sister, was talented in magic. It was everything that seemed to matter to her mother and her stepfather. Ever since her sister had come into the world, Jade had lost their attention and devotion.

Jade had to acknowledge that she was excited when Amraelt was born. She knew she would have a cohort that would do her bidding, one that would follow her word as only a blood-sibling would. Jade could see her mother even now as she held Amraelt up in the air and upon the pedestal because, unlike Jade, Amraelt was not born from the rape of a man that would forever stain Jade's existence. Jade thought her mother ugly, from her physical appearance all the way to her soul. Her mother would tell Jade how much she looked like the man that gave her life. He was never revealed to Jade, but her mother said he was near.

Amraelt was born from love, and from that love, the girl grew in ways that Jade could never attain. Jade's stepfather had vowed to be father to her when he and her mother were handfasted. Yet when Amraelt was born, his loyalty to Jade ceased. There was no one more special than Amraelt. There was no one more beautiful than Amraelt. When Amraelt showed magical ability, there was no one more talented than Amraelt. *Amraelt this and Amraelt that. Amraelt. Amraelt. Amraelt.* Jade let resentment boil in her craw throughout her adolescence.

Her mother was surprised when Jade came home one day and announced her name had changed from "Jadelyn" to simply "Jade," but her parents supported her, accepting that children need to find their own identity. Not long after, Jade went on an excursion to the docks of Bevisson. It was a place that no young lady was seen as it was full of bandits, the Goddess' followers, and all things that went against her parent's teachings of love, acceptance, and being a good person. Jade found her people there.

She had a relationship with a man, who was sensual, mysterious, and deadly. He spoke of misdeeds, lies, and curses to her. The more he taught her, the more she wanted power. He began teaching her the ways of the Goddess' magic. Jade learned that if she wanted to be more powerful, then she must give the Goddess a sacrifice or offering to prove her loyalty and worth. At first, she followed his every instruction and began sacrificing cats along the docks. She would find one that wanted to be fed, purring away as Jade pet the animal until she found herself squeezing the life out of it. Before long, she had become skilled at killing the animals and calling out Her name before they died. She had been with the man for more than two years when her mother caught her embraced in his arms. She pulled the two lovers apart, standing between Jade and her lover. Her mother screamed at the disgrace—her daughter in the arms of a man who was twice her age and a dockhand, no less! Jade ran off, furious.

"I hate them. I hate them all!" Jade wailed into the air. "I want them to pay for *everything!*" A robed woman appeared then, tilting her head to the side.

"Is that what you really wish, Jade? Or do you wish for more?" Jade wiped her eyes, glancing up at the robed woman. The woman's face was obscured, and all Jade could make out were vague features. "I will grant you your desire, but you must feel Her power and accept whatever she asks of you. Do you?"

Jade nodded. "Oh, yes! Wholeheartedly, yes!" Jade moved closer to the woman, prostrating herself before the embodiment of her Goddess.

"Rise, child of Mykondra! You will be more powerful than you will ever know! I think you know where to begin your journey."

Jade raised her head toward the woman's face.

"I do."

A smile curled Jade's lip. From under her robe, the woman presented Jade with a sheathed sword blessed on the altar of the Goddess. Jade took up the sword from its sheath and raised it over her head as she proclaimed, "In Mykondra's name!" She replaced the sword into its sheath and tied it to her belt.

"Follow us, Jade, become one of us!"

The woman removed her cloak and draped it over Jade's shoulders, then disappeared. Jade sprinted along the dock, concealing the sword in her cloak. She arrived at her lover's shack where he waited for her in bed. She uncloaked and sauntered over to the side of the bed like she had done many times before. He reached for her. She unsheathed the sword. He became excited, unaware of her intention. She raised the sword, closing her eyes as she let it fall. "For Mykondra!"

He tried to get away, but her strike was quick. Blood splattered the interior of the shack, and she couldn't look at him. She turned her head, feeling nauseous. She dragged the sword out of the shack and along the dock, scarring the wood as she went. She sat down, exhausted yet invigorated.

Well done, my child, a voice whispered gently on the wind.

Jade ran across through the docks with the cloak, hiding the sword and the blood sprays. She had cleaned up her face and prayed that no one would be wise to what she had done. She reached her cottage. Opening the door, she waited to hear her mother's exasperated voice coming from the kitchen.

"Amraelt, is that you darling?" her mother sang out toward the entrance. Jade unrolled her cloak and took the sword out of its sheath. She headed into the kitchen and her mother turned around. Jade announced her presence.

"No, Mother. It's not your precious Amraelt. It's me—and today I am sending you to my Goddess." It was an easy swing. There was no hesitation, and her mother was down. The release of all of her resentment and teen anger just faded away.

She waited in the parlor, sitting quietly in a chair for her step-father to return. The wait wasn't long, and Jade greeted him at the door with Mykondra's name and sword. As she increased her victims, her skill became more honed. Three down, one to go. But this last one would need special attention.

Jade locked up the cottage and wrote a note and attached it to the door. It told Amraelt not to go inside the house but to meet Jade at the dock house. Jade watched the door from a distance just to make sure that Amraelt followed her instructions. Her sister came home, noticed the door, and swiped the note from the nail. She ran to meet Jade, who was just ahead of her. Jade stood sentry at the dock house, breathing hard from the effort of keeping one step ahead of Amraelt.

"Jade, what's going on? Your note said to meet you here. Is everything all right?"

Amraelt was dressed in a white chemise. With her reddish-blond hair flowing around her face, she seemed angelic. Jade moved forward.

"Amraelt, it's Mother. She's taken sick. I had to bring her here."

"Here, Jade? To the dock house?" Amraelt was hesitant, but still trusted her sister.

"Yes, see for yourself. She's just inside."

Amraelt entered in front of Jade to find her mother, and Jade hit her hard with a rock, knocking her out. Jade carried her unconscious sister to the temple. She told the priestesses within of her plan to eliminate the girl, but first she needed to take the power of her sister's magic for herself. Jade told them of the cloaked woman and of her wishes for Jade. She presented the sword, and the priestesses knew that Mykondra herself had indeed visited Jade in that alleyway. They began preparing Amraelt for sacrifice, and after waking the girl, they made her say a transference spell that gave her magic to another. Amraelt begged for her life, pleading with Jade and those around her. Jade leaned over and soothingly smoothed Amraelt's hair away from her face.

"Don't worry, Amraelt. I'll bring you to your mother and father." Amraelt breathed a sigh of relief, believing Jade.

"For Mykondra!" Jade brought down the sword and then raised it until the priestesses with her had to stop her hand. Jade stabbed Amraelt forty times. She looked up at the statue in the temple, raised an altar cup full of Amraelt's blood to the Goddess' likeness, and drank from it. A warmth that Jade had never felt before overtook her, and she could feel the rush of the magic running through her veins. It was a feeling that Jade would desire ever after.

The thoughts of her wrath against her family gave her more power. *These two should be down on their hands and knees, begging for the life that I have allowed them to have. I could take either on a whim. They will prove useful in due time; I am sure of that.* She smiled maliciously.

Blaze had left Snip with Venom and Spider while he continued his training. Returning to the guild, he was surprised that it was empty. Blaze called for Snip, but she wasn't in the guild at all. He knew he'd have to locate the girl, but there was time for that. His mind replayed Jade's words and certain ones reverberated. He shook with fear, for he knew Jade was capable of anything. He needed to feel safe again, so he dashed to Locke's door. On the door, the wizard's face stared, silently criticizing the occupants of the common room. The carved image made Blaze even more uncomfortable. He reached for the door's handle, but it refused to turn. He became desperate. He banged on the door and the walls creaked their silent answer.

"Master Locke, please! Open the door! I need to talk to you! Please, open the door!" Blaze banged again, leaning into the locked, solid-oak door. He spent what seemed like hours leaning and banging his fist against it. He called until his words turned to pangs of sobbing. He fell to his knees, resting his head on the door and there he calmed himself. "Master, I need you."

Footsteps outside moved him to his feet. He felt light-headed and turned to tend the fire to disguise his distress. Some of the girls were back. He could hear their laughter, and he cringed at Nightshade's cackle. A single thought washed over him: *Why in Mirias does Venom actually like her?* The door swung open. He kept his place at the fire, staring blindly into the burning embers. Like tongues of flames, Jade's words burned inside his head. He wiped his gloved hand across his face, smearing dirt, ash, and tears so that his face was encrusted with filth.

"Blaze? What in the world are you doing?" Blaze refused to answer Nightshade. He remembered his injured arm, and it suddenly began to throb violently. "Fine, don't answer me. But I took your sister for a little walk. She's very amusing. Actually, Blaze, she knows *a lot* about you. I filled her in on a few other details, and we both agree that you're useless."

Snip grinned, tilting her head to the right. Blaze saw her out of the corner of his eyes, and it angered him that she was so easily manipulated by Nightshade. A fire of rage blazed inside him. He seethed in a fury that made him want to attack them both. But he refused to give in to the frenzy, and instead he bolted out the door.

"What's wrong with him?" Snip's voice followed him out the door.

"When you're talking about Blaze, it could be anything. Come on, Snip, I'll teach you the ropes around here."

Blaze ran without looking back until his anger started to subside.

The day of the competition arrived, and Blaze waited in the competitor ring. The tourney grounds were filled with spectators, and Blaze could feel his heart pounding hard in his chest. Aldric stood next to Blaze, where he noticed Blaze's reluctant expression. He smiled and waved at Blaze, but Blaze stared beyond the blond boy's head. His eyes were scanning the audience for Jade. He had bandaged his arm and set it. He shouldn't be here in the competitions today; he was responsible for Snip, and he knew his life depended on it. He felt sick, his stomach tied in a knot. He swallowed back the desire to retch. His eyes caught Aldric's, and he returned his mind back to the competition at hand.

The fierce competition between the two boys was one-sided. Aldric was happy that Blaze joined him in the tourneys, completely unaware that Blaze tried to best him. Had Blaze known of Aldric's naiveté, he probably would've found another way to best the younger boy. A contestant's number was called, and Blaze was thankful that it wasn't his. His mouth was dry; he could use some water. His palms sweated and he could feel his pulse racing in his neck.

Aldric excused himself from the group as his number was called, smiling all the while. He patted Blaze's shoulder, hoping to reassure Blaze's confidence, which seemed to have slipped away. Blaze mistook Aldric's touch as a gesture of superiority. Blaze scowled at Aldric and watched him with anxious hope for Aldric's failure. However, Aldric's performance was remarkable and even made Blaze's prior accomplishments at the tourneys pale in comparison. Blaze's head spun and he sat down against the wall. A few more competitors entered the competition ring, but Blaze didn't care. The proctor called his number and no one appeared. Again, the proctor called with the same result. The third and last time, the proctor called; Blaze appeared. An explosive applause from the audience caused Blaze to circle the arena. He bowed at King Kiril and Queen Thalasa before moving toward the obstacle. He thought he noticed their polite bow at him as well, but he must've been wrong. He reached the starting position to the obstacle and raised his arm to signal his readiness.

An arrow struck the starting pole and Blaze ran to the first pillar. It was no taller than the windows of Lords and Ladies and Blaze had been training heights well beyond this one. But at the very moment of his ascent, Blaze's arm responded uselessly. The two fingers on his right hand supported his entire weight and he could feel them beginning to slip. He was too far up to just jump down, which would show his failure. He glanced across the competition ring and his eyes fell upon Jade's smug expression. *Worthless little scum*, she seemed to say. *What a mistake you were!*

He snarled at Jade and found the strength within to continue climbing the pillar. His entire attention rested hard on the climb. He raised his arm and caught the next handhold, lifting his body as though it weighed a ton. The pain clearly showed on his face. He was covered in sweat, and his left hand slipped its hold. He flailed his hand back to the handhold and successfully caught it. He was nearly at the top. His thoughts wandered to the running clock: he was behind his competition. There was nothing else he could do except finish. Blaze reached again with his injured arm, relying on its normal reactions; he grasped the next to last handhold. Blaze's right hand stretched to reach the uppermost hold, and he felt it with his fingertips. He clawed at the hold and his fingers were able to grip. He swung his body across the pillar, but the two small fingers slipped. The momentum of his own movement and gravity pulled at him, and he was at their mercy.

He plummeted hard, landing on his back. The force of his fall spread the dirt on the ground and produced a dust cloud. The crowd watched, mystified by Blaze's mishap. He lay there, enveloped by a deadly silence that hushed the grounds. *Worthless. I'll make you pay.* With the realization that Jade had done this to him through either her words or some other means, Blaze stirred. The crowd roared with cheers and claps, relieved that the boy was unharmed. Two tourney clerics moved to Blaze's side. They were quick to get him up and encouraged him to walk off the grounds while they waved to the watching crowd. Blaze bowed his head, took a deep breath, and raised his arm in a gesture similar to his starting position. The crowd clapped harder.

The clerics escorted Blaze back to their tent just to the side of the tourney grounds. Pain forced him to sit and they scrutinized his injuries. The warmth of their hands soothed his pain, but he prepared to run when Cleric Selman sauntered up.

"I'll take it from here, Cleric Adica and Cleric Rew." The two clerics glanced at each other yet bowed down to Selman's local authority. Blaze raised his eyes to meet Selman's steady gaze. Selman pulled the gloves off Blaze's hands. Blaze shuddered, yet kept his eyes fixed on Selman, meeting his eyes. "Mm-hm, I knew it was you, thief. Cleric Lania pointed you out from amongst the competitors yesterday at sign-up. So what are you doing here?"

"Isn't it obvious, even to someone as simple as you, Cleric?" Blaze baited the older man. A cheeky smirk emerged on Blaze's face. Selman raised his arm in anger, but the forward movement of the two Venesial clerics nearby made him lower it, resting his open palm on Blaze's head. He patted it as though Blaze was a dog while smiling at the two other clerics. He returned his attention to Blaze.

"Oh, I see." Selman detected the older injury. "Apparently, thief, you are looking to get free healing. You faked this little stunt of yours, didn't you? Very clever, son of Rhatt, very clever. I must let Cleric Lania know of your treachery. You are worthless." *Worthless.* "Did you hear me?" Blaze blinked, reliving his encounter with his mother. Sadness and fear crossed his face. The healer grew quiet at Blaze's refusal to speak. Selman healed Blaze, but just to the edge of injury again as instructed by Cleric Lania. Then Selman retreated to find Lania and report back to his superior.

Clerics Adica and Rew intercepted Blaze who moved in obvious pain. He glared at them, but they were steadfast in their efforts. They held the teen in place and began their own healing. Blaze felt their hands and pulled away, cringing in fear. He grabbed his gloves and ran as fast as he could, given his still-present injuries. The two clerics shook their heads and shut their eyes out of shame of their Ballardtonian counterparts.

CHAPTER 13

BEST

THE SEASONS TURNED until the tournaments came back
around. Blaze was certain that Aldric would outshine him,
but he was still going to try to best the boy. Aldric flaunted
his win from the year before, which made Blaze seethe with anger.
Blaze sat on the newly installed benches with the other competitors; however, Aldric was nowhere to be seen. A sly, confident
smile flickered across Blaze's face. This would be his year, no doubt.
Venom sat to his right and talked incessantly in Blaze's ear, but
Blaze was lost in his own thoughts.

"Don't you think?" Venom's voice interrupted after he repeated
himself several times. "Huh? Yeah." Blaze agreed with Venom simply to shut him up.

Blaze looked out at the tournament grounds smugly. He was
ready to take this, but still had to wait until it was time. *What time
is it anyway? It has to be close to start time. Where is Aldric when you
need his stupid time piece?* Blaze's eagerness outweighed his patience.
He looked toward the sun and held out his arm skywards, hoping
to discover the precise time as he had been taught by Mason. This
was a skill learned by every scout in their career's infancy.

"Blaze? Blaze?"

"Yeah?" Blaze reluctantly answered as he concentrated on the
sky.

"What are you doing? Sit down!" Venom's face reddened as he glanced at the other competitors and he pushed Blaze's arm down.

"Just trying to tell what time it was. It's just about three." Blaze glanced at Venom questioningly, but he was proud to use a learned skill.

"Yeah I know, but I didn't have to do that strange arm thing. I know it's three because the king just arrived in his box!" Venom pointed toward the royal boxes that sat just to the left of their benches, deflating Blaze's moment. Blaze said nothing as he slumped back down onto the bench. His attitude perked up a little when he again realized that Aldric still hadn't arrived. He smiled confidently. Blaze looked out to the tournament's proctor who would proclaim that all contestants must now be in attendance. Blaze leaned back, rested his elbows against the upper bench, and waited for the announcement.

The proctor walked with precise posture out onto the middle of the field. A movement to Blaze's right caught his eye. The proctor trumpeted a horn. Blaze sighed with resignation as two boys ran up as fast as they could toward Blaze and the competition area. The proctor bowed to the royals.

"Attention, attention! Kind King Kiril and Queen Thalasa, may I present the competitors of this year's wall climbing tournament." The proctor waved his arm, indicating the group of competitors. The two boys stopped, bent over from their sprint and holding onto their knees in front of Blaze and Venom, breathing heavily. "All those in attendance are the competitors; any others will forfeit their registration. Let the tournaments begin!"

An arrow shot out from above the king's box, expertly finding its mark on the starting post.

"Whew, Silwyn, we made it!" Aldric smiled, speaking to his well-dressed companion he kept in tow.

"Aldric, I shouldn't be out here; I thought we were going to watch," Silwyn whispered, completely aware of the seething eyes upon them both.

"Oh, don't worry, Silwyn!" Aldric looked toward his fellow competitors. Blaze glared back, but Venom laughed at the two misfit boys. Aldric was dressed as was typical for any peasant boy in dirty, worn clothes and Silwyn wore lightweight, elfin, silver-woven clothes under soft kid leathers. A silver circlet crowned Silwyn's head. Pale silver eyes that had a saddened softness to them rested in a moon-kissed face.

"Blaze, I want you to meet my new friend, Silwyn. He's an elf! He's from Nashira! Silwyn, this is Blaze. He's in the guild with me, too. Oh, and this is Venom."

Blaze moved his glare from Aldric to the elf. Aldric grinned at Blaze. Blaze sensed that Aldric was gloating yet again so he responded coldly and rudely.

"You're no elf! You look more like a specter than any elf I've ever seen," Venom guffawed, bending to his knees while grabbing Blaze's arm.

"Venom's not wrong." It was all the sentiment Blaze could muster.

Blaze glanced sideways at Silwyn and leaned over suddenly, whispering in Venom's ear. He glanced back at Aldric and Silwyn, then Venom snorted a laugh in response to his whisper and a wicked smile crossed Blaze's face. Silwyn felt intimidated although he showed no reaction. His impassive face had been learned through countless years of a Nashiran upbringing. Nashiran elves were known for their calm dispositions and ability to remain proper in all instances. Shortly, Blaze's number was called, and he deliberately bumped into Silwyn. The elfin boy felt his pouch being removed. He glanced up at Blaze and spoke quietly.

"It's spelled."

Blaze heard Silwyn's soft words and quickly dropped the pouch at Silwyn's feet. Blaze continued on his way to the arena and Silwyn watched after him.

Blaze grinned triumphantly as he returned to the competitor's area. He had done very well and expected he would place first. His time was faster than everyone's and though there still were more competitors, Blaze was not worried. He happily jumped next to Venom, who shouted, "Huzzah!" and hand slapped him. Venom was not competing; he was there to support Blaze. Blaze would do the same when Venom competed in knot tying later that day. He searched the stands, hoping that Jade hadn't returned for the Festival. Thankfully, Jade wasn't there. However, he did see Snip in the crowd. His eye caught hers and she made a face at him, so he turned away. Next to be called was Aldric. He straightened his clothes and patted Silwyn on his arm.

"Good luck, Aldric. I'm sure you'll do well," Silwyn encouraged.

"Yeah, good luck," Blaze said, and then haughtily under his breath, added,"You're going to need it."

Aldric looked at Blaze with a sincere expression and smiled as he walked out onto the tournament grounds. Blaze watched the elf that stood before him. *Royal birth, no doubt. Why is he not accompanied by his nursemaid?* Then it hit Blaze. *Oh, I get it. His nursemaid must have abandoned him to go do gods know what. Even those of royal birth are just surviving like the rest of us!* Blaze's profound thoughts were interrupted by Aldric's return. He could hear the crowd cheering.

"You did very well, Aldric."

"Yeah, I know, Silwyn, but I couldn't have done it without you. I'm so glad you're here." Aldric smiled at Silwyn, and Blaze narrowed his eyes. Venom watched the final competitors and soon they were all waiting for the announcement of the standings.

"You totally got this, Blaze." Venom leaned in and whispered to his friend. Blaze waited with confidence. He held his head up, chin in the air. He took a deep breath and slowly exhaled while a smile came to his lips. The proctor reentered the center of the tournament; this time, he carried a scroll with the list of competitor's numbers and their placing. Blaze knew his number was on that scroll and what place it occupied.

Top coin, he grinned.

"My lord, my lady, dear Timerians, and honored guests, I have here in my hand the results of the tournament for wall climbing. I extend our king's and queen's gratitude to each competitor for their abilities and participation." Blaze scoffed at the very notion as if the king and queen really cared about the little thieves that ran in this tournament. Venom, however, seemed to believe that the king appreciated their efforts and truly cared for them. Blaze thought Venom was sometimes naïve, but he'd never express it. The crowd cheered again for the competitors and some of the vain competitors moved forward to take center stage. Blaze stayed in the background, waiting. There was no reason to stand out—his score would do that. The proctor began again when the crowd subsided into silence.

"My dear friends," he raised his arms, reestablishing his control of the audience, even though they had already been silenced."I present, in fourth position, number nine!" Blaze watched as number nine walked forward to collect his token prize. Number nine had been one of those competitors who had risen, accepting the audience's cheers, and again the audience roared with applause. Blaze looked away, annoyed. *Come on, next position. Get off the grounds, you dolt.*

"In third position, may I congratulate number seven!" The crowd responded enthusiastically. The proctor waited as number seven took her award, congratulated her personally, and sent her back to her seat. When number seven sat, the proctor began again. *This is taking forever! Why is it taking so long? Does the proctor need to make sure everyone sits down before announcing the next winner? Second position is number twenty-one. And in first place is me— number. . . .* "Seventeen is in second place. Congratulations, number seventeen! It was a great showing."

Blaze stared at the proctor, shocked that he had only taken second position. His dumbfounded expression remained on his face all the way to the proctor. He looked at him, took his prize, and asked quietly, "Who came in first?" The proctor smiled and told him that he did very well, but the next winner bested him by just a bit.

"Better luck next year, son."

Blaze turned on his heels and furiously walked back to his seat. His face showed his anger and unrest. When he had settled, the proctor began to speak again. Venom patted his shoulder, but Blaze shrugged him off.

"Good placing. That's a couple of silvers for second," Venom whispered. Blaze nodded, but inside he seethed with contempt.

"In first position—and I'm sure you'll all agree this young boy did an amazing job, especially for one his age—it is my pleasure to present first place to number twenty-one! Please come up and receive your prize and silvers!" Blaze sat motionless as he glared intently at Aldric, who acted surprised at his win. He hugged Silwyn, then moved forward toward the proctor. He was engaging and the crowd's applause was worthy of a jousting tournament. "Huzzah! Huzzah!" came the cheers from each section. Aldric took in every breath as though it was his last living moment. He pumped his arm in the air and began chanting along with the crowd.

"Huzzah!" Aldric yelled.

"Huzzah!" the crowd responded.

"Huzzah! Huzzah!" Venom joined in. Blaze punched him. "What?" Blaze glared at him. "Oh, yeah. Sorry." Venom folded his arms across his chest and looked angrily at Aldric. Aldric was now moving about each section and getting hand slaps from the spectators seated close to the ground.

"Okay, all together, one last time! HUZZAH!"

"Huzzah!" the audience cheered. The king, queen, and courtiers all added their own voices. So did Venom. Blaze did not, and he punched Venom again, but Venom didn't care. Aldric skipped toward the proctor with his blond hair bouncing up and down. The audience was quiet. They were listening for the quiet exchange of words, but Aldric shouted in the proctor's smiling face in order to be heard by all.

"HU-ULLO!"

The proctor didn't seem to mind Aldric's loud voice.

"Congratulations, son! Your speed was very impressive. On behalf of the king and queen, I present your award." Aldric beamed. His smile was brighter than the sun. He thanked the proctor and then turned toward the crowd. He raised his prize and another"Huzzah" rang out. The king and queen smiled. The king sent a messenger down to the stands to extend a dinner invitation to the young winner. The messenger intercepted Aldric as he ran back to the competitors' area. He nodded and trotted back. He grabbed hold of his new friend's sleeves and told him the news of his great fortune. Blaze glanced back and forth from Aldric to Silwyn. *What did Aldric say before?* Blaze replayed the day's events in his mind's eye. *Oh, yeah, I remember. The elf said, "You did very well, Aldric." And then Aldric said, "Yeah, I know, elf or whatever, but I couldn't have done it without you. I'm so glad you're here." I couldn't have done it without you! I couldn't have done it without you!*

Blaze could almost see the interaction between the two boys again with brand new eyes. He remembered Silwyn's words to Aldric just before Aldric went to compete."*Good luck, Aldric! I'm sure you'll do well!" That's it! Aldric beat me because the elf trained him! That little brat! I'll show him.* Blaze had no intention of doing any physical harm to Aldric, but he was livid. The elf was to blame for his loss.

"All winners, please see me before leaving the tournament grounds!" the proctor yelled above the dispersing crowd. Blaze walked over to the proctor and received his two silvers. Venom walked beside him.

"This reeks of Adoon's poison!" Blaze said to Venom as they walked down King's Highway.

"I know, there are so many people on the highway today."

Blaze turned on him. "I'm not talking about the amount of people here! The elf trained Aldric so he'd be better."

Venom thought about Blaze's realization, and with renewed clarity, Venom grabbed Blaze and halted his rage.

"Do you think he'd help me with my knots?" Venom inquired.

"UGH! How can you say that?" Blaze screamed in Venom's face and stormed off. Venom looked after him, frozen in mid step.

"Easy. I want to win," Venom hollered after Blaze. "Don't forget to come back for my tourney!" Venom shrugged, turned around, and went off to locate Spider so he would be there for the knot tourney.

"An elf! An elf! Where and how does that brat find everything? Is it the dungeon? No. You'd be more likely to find a *dragon* than an elf looking to train you! Wait a minute! I know where I can find an elf to train me, too. Aldric you numbskull, you're not the only one who can get help to win the tourneys! Ha!" Blaze ran between the carts and pounding hoofs of travelers' wagons on the King's Highway. Drivers cracked whips over Blaze's head angry that he had disrupted their path and panicked their horses.

CHAPTER 14

TRAINING

THE TREE STOOD AS IT ALWAYS HAD. It was in full summer bloom, with a knotty, old trunk and limbs that extended high toward the gods and spread outward to hide things within its branches. Blaze ran up to the tree and leaned into the trunk. He looked through the leaf coverings. *Now what did he call himself?* Blaze couldn't remember. *Ah, it doesn't matter.* He had never thought he'd need to remember the name. Aside from a few squirrels running through the branches, Blaze could see no other occupant. *The elf must not have come to the Festival this year.* He pushed away from the trunk, disappointed. The shade of the tree shielded his eyes against the blazing sun on this midsummer day.

As he stepped out from underneath the tree's sweet shade, Blaze could feel the sun beating him down, just like his humiliation. Covering his eyes from the sun, he looked up into the rich blue hues of the summer sky with white fluffy clouds that looked as soft as the fluffed beds at Lords and Ladies, but none of this pacified him. Blaze sighed. There was still a chance that the elf might be inside the sanctuary of the tree, but it would require Blaze to physically climb it. He decided that it was worth the effort. If he couldn't find the elf, then maybe he could find remnants of the elf's visit. He had hoped the elf had come this year to spend his days under the influence of ale and in the shade of the tree; however, now Blaze doubted it. His thoughts returned to Aldric and the richly dressed

Nashiran. *I couldn't have done it without you! I couldn't have done it without you!*

The words echoed through his mind as he climbed the twisted trunk of the oak, his face reddened with the fire of anger. Tears of humiliation and loss filled his eyes. The entire guild knew once again that Blaze was bested by the Little, and he wouldn't ever hear the end of it. He could hear Dorken's and Pip's taunts now:"Blaze, you came in second to that Little again! What a failure!"

It was his fastest time, but no one would care. He was a failure. *A failure, again. Always a failure.* Blaze pictured his master. Within his mind, he could see Locke looking at him, shaking his head in disbelief and pity. Locke had witnessed each of Blaze's pathetic failures, and Blaze hated that Locke knew all of them. He would never be anything beyond that.

As he reached the main branches of the tree, Blaze stopped. He believed the elf would have been higher up. However, Blaze suddenly felt exhausted. It was probably due to the strenuous activities that the tourney required to achieve merely second place, or perhaps his loss of energy from the emotional highs and lows. Either way, the tree offered comfort to Blaze's worn body. There was a slight breeze that rustled the leaves and kissed his skin as he reclined in the crutch of the branches. *Failure. Always a failure. And Locke knows the truth of just how many failures I have had.* He drifted into slumber as his mind wandered back through time.

* * *

Within the outlands of the Ballardton dungeon, an outstretched hand lay in the overgrown grass covered by brush, and a pungent odor of decay lingered in the hazy air. Blaze, a third of the way through his fifth turn-year, tripped over the hand. Not realizing what he had happened upon, he kicked it with his tattered boot, and the hand released a gemstone that was nearly the size of his own fist. It was soiled and covered in stringy muscle and the rotting flesh of decay. He reached down and lifted the gemstone, rubbing it against his coarse tunic to rid it of the waste that made it appear more like an ordinary rock than something of value. The dirt clung to its surface, darkening it with an opaque film. He spat upon it, attempting to use his saliva to wash it more effectively.

At that precise moment, he felt a warm liquid between his own skin and the cold stone.

He lifted the rock and noticed his hand was bleeding from a cut assumedly caused by the stone.

He fingered the stone while he wrapped the plaits that held his tunic closed across his palm as a makeshift bandage to stop the bleeding. He wondered about the stone. He felt no rough or jagged edges, but that meant nothing. He shrugged and put it in his pouch, then darted off toward the King's Highway and back to show Dorken and Pip. Pip, in all ways, had the best reactions, while Dorken scorned Blaze's attempts at everything.

By the time Blaze reached the fountain near the guild's house, the weather had turned dark and gray, and the winds were creating wild high gusts. He looked quite the sight. His tunic billowed in the wind and his overgrown black hair danced wildly around him, at times whipping him nastily across his face. His skin was paler and pastier than usual, and his dark eyes became larger and darker, indicating that a sickness was upon him. He staggered as he walked, causing the onslaught of hurried travelers to open a path out of his way. Yet he felt only excitement and perceived himself to be quite able-bodied.

He walked, or rather tripped, into the guild house, causing the door to swing violently open.

He didn't bother to close it.

"Hey, do you live in a barn?" came the ageless remark from the guild's occupants. He ignored the comment, or simply it didn't strike his ears. The sudden burst of wind brought Master Locke into the main quarters. He gazed, troubled, at his charge.

Blaze stumbled up to his master. An impish grin rested upon his face that made the boy appear possessed. He reached down and attempted to release his pouch from his breeches. The pouch would not detach, making the boy more frustrated and embarrassed as the seconds ticked away.

Unbeknownst to Blaze but apparent to his master, a black magic swelled around Blaze and enveloped his whole being. His aura was black as the dark goddess' heart. Locke reached down and caught the boy's left hand with the cording wrapped tightly around it. His fingers were cold and lacked color, the hand was drenched in blood, and the lacings were saturated and sticky. He didn't know how the boy remained conscious, let alone standing. Blissfully confused, Blaze still tugged at his pouch.

"Wha—? I have . . . sumting . . . if I can jus—get it to come off. . . ." Locke picked his charge up off his feet and held him eye to eye. He saw it there across the boy's ashen face. It was just a glimmer, but it was there, nonetheless—the beginning of a possession. Locke was not going to let that happen to Blaze. He called the others into the room.

"Pip! Dorken! Bring Master Zoryk here immediately! We have no time to lose!" The two apprentices jumped to their feet and were out the door before their master had completed his sentence. To Blaze, Locke simply and quietly whispered, "It's all right. Rest." Locke placed the boy on top of a straw mattress. Blaze protested, still insistent on retrieving the pouch, and stood back up. Angered, Locke grabbed the boy and eased him to the ground. *If Zoryk doesn't arrive soon, it may be too late*, he worried. "How do you get yourself into these messes, Blazey?" There was no answer, but none was expected. Within moments, Zoryk arrived, carrying a satchel of herbs and a large book. Pip and Dorken followed behind.

"Sorry it took me so long, Locke, I couldn't find my book. What seems to be the trouble?" Zoryk rested his eyes on the boy. He had come to know the lad and been glad to see how much he had grown, amazed that his magic was no longer viable. The loss of the child's magical aptitude was *such a disappointment.*

"He's the trouble . . . again." The final word was barely uttered, but Pip heard it. Without hesitation, Zoryk opened his book, turned to a page somewhere near the middle, and began chanting. His body swayed with the rhythmic words. Blaze gasped and fell limp under Locke's grasp.

"Locke, secure the doors and windows. The demon comes. I also need the cursed object, to which the demon is linked. We have to connect it to the magical opening by placing it on the spot. We cannot destroy the object, else we destroy the boy. And I don't think you want that to be the case here."

Locke motioned to the younger thieves, and they began to seal the guild. Locked reached inside Blaze's boot and removed his dagger. Locke smiled to himself at the fine craftsmanship and delicate ornaments on the pommel. *Quite a find*, he thought. Locke lifted the boy's tunic and located the pouch. The pouch was illuminated by a bloody red hue. Using Blaze's dagger, Locke cut the ties and let it drop to the ground. Zoryk began throwing herbs over the boy while reading aloud from his book. A wild twisting wind began rattling the guild.

"Pick it up! I need the object on top of his wound!" Locke picked up the pouch, pinching the ties between his forefinger and thumb. Then he laid it on Blaze's open palm.."Not there, Locke! Upon his breast, the magic is deepest there!" Locke dropped the pouch onto the middle of Blaze's chest. Still, Zoryk was annoyed."Can't you see it? Rip open his tunic—then you'll see!"

Locke did as he was told. He could see it now—a spot just above Blaze's heart. The mark swirled with evil magical energy. Locke dropped the pouch onto the spot. Suddenly, the wind blew the door open, and Dorken rushed to close it. He murmured under his breath that the little rat wasn't worth all this bother and yet, he watched with concern. Locke intently watched Blaze's chest rise and fall. He was relieved that the boy still breathed. Locke stared at him, almost seeing him with new eyes.

In his short years, Blaze had been unlucky in his pursuit of thievery. This was only one time in a long series of similar encounters that the boy had had with dark magic. Locke knew this wouldn't be the last, unless Zoryk couldn't fix the infliction. *If he can't fix it*, Locke thought, *we would . . . no, I would lose him*. It was a thought that trickled through his mind and his heart sank. He watched as Zoryk prepared another batch of herbs. The boy trembled and began to groan. The voice erupting from his throat took on a guttural tone. Zoryk, Pip, Dorken, and Locke's eyes widened. It was true—the demon was coming! A bang on the door turned Pip's and Dorken's heads back around.

"Hey, let us in!" It was the other thieves coming home near the end of the day.

"Go away! Come back later!" was the response from Dorken as he and Pip held strong against the door. Grumbling, the band of thieves left. Locke was relieved that the others didn't fight hard this night.

Zoryk had kept the beast at bay, but he was fighting to keep control. His hands were raised, outstretched, and readily releasing his magic. Zoryk was old by human standards, more than thrice Locke's age, with gray hair and blue eyes that still danced with enthusiasm. Zoryk was no longer a practicing master mage at the Magic Guild but had retired to a small cottage in Ballardton and offered Locke his assistance when called upon for work at the guild. He didn't wear the rich purple robes of the mages but rather those of a humbler blue with patches that would make his appearance more like that of a bumbling professor. However, his appearance told nothing of his incredible skill as a mage. A thunderous blow knocked first on the door, then on the shutters. It moved quickly from one place to another. Pip, annoyed that the band of thieves returned, spoke first.

"Go away! Come back later!" The knocking ceased. Pip looked at Dorken and they both turned in Locke's direction but never caught his eyes. Locke sat listening. Zoryk's power was weakening.

"Give me my hand!" Blaze sprang upright, his hand outstretched toward the window, his voice was distorted, his eyes red and unblinking. His lips started to blue in anticipation of the end. The shutter crashed into the thieves' guild, followed by the severed hand from the dungeon outlands. It grabbed Blaze's throat. Locke, not knowing entirely what to do, acted on pure instinct alone. He reached down, found Blaze's dagger, and began hacking at the severed hand. Likewise, Pip grabbed a morning star that lay near the door and began swinging.

"Yes!" shouted Zoryk. "Yes, smash it!"

Pip moved in for the kill. He was going to stop the demon by destroying the hand in one fell swoop, although one blow from the morning star and there would be no chance of Blaze's survival. Locke, sensing Zoryk's meaning, ripped the star from Pip's hand and shattered the gemstone. With the final blow, the hand released its grip around Blaze's neck, falling lifeless to the dirt floor.

* * *

Blaze awoke with a start and nearly fell from the tree. He shook away the dream. The sun had fallen deeper toward the horizon. Looking through the branches toward the east, Blaze saw the first hint of Luminessa just above the tree line. He stared at her. She shone her full face this night. *It will be an easy night to see and a good night to work.* He thought about the day again, then moaned to himself that he had probably missed Venom's tourney.

Then he remembered that the opening ball, called "First Ball," was this evening. Not that he would attend. It was only for the nobles, and he had no place there. Some of the older thieves would talk about how they attended the ball, but either they had gotten caught and thrown out or they melted seamlessly into the crowd. Of course, you'd have to get the right clothes, walk the right way, and have all of your fingers. Blaze believed that he was unable to do any of that. Besides, while they were fooling around pretending to be nobles, Blaze was at the inns seeing what goodies the nobles had left behind.

A wine sack fell from above and hit the ground with a thud. Blaze smiled and glanced up. He heard someone grumbling, but he couldn't make out the words. He hoped they were speaking Drisanian. He moved from his spot and found what he had spent the whole day waiting for.

The elf was unfazed by seeing someone else climbing up to meet him. Blaze smiled at the elf, whose name still evaded his memory.

"Um, hi! I'm Blaze; we met a few years ago when I was training for the tournaments and you were here then too." The elf laid out on a platform that had been erected in the tree in case of attack from the north. It had become a perfect resting spot for wary travelers and for one bored Drisanian Border Patrol captain. The elf met Blaze's gaze and lazily smiled at him.

"I come here a lot (hic)," the elf interrupted. "I don't really remember that 'cause I . . . well (hic) just don't."

Blaze furrowed his forehead and wasn't surprised by what the elf had recollected.

"Yeah, well . . . Um, well, you told me back then . . . that you'd be willing to train me and, um . . ."

"Oh, yeah! Definitely! It would be better than sitting in this foul tree for the whole summer. And if I hadn't (hic) mentioned it before, I am one of the captains of the Drisanian Border Patrol."

"Uh, yeah, you mentioned it. But I've forgotten your name."

"Oh, that's okay. It's Telmarn, or 'Marn for short. It's actually based on the Goddess Marnie's name. You'd think my *sister's* name would be based on a goddess' name, her being a girl and everything, but somehow *I* got stuck with it. My sister's name is Telmar (hic) and everyone tends to mix up our names, but we're twins, so, it's okay (hic). I wish I could get rid of these cursed hiccups!"

"Stop drinking, and they'll probably go away," Blaze said under his breath. The elf heard him and laughed wildly.

"You're a funny lad. What did you say your name was?"

"Blaze."

"(Hic) *That's* a name that will be burned on my mind forever."

"Like I haven't heard anyone say that before. Will you train me?"

"I already said I would." Telmarn moved closer in the tree to Blaze. Blaze could smell the sweet, foul smell of honeyberry wine on his breath. He turned up his nose and tried to move his head away from the elf's breath. "I will see you here tomorrow, Blaze. We will begin at sunrise. What (hic) tournaments do you have coming up?"

"Well, I just completed wall climbing. Next up is dagger throwing and then lock picking."

"Lock picking? I don't know much about that." Telmarn scratched his head. "But I'll help you with dagger throwing and if you want to learn how to carry a sword so it feels weightless, then I can help you with that, too (hic). Damn hiccups! Maybe teach you some swordplay?" Blaze nodded in agreement. *Anything,* he thought, *to beat that little cheeky brat!* The elf looked around, nearly falling out of the tree. Blaze held his breath, but then Telmarn regained his footing. Blaze relaxed. It would be just his luck if the elf fell from the tree to his death and left Blaze responsible.

"Do you need help finding something?" Blaze asked nervously. Telmarn nodded. "Yeah, I'm looking for my (hic) sword." Telmarn twirled like a dog chasing its tail. Blaze half smiled.

"Does it have a blue scabbard? And the pommel is gilded in silver with a shield on the tip?" Blaze stared directly at the sword.

"Yeah, did you take it?"

"No. It's hanging off your belt," Blaze stated flatly.

"Oh (hic), 'scuse me. So it is! Here, let's see if you can hold my sword up. It'll give me a baseline as to where we will start tomorrow. . . . But first I have to catch it!" Telmarn twirled until he caught the blasted sword. Blaze bit his lip and wondered if Telmarn excused himself for hiccupping or for the accusation. Trying to wrap his mind around the thought, Blaze decided that the elf was apologizing for hiccupping. The elf struggled as he pulled the sword from the scabbard; however, he held it with comfortable ease. His natural muscle memory had overtaken his lack of senses and Blaze suddenly had a glimpse of why the elf was head of the Drisanian Patrol. "Okay, Blaze, take hold of the sword."

Blaze stood up and reached for the sword. It had a beautiful blade with a fuller that ran three quarters up the blade with an etching of Drisanian writing. Blaze wondered if this sword had a name. The grip was wrapped with copper, complete with a wheel pommel that was pressed with the crest of the Drisanian Border Patrol. Blaze lost control, and the sword fell hard onto the platform, gouging the wood. Blaze tried using both hands to lift the hefty sword. It rose momentarily and then fell back into the floor. Telmarn staggered forward and pulled the sword from the floor effortlessly.

"Not a bad attempt. I'll have to get you a practice (hic) sword to start, I think." Blaze frowned, which didn't go unnoticed by Telmarn. "Don't worry, lad. It just takes practice, like anything in life. I bet when you first held your dagger, you held it wrong." Blaze glanced at his dagger that dangled from his belt. He couldn't remember the first time he held one. There was always one at his side, though they had changed over the years. His current blade was made of hardened steel with overlaid silver from pommel to tip. It had intricate etchings that appealed to his eye. He had found it as he walked along King's Highway. It had jumped into his hand and had been on his left hip ever since. He reached down and tugged on the ties that held it to his belt. The dagger fell deftly into his hand.

Unbeknownst to Blaze, Telmarn watched with interest. The elf sized up the adolescent's skill and speed, cocking his eyebrow in appreciation. The dagger was twice the size of the boy's forearm and deadly sharp. Blaze's care of it was remarkable, which showed Telmarn just how committed the boy was to his weaponry. Telmarn reached out and grabbed the boy's wrist. He held Blaze's hand in midair for a moment. Blaze's eyes questioned the elf's intentions, but after a brief moment, the elf released Blaze. Blaze restored the dagger to its place on his hip. Telmarn watched him and then turned aside.

"(Hic) What happened to your hands? Your arm is weak." Telmarn kept his eyes on Blaze's dagger.

"My hands?" It wasn't really a question, but Blaze wasn't quite ready for the inquiry so soon. He inhaled, smirked, and replied haughtily, "Nothing—they're the same as yesterday."

"Okay. But if you want me to train you, then you need to trust me."

"That goes both ways, doesn't it?"

"You (hic) came to me, remember?" The elf looked down from his perch on the platform. "See you tomorrow, lad, training starts then (hic)." Blaze watched after Telmarn as the elf jumped down and retreated down King's Highway. Blaze sat for quite a while on the foliage-covered platform. He removed his gloves and stared at his disfigured hands. *I don't think I can do this.* Just as doubt rose in his mind, so did Aldric's voice: *I couldn't have done it without you!*

"I'll be here." Blaze narrowed his eyes and swore his commitment to training.

The sun rose to its zenith before Telmarn arrived at the tree. Blaze squatted at the base of the trunk, waiting. He was annoyed but understood Telmarn's warning that he had searched out the elf and not the other way around, so he had to be patient. In order to pass the time, Blaze counted the number of travelers that passed by the tree. He fingered a key that was dropped from a cart going away from Ballardton. He recognized it as one from Two Realms Inn. When Telmarn arrived, he secured the key in his pouch and rose to greet the elf.

"Hi!" Blaze greeted Telmarn with joyous relief.

"Hello. Blaze, right?" Telmarn was more soft-spoken than he had been previously and seemed not as jovial as before. Blaze raised his eyebrows, surprised by the serious elf that approached.

"Um, yes, sir."

"Thank you. You can forget the sir, nonsense. I'm just Telmarn or 'Marn, but I think I've mentioned that before." Telmarn ran his hand through his hair. His brown hair stuck up, responding to the movement. Blaze stared at Telmarn and furrowed his brow.

"Are you okay?"

"Yeah, I'm fine. I just need to clear my head." Blaze glanced around, looking for the wine sack that he was sure would appear. Telmarn reached into his cloak and pulled out a green handkerchief with a Drisanian crest. He wiped his brow and then replaced it into the hidden pouch in his cloak. Telmarn sighed. "Right, then. The reason I was late is because I was at the market getting you a training sword. They didn't have any that were crafted to my liking, but this one is acceptable for now." Blaze stood wide-eyed. "Oh, it isn't really that great, Blaze, so don't think it is. The traders from Doralis weren't here yet and they are known for their blades. When they arrive, I'll get one that is better. Here, take hold of it." Telmarn presented the sword to Blaze and honored him with the respect that was due someone of nobility. However, Blaze did not reach for it, nor did he react at all. Telmarn was taken aback. "What's wrong? Take up the blade, Blaze; I can't train you if you don't hold the sword." Blaze said nothing, but he lowered his eyes. Telmarn followed Blaze's glance.

"I don't want to be trained anymore. Okay, bye." Blaze turned to leave. Telmarn, confused by the child's behavior, grasped hold of Blaze's arm. Blaze turned back and stared daggers at the elf. Telmarn reacted with surprise and released him.

"Wait. I've gone to all this trouble. You owe me an explanation. So, what is going on?" Telmarn rested against the trunk of the tree. Blaze looked down and sighed. He mumbled to his feet quietly, but his mumbling didn't reach Telmarn. "Wait, I couldn't hear you, Blaze. Please talk to me and not to your feet." Blaze looked up and his eyes showed the hurt he was feeling. It was an expression that Telmarn was not expecting. "Did I offend you?"

"No, uh, well I don't think I can hold the sword . . ."

"What? Why not?"

"Because of my hands." Relieved, Telmarn smiled slightly.

"So, what about your hands?"

"Yesterday, you asked me what happened to my hands." Blaze hid his hands behind his back. "So. . . . I think you know that there is something wrong with them."

"Ah! I see. I was not really myself yesterday. I'm sorry if I offended you." Blaze bit his lip, showing his immaturity. "Here's the deal, Blaze. I'm not here to judge you. I just want to help you. I think you have some good skills that we can build upon with the sword, and I want to help you to improve. Will you allow me to train you, as that was why you sought me out?" Blaze nodded, and Telmarn smiled. "Great." Telmarn's words made Blaze smile.

"Okay, but this is harder than holding a dagger."

Telmarn smiled in agreement.

"Yes, it is. However, you'll be able to build up the muscular strength to hold it with ease. Everyone has difficulties at first. Okay, let's see. Where should we begin?" Telmarn sat down on the platform, lost in his thoughts. Every now and then, he shook his head. "I got it. I want you to spend the day until our next meeting holding the sword up. That should be enough time for you to get the muscle memory to work with it. So that ends our training for today." Telmarn rose and jumped down from the platform. Blaze stared after him, amazed that he waited the whole day for less than five minutes of training.

He did as he was told and spent the entire evening on the platform. He held the blasted thing up, swapping from one arm to the other until his muscles shook from fatigue and he needed to give in to sleep. His head nodded, but he kept remembering Aldric's words to the elf. With that knowledge, he kept himself awake and determined. By the time the sun began to rise again, Blaze was sound asleep and the sword lay on top of him.

"Good morning, sunshine!" A gentle shaking roused the sleeping boy. Blaze mumbled and swatted away the morning greeting."Come on, Blaze! I thought you wanted to be trained this morning?"Telmarn stood over the boy, leaning on his sword. Blaze rubbed his eyes while he turned his head up toward the elf. In the morning light, Blaze stared at Telmarn. A broad smile claimed the elf's entire face while his dark brown hair curled around his flawless skin. Blaze thought for a moment that he must be staring at the mortal figure of one of the gods. Blaze's eyes widened— could Telmarn possibly be the God Cerenth? It would make sense: Telmarn had Telmar and Cerenth had Rhiun: twins. *What was to prevent the two gods of light from coming down and having a bit of fun with the mortals?* Then Blaze thought of Telmarn's behavior in the past and dismissed the resemblance. He was positive that the gods wouldn't get drunk on golden mead, like Telmarn did. If anything, Cerenth would probably have frowned on such pedestrian spirits. He dismissed the thought and rose.

"I did like you said." Blaze searched the platform for the practice sword. Blaze searched the platform for the practice sword, which had fallen to his side. Telmarn tossed a small sack of two egg sausage pies to Blaze then gently placed a glass bottle with milk next to Blaze's left, understanding which hand was Blaze's dominant.

"Eat and drink up. Eating well is important, especially when you are training. It will help with your endurance. Then I'll test your new abilities. Down on the ground."Telmarn swiftly leapt from the platform with pure grace. Blaze swiftly stuffed the pies in his mouth and chugged down the milk. In no time, Blaze followed Telmarn, landing with a thud. He felt discouraged and cumbersome. His own inadequacy went unnoticed by Telmarn, who offered his open hand to Blaze. Blaze refused it, rising without help.

"Okay, Blaze, take up the sword. I want to see how much you have accomplished since yesterday." Blaze glanced away and tightened his grip on the sword. *Yeah, like you'd really be able to see a difference from our whole five minutes together!* Blaze picked up the sword and held it with minimal difficulty. "Good! See what a little practice can do?" Telmarn's smile widened.

"Now what?" Blaze's annoyance was obvious.

"Let's see what you already know. That'll give me a good starting point." Blaze nodded. "Come at me."

Blaze rushed toward Telmarn, similar to the way the competitors in the knight tournaments did. Telmarn sidestepped Blaze's momentum. Blaze followed through in his attack, swinging the blade toward Telmarn's new position. The switch in direction caused Blaze to falter, and the blade sunk into the ground. Blaze rose; his heart felt like it was going to erupt out of his chest and he was drenched with sweat. He swallowed hard. Telmarn could see the anger and humiliation in Blaze's face, which was smeared with dirt. There was a red glow over his cheeks; however, Telmarn sensed the boy was reassessing his next attack.

Seconds later, Blaze lunged again. Telmarn shifted his weight, causing Blaze to somersault and miss his target. The teenager jumped to his feet, not missing a beat. He quickly regained his footing and leapt at Telmarn again. The sword's blade caught the ground. Blaze's grasp waivered, and the sword dropped from his hand. Blaze shrunk to his knees, exasperated. Telmarn moved forward and retrieved Blaze's fallen sword.

"Good! With some training, you will be quite a fast swordsman. We'll train every day at dawn. Is that acceptable?" Blaze nodded. "Great. It'll be cooler at that time. We can continue through to the end of the Festival. Maybe about an hour a day to start."

Blaze agreed.

For the next few weeks, Blaze met Telmarn every morning. Telmarn stayed sober and Blaze learned how to anticipate an attack. He was learning many skills that were used by the Drisanian Border Patrol, and Telmarn began to wonder if Delrik would consider allowing him to take Blaze back to Drisana at the end of the festival.

"Today, I am going to explain the importance of knocking someone off-balance using their own momentum. Sometimes, like our first lesson together, you don't need to even touch the other person. Remember to watch for the position of my hips and then look at my feet but keep your head up."

Blaze's eyes were wide. As the lessons progressed, Blaze was becoming quite able to anticipate the elf's next move. By the end of the hour, Blaze was ready for the next lesson.

"Would you like to stay longer today and try to put it all together?" Telmarn asked.

Blaze considered all the coin he was sacrificing. Over these past weeks, he had even forgone the tourney that he had originally sought help to win, but if he could enter the swordplay competition next year, then it was all worth it. Those tourneys had prestige and real serious pots. He shrugged.

"Yeah, I can stay." Blaze never called Telmarn by his name, or his nickname, out of respect. He simply left that formality off of his sentences.

"Perfect. Now, let's put it all together. We'll have a short melee for a bit, and then I want you to come in for the attack when you think you're ready." Blaze agreed. He started in the ready position, sword raised, waiting for Telmarn to start. Telmarn moved forward. He held his sword two-handed, keeping his grip high and close to the guard. Telmarn struck Blaze's sword. The sound of clashing metal rang out. Before too long, they were engaged in a dance of blocks, parries, and attacks. As Telmarn moved forward, Blaze moved back, and vice-versa. Telmarn was pleased with the young teen's accomplishment in such a short time. After they had moved into the flow of the fight, Blaze moved in to perform a feint, but when he did, Telmarn spun around and kicked Blaze to the ground and held the sword to the boy's neck. Blaze was surprised and accepted the defeat.

"That was much better, Blaze. I am quite impressed. I changed the plan because I really wanted to see you take full control of the flow of attack." Telmarn smiled reassuringly. Blaze stared emotionless at the ground. His confidence waned. "When you're ready, let's give it another go."

Blaze inhaled a great breath then he released it slowly. He rose as he did, his eyes narrowed with anger and frustration. Blaze snatched his sword from the ground and moved to face the elf once more. Telmarn raised his sword, ready for another attack. Blaze swung the sword back to claim his first strike, but the blade resisted and stayed behind him. Blaze saw Telmarn's expression change from jovial to concerned.

Constable Sterling stood behind the youth, binding his sword with a swordbreaker. He took control of Blaze's blade, for the mere sight of Rhatt's brat with a sword in hand was enough to enrage him. In addition, the Drisanian drunk was training the brat in swordplay. Diplomatic matters required a delicate hand, but Sterling was anything but delicate. The child was a Timerian, and as such he was required to follow Timerian rule. If it were entirely up to Sterling, the thief would've been locked up tight within the vault until his death. To the constable's dismay, the youth's master had become involved and released the brat. Sterling knew the teen's type: born to thieves, stealing for more than just survival, which would eventually lead to higher stakes. He hoped Blaze would jump in over his head and cross the wrong group, giving in to a premature death. One could definitely hope. One could also pray. One could also move destiny's hand.

"What is it?" Blaze asked Telmarn, confused by the elf's inability to move and the loss of control of his sword. Blaze turned around and faced the enraged constable. The constable breathed hard, flailing his nostrils. Air brushed against Blaze's face. Although he knew what the constable was capable of, Blaze narrowed his eyes in defiance.

"Well! What have we here?" Sterling pulled the sword out of Blaze's hands with the swordbreaker's tines.

"Please excuse me, Constable. I was just helping the boy . . ."

"Shut up! It is against Timerian law for a foreigner to assist in the training of swordplay. One must be schooled in this area by an acceptable teacher like those at the Ballardton Blade Academy." Sterling returned the dagger to its scabbard.

"I assure you, My Lord, that I am qualified to train the lad. . ."

"This lad, as you so quaintly call him, sir, is a well-known thief, and has a shameful reputation. It is forbidden for someone of his stature to be trained in swordplay, openly or secretively."

"My Lord, all children should learn the art of swordplay. It will enhance their future, especially if they decide to enlist in your country's able army."

"Please excuse me, my *lord* Drisanian. I must apologize. You must not be aware of Timerian laws. According to Timerian rule, there will be no training of any persons who have entertained a life of ill repute and have been determined dangerous by the local constabulary. Said person will have restrictions placed upon them in regard to swordplay and, likewise, the trainer will be accountable for their future actions, which may result in public hanging. The statute of limitations will be annulled due to the anticipated severity of said person's actions and intentions. Thus, they will be executed with said person's instructor publicly. Therefore, my lord Drisanian, I will request that you immediately desist these actions, or you will be deported forthwith and held quite accountable for the bra . . . boy's future actions. In addition, my lord Drisanian, I will remind you of a fortnight hence when your own actions of disrepute drew the constabulary's attention. Or should I spell it out for you, my lord Drisanian?"

Sterling glanced at Blaze, making sure that the Timerian guttersnipe didn't run off. Then he turned his attention entirely on Telmarn, and with each word he took a step closer to the elf for dramatic emphasis.

"Drisanian, I am referring to your own action of being in a state of undress while engaging in a variety of quite public activities that ended with your lordship nestled amongst the tourney stands in a drunken stupor and, most indecently, spread out like you were waiting for someone to provide services." Telmarn turned scarlet.

By this time, Sterling stood in front of Blaze, who decided to retreat before Sterling returned his attention to him. Cautiously Blaze bent forward and laid the sword at his feet, and carefully took two light steps backwards. Sterling must have sensed Blaze's retreat because he reached behind him, grabbing the thief's tunic and subsequently gouging the boy's chest with the metal tips of his gauntlets. Blaze struggled ineffectively to rip his tunic and escape Sterling's grasp. Telmarn stood, dumbfounded. He knew he could do nothing to help the boy at this point, but once Sterling left, Telmarn knew he could call his sister and half-brother for help. It was the only option; Sterling had him with his conviction and he knew it.

Grabbing the boy's wrist, Sterling subdued him by pressing his thumbs into the boy's pressure points. Blaze's palms fell numb and his wrists ached from the intense pressure and the rupture of skin. Blood oozed around Sterling's thumb tips, but the boy's continued defiant stance angered the constable further. Sterling guided Blaze to his horse and tethered the boy to it tightly. Blaze was unable to move and noticed bleeding under the iron-clad tethers. Sterling removed the horse's crop, cut open the back of Blaze's tunic revealing soft skin, and firmly struck Blaze's back. Blaze bowed his head into his chest to save his head. His back burned and Sterling continued his assault.

"Stop. Stop. Stop! STOP!" Blaze's words gradually grew in volume, but they landed on Sterling's deafened, uncaring ears. Sterling continued beating the boy, but his arm was halted by Telmarn's interception. Tears flooded the elf's eyes and wet streaks ran down his reddened face. His intervention would be cause for him to forever be banished from Timeria, and possibly imprisoned or executed. No, Prince Delrik would make sure that didn't happen—this was cruelty to children, and as a Drisanian, Telmarn could not let the child be hurt any longer. Banishment would be the logical result after Delrik's plea for Telmarn's life.

"Drisanian, you just signed your own death warrant!" Sterling smiled menacingly.

"So be it! Here, run home as fast as you can." Telmarn sliced the tethers that bound Blaze's hands. Blaze said nothing, but there was a question in his eyes as to the elf's fate. Telmarn nodded and gestured for him to go. Blaze turned and ran to the safety of the guild.

As Blaze reached the sanctuary of the guild house, he stopped. His fear of the constable was not strong enough to push him any further. Blaze realized that his retreat to the guild would have its own consequences and those consequences would be lifelong. Sterling, Blaze knew, would eventually leave to seek bigger fish, thus leaving him alone. But his own reputation at the guild was already tarnished by his innumerable failures, and he was not ready to face another mark on his ability. His back stung with the lacerations from Sterling's crop and his chest burned from the sharp gauntlet. He knew he could withstand the pain and let the wounds heal naturally, allowing the scarring that would accompany them—it would be a reminder of Telmarn's bravery of standing against Sterling.

Looking around, Blaze could see Venom heading down the street carrying Lennnowen, who had a busted seam, while attempting to push the fluff back into the softie. Blaze raised his eyebrows deducing that Venom was returning from his brother's shelter. Venom paid annually for the protection spell to be renewed. As far as Blaze knew, nothing had ever returned, not the gnashers and not the Lupin. Blaze was sure that everyone knew the child dwelled in the cave, but they said nothing, nor did they ask Spider to leave.

Blaze waited until Venom had retired into the guild to stealth away up to the youngster's sanctuary avoiding any questions Venom had that may be intrusive.

"Hey, Spider!" Blaze greeted the boy, trying to disguise the pain that he was feeling. Spider's grin welcomed Blaze with exuberant glee. The younger boy was pleased when anyone came to visit him. To add to the cave, Spider collected pine needles. He enjoyed the smell and also walking on them. The boy was lonely, but Venom refused to let Spider stay in the guild. Spider had welcomed Snip and even showed the cave to her. They had become close friends and she would sometimes stay with him just because she didn't want him to be alone all the time. She even convinced Venom to stay with Spider, and sometimes he did. The weather was beautifully warm and Blaze was surprised by how cool and refreshing it was inside. Spider readied a place for Blaze.

"Blaze, Venom's not here. He just left." Blaze averted his eyes.

"I know."

Spider was concerned, and it showed.

"Are you in trouble?"

Blaze did not respond. Spider moved closer to him, but Blaze busied himself with some of the pine needles that nearly carpeted the sanctuary. "You're hurt!"

Blaze shot him a look of anger. Spider lowered his volume and repeated himself. "You're hurt. You should go to the healers."

"No."

"But if you're hurt, Blaze, they can help you." Spider's simplicity was refreshing to all but Blaze. The child was, at times, simple-minded; it was a fault that Venom spoke of only to Blaze. Nevertheless, Blaze still liked Spider. He pulled off his ripped tunic, cringing as he did. Spider assisted until Blaze pulled away. Innocently, Spider stared at Blaze's chest. The scrapes reminded Spider of animal claws, but he said nothing. He wondered who or what Blaze had crossed this time. Venom had told Spider of Blaze's catastrophes: the loss of his fingers the first and second time, losing the tourneys, and other things that Venom made up or enhanced. He hoped Blaze would confide in him, although he knew that to ask would probably cause Blaze to flee. Spider did the next best thing. He gave Blaze a side hug after he noticed the lashings on Blaze's back. It meant, *I am worried about you and I care about you.* Blaze twisted until Spider let him go.

"Do you want something to drink? I have a birch beer skin."

Blaze declined Spider's generosity.

"Spider, can I just stay here for a little while? I just need to rest a moment."

"Uh-huh. If I don't feel well, I always go to sleep and then I feel better when I wake up." Spider smiled at Blaze. "I'm going to have some stew. Venom brought it. It's really good. There might even be a piece of meat in the bottom, but Venom wasn't sure."

Blaze lay down on his side with his back facing Spider. The marks on and around Blaze's shoulder blades were irritated and red. Spider held his breath until he knew Blaze was nearly asleep. "Guard thee waking / Guard thee sleeping . . ." Spider began reciting a childhood prayer that he said nightly.

Spider's voice crept into Blaze's sleep. He could hear Spider in the distance as he walked through his pain and into the darkness that was his own mind.

"Guard thee from all dark things creeping. . . ."

Blaze woke out of a fever in a tent walled in vibrant silks. The colors were rich and draped asymmetrically about the tent. A woman was praying at his feet. About her head, she wore a garland of flowers that enhanced her silk robes. The woman blended into the tented room: she seemed to be a living extension of it. Blaze rubbed his eyes as they still desired sleep. The woman rose and smiled. Its sparkle brightened the room.

"You are safe, child. Do not worry."

Blaze removed his hands from his eyes and gazed thoughtfully at the woman. She had smooth, rich, ebony skin with beautiful features. Blaze wondered if he looked upon King Eldon's wife, the Goddess Solana; she was the goddess of motherhood and fertility. He stared at her in awe as she approached his bedside.

"Are you a goddess?"

She chuckled and smiled with amusement.

"Why would you ask such a thing?" Blaze shrugged.

She smiled proudly at him. "No, sweet child, I am no goddess. I am Hende-Li from Pyrrin." She reached to touch his forehead, but he pulled away. She did the same.

"Pyrrin? You're from Pyrrin?"

"Yes."

"Oh, so you're a noble?" Blaze tried to bow from the half lying, half sitting position that he found himself in.

"No, sweetheart. I am just a woman. You judge me for what you think I should be. I know your friend, Spider. He is a good boy. He brought you here. You will be better now. I myself am known as a builder." Hende-Li and those like her were special people who remained in the hearts of the people they touched because they made a positive impact on others. Hende-Li turned away from Blaze. She moved to a cooking pot hovering over a small fire. "Is your belly talking to you?"

Blaze slit his eyes, confused by the statement. He felt simple and he was ashamed that it was true. Hende-Li turned and noticed the boy's reaction. Again, she smiled. "I am most sorry, child. Please forgive me. In Pyrrin, these words are spoken to ask if you are hungry. In Timeria, I need to ask differently. Do not think ill of yourself. I did not express myself in your terms."

Blaze said nothing, just stared at her. His trust was dwindling fast.

"How do you know Spider?"

Hende-Li rose, carrying a bowl and spoon. The bowl contained a Pyrrin stew that was made mostly of fruits and vegetables. It was a traditional staple on the small, festive island.

"Good question. I have known Spider for a few years. I have been honored to represent Pyrrin at this Midsummer Festival. I also know some healing magic, amongst other things."

"What other things?"

"Oh, you know, things such as tradition and culture. I am privileged to learn of other people's cultures, and I have changed as a result of knowing such things." She gleefully grinned at him whilst handing him the stew. Blaze said nothing, but he reached for the bowl. Hende-Li returned to the stew pot and dished up a bowl for herself. She sat away from Blaze, giving him plenty of space. She began to eat. Blaze, happy to see that Hende-Li was eating her own stew, started to eat as well. The two strangers ate in silence.

CHAPTER 15

LEAVING

BLAZE SPENT THE ENTIRE MONTH with Hende-Li, but then the time had come for the friends to part. Blaze needed to return home to the guild, so he said farewell to Hende-Li, who was traveling to Springfloressey, the sprite kingdom, and from there to parts unknown. She hugged Blaze.

"I am very proud of you, Blaze. Good luck. Be safe and be smart, my little brother. Look for me; I will be here again. Remember, there is love in life. Find it and your life will change for the better. We are family."

Blaze nodded, his eyes welled up, and he hugged her back. Tears stayed in his eyes as he silently wished he could go with her. Blaze pulled himself from her, returning to the guild.

Blaze entered the guild house through the back entrance. He sighed as he rounded the back of the building, but once there, he had a hard time comprehending what he saw. Everyone was standing outside. A large carriage stood in front of the guild. It had a crest, but Blaze couldn't see it from where he was standing. He slid up next to Dellanie and asked what was happening.

"Aldric's leaving—that should make you happy." Dellanie smirked and jabbed him in his side. Personally, she was indifferent to Aldric. Blaze smiled broadly; he was overjoyed.

"Leaving!" Blaze let out a devilish laugh, which surprised him as well as Dellanie, who raised her eyebrows and looked knowingly at him. He shrugged with an impish grin.

"Don't enjoy this so much, Blaze, because it seems that Aldric is a prince of Drisana. That man standing with Master Locke is the crowned prince of Drisana *and* Aldric's father. You remember that stupid timekeeper that Aldric wore around his neck on a string. . . . Well, that was the key to who Aldric was. Oh, and not to mention, the crowned prince's name is Delrik, which is really close to Aldric, too. It is so obvious, if it was a gnasher, it would have bit us."

Delanie continued on, but Blaze wasn't listening any longer because he was lost in his own thoughts. Visions of Telmarn swirled through his head. He could recollect everything and every meeting he'd ever had with the surly drunk. He remembered the twin captain's conversation many years before, but he had never connected any of the names together. It was such an unbelievable course of events. No wonder Aldric bested everyone in the guild.

For a moment, Blaze felt insignificant. He looked around at the assembly and drank in their reality. *If Aldric is a royal, then who else could be?* His eyes fell on Venom: mystery surrounded his and Spider's arrival. He stared at his best friend with renewed interest. *Who was Venom, really? Where did he come from and why does he hide Spider away?* His mind attempted to wrap itself around Aldric's newfound family. Life in the guild would be different now without the stifling little runt who was running off to live a life of incredible wealth and power, with all the food Aldric could ever want. Blaze hoped Aldric would remember the harsh life he had lived at the guild, but that maybe too much to hope. Blaze breathed in deeply. He stared unblinking at Master Locke.

The master was smiling with his arm over Aldric's shoulder. There was something about Locke's expression that stirred Blaze's anger. Ah, yes—it was a fatherly pride that Locke bestowed upon the new elvin noble. It was that pride that bore into Blaze's soul, the pride that Locke never really gave to anybody except to Aldric. *He* only saw Locke's pity and disappointment. Blaze turned with a huff, beginning what he thought would be an angered march away from the lot.

"Blaze! Wait! Blaze!" Aldric called, running up from behind him.

Blaze hesitated, but he did not turn toward the boy. Aldric caught up to him and his arms wrapped tightly around Blaze's rib cage. Blaze felt trapped under Aldric's heavy embrace. He knew he couldn't look at the others for fear of dying of embarrassment. He could feel Aldric's head leaning against his back and his breath warming his tunic. With a sigh, Blaze turned around and pulled Aldric's arms off of him. The boy grinned up at Blaze, who in turn made a face. Aldric waited expecting a reaction from Blaze.

"What?"

"I'm leaving."

"Yeah, I know. So what?"

"I'll miss you," Aldric whispered. Blaze furrowed his brow and laughed.

"Go on, Aldric, go enjoy your new life. They're waiting for you." Blaze gestured with a dismissive wave and pushed Aldric toward the carriage. Tears filled Aldric's eyes, and he embraced Blaze again.

"You're like a brother to me. We had some fun, huh?"

Fun? By the Gods, Aldric! Blaze stared dumbfounded at Aldric and shoved him away again.

"Go! Get out of here, Aldric! Just go!" Blaze barked.

Aldric smiled and winked at Blaze, then turned and skipped back to his future. Locke scolded Blaze with his expression and then returned his amiable expression to the Drisanians. Blaze marched off down the road, heading toward King's Highway and away from the guild. He realized that he'd hear about his behavior from Locke later. As he marched off, his anger subsided and was replaced by loss. He hesitated at the fountain, just past the storage houses, and glanced back at the guild house.

Blaze sat on the fountain's edge. Everyone looked much smaller from this distance. It seemed like the goodbyes continued on for half the day, but finally the royal carriage with the Drisanian seal was filled, adding one extra passenger. The carriage drove past the fountain. Blaze kept his head down, but his eyes followed it. He caught a glimpse of Aldric, who waved his goodbyes as the horses trotted along and turned onto King's Highway.

As the carriage turned, Blaze moved his head to watch it leave. Telmarn rode behind the carriage, and his expression was stern and set. He nodded his acknowledgement of the thief. Blaze scowled and turned away. He returned his gaze to the retreating carriage, hoping for just a glimpse of Aldric's new life. After some time, he turned his eyes back to the thieves' guild.

"Lucky for me, I was born here. There's no need to look for something else. I'm not going anywhere." He closed his eyes, wishing for something more.

Blaze entered the common room, annoyed by Locke's display at Aldric's departure. He searched the room for someone to complain to about Master, but those in attendance would not have understood Blaze's feelings. Older thieves discussed their recent missions eagerly with each other. Nightshade and Jewels huddled together, and their eyes watched Blaze cross the room. Nohan busied himself with sewing Littles' clothes. Blaze thought Nohan wasted his time repairing the old when new could be swiped from any farmer's clothesline. Gavin sat leaning against Nohan, engaged in a conversation about the benefits of stealing pies from Borintak. Nohan nodded his head every so often to look like he was interested in Gavin's conversation. Littles played marbles in one corner of the guild, unaware of the injustices they would face as they aged. Discouraged by the lot, Blaze flung himself onto the floor in front of the fire on top of a pile of worn blankets. He watched the fire that rose from the fluorescent red embers. He took solace in its unique beauty.

The fire burned hot this day. He watched the bright blues and deep indigos move around the fire. The flames were erratic and spontaneous in their movements, yet they stayed close to their ember home, afraid to travel any higher lest they lose their identity. However, the consistent reds, yellows, and oranges of the flames stayed true to themselves.

The other thieves moved about the guild house, readying for slumber. Blaze paid no attention to their movements. One by one they prepared their belongings in a keepsake hole under a short, wooden platform that they used as a bed frame. Master had afforded the luxury to those who followed his newly established "no weapons in the guild house rule," which eliminated altercations and any other unnecessary act against the building itself. Blaze glanced at the dagger that was embedded deep into the wall near the door. It hung there like a coat hook. More than two months ago, Dellanie had thrown it hard between Blaze's and Venom's heads that it sunk deep in the wood, and there it stayed. Everyone had attempted to remove it from the wall, but it stayed as strong as Ballard's dragon protection magic. From that moment on, Master had issued the rule and left the dagger in the wall to remind everyone of its justification. If someone forgot the rule, Master would point accusingly at the dagger. He made the mandatory decree and placed a large chest near the door for all weapons.

Gradually, Blaze drifted off into his own sweet slumber. He hadn't been asleep for long when he woke himself up. He felt eyes on him, similar to the hypnotic eyes of a cat. Blaze shot up and blurrily looked around. The others were asleep. He rubbed his eyes to return his natural vision. He saw her now. She wasn't staring at him per se. Dellanie sat crisscrossed upon her bed in a"let them eat cake" royal fashion. Her back was perfectly erect and her head summoned her due respect. Her eyes barely moved to catch Blaze's reaction, which was open and obvious. He cocked his head while finally noticing what made Dellanie seem so noble. It was the emeralds that danced in the firelight around her head. She wore a dangling necklace of perfect emeralds and a matching crown, and further investigation discovered rings and bracelets. Her neck sparkled and her head glistened. He glared and wondered how Dellanie achieved such finds and why was she wearing them instead of selling them to Master. Dellanie's mouth twisted ever so slightly to a nearly invisible, smug grin.

"What are you doing, Dellanie?" he finally queried.

"Whatever do you mean?" She lowered her eyelids and peered down her nose at him.

"You know what I mean." Blaze gestured toward the crown and the other jewels.

"Oh, the-ese! Well, isn't it obvious, Blaze? I am Dellanie, queen of all I see!" Her smile burst into a full grin that she tried to suppress. Blaze joined her in her folly. He looked at her differently for that moment. Dellanie's brown hair seemed to catch the light, blinding his senses. Her head leaned slightly against her shoulders and it felt more sincere. The aura of green enveloped her and made her look dazzling. Blaze stood up and with exaggerated gestures, he bowed to her. Dellanie laughed, and Blaze smirked with childish fancy.

"How can I serve you, my queen?" He swung his arm, offering her the world. She beamed with the same delight. He quickly searched the room, looking for a proper offering to the queen. He grabbed ahold of Venom's belt and curled it around in his hand."I have before me, Queen Dellanie, a golden snake that will honor you, Your Highness." Blaze lifted the belt high above him, showing her the gestures of the royal staffers that would befit a true queen. She reached out for the small bundle as if it were that of which he spoke.

"That is the least you can do for your queen!"

For the brief moment that passed between them, it was as if they were entirely alone. It wasn't until a pillow was thrown at Blaze that they realized they weren't. Dellanie removed the jewels and secured them under her bed. Once secure, she glanced up at Blaze.

"Did you hear about the castle?" Blaze stared at her blankly."I didn't think so. The townsfolk are swarming bees abuzz that important news will arrive tomorrow."

"What are those stupid bees saying now?" Blaze felt a familiar twinge of anger rise up inside him.

"There is news from the castle. Apparently, something very big is happening. And you know if it is a big event, there will be food for all." Blaze frowned.

"Maybe the queen is having another baby. Then we'd have to wait until its birth for the celebration."

"Could be, Blaze, but I've heard buzzing whispers from Ceretheena castle." Blaze's eyes widened and Dellanie grinned clearly gauging Blaze's interest."I guess we'll find out when the bellman returns tomorrow." Dellanie folded her pillow in half to double its size while reaching for her blanket.

"Yeah, we'll meet up tomorrow at the bellman." Blaze smiled.

"And Blaze," Dellanie whispered,"I'll read it to you." Blaze nodded.

"Yeah, thanks, that'll be nice." Blaze pierced his lips trying to conceal his feelings of inadequacy and appreciation that Dellanie would do that for him. He resumed his spot on the floor studying the fire. He laughed at himself for the foolish fancy that was uncharacteristic of them both. Silently, she did the same. He looked back at her and she lay in her bed, presumably asleep. He turned back to the fire and became a scholar of it until he drifted into his dreams. Tomorrow would be different, he knew. Important news from the castle, there was no doubt that he was going to be there with Dellanie when the bellman arrived.

The next day came and Blaze slept in, but by noon he was out in Ballardton, searching the ground for coppies or any coins that dropped between merchants. From there, Blaze ran to the horse traders' stands. There were many new mares, and he fancied a beautiful fee-stallion. The fee-horse was ghostly blue-white and he had only heard stories of them from Skelly, but he knew this had to be one. The horse trader shooed him away or else she"was going to call the constables."

He found himself at Two Realms Inn, begging at the back door for scraps or stew. He was saving his coins for a sword from Doralis. He was rewarded with a ladle or two of stew and then waved on. After the stew, Blaze went looking for the Doralis trader. He eventually inquired about the trader and discovered that they had just arrived but hadn't unpacked yet. Dusk was falling and Blaze realized then that he needed to run to hear the announcement from the castle. He dashed across the market to the center green. *I'm late. I'm late,* Blaze scolded himself as he bolted across Ballardton. *Dellanie, please still be there. I am forever doing this! Important information from Venesial and Ceretheena castles and I am late! The last time was the return of the duke and his family along with the feast that followed! I'm such an idiot! Maybe they're right, maybe I am simple. Of course, I am! Oh, look there's the bellman! Is it the lady or man today?*

The man hammered a scroll to an information board just next to the tourney grounds. The bellman's spot to cry out the news was an overturned wooden crate, which was neatly tucked behind the board for tomorrow's use. Blaze skidded to a stop, frightening the man. Upon seeing the young thief, he huffed a discouraging sigh, then continued working on his task. Blaze breathlessly forced out his words,"What's today's news?" He smiled at the bellman and leaned nonchalantly against the wooden board's supports.

The bellman coughed and cleared his throat."No defecation in the fountains per order of the Lord Mayor. Uh, anyone caught selling without a permit will be fined. Uh," the bellman finished hammering the final nail."Just read it, lad. Or get someone else to read it. I'm going home." The bellman tossed his hammer into a leather satchel next to him then rubbed his throat. Blaze felt betrayed. The bellman always took the time for him. Why wasn't he now?

"But . . . news from the castles . . ." Blaze began again.

"I'm done. Go ask those folks." The bellman gestured toward an older group of people who stood nearby, clearly upset by the bellman's news. Blaze looked back at the bellman, who grabbed his tool bag and strutted away with determination not to be caught by another soul. He was too late. Blaze watched after him, his mouth gaping and brow furrowing, then turned his expression into a frown. He glanced in the direction of the elders, then glanced back at the board.

He searched for Dellanie, but she was nowhere to be seen. *She could have stayed a little while longer.* He sighed and glanced back up at the board.

He stared at the scroll. Letters leapt off the page, spinning with a randomness all their own. They floated above the parchment. He lifted his finger and held one down. He tried to identify it. As he did, it shook with fear until another letter ripped off the page and caught Blaze's attention. He released the letter, which danced away uselessly. He closed one eye. Some of the letters hid from him. Others frantically ran off the page, escaping his view, but they could only retreat so far. He blocked them from his vision with his hand. The crest of the Timerian monarchy came into view. This is the news from the capital, he assumed. He peered with all his strength of focus, removing his hand and hoping that the words would cooperate just this once. But they refused to abide by his wishes and they moved violently, jumping toward him and away. He turned from the parchment. It was no use. He glanced back at the group, which was growing in numbers, all a flutter with the news that he so desired to learn.

" . . . feel for the queen. So horrible!"

"Devastating. We should declare all-out war on them." Blaze watched while each person gave their own reactions. He felt an excitement rise in his belly, similar to the anticipation of the Festival. He listened but still gathered no real information. He entered the group, shaking his head in despair as he had witnessed others do.

"It's just too sad; and to think, she took him to her breast and she didn't know," a woman in a white apron remarked.

"Well, she has nannies to look after the lad; I imagine it'd be easy not to tell your own when you have others caring for him," another scholarly woman observed.

"And don't forget he survived the plague that took the life of the baby princess. So much death! May the Gods watch over them! May Solana help Queen Thalassa heal. May Cerenth guide His Highness."

"But to have the prince replaced by a changeling right under their royal noses and then to discover that the real prince died many years ago. Poor Queen Thalassa and King Kiril! They had a hard

time getting that one—it is up to the duke to provide the heir now."
Blaze's eyes widened finally learning the important news.

"Oh, who do you think it'll be? Beautiful and elegant Princess
Valorie, I'd say. Well, definitely not her vulgar sister, the years away
were not kind to that one at all! So wild!"

"Or maybe it'll go to the boys, Prince Tarn or sweet Prince
Derry."

"Oh, yes, it must go to Prince Derry. After all, he was the one to
reinforce Lord Ballard's dragon protection spell during yule. He is
such a magical prodigy!"

"Or it could be little Princess Lecksa, born in the prophecy time.
She is so cute with her button nose and auburn hair. I'd be okay
with either her, Prince Derry, or Princess Valorie."

"But it really is horrible about the king's son."

"Yeah, I know. May Marnie watch all the missing children
tonight."

The whole group dispersed leaving Blaze alone in the night.

Rhiun

Cerenth

Part Three
Realm of Light

Vassyr

CHAPTER 16

PIES AND THE FESTIVAL

THE SEASONS TURNED as oft they do. Blaze had spent a good part of the year standing in front of the entrance to the dungeon, yet his feet refused to move any bit farther. His heart raced and his mind screamed. His own failures or perhaps something from his early youth prevented his body from entering into the ruins. Blaze stood gazing at the entrance. An unholy noise resounded from inside the entrance, sending Blaze bolting from the place.

By the time Blaze had reached the markets, his fear had subsided. The markets were filled with patrons and Blaze grinned with delight. He strolled through the markets browsing, not at the wares on the stands, but at the purses attached to belts. The pouches seemed thin in most cases, but there were those that seemed to glow. Blaze felt the familiar tug on his soul to move closer. An uncontrollable urge to take one pouch in particular was overtaking him.

A richly dressed girl, presumably a noble, was darting in and out between the stalls. She moved gracefully between Blaze and the pouch, alerting the owner to look in Blaze's direction. Blaze quickly turned around, indifferent. He glanced at the girl and narrowed his eyes, disgusted at the loss of her pouch. He watched her. She acted strangely, smiling at people as she passed them. She spoke in a strange tongue and waved to people around her, blond curls loosely hanging around her radiant, blue eyes. He followed her for a while and watched as she tried to ask about a scarf. She pulled out her pouch and shrugged. The vendor pulled an ebon coin from her pouch and shoved the scarf in her arms. The girl wrapped the scarf around her neck, secured her pouch, and continued walking toward the pie stalls. Blaze kept vigil and walked two stalls behind her. Her hair bounced and glistened like the sun. He had never seen anyone's hair do that before. She gestured to a pair of patrons about their birch beer skin and they pointed to a stall. She nodded, then fluttered to Borintak's stall and bent over to pick up the pies that were within Littles' reach—Gavin's pies. Blaze effortlessly quickened his pace and reached the girl as she was poised to purchase her selection.

"Don't buy pies from him! He's rotten." Blaze glared at the seller, who was waiting on another patron. He grabbed the girl's arm. She blankly stared at Blaze, who repeated himself slower in Common. She shook her head and pulled away. Blaze motioned for her to follow him. She was surprised at herself that she did. She pulled away momentarily and attempted to replace the small pie that she had taken, but it fell on the ground. Blaze motioned to ignore it.

"It's probably poisoned anyway. Come on."

He led her gently by the elbow to Nerapi's pie stand. The pie seller was a large man with large hands. He had a cheery smile that reminded her of a jolly old soul. The boy motioned with both his hands and spoke slowly again."Good pies. Here. Eat."

She turned and glanced at the pies behind the seller. *Good*, he thought, *she's making a choice.* He left her behind in search of better pouches.

No pouches matched the one that the girl had on her belt. Night was beginning to unfold. He returned to the fountain and sat on its edge when he noticed that there were some stones that were different under him. Intrigued, hungry, and bored, Blaze straddled the fountain's base and began scraping away the mortar with his knife. *Maybe there was something buried there,* he thought; *maybe there was some treasure.*

Metal against rock scraped in loud, echoing dissonance. He worked diligently on the task until he had removed the mortar from around one side of the stone. He peered into the hole that he had made. He could see something—anything would be worth continuing the task. He started working a little harder when a shadow moved behind him. He jumped, startled to see her. He looked around at the buildings nervously.

"You shouldn't be here!" he said frantically, hoping the girl would understand this time. She just stood there dumbfounded while smiling and nodding her head and speaking in a tongue he didn't understand. *By Eldon's crown*, Blaze thought, *she's beautiful enough to be a goddess; but a goddess would be able to understand Common.* He checked to see if anyone was nearby, and they weren't. He knew the darkness would come for her. He grabbed her by her arm again and hurried her down the street before anyone else could sense her. He brought her right into the guild.

The door opened and he entered dragging the girl. The girl tripped on her way into the guild, falling into Blaze, who caught her. The door swung closed. Blaze glanced around and noticed that the guild was full. The closing door drew the other thieves' attention. Whistles, laughter, and catcalls resonated throughout the room. The girl regained her footing and stood, trying to shrink into the woodwork. Blaze held her arm still. She smiled nervously.

"Hello, I'm Goldenrod, but you can call me, Goldie. I'm from Mahdurna." She waved. Her words in Mahdurnian were garbled noise to the band of children, who took a quick interest and moved in closer, pawing at her clothes. A toddler pulled on her dress. Blaze held her closer.

"Ooh, pretty," the little girl said as she rubbed the fabric.

"Hey, Blaze! You're not supposed to bring everything *with* the pouch!" a voice taunted from the circle.

"Well, that would be the only way *he* could actually get a pouch without losing his fingers!" another voice taunted.

"Yeah, he doesn't have many left so he's got to hold on to what he's got!" the first voice retorted. Laughter erupted in agreement. Nightshade sauntered up to the front, pulling Goldenrod from Blaze's grasp.

"It's okay, Miss. No one is going to hurt you. Come in and meet all of Blaze's friends. This is Nohan2—we call him that because he doesn't have a hand, see?" Nightshade grabbed Nohan's arm and shoved it into Goldenrod's face. Goldenrod shrunk away.

"Leave her alone, Nightshade! She's scared out of her wits. Give her back to Blaze to take her home." Nightshade ignored Nohan and continued on her trek around the guild. Nohan's eyes scolded Blaze for bringing the girl here.

"Here, you can sit here," Nightshade said as she led her to the dining table. The circle of children had turned, following the girl who couldn't speak in their language and keeping Blaze from getting closer. Nightshade untied Goldenrod's cloak, handing it to someone behind her. "You look tired—take off your belt."

Nightshade slid her knife under Goldenrod's belt, but Goldenrod held onto it tightly, preventing Nightshade from taking her pouch and eating knife. She gave Nightshade a knowing smirk while holding tight to her belongings.

"Okay, I get it. This is like my high school. You're trying to intimidate me. You must be the mean girl and I guess he's the jock. You, my pie friend, are trying to set me up. I thought you were nice," Goldenrod said in Mahdurnian. Still, no one understood her. A much older man approached the table. His gray beard distinguished him as many years older than the teenagers who flocked around Goldenrod. He sat down across from her. He raised his arm and pointed his finger at her.

"Don't worry. I do understand Techniumian and it's close to Mahdurnian," the man said. Goldenrod looked surprised and happy to be understood by someone, even a stranger. "They don't understand it—any of it. The girl who is sitting next to you is Bella Donna. Their names don't translate. The jock, as you so quaintly put it, is Poison Dripping. The one, your pie friend, who brought you here, is Fire Raging. Do you know where you are? You are in our guild. I guess you can think of it as a frat house that you never really outgrow. What's your name?"

"My name is Goldenrod. The boy, Fire Raging, was it? He helped me get a pastry. I got a little bit lost, and he dragged me in here. I was looking for the inn; I think it is called Two Kingdoms or something like that?"

"Two Realms Inn. You are completely off course. I have known these people for many years. You must be wary of these folks, Goldenrod. Fire Raging and Bella Donna are dangerous people. Poison Dripping . . . well, we haven't quite figured him out yet, but he and Bella Donna have a relationship. There are others here that you can't trust, including yours truly. Some of us will sell you down the river as easily as stealing a sweet pie."

"Hey everybody, look what we captured!"

Some of the surrounding thieves looked back at Dorken and Pip as they entered the guild, but returned their gaze to the girl. Dorken and Pip held a brown sack away from their bodies. Blaze didn't dare back away or even turn away from Goldenrod. He was unsure of what his guildmates were going to do and he had an uncharacteristic urge to protect her.

"What is your name, sir?" Goldenrod asked the older man, narrowing her eyes.

"My name is unimportant, but at one time, I was age mates with the young ones who surround you." Goldenrod was taken aback. He was nearly three times the age of the teenagers.

"I don't understand. Why? How?"

"I'm mostly human—more mortal than the ones here. These others are Timerian, the country that you are in. They are a mix of many races."

"Hey, Pigeon!" Dorken called across the room.

"Leave me alone, Dorken. I'm not interested in your troubles today," the Techniumian man responded in Common. Goldenrod looked confused. Dorken was examining the bag that Pip had in his hands. A portion of the outside of the bag encased Pip's finger.

"Hurry up! Dorken, I think it just broke my finger," Pip said, somewhat desperately.

"Don't worry, Pip, I've got this . . . Pigeon, take a look at what we found just outside. A bird! I think it's some kind of hawk. We startled it with a stone—hit its little head. Dead-on aim! It'd make you a nice snack. We know you like hawk meat. Personally, Pip and I think it's too tough, but it's a Techniumian thing, right?" Pigeon waved two fingers for Dorken and Pip to approach him. "Here, take a look." Pip gave the bag to Pigeon just as the creature released Pip's finger. Pip examined his finger, which had a strong red ring around it, and he rubbed it carefully to soothe the skin. Pigeon opened the bag, and the hawk popped out its head.

"Hey! Give him to me!" Goldenrod said in Mahdurnian, pulling the bag out of Pigeon's hands. Pigeon clearly understood the sentiment, if not the words. "That's my friend Keir. He helps me. He's a bird sprite." Goldenrod looked at Keir with concern. Keir turned his head, evaluating the danger that sat next to Goldenrod. He squawked and expanded his wings, escaping the sack. He flew upwards and perched on a rafter. He shook off the stoned daze and suddenly had complete clarity. His eyes took in the sight of the one who brought his friend Goldenrod into this danger. He jumped off the rafter and took flight, aiming right at Blaze. Blaze protected his head. The bird missed and recalculated his next attack with precise reflexes and turns. "No, Keir! Stop! Don't hurt him!"

At once, all of the guild members jumped up to grab ahold of Keir, but his small bird form eluded capture. Dorken picked up his slingshot and shot at the bird with a small stone. It missed Keir completely, hitting a Little instead. The Little was confused for a minute, then continued her own pursuit of the bird. She picked up the stone and threw it back at the bird. Keir, attempting to dodge many stones as everyone now worked to capture him, misjudged his movements and was hit by a flying belt knife. A small abrasion made him take a reprieve in the rafters again. Hiding for a moment, he rested just enough to heal himself from the wound. The noise below was disturbing. Benches were being stacked on top of the table to try and reach the small creature. Goldenrod pleaded with everyone to stop and leave him alone, that he was only protecting her and would not hurt anyone. Venom pushed Goldenrod out of the way as he started to climb the makeshift structure.

Keir took flight again. He returned for another attack, flying around Venom, who stood awkwardly on top of the benches. Venom lost his footing and fell, knocking into Nightshade with his body and the uppermost bench. Keir extended his talons. He wasn't going to let anything happen to Goldenrod. He headed again for Blaze. He grabbed Blaze's shoulder and ripped the boy's tunic. Keir turned to see Nightshade heading for Goldenrod with her dagger drawn.

"I'll get it to stop!" Nightshade exclaimed as she lunged at Goldenrod, but Blaze pulled the Mahdurnian girl out of harm's way. Blaze told Goldenrod to run and pointed for a side door, which had been Jade's room when he was an infant. It was now a room for storage and it locked from inside. Goldenrod would be safe there until he could get her out of the guild unseen. Blaze pulled Goldenrod closer to the door but Nightshade repositioned herself for her next attack. Blaze jumped in front of Nightshade and disarmed her by grabbing the blade of her knife—a trick he had practiced with Dellanie for years. Keir returned his gaze to the girl thief, but his true quarry was Blaze. Blaze glimpsed Goldenrod running out the side door. He screamed, "No!" as the bird attacked him, talons drawn, and scraped his chest to make bloodied wounds. He batted the stupid bird away.

Someone jumped up and tried to grab the bird. Keir grabbed his hair and he batted the bird away again. The bird carried a clump of black hair off in his talons, dropping the hair to the floor just as he rounded back to attack again. The children threw things at the bird, knocking him down once or twice. He regained his senses and flew upwards to the highest windows in the guild. He rested for a moment.

"Dinner! Let's roast it!"

"Knock it into the fire!"

"Hit it with a broom!"

"Grab a knife from the chest! Carve it up!" excited voices yelled.

The bird flew around again, readying himself for another attack. Daggers, knives, belts, and pouches all flew into the air. Blaze found his own escape and quickly ran toward the dark temple, surmising that the girl wouldn't have gotten much farther than a foot out of the guild before the priestess approached her.

"Wait!" Blaze yelled as he noticed Goldenrod talking to one of the dark priestesses.

The priestess wore white robes and was significantly taller than Goldenrod. The woman noticed the boy running at full speed toward them, followed swiftly by the small hawk. With a wave of her arm, she and Goldenrod were gone. Blaze screeched to a halt and Keir transformed to human right in front of him. Keir turned with his dagger drawn, confronting Blaze.

"Way to go, *Bi–ird*!" Blaze drew out the word, turning the sound into a long 'u'. He stopped, unaffected by Keir's stance. "Look what you did!"

"It's your fault, *Thief*! You put her in danger."

"Right, like *I* came in the guild screeching and flying around like uncooked food. I'm going to save her!"

"No, *I'm* going to save her, *Thief*."

"Get out of my way, *Burd*!"

"I'm not stopping you, *Thief*!"

The girl was more trouble than she was worth, having been taken into the Dark Temple by the priestess. There was no thinking in this matter. Blaze drew his dagger and sprinted toward the entrance. *No*, he thought, *it would be stupid to go in and face a direct attack*. It could get him captured too. He stopped for a moment, walking in a circle to ease the internal desire to rush directly into the heart of the temple. Blaze was not a thinker and he believed that he was stupid in most things, but getting in and out of the temple would require all of his sense and all the good judgment that he could muster. He interrogated himself: what did he know?

He knew that the constabulary looked away from matters involving the temples. He knew that Goldenrod was valuable to them in her naïve innocence. He knew that Jade was somehow responsible; after all, it was her temple. He glanced at his arm, the ringed scar becoming painful as his thoughts drifted to the many times he had had run-ins with the temple, with and without Jade.

He knew he would have to enter the temple, and he prayed to Eldon that he would go undetected. Blaze tucked his dagger away into his belt. He scrutinized the lower windows of the temple. Above him, there were large stained-glass windows depicting the Goddess murdering her parents in the name of the dark. He crouched to find the latch. No picking tools needed here—he had opened it once before. He dug into the frame. Realizing his fingers had grown considerably, he grabbed his dagger and made an opening just larger than his left index finger. He inserted his finger and swung the metal latch open. He gently swung the glass forward, allowing him to easily slip down onto the wet stone floor. Once in, there was no time for thinking—he'd act on instinct alone.

His boots slipped underneath him, but he kept his balance. Water flowed down the hallway. He knew approximately where he was in the temple. The refuse was nearby; the smell filled his nose. He covered his nose with the neck of his tunic, wishing for the linen face mask he had worn at the castle. He hoped the temple's incense would conceal any stench that he attracted. Sneaking through the hallway, he heard voices up ahead.

Blaze hid behind a statue of Lady Mykondra. He wished with all his might that the statue was just a replication in stone of the being he had once seen come alive as he witnessed his father's demise. The statue was beautiful and enticing. Her beauty lured her followers to their death. It was said that the Lady herself tested the Dark Priestesses. Blaze glanced around the statue.

In the rotunda, just ahead of him, there were three robed figures. Blaze knew they were all female because Jade had told him that there were no male priests. She was still striving to become a priestess officially in Cadmaria. She had tried for many years in

Ballardton, but to no avail. She had tried to cut off Blaze's arm in infancy and even sacrificed Rhatt. There were more attempts of which Blaze was ignorant.

One of the figures stepped into the light. Blaze watched the woman intently. He could sense her urgency. Her white robe rustled with each movement of her arms and head. Her immense hood disguised her identity. A light caught his eye as it illuminated the gemstone on her ring. Blaze recognized that jewel as one with which the priestess hypnotized would-be followers.

He knew that he should follow this trio if he had wanted to discover the girl's whereabouts. Blaze huddled back down behind the statue concealing himself. He waited for the sound of footsteps, footsteps that he would mimic to eliminate any suspicion that they were being stalked. Music echoed through the temple, and with its arrival the trio moved swiftly down the hallway to the right. Something was happening, and Blaze hoped that it wasn't a sacrifice to the Goddess.

Blaze kept to the walls, staying hidden in the shadows. When the trio hesitated, Blaze hesitated; when they walked on, so did he. As he passed walls, he noticed openings and mapped their whereabouts in his head. He moved his hands over one of the openings. He curled his fingers around an edge of stone. He heard the trio moving ahead of him. The stone silently slid aside, revealing a stone staircase. The music was louder through the opening. He knew that the trio would be attending and presiding over the altar. The altar, he knew, would be near music. He changed his direction and entered the staircase.

As he left the hallway, the stone returned to its original placement, concealing Blaze. The staircase was dark, but dry. Darkness encased him. Blaze nimbly ascended the stairs, taking quick, quiet strides. The stairway turned to present a crossway. Blaze walked into the left stairwell and stood listening for the music. He thought for a moment that it was growing louder, only to discover that the music sank into silence. He turned back to the crossway, taking the other route.

The music began to play faster. Blaze knew that this indicated that the service would soon start. He sprinted until the music became too overpowering to continue. His ears hurt. He wondered where the bird was. *He probably started from the top*, Blaze reasoned. *It doesn't matter*, Blaze thought as he peered through another opening. *I'm only counting on myself.* From his boot, he selected a different dagger, a foot-long blade with an obsidian hilt that was sharp as a surgeon's instrument. *Dellanie won't miss it,* he mused, a grin curling his lips with pride that he had been able to steal it from her.

From his vantage point, he could see the priestess moving across the room. Sitting in pews, the followers sat entranced, chanting incoherently. Blaze wondered if they knew what was transpiring. He poked his head through and noticed the white priestess standing at the altar. He knew who she was. Her name is Elanit, and she was high priestess of this temple. Blaze had seen her his whole life. When he saw her in the streets, Blaze hid from her always. She addressed the congregation, her arms outspread. Her followers mimicked her words. Blaze snuck out into the aisle. The light from the red and black candles flickered, casting blind spots that hid his position. He moved into an empty pew and crawled along the kneeler, carefully avoiding his dagger's blade. Halfway across the pew, he heard everyone rise to their feet. He glanced over the wooden rail and saw that Elanit had begun to invoke powers to a ceremonial knife. Blaze's eyes widened as he realized the knife's importance. It was a dragon-shard knife that contained an enormous power, which pulled Blaze's soul to it.

Blaze could hear his father's voice in his head: *It is believed, Blazey, that a dragon-shard knife will capture the souls of its victims held there with its pommel. This is one reason why our Goddess is all-powerful.* Blaze stared at the knife. He wanted it, even though he knew the dark Lady Mereen would have cursed it. It could easily slice through enchanted steel. Made from a rogue dragon's scale that had broken in a duel, magic could not dull its edge and only a God could destroy it. The blade was made from a Dust Dragon's scale, which are loyal only to the Dark Goddess. The pommel was made from the claw of a Mist Dragon that was killed by the same Dust Dragon whose scale made the blade. Once assembled, the claw was soaked in slugslime venom to disable its natural light properties. Blaze moved along to the far end of the pew. His heart, pounding in his ears, deafened him.

"Followers of Mykondra, may you see Her power is good and just as she destroyed the evil ways of her parents, allowing her to become our Queen in her own right! We follow you, Most Powerful One. As an act of your great power, Lady, we beseech you to give

us your wisdom, as we come forward to claim your mark." Elanit
gestured for the congregation to come forward. The people walked
in line up to the altar.

Blaze's eyes widened in disgust that these people would willingly
offer themselves to Queen Mykondra. Each parishioner carried a
physical offering for the Goddess in one hand. Their other hand
was held palm side outward as they stood waiting their turn. The
dead-eyed line leader approached the High Priestess. Elanit stood
stoically and slashed his hand with the dragon-shard knife. She
motioned for a priestess to remove the offering. Elanit also summoned another priestess to her side who collected the blood from
the wound. Blaze watched as Elanit continued through the whole
line in the same manner as the first. Once completed, Elanit walked
to the statue of Lady Mykondra and offered the bowl of her followers' blood. Elanit bowed and blessed it in Her name.

The blood boiled, producing bubbles that floated up to the statue,
the red orbs landing at its mouth. After devouring the bloody orbs,
the mouth licked its lips, smiled, and returned to stone. Blaze was
so mesmerized that he never noticed a set of clear, blue eyes sitting
above the mouth, which stared at him hungrily—eyes he had never
gazed upon, eyes that could see a glowing, visible scar on his arm
that indicated that he belong to Her.

"In Her name, I bless you. In Her name, I give you the power to
carry out Her decree. Oh, Queen, we follow you to the darkest ends
of Mirias with your trusted and loyal companions: Lady Mereen
and Lord Adoon. Lady Mereen, who is forever at your side, wielding the sword of the righteous and Lord Adoon, who attends to
your will through his crux of tribulation. We follow you!"

"We follow you!"

"We follow you. We follow you as you take the necessary path
to eliminate your foes and bear our rights against the Twins and
what they take from your realm as they try to destroy and collect
the souls of your flock. We bear witness as we convert one of theirs
to your enlightenment. Bring him forward!" Blaze pulled back
fearfully. Noise from the congregation made him turn his head as
robed figures dragged a barely conscious merchant forward. His
head drooped; he had clearly been beaten. Blaze gasped inaudibly
as they passed by him. They forced the man to drop to his knees in
front of Elanit. He mumbled incoherently to the Twins of Light to

protect him. The congregation began an incantation to invoke the Goddess. Elanit yelled above their spell.

"Turn him, Beloved Queen, to trust and see the right of your ways. Allow him to help in preaching your word through his daily work. I beseech you to help his soul and heart see the Twins for what they truly are! My Queen, afflict him now!" A white light erupted from the altar, blinding Blaze as it enveloped the room. Blaze covered his face in an effort to protect himself.

The light subsided and the merchant stood. He cried out, "I see! I follow Her and I understand Her beauty." He turned toward the congregation. His eyes were dead of emotion. His face was blanched. Those who had dragged him to the altar welcomed him into their fold. He hugged each of them and professed his love for the Lady and his newfound hatred for the Twins of Light, Cerenth and Rhiun. The congregation cheered and clapped when the merchant greeted them with handshakes and hugs.

"Finally, I ask you. Do you find yourself within Her embrace?" Elanit moved closer to the pews, arms outstretched in blessing.

"We do!"

"Then go forth into Mirias and spread Her good word through your acts and life. May the Queen forever have you in Her palm!"

The congregation emptied out of the room, seemingly normal in their affairs as they socialized with each other. Blaze waited until the room was still before he stealthily crossed the room. He moved up the stairs to the chancel. The lush carpeting reminded him of Lords and Ladies. He crept alongside the altar. Blood smeared the table. He wondered how many had been sacrificed here. He knew that the girl's fate was grimly close. He slid into the apse and a tiny, locked door caught his eye. The door was no bigger than eight inches by five inches. He glanced around and pulled out his kit. He removed his left glove and tucked it into his belt. Sand that gave his gloves weight and the illusion of fingers spilled out onto the floor. His presence would be known. He spread it out on the rug with the toe of his boot. Blaze listened intently for a telltale click that signified the lock's release.

The door gently opened slightly. Blaze pulled on it, opening it wider. Inside was a box, a holy item, he assumed. The box was adorned with gold leaf and the image of two upside-down shields and Mykondra's mark etched into its lid identified it as belonging to the Dark Queen. Blaze frowned—nobody would buy or touch such a thing outside of the temple. He lifted the cover to reveal a fully articulated arm and hand, the humerus severed clean through at the same spot that Blaze's arm wore a scar. Only this baby hadn't been so lucky. Blaze suddenly felt a deep bone-chilling pain in his arm. He dropped the box. The arm bones bounced out, sounding like sticks clacking together. The box rested underneath the altar and cloth. He went to reach for it, but his body hesitated. As he began to reach under the altar cloth, a strong stench of fountain filth and rodent decay halted his journey; he recoiled from the altar, leaving it undisturbed.

Blaze returned his attention to the little compartment. Its depth was deceiving. The cavity stretched back to Blaze's full reach. At the back, Blaze's bare fingers touched cold metal. He grabbed the hoard, pulling it toward him. As his hand emerged from the compartment, he was shocked at the handful of gold jewelry now in his possession. The offerings, Blaze realized. The followers had offered up their most valuable possessions. *For what?* he wondered. Blaze worried about holding the jewelry. He couldn't remember if they had blessed the offerings. If they had, he was already dead. He took a moment considering what he should do. *The girl!* He'd almost forgotten about her. He stuck a couple necklaces into his pouch and threw the rest back into the compartment. He hurried now. *Stupid, Blazey! How could I forget?*

From the altar, he grabbed his kit, tying it underneath his tunic. The compartment door swung open and he attempted to close it, but to no avail. He now realized that he didn't have time for all the details needed to hide his crime. How could he have gotten so caught up in this that he forgot that the girl was in peril. *Ugh! It's no wonder Master never sent me on any missions! I completely forgot the reason for being here! I'm so stupid!* He ripped his glove from his belt and replaced it on his hand. The unstuffed fingers flopped uselessly.

Blaze crept through the back of the apse, following a corridor that opened to a small sanctuary, and once there looked up at the windowsill. Sitting perched and watching the ongoings was a small, forest hawk, waiting for his moment to attack. Blaze realized immediately that it was Keir, Goldenrod's bird-sprite. Down below, surrounded by stadium-style seating, was a small stage. Sitting in an enormous throne with her arms tied with blood-soaked and blessed ligatures, Goldenrod sat motionless. *Is she dead?* Blaze wondered, but then he realized had she been dead, Kier would have already been attacking. *No, she's spelled, I think.*

Keir caught Blaze's eye. They'd have to do a synchronized attack. Blaze glanced back at the stage. There were maybe three robed figures. Elanit hadn't yet taken her turn at the girl. The two of them, Keir and Blaze, just had to overtake the three people, who seemed to be of smaller statures. Blaze looked back to Keir. He pointed at the two people who were standing on the ground, possibly appointed as sentries, and then he pointed to himself. He pointed at Keir and then at the person standing over Goldenrod. Keir nodded. Blaze counted them off: *one, two, three!*

Blaze ran, storming out in plain view and screaming loudly at the sentries with his blade drawn. They immediately prepared for the attack. Blaze ran, skipping stairs as he did. From underneath their robes, the sentries pulled out daggers. As Blaze reached the bottom stair, Keir took flight.

Keir flew straight at the sentinel near Goldenrod, his talons poised to land. The razor-sharp blades reached their target as he landed in the robed woman's face. She grabbed him, but he held on, ripping into her flesh. Blood poured down her face, reddening her pristine robes. She grabbed Keir and began to choke the little hawk. Keir let go and flew swiftly out of her reach, shrieking in anger.

Blaze fought off the two sentries. They lay bleeding on the floor. There was no time for mercy. Keir's screeching and his own screaming would surely call the others to the room. Regaining his stance, he hopped onto the stage. He looked to the ceiling for the bird, but he didn't see him. Not waiting for Keir's assistance, he ran to Goldenrod. He tried to revive her; she groggily roused to consciousness. Keir landed next him, his transformation having occurred in midair. The boy who now stood next to Blaze started working hard with his own dagger on the ligatures. Blaze worked the right and Keir the left.

"I know a way out of here, Burd. There's a back way." Blaze cut through the ligature, replaced his dagger in his boot, and gently touched Goldenrod's cheek. The second ligature gave way with a snap of the band. "Goldie, are you all right?"

"Hm?" was Goldenrod's soft reply.

Blaze picked her up and carried her over his shoulder. He stumbled for a moment, readjusted her position, and started to run to the back of the stadium.

Keir ran behind him, but quickly caught up.

"If she gets too heavy, Thief, I can carry her."

"Shut your beak, *Burd*."

"I was just trying to help."

"Keeping quiet would be the best help." Keir stopped reaching out to Blaze. Blaze stopped again, readjusted Goldenrod's weight, and carried her nonstop through the tunnel. Keir transformed back into his bird form and led the way.

"Follow me to Two Realms Inn; she'll be safe with the Drisanian prince. I will alert my brother, Kyreek. He's on guard now." Blaze nodded. The two began to travel into the woods. Blaze sprinted around trees and over brush. Bindweed caught his legs, but he worked his way slowly out of it after nearly tripping and losing his teetering balance. Following Keir was difficult as the bird swooped in and out of the trees: he found the easiest path for himself from his lofty perspective, but there is a difference for earthbound creatures, and Blaze ran through raspberry thickets. The thorns tore his clothes and trapped him for what seemed an eternity. He struggled to free himself, nearly dropping Goldenrod.

As Blaze struggled to trudge through the forest, Keir went ahead to alert his brother, Kyreek, who was flying sentry around Two Realms Inn. Kyreek was a cooperi hawk-sprite. In sprite form, Kyreek squawked out an alert to the Drisanian prince to follow Keir back to Goldenrod. The alert was immediately recognized, and Prince Delrik opened a window on the second floor. He caught Kyreek on his arm and the hawk-sprite relayed the news of the alarm. Keir, satisfied that the prince would soon arrive, took flight again retracing his path.

"Where is that *stupid Burd*?" Blaze looked to the sky: *nothing*. He knew he didn't need Keir. His shoulders started to ache under Goldenrod's weight. They had crossed many types of plants and thorns throughout their trek. The sticks that slapped them were brutal enough, but when they ran straight into nettles after losing sight of Keir, Blaze cursed the bird for not being there. Blaze stopped, placing Goldenrod down gently against a rock with her head resting on his shoulder. "We can do this. I know we can. I hope they're not following us. Damn, my skin burns." If he had only carried her for a short stint, it would have been very easy, but the distance he was going was torture to his muscles. He worried that he wouldn't make it to the inn. He thought he should go somewhere closer. Marnie's gardens and Solana's temples were close by. All he had to do was follow the tree line. With his newly selected destination, Blaze felt a renewed strength to carry on.

Keir flew as fast as his wings could carry him. He circled back around toward the dark temple. He had to make sure that Blaze and Goldenrod were not being followed. He kept his distance, but to his dismay, the temple had started to make chase. Blaze had continued following a straight trail through the brush, and his path was trampled, making it easy to follow him. Keir thought that he might have to teach the thief ways to disguise one's trail, but of course that would be for a later time. Keir flew faster to alert the thief of his assailants.

As Blaze reached the end of the forest, he was met by a cow chewing on grass. It stared at him for a long while as Blaze twisted and turned to avoid the dung landmines, which were scattered around the farmland. After finding a clearing with some clean grass, Blaze rested. He looked to the sky. The sun was setting. The moons would start to rise and if memory served him, Luminessa was in its dark moon phase. No light to start, just a darkened shadow until the next moon showed its face.

"Goldie, are you okay? Are you thirsty?" He pulled out a water skin from his belt and, gently holding her head, poured the sweet liquid onto her dry lips. She barely moved. He pulled her close to him and noticed that she would need a healing. *I have to get her to Solana's temple quickly.* He took a quick swig from the skin and gently raised Goldenrod back over his shoulders. A high-pitched screech alerted Blaze's attention to the sky. The call continued again. *Burd? Why is he circling?*

The assailants emerged from the woods. Blaze could see them just below Keir's circle. He dashed across the plains, forgetting about the cow's excrement. Keir caught up to him. Keir flew parallel to Blaze, and the three continued their course.

"They're gaining on us, *Burd*! Solana's temple isn't that much farther. She needs a healing and sanctuary."

"You can do this. Go to Two Realms Inn, *Thief*. Her family is there! She'll be safe and her aunt is a healer." Blaze stared at the bird, wondering just how far Keir thought he could carry the girl without losing his stamina.

"Okay, but I don't know if I can outrun them. The darkness always follows me."

Keir didn't hear the last part as he flew off to attack. Screams carried across the field as Keir made contact. The bird screeched and called to Kyreek, telling him of the change of plan. Kyreek returned the call, notifying Keir of his acknowledgement of the message.

Blaze jostled Goldenrod as he ran; she started to rise. Her mind was regaining clarity.

"Fire Raging, what's going on? Put me down!" She spoke in Mahdurnian. She struggled to get down, but Blaze held fast to her. He rounded Marnie's garden and turned onto the side road. It was less rough that way and he could make up time and distance. He could see the inn just across King's Highway. His muscles screamed in agony, but he carried on. Blaze scampered across the highway, dodging carts and hooves.

"Damn children, get out of the way!"

Upon reaching the inn, Blaze was met by an older boy who looked very much like Keir, although he was much closer to adulthood. The boy's clothes were similar to Telmarn's. The boy cleared his throat. *This must be Burd's brother, whatever his name is.* He ran to meet Blaze and take Goldenrod to safety before the prince's arrival.

"For lack of a better name, I will call you *Thief*." Breathing hard and weak-kneed, Blaze nodded his approval. "My name is Kyreek. I am a member of the Drisana Border Patrol, and I will help Lady Goldenrod now. We can protect her. Her aunt is on her way; she is a magical healer—one of the best, actually. Drisana owes you a debt of gratitude, sir. Thank you on behalf of Delrik, Crowned Prince of Drisana."

Blaze passed the girl to Kyreek, who carried her in his arms.

"Okay. Um, keep her safe, okay?"

Kyreek nodded, giving Blaze permission to run off and seek refuge in Eldon's temple, which was just a short distance further.

The moons rose and fell in the sky five times while Blaze sat along the side of the road waiting to catch sight again of the girl. He knew he couldn't see Goldenrod again, but she was all that kept his thoughts. He walked about the camps, unaware that he was even searching for anything, until he saw the familiar Pyrrin scarves announcing Hende-Li's return. Blaze ran full throttle to her tent. He could smell the familiar scent of her cooking and the Pyrrin perfume that was caught in the wind. Just outside of her tent, he stopped, causing dust to waft up. Hende-Li exited her tent, and when she saw him, she wrapped him in a large bear hug. He accepted her affection, and then she walked him around to show him off to her companions.

"This is my little brother. My little brother! Oh, how I have missed you!" She held him again, protecting him against all of the injustices in the world. He smiled, genuinely happy to be with Hende-Li. She showed him more respect than anyone else, and he was honored to be able to call her family. He blushed as she showed him off to her neighboring campers. When they returned to her tent, she turned him to face her. He was humbled by her affection. "Now, let me see how much you have grown! Little Brother, you have grown into a handsome young man. Yes, sir. No doubt about that! The Holy Ones did bless us with good looks, didn't they?" She leaned into him and they gazed into a mirror mounted on a post. "These two are something else." She did a little dance and Blaze tried to copy her moves. They were laughing, clapping and dancing the whole time. Hende-Li even taught him a Pyrrin dance. "You're a natural, Blaze!" They frolicked together for close to an hour.

"Hende-Li, I love how I can be so free with you!" He stopped, exhausted, yet content.

She breathed heavily from dancing hard and laughing with him.

"That is because you are with family, Little Brother. You can be who you are when you are with family. No one judges you. We just love you." Hende-Li sat down on cushions that encircled the cook fire. Everything was Pyrrin style. Bright-colored silk scarves and large brocade floral cushions that were more comfortable than the beds at Lords and Ladies were scattered on the floor, filling Hende-Li's space with colors, joy, and excitement.

"Oh no! Oh no!" Hende-Li hastily pulled the meat off of the cook fire. "Look at that, I've gone and burnt the meat!" Blaze peered at the meat; it was charred, but definitely still edible.

"No, you haven't, Big Sis." She glanced over at him, smiling with pride. "You just need a sauce to cover that up. When I worked at Ceretheena Castle, the cook would sometimes have us younger staffers help out with cooking, and I did just what you did. Cook put the meat in a sauce, and no one noticed." She agreed, and using a long-handled fork, she dropped the meat into the au jus that was simmering at the edge of the fire.

"Smart thinking, Blaze." He liked that she called him smart. "I didn't know that you worked at the duke's castle. I just rode by about a week and a half ago. I couldn't believe that it was alive with jubilation." Hende-Li scooped some green silky leaves from a dutch oven that was to the side of the pot of au jus and then placed the meat on top, plating it all on etched, burnished-copper plates. She handed it to Blaze with a fork.

"Ceretheena is active again because the duke and duchess have returned. Oh, I don't need a fork, I have my eating knife." She smirked a knowing smile at him. She plated her own food and then poured the rest of the au jus dividing it between their plates.

"Now don't you worry about your eating knife, this is not mutton. The meat will be extra tender, and it will be what our dear God, King Eldon, is eating tonight with his queen, Goddess Solana. Mm-hm. The Gods know that life is best served spicy."

He pierced the meat with the fork and brought it to his lips. It was spicy, sweet, and juicy. Nothing he had ever eaten could compare to Hende-Li's cooking.

"So tell me Little Brother, what engages you now?"

"Mm, this is really good." He looked up from his plate. He finished chewing and swallowed the whole mouthful quickly. "Well, I have been helping this girl who is from another place."

"Another place?" Hende-Li was well traveled and had seen most places in the world, so this fact piqued her interest. "Where is she from?"

Blaze stopped eating and glanced up at Hende-Li.

"Oh, she's from Mahdurna." He waited to see her reaction, as the word seemed to strike fear into many.

"It's a lovely place. The people are unique, their language difficult, and their transportation odd; but different is sometimes a welcome change." He sat back on the cushion and dreamily thought about Goldenrod. "Does this girl have a name?" Hende-Li could see the difference in his demeanor. He was wistful, enchanted, and blissfully spellbound. *His first love. How sweet and endearing.*

"Yes, her name is Lady Goldenrod, her family is from Drisana, but she's actually from Mahdurna." He glanced sideways at Hende-Li, checking to see if she was still listening. She nodded confirming her interest.

"I think she sounds beautiful and may be worthy of knowing

you." He blushed from her comment, then finished the last bite of his meal. This included the greens at the bottom, which he wasn't really keen on eating but did anyway because Hende-Li was so kind to share her food with him, and the least he could do was eat it all. She handed him her plate. "You know where those go."

"Yes, Big Sis. I can wash them."

She smiled, and while he washed the dishes in the kettle drum by the fire, she dried them. When all was washed, dried and put away for the next meal, she invited him to stay as long as he wished. "I'd like that, Hende-Li, but I will have to go back to the guild house now and again."

"Yes, I understand, but do not be a stranger here. This is also your home. So . . . please tell me more about your Goldenrod."

Long into the evening, Blaze spoke of Goldenrod and everything that had happened, the first being her visit at the guild. He spoke of how he wished he hadn't ever taken her there because the others treated her cruelly. Then he went on to tell the tale of the most recent event in the temple. Hende-Li was worried for him, as to enter the temple could be seen as an unholy move and would give attention to both him and Burd, as Blaze so sweetly called the bird-sprite. When he finally fell asleep, Hende-Li prayed over him, asking many different Gods to watch over him and hear her plea to keep him safe. She prayed to Solana, the mother of all mothers; to Wyssa, for her healing assistance; to Hala to keep him from death; to the Twin Gods, Rhiun and Cerenth, for their wisdom, spirit, and magical keeping. She felt the warmth of the spirit upon them, and she settled in for the night.

In the morning, Blaze woke after Hende-Li and they ate breakfast together. She lit incense and sprayed perfume to honor the gods. She cooked with the spices she brought with her from around the world, although she preferred Pyrrin ones most of all. This morning she served up a tasty egg scramble. Blaze was taken aback at the heat from the spices. He was not used to such flavors, but he was enjoying Hende-Li's food—spices and all. Hende-Li hurried the boy along so that he could go out and find the young lady. She knew that he was eager to see the girl, even though he had sworn off seeing her ever again. Hende-Li reminded him that he probably should make sure she was okay and see if he could find her. She knew that the First Ball was approaching and a newcomer like Goldenrod would not want to miss such an event.

"Head to the markets, Little Brother. I would be surprised if you do not see her there."

"But Hende-Li, I don't know if I want to see her. I completely failed between bringing her to the guild, and then letting her be taken to the temple where she was nearly killed," Blaze said, worried. Hende-Li smiled, remembering her own first love and how special that first one can be. Actually, she had married this love, but he stayed in Pyrrin and was content to let her wander as she needed.

"Bring home all those brothers and sisters, Li. I'll feed them all," her husband always told her before she began her travels. One day, she knew she would bring little brother home with her.

"Now don't you go worrying about any of that, Little Blaze," she said to her friend. "I'm sure she appreciated you getting her out of that terrible place. Go on now. Scat! I'll see you soon." He did as she said, but not before hugging her again.

Blaze left Hende-Li's tent with a full belly and the Pyrrin song that Hende-Li was humming while preparing breakfast stuck in his head. He went to the market as instructed and was strolling through the stands when he caught sight of Dellanie peering at a Drisanian toy. Blaze sauntered up and leaned in to look at the toy as well. Dellanie glanced at him.

"You smell funny. What happened to not smelling like anything?"

Blaze grinned and sniffed his tunic. The fragrance of Hende-Li's perfume and spices were infused into his clothes.

"I know. I ate well."

"I see."

"Why are you just staring at this?"

"It moved when I started by it earlier. I want to see it move again." Her nose was inches from the top of the toy. Blaze caught movement near the bottom.

"It just did! Right there, on the bottom!" He pointed at the spot with ebullience. Dellanie looked around the bottom and saw nothing. "I think it's elf magic," Blaze noted.

The vendor approached, chuckling.

"No, children. There is no magic involved in these at all. Everything is handmade and meant to move. This particular one has been wound up and different animals appear when the coils are released. Here, it will move on your side again, young miss." Sure enough, the little figure popped out, nearly hitting Dellanie's nose. The children laughed, not at the joy that the toy brought,

but more because of its uselessness. They found their way around
the stall, pressing buttons and watching the reaction of the
toys. One played a lute, another banged a drum; they put them
together, and they played in harmony. Another opened with secret
doors like the first. Dellanie and Blaze enjoyed just watching the
things move, but they really had no purpose, and they mocked the
toys by mimicking their movements. They had been at it for over
an hour when one caught Dellanie's eye. It was a horse and rider.
Press down on the rider and the horse galloped a yard while the
rider's clothes switched to plate armor and the little knight raised
his sword. The tiny individual plates flipped and flopped, ending
with a click-clack when they turned over. Blaze pressed the knight
again and the knight's armor changed back to riding clothes.
Dellanie and Blaze laughed at it. Blaze made fun of the lack of
technique of its sword arm.

"Make it do it again." There was excitement in the children's
voices and it didn't go unnoticed by the vendor, who smiled to himself. He did nothing to stop them from playing with it, but instead
strolled over to them.

"That is the Dragon Knight. I thought it would do well here
at the festival since it is fabled that a Dragon Knight was from
Timeria once upon a time." Blaze started to pull Dellanie away as a
crowd started to form; he didn't like the attention from the vendor.

"I want it," Dellanie announced softly to Blaze.

"Why?"

"I don't know, I just want it." She grabbed it from the tabletop
and held it close to her chest, so no one could retrieve it from her.
Blaze tried to take it from her, and she turned her back to him.

"You can't steal it, he knows you have it. He keeps watching us.
And it must cost a king's ransom . . . it's a Drisanian toy, after all."

There was something magical about the toys from Drisana. It
was the one place in the world that allowed their children to be
children until they grew to adulthood. All children also went to
school and learned lessons, arts, sports, and fun games that taught
children to be on the border patrol. The toys were special because
they were intended to make children happy and enjoy imagination
and life. It was the opposite of Ballardton, where survival was all
that mattered.

"I don't know what you're going to do, Del. I think it's foolish to want it, but do you want me to distract him?" Dellanie thought about it.

"I want to buy this." Dellanie surprised Blaze by approaching the vendor and declaring her purchase. He had already planned to push a toy off another table, allowing Dellanie to escape. The man looked at her and Blaze, assessing their buying ability. He glanced down at her shoes. Her boots were a fine quality but the leather was starting to wear through with small holes and threads along the seams. He could see that she needed new soles as they were worn along the edges. He glanced at Blaze's feet. The boy's boots were nearly bursting. The toes had started to rip and the soles were worn through along the back heel. The vendor wondered if it caused his feet to hurt. Looking at what people wore on their feet told the vendor a lot about the people to whom he sold his wares. He looked to his left, and the feet that approached wore fine leather boots, with perfectly soled heels. The wearer clearly took pride in their shoes: their polish made everything shine. The owner of those boots would pay more than these two pairs of very worn boots, that was for sure.

"Certainly, I would have to sell the Dragon Knight for eight golds." The vendor spoke in a loud voice to show there was no discrimination of price. Blaze's eyes widened, and his head fell. He was crestfallen. Dellanie leaned in and whispered to the man that she had a tiara and jewels and would like to barter. The vendor raised a finger, causing Dellanie to wait. Blaze tugged on Dellanie's tunic—he wanted her to get out of there and run with the toy. However, the man with polished boots walked out of the stall, and then the vendor spoke openly, but in a hushed tone in case more polished boots arrived. "However, my dear, the Dragon Knight seems to have taken quite a liking to you, and I would like to see that he stays with you. Nothing would bring me more pleasure." Dellanie stood there agape at the notion.

"Wait. *What?*" Dellanie was looking to see something amiss.

"Young miss, there are some times when you are aware of the needs of others. In this case, I believe you need to experience the joy this toy will bring. It is yours. I am not in the business of trades, and I am sure your tiara and jewels will look more lovely on you than me. Here is a sack to put the toy in. Enjoy." Dellanie put the toy in the muslin sack and scurried off before the man could change his mind.

Blaze followed behind Dellanie until he saw Goldenrod walking the stands just ahead of him. He darted in between the stalls and hid amongst some barrels and crates. He knew he was well hidden. He could no longer see Dellanie from his vantage point, but he raised his eyes to the sky, wondering what she was going to do with that little knight. Then he peeked out and followed Goldenrod with his eyes, his breathing heavy as the girl moved closer with such grace and beauty. He wanted to speak with her, but he feared her reaction, and so stayed sequestered.

Goldenrod was wearing a blue dress that identically matched her eyes. Her dress sparkled, catching the morning, sunlit rays. Her hair was gathered into a long thick braid that started at the nape of her neck and flowed over her shoulder and down to her waist. Intertwined in her hair were soft, white flowers that grew in Ceretheena. The small flowers dipped and bent with the curl of the braid. Goldenrod walked slowly, unaware that Blaze was nearby.

He kept watching her as she floated through the crowd. The morning patrons walked amongst the stalls and vendors were actively hawking their wares. As Goldenrod passed, people noticed her; she smiled and nodded her head in greeting to each one. They responded similarly. Every now and then, Blaze noticed that Goldenrod seemed to talk to herself. The sounds were foreign and harsh to Blaze's untrained ear. He realized that she was engaged in conversation with herself in her native tongue. Blaze watched her, bewildered. As she closed in on him, he sank deeper into his hiding place. She moved with the grace of a deer, and he fell for her again.

"Blaze?" Goldenrod called out in Common above him as she reached his hiding spot. He glanced side to side; it was impossible for her to have seen him. He had secured his spot and without proper training, there would be no way that she could have located him. "Blaze?" she called again. He crouched down, hidden by the shadows of new dawn. She hesitated in front of him, spoke her native tongue, and then continued on through the market. He watched her perambulate across the market. Nary a rustle from her dress was heard and she danced a ballet that was known only to her. It all spoke to the refinement of nobility. He thought she was more beautiful than any creature he had ever laid eyes upon. He stood up, entering the light of day, assured that she was far enough away from him.

Suddenly, Goldenrod turned, and her gaze captured his eyes. He had wanted to escape back into the shadows, but instead stood there in awe of his unlikely good fortune. She waved and ran back toward him, calling his name. His face reddened, and he was unsure of his own actions.

"Hi! I think I saw you, Blaze." Her grin was genuine, but she moved her head to her right and shushed the air. Blaze did not question her actions. He briefly thought she might be unstable but then he fell into the pools of her blue eyes and dismissed any thoughts other than heartfelt feelings. "Are you, um . . . okay, Blaze? You seem . . . distracted." Blaze couldn't hear the silent voice that whispered back in Goldenrod's mind, translating his words and helping her along as they walked. The bird-sprite hid under her braid, which created a safe perch and a way for her to learn and translate the language that she did not know. Her aunt, Princess Eloine of Drisana, had taught her enough key terms that she was able to be out on her own as long as Keir was her companion and guard.

"Uh-huh." It was definitely not a loquacious remark, but it was all he could muster for the moment. Goldenrod had a slight tilt to her head, and there seemed to be sunshine coming from her smile.

"Will you walk with me?"

Blaze nodded.

"Good. I was hoping that you join me at . . . plays, is that right?" She glanced upwards, as though one of the gods had whispered in her ear the correct answer. Blaze followed her gaze. "No, not plays . . . tourneys. Yes, that's right." *I think my mother used to talk to me in Common when I was little. I think I remember some, Keir!* Goldenrod said to Keir in Mahdurnian. She beamed with pride. "Blaze, join me . . . at . . . tourneys?"

"I can't, Goldie. We . . . um, I'm not allowed at the opening. The constables . . ."

"Well, that's no right! I will tell them so!" Goldenrod began to storm off, when she suddenly stopped with Keir's intervention, turned back, and stood at Blaze's side. "Okay . . . you walk me around Ballardton?" Blaze sheepishly smiled.

"Okay."

Goldenrod caught Blaze's hand, and they walked hand in hand out of the marketplace. She noticed that he smelled like cologne and spicy food, but she never mentioned it to him. It was easier to leave some things left unsaid, especially when translating was so difficult.

The unusual pair of nobility and commoner did not go unnoticed. Venom watched the pair with a twinge of anger in his heart. Nightshade sauntered up next to him.

"How does this make you feel, Venom?"

He glanced toward her, his face open with the anger in his soul. However, his expression quickly changed and his face relaxed.

"It's nothing, Nightshade. It's just . . ."

"Oh, I know, Venom. He'll leave again like before, and he'll leave you behind. Brothers shouldn't leave each other . . . ever. Isn't that what you said?" Nightshade glanced sideways toward Venom, grinning wickedly. She searched the crowds, making sure Dellanie wasn't around. *That stupid girl always makes things difficult for me. How many times has she squelched my ambitions? One day she'll get what is coming to her.* Nightshade enjoyed playing cat and mouse with two of her year mates. She pawed at Venom, who reached for her, only for her to pull away again.

Venom was the easiest toy because he had an attraction to her as well. It showed when he had tried to kiss her some time ago. She ran her dagger into his side and told him to "get the point." It was a standing joke at the guild, but she knew she could still manipulate him to do her will and the only cost was a kiss. However, Blaze was a toy that she sometimes had a hard time manipulating. He had a strong sense of self. His weakness was his desire to be included and respected by Master Locke. Nightshade scoffed at Blaze's uselessness, but Venom was useful, and he could be persuaded very easily to do her bidding; it was as easy as it had been to make him cut off Blaze's fingers because of his "disrespect."

"You know, Venom, I know these two men that need an assistant who wants to make a good amount of coin. Do you know someone who would be interested in being an assistant?" Lace arrived just as Nightshade wrapped her arm around Venom's shoulder, pressed her body into his, and guided him away from the highway.

After showing Goldenrod around Ballardton, the two stopped near the entrance to the tournament grounds. A ten-foot, hand-painted sign stood erect in front of the entrance gate.

"What say it, Blaze?"

Blaze peered at the sign as if squinting would suddenly give him insight as to how to read. He glanced side to side.

"Um . . . let's see . . . it . . . um, says . . . that today is . . . um . . . the . . . uh . . ." Blaze looked around the wooden sign and noticed swords and armor. "Oh, it's a warrior's tourney!" Blaze was so proud of himself that he exuded excitement.

"Oh, Blaze, Delrik tourneys talk to me. Please we go?" Blaze's grin faded and he backed away. *I can't go in there.*

"Remember I told you I cannot go with you, Goldie." Blaze turned to leave. Horns blazed a joyous tune.

"The tourneys are . . . starting! Please come me? . . . Please?" Goldenrod persuaded Blaze, but his face showed reluctant disgust. Her continual pleas moved his feet forward. Inside the tourney, Blaze and Goldenrod sat in the stands. Blaze had never watched other tournaments in the stands. He would sneak in and watch under the stands until he was chased away by the tourney guards. Today, the tournament was for squires, knights, and warriors. Blaze leaned forward, resting his elbows on his knees. He wanted to keep holding the girl's hand, but he didn't know how to approach the gesture. Goldenrod moved closer to him; her body pressed against his side. He scooted over to give her more room. She followed him until he could move no further. The warmth of her leg was soothing. He closed his eyes and felt the moment last for eternity.

"Blaze? Blaze?" Blaze's eyes snapped open, and he gazed into hers. He could see himself in them and he had the desire to flee from such beauty. He rose to leave; she held his arm, so he sat back down. He wanted to look at her and tell her that he was scared. His heart sank, knowing that he'd have to lose her. He stared at his feet as he leaned forward. She imitated his movement and looked hard at him. His black hair hid most of his pale face, but what she could see was worry and heartache. She felt for him. She placed her hand on his arm and he cringed away. Confusion overtook her senses and she pulled back. He turned and gave her a look of vilification. "Blaze, I . . . sorry . . ." Before she could finish the sentence, he had fled from her. "I don't know . . ." Quiet tears poured down her face as she caught him leaving back through the gate. *I don't understand, Keir.*

❖

Running away from Goldie and all that she made him feel, Blaze turned back to what he knew. He ran back to the guild house. It seemed that everyone was there, and they were talking about nothing and everything. Venom caught sight of Blaze and pulled him into the main quarters. Blaze refused to talk, but Venom was rattling on and on about Nightshade. All he wanted to do was yell for everyone to just shut up but instead he stayed quiet, allowing Venom to carry on. It was what Blaze called First Ball Hysteria. Many of the older thieves who had left to join other guilds returned to Ballardton for the event, taking up space that was normally owned by those who lived there. But Blaze understood that at one time or another, this was their home and he acknowledged that he, Venom, Dellanie, Nightshade, and the rest of his age-mates would probably return to do the same. The visitors to the guild were all members of the guild, but of different calibers, and some had advanced to master thief. To be a master thief was one of the greatest accomplishments, as one could start their own guild or attain wealth through their high ranking.

"I can't believe they are taking up all of the space in here," Venom remarked. "Is it me, or are there more of them this year?" Blaze looked around. Venom was right, there were more of them this year than last. He searched the room for Mason, but he wasn't there. His eyes caught sight of Denalisa and Barden. He cowered away, not wanting to be seen.

"What's wrong, Blaze? What do you see?" Venom followed Blaze's eyes and a huge smile crossed his lips.

"Denalisa! Denalisa is here!" Blaze hushed him, but it was too late. Venom had already drawn the attention of the entire group, especially Denalisa and Barden. Denalisa nearly danced across the floor as she dodged people throughout the quarters. Barden followed her happily. She smiled and waved, calling Venom closer.

"It looks like she wants you, Venom."

Venom waved back eagerly. Denalisa hopped up to them both. She caught Blaze's arm and held Venom's hand. Both boys immediately noticed her protruding abdomen. Barden wrapped his arms around Denalisa as he came up behind her. She turned and pressed her head against his chest. Blaze scowled at the show of affection.

"Congratulations! You're going to have a baby!"

Barden tightened his arms around Denalisa and placed his hands on her belly proudly.

"Nope, not just one. We are having twins! It was confirmed by Solana's temple and everything." Denalisa leaned back against Barden.

"Barden, sweetie, I'm feeling so tired. Can you get me a chair and rub my feet?" Barden kissed her cheek and ran off in search of a comfortable chair from upstairs. "That'll keep him busy for a bit. Oh, it is so good to see you both. I wanted to show you the babies . . ."

"You do realize that they aren't born yet, right?" Blaze flatly stated. Venom swallowed a chuckle. Denalisa released her grasp on them and countered her balance with her hand resting on her lower back while the other hand rubbed her stomach.

"I do. They are coming soon, but we had to make the journey here. It was mandated. I had to come too. I couldn't be without my dear Barden. These two are going to be born here."

"Ha! Just like Blaze! You won't be the only one to say that now, will you?" Blaze narrowed his eyes at Venom unamused by his comment. Venom walked up to Denalisa and gave her a hug, nearly knocking her over. He placed his hand on her belly and leaned down to talk to the two babies.

"Aw, Venom, that is so sweet." Barden arrived and led his pregnant wife to the chair, which he placed next the fire for comfort. Venom stared at Barden, who unlaced Denalisa's boots and started to rub her right foot. Denalisa instructed Barden where to rub and when Barden found the spot, she leaned back, satisfied.

"I can't stay here." Blaze was feeling overwhelmed by the excessive amount of noise and the company.

"Huh, did you say something, Blaze?" By the time Venom turned around, Blaze was already gone.

He hoped that he wasn't going to bother her as he came up to her tent. *After all, she did say I was welcome anytime.* Blaze moved a scarf out of his way as he walked into the tent. Hende-Li looked up from her book. Her smile was welcoming and open. She placed the book upside down and jumped to greet him. She wrapped him in a bear hug and Blaze hugged her back.

"Is it all right if I stay here?"

Hende-Li pulled back, giving him a you-know-better-than-to-ask look.

"You know you belong here, Little Brother. Don't ever feel like you need to ask. Come and go as you please. This door or curtain is always open for you. Are you hungry? Of course you are; here let me get you some of my fabulous stew." Hende-Li served the stew up for Blaze and set a place for him to eat and sleep. Blaze took the meal and ate it slowly as Hende-Li preferred. "Good job. You can't really find something enjoyable if you voraciously eat your food."

"I know—I'm trying." Blaze sat, contemplating the bustle at the guild. *Why did Denalisa and Barden show up?* Hende-Li picked up her book again, but she kept her eyes on Blaze and noticed his pensive stare.

"What is eating you?" she questioned after a brief time.

He glanced at her, expecting to catch her eyes, yet her eyes were absorbed in her book. He furrowed his brow and then shook it off.

"Nothing really, Hende-Li, just some people back at home that may serve to be trouble. Mmm, this stew sure is good. Every time I go back in for another bite, it's like tasting something for the first time." Hende-Li nodded her understanding, taking in his statement about trouble. She read another few lines of her book, then placed it upside down on her knee.

"Life may serve you up something to your liking, but it's what you add to it that makes it memorable." Blaze stopped eating with his spoon halfway to his mouth. Once she finished, he ate the spoonful.

"I guess we're not talking about the stew anymore." He smiled.

"Take it as you will. Go on; finish up. I have a book to finish."

Blaze ate the rest of the stew quickly, but not without manners. When finished, he washed the bowl and spoon and placed them in the drainer to be put away as he went to retrieve a towel for drying.

"Don't worry about the drying. I'd rather you sit down here." Blaze did as he was requested.

"What do you want to talk about, Hende-Li?"

"You know, I know where you live, Blaze and I don't care. You and your friends are good people. I have heard some talking that drifts on the wind and on the tips of birds' wings." Blaze leaned forward, resting his elbow on his knee as he focused all of his concentration on Hende-Li's words. "That talk is undercurrents of strife that will take our world to new unexpected places, but the surface of the river knows nothing of those undercurrents so it stays steady and true." Blaze didn't really comprehend her meaning this time.

"I don't understand, Hende-Li."

"Sometimes, Blaze, when we aren't looking, things are happening around us, but we are so involved in our own lives that we are unaware of problems that may eventually touch our lives. Keep your eyes open, Little Brother. There is more around you than you can see. There are many at your guild, are there not?"

"Yes, but how do you know?" Blaze looked at her with surprised suspicion.

"Because, my dear little brother, the Queen of Nashira has arrived at Festival this year and it is not to retrieve that wayward, fair-haired prince of hers; likewise, all of the great leaders have come upon this place. Their interest is in a country elsewhere." Blaze glanced sideways. *Why is she telling me this?* Hende-Li tilted her head upwards, gazing at the tent ceiling but clearly miles away in thought. "There will be missions and assignments to each guild across all countries looking for more intelligence. I fear that you will be called to join these undercurrents and my heart hurts at the thought."

"Don't worry, Hende-Li, I have never been on a mission and I've been at the guild for my whole life. I was born there," he said with a grin worthy of Aldric. Hende-Li leaned forward and kissed his forehead, then got up and went to put away Blaze's dishes. After her duties were complete, Hende-Li returned to her seat.

"Now, Little Brother, tell me of your young lady friend. I will assume you spoke to her again." Hende-Li picked up knitting from a basket and leaned in for what she had hoped would be a lighthearted love story. Blaze was embarrassed. It had been Goldenrod's touch that sent him fleeing at the tourney. He was fearful of an intrusion into knowing him and what he kept secret.

"Yes, I did talk to her," he reluctantly admitted, blushing. "We ... she has the most beautiful eyes that sparkle like blue water in the sweet summer sun, her smile could stop a war, and she wants to talk to me—to *me*." He gestured at himself, astonished.

"She sounds perfect, Blaze."

"Well ... almost. She can't speak very well." Hende-Li clapped her hands jovially.

"Yes, don't worry about that, Little Brother. She has made herself known. Her words will come without breaking."

An eruption of musical folly began to play outside and Hende-Li rose, taking Blaze's hand in hers. "Come on, this will be fun. The Glenblathan Pixies have begun their merriment in honor of the yellow moon, Keltainen, who shows her whole face and rises to zenith tonight." Hende-Li clapped in time with the music. Pixies, as far as Blaze knew, were bothersome creatures that pulled hair, turned milk sour, and pricked babies to make them cry. Blaze, not wanting to disappoint Hende-Li, narrowed his eyes as he looked down on the four-foot-tall, winged creatures that trooped forward in procession toward them. A memory of a sign over his head blinking out the letters "t-h-i-e-f" soured his expression. Hende-Li noticed and tried to change it by moving her arms to the music. As the pixies passed the tent, shorter ones flew up to Hende-Li and blew sparkle dust on her. She twirled in delight. Then the pixies started toward Blaze, but they noticed his air of disgust and flitted away to the next tent. Hende-Li noted his appearance and stance as he crossed his arms, closing in with his hatred. Hende-Li drew in a breath and led Blaze back into the tent to his seat. While he sat, he could see sadness on Hende-Li's face.

"What's wrong, Hende-Li? You look unhappy. Oh, I know." Blaze glared and directed his anger to the entrance. "You didn't like the sparkly stuff on you—stupid pixies. They're so ugly, with their translucent, sparkly wings. They're always such little pests, making people mad." He turned back to Hende-Li and began to speak again. "Did they hurt you?"

She pressed her finger to his lips, hushing him to silence. She closed her eyes, still keeping her position, and for some time she remained quiet. A soft wind filtered into the tent, engaging the scarves in a dance that moved in time with the pixies' music. Watching it deflated his anger. Blaze went to speak, but Hende-Li began before his breath.

"No, they did not; but I imagine they did you at one point or another. One thing that distresses me is your ridicule of their per-sonness, calling them 'pests,' just as some people refer to them as 'bugs.' They are equally needed in the world as you yourself are. They are people like humans, elves, sprites, the Fee, and any other that I may not have mentioned. I want you to always remember this, Blaze. A person, no matter who they are, shouldn't be judged by their features because no matter what, two people fell in love and created the one. When you showed your anger toward these people by your expression and your words, you took away their importance and made them less. I know that you were only saying those hurtful words out of your own experience and what you have heard others say, but you need to think for yourself. And I know you can. At some point, you will learn to see others for their gifts and know when to walk away from those who give nothing and always take."

Blaze felt terrible. He didn't want Hende-Li to be disappointed or angry; he wanted to make her proud. He bowed his head, wishing that he could say anything that would make Hende-Li feel differently about him, but nothing came to mind.

Hende-Li escorted Blaze outside. She shook some of the pixie sparkle dust from her clothes onto him. He didn't complain, nor did he show any enjoyment. He sighed. He guessed the least he could do was to try to understand their culture. He was determined that all he was going to learn would just reinforce what he already knew. Pixie music was upbeat and airy, with bells that were pounded gently with mallets. The music was inviting and uplifting. Hende-Li danced next to him, becoming enchantingly moved by the mystical songs. The songs traversed seamlessly from one to another. Hende-Li spoke in his ear as each part of the ceremony was introduced.

"Each clan of pixies is related to the petals of different flowers. These here are Trendapheel Pixies because the colors of their wings reflect the rose—stunning. This clan coming up to join the dance is the Kelta clan. They are the night bloomers, or the trumpeters, of the pixie world. They are the ones who we are celebrating tonight. Notice the sleeves of their outfits; they are tubular like the cestrum plant that their clan is associated with. Like the yellow moon, these pixies have wings that are soft shades of yellow. Because this is the Kelta clan, the other clans have come before. We watch with our eyes fully open, Little Brother, and we understand with our heads and our hearts."

Blaze watched, trying hard not to miss a single flutter of a wing.

The Kelta Pixies trooped into a circle around the maypole. They each grabbed a long ribbon. The ribbons tonight were white, yellow, and green. They paused, waiting for the right note to begin; within minutes, the pixies were weaving in and out and around until all ends were wrapped. The ends handed off to a pixie from a completely different clan. They secured the ends, while the Kelta Pixies fluttered around the pole. Together their wings fanned the air, creating a soft breeze. Blaze was surprised that pixies came in so many different colors. Their wings were tinted with shades that matched the colors of their distinct clan. With the pixies hovering above everyone's heads, clansman invited individuals from the tent camp to join in the dance to honor the Keltainen Moon. Blaze watched as the moon rose higher in the sky. A pixie took Hende-Li's hand, and Hende-Li grabbed Blaze's to have him partake in the festivities. He had never done so before. Hende-Li released him when two pixies flanked him and reached for him. He held their hands; he was over a head taller than they were, but it didn't seem to matter to them. He danced and when everyone started to sing, he sang. It was acceptance; it was love; it was pixie culture. *Everyone is invited! This is great!* Soon they released hands and everyone spun back out. The pixies in the air spun up and down, circling into a dance of a yellow ring. In the middle of the ring, Keltainen shone her light. Sparkle dust flew out, sprinkling across pixies and those in attendance. Hende-Li took Blaze's hands and the two spun, twirled, and danced well into the night. He stayed at Hende-Li's tent into the early morning. He slept for a few hours and then headed back to the guild.

Blaze opened the guild's door, humming the tune of the dance. He was covered in sparkle dust and he didn't mind. It was for luck, after all. The next time a pixie wanted to sprinkle sparkle dust on him, he'd be honored and accept it. Pixies weren't so bad. He smiled, realizing that Hende-Li was right. She was always right.

CHAPTER 17

FIRST BALL

THE GUILD WAS BUZZING with the chatter of the Midsummer First Ball that officially began the festival. The females of the guild prattled on about dresses, who would attend the grand event, and if they themselves were going. Blaze tightened his jaw and Venom caught his expression.

"I know, isn't it ridiculous how they ramble on? What in Hala's realm is all over you?" Venom stared, repulsed, at Blaze's sparkle dust as Blaze went to sit next to him.

"It's pixie sparkle dust. It's for . . ." Venom hushed him.

"I don't want to know, and I don't care. You must have been with that weird lady who Spider likes from Pyrrin."

"She's nice. You'd like her. She calls me . . ."

"Let me guess—Little Brother. Guess what? She is a flake and fraud. From what I learned, she's not even really from Pyrrin. She calls everyone who is a boy Little Brother and every girl Little Sister. I learned all this from one of the other tent campers, who was really from Pyrrin. Did you at least take something from her tent? I did. She had these huge gold earrings. They brought a few silver. 'Unusual in these parts,' said the trader. Now, go get cleaned up and if you want to sit next to me, you'll have to get rid of all that pixie-nonsense that is all over you."

Blaze was crestfallen. He got up and went to get cleaned up in the river. He jumped in the water and the waves washed over him. He felt a quick pull underneath him. He smiled. *Undercurrents.*

After his dip in the river, Blaze sat at the edge of the bank. He decided to dry off in the sun. He didn't really care about First Ball or even what Venom thought about Hende-Li. She made him feel special—a part of her family, a family that loved each other, who didn't try to hurt or backstab each other. She didn't even care that he was missing his fingers. She liked the person he was. Not one other person could say that . . . not even Blaze himself. Venom saw him outside, sitting alone in the sun. Blaze heard him approach, but he didn't turn to greet him.

"I'm glad to see you got rid of those silly sparkles. Now you'll be safe from those stinking pixies." Blaze nodded."I bet they did that to you to tie your hair in knots or to come after you in your sleep." Venom wrung his hands, portraying a pixie.

"You think so?"

"Definitely. You should spit thrice on the ground for good measure." Venom spat and anticipated Blaze to spit with him."Why aren't you spitting?"

"Because I don't think they have evil intentions."

"Who are you?" Venom exaggeratedly asked.

"I think Hende-Li is a good person. She accepts me for me and she says I'm part of her family. I don't want you talking badly about her. The pixies spray sparkle dust on people for good luck. The only way you'd know that is if you learned about their culture. Sometimes people do things that are weird because it is what is normal for them even if it isn't normal for others. I know that now." Venom got up and knocked on Blaze's head like a door.

"I think you have been replaced by a changeling. Poor changeling, you aren't going to get much from changing places with Blaze." Blaze stood up, then hauled off, punching Venom hard and splitting his lip. *That's for taking the earrings.*

"Shut up! You're an idiot, Venom!"

Venom laughed, rubbing his face and tucking his lip inside his mouth to try to stop the bleeding. The metallic taste filled his mouth. He swallowed his saliva, trying not to reveal that Blaze's punch was painful or even bothersome.

"I thought we *both* were, but then you go and get all insightful and crap."

"Are Denalisa and Barden still here?" Venom nodded."Did they say why they are here?" Venom pulled out an apple from his pouch and began cutting into it with his dagger.

"You want a piece?" Blaze shrugged. "Yeah, they're here for First Ball, and Denalisa wanted to show off that she was having two babies at once. You know, the normal crap that the Olders do to show off how special they are." Blaze sat in silence, wondering if that was their true reason for being at the guild. After chomping on his apple, Venom spoke again. "Is that Mahdurnian girl who you have been following around like a puppy going to the Ball?"

Blaze dreamily thought about Goldenrod. It had been so long since he had seen her. His heart jumped a little thinking about taking her to the ball. However, he knew that he could never go to the ball with her or anyone else. Hende-Li hadn't calmed his worry or feelings.

"Is she your girlfriend?" *Girlfriend? Girlfriend.*

"Stop being an idiot." Blaze walked away, leaving Venom calling after him.

Blaze's thoughts drifted back to the girl. *Was what Venom said true? Could she be my girlfriend? No, there's no way—I am just a thief and she is a noble. No one would ever let me near her.* Blaze was not wrong; she was above him. Look at all the trouble he had caused! It had been awhile since he had actually seen her and her bird. He hoped to see her again, but his retreat had been so quick and sudden that he figured she'd have forgotten him. *Nothing really to remember.* He began to walk toward the market stands. Blaze searched the alleyways that separated each stand. It took about a half-hour to find her, but she was there, looking at fabrics for dresses. A woman stood next to her and they spoke in a tongue that Blaze didn't recognize. He stepped back behind the bolts of fabric and crouched down. He watched her.

He saw the way she tilted her head when she talked. He held his breathe when she smiled in his direction, though she did not see him. He hid until a patron came to buy the fabric he was hiding behind. The woman screamed, and he knocked over the rest of the bolts trying to scramble away. Heads turned in his direction, and Goldenrod smiled gleefully when she noticed him. She ran to catch him as he tried to make his retreat. She grabbed his hand and pulled him to her companion.

"Aunt Eloine, this is him—Blaze. Did I say that all correctly? Keir is not with me so I am worried that I have made a mistake."

"Yes, Goldie. Everything was spoken in perfect Common; you are learning so quickly." Pride was shown on Eloine's face. She nodded to Blaze. "It is a pleasure to meet you, Blaze. I wanted to personally thank you for helping my niece."

Blaze found no words. Goldenrod held him by her side while her eyes sparkled with admiration. He bowed his head, fearing the lady would discover that he was a thief. It was obvious; he knew just how much he stood out amongst those in attendance. He was happy that he wasn't covered in sparkle dust and silently thanked Venom. Goldenrod spoke again to her aunt in the other tongue, then addressed Blaze.

"We are going to eat at Two Realms Inn; would you like to join us, Blaze?" Blaze glanced up at Goldenrod, whose expression was expectant. She nodded her head, encouraging him to say yes. He felt that he could not decline based on Goldenrod's expression and her hold on his arm.

"I guess."

Goldenrod glanced at her aunt who nodded her head. Turning back to Blaze, she grinned. Blaze smiled coyly at her.

"So, Blaze, have you always lived in Ballardton?" Goldenrod inquired as they waited for their food at the inn's restaurant. He nodded his head. Blaze's quiet demeanor was intriguing to her. There was something about him, something she couldn't explain. Her boyfriend back home was arrogant, self-righteous, and enjoyed having Goldenrod on his arm for decoration. Her rebellion had led her to leave to find her mother, a quest that had led her to Drisana and then to Timeria to enjoy the luxuries of the Festival. Now he was only a memory, and Blaze sat next to her. Blaze was dangerous, she knew, but her aunt was allowing her to keep company with him. There was softness to Blaze's personality—for instance, the unobtrusive way that he helped her with the pieman and the way he hid from her in the marketplace. She wondered now if he had waited for her. She hoped that he had. Blaze glanced around the room. Goldenrod wondered if he found that for which he searched.

Blaze's eyes had settled on Goldenrod's sunlit locks. She smiled at him and her eyes sparkled, wrinkling the outer edges of her eyes. He smiled back, only to turn away when she caught him. He glanced at Goldenrod's aunt. He thought Goldenrod the most beautiful girl he'd seen, but he could see that the natural grace and elegance of her aunt would catch the attention of most. Blaze looked away from the table and was anxious to leave. He wiggled in the chair, turning every chance he got.

"Do not be nervous, Blaze. You are amongst friends." Eloine comforted him.

The food arrived within minutes, and by the time the waiter left, the table was full. Aromas that Blaze had dreamed about were set before him. He felt his mouth water and he drank in the smells and sights. There were days when food was scarce, especially when he wasn't able to locate anything worthwhile to bring back to the guild. Those were days that Blaze just stayed away. During the Festival, pickings were good; however, he had never been treated to such succulent local fare as that which sat in front of him. Blaze waited and watched as the royals laid their napkins upon their laps. Blaze mimicked their actions. Next, Eloine asked if she could serve everyone. Was Blaze imagining it, or was Goldenrod also mimicking Eloine's gesture? No, it couldn't be; she had to have been just accustomed to the rites of dinner feasts. Eloine filled their plates to her own liking. Eloine nodded when everyone was served. Blaze looked at the silverware and chose the spoon, as it was the most recognizable utensil. He was delighted and relieved to see that it was also the tool that Eloine and Goldenrod chose.

The food served to the nobles was better than any Blaze had ever tasted at the inn before. He had to hold himself back from asking for more, though he desired it. By the end of the meal, Blaze was fuller than he could remember in recent history. Eloine and Goldenrod talked about her dress for First Ball and Blaze lost interest in the conversation, distracting himself by watching the barkeep. He was a slim man with a long nose that reminded Blaze of a weasel. His hair was gray on both sides and black in the middle, reverse skunk style. Blaze nearly spit when he thought of it. The other patrons were as well-dressed as Goldenrod and her aunt. They, too, were bursting with enthusiasm about First Ball.

"I hope to see the duke and duchess since they have returned."

"My dress better be the only one like it."

"I hope that Princess Valorie will dance with me. She's such a beauty."

"My son has as much opportunity to marry the princesses as anyone. I have already gotten him on their dance cards. He is also dancing with a Drisanian lady. Oh, I think that is her. She's pretty. I wonder if she has any land." When the woman mentioned Goldenrod, Blaze glared at her.

"Blaze, are you going to First Ball? We could go together, kind of like a date." Blaze raised his head from his food plate, eyes wide. He encountered Goldenrod's blushed, anticipating expression. He smiled shyly at her and glanced sideways at Eloine.

"No." He returned his attention to his plate. It was entirely empty, but it gave him a safe spot to stare and think. Goldenrod immediately deflated and protested. Eloine calmed the teenager's complaints with a comforting look. "I should go. Thank you . . . for the food." Blaze stood up to leave. Goldenrod caught his arm.

"I'll see you after the Ball, then. It's okay, but you understand that I will be going." Blaze didn't turn to face her.

"Yeah."

Blaze walked back toward the thieves' guild. He didn't really want to go back. His heart desired to stay with the girl. Goldenrod had taken him by surprise, and he really didn't know how to handle the crush he had on her. He wondered if she really liked him for who he was or if it was that she pitied him. He hoped the first was the case. First Ball was not a place for someone like him. He had no idea what to expect at such a grand venue. He would often watch through a rooftop window. The dance was always given by the mayor and his mayoress in honor of the Timerian royalty and was held in the great ballroom of the mayor's manor. It also officially started the Festival. The constables had a tendency to look the other way while the guttersnipes sneaked a peek at the royals. There were times, especially when a specifically well-renowned royal would come to First Ball, that the court would offer a gated entrance for spectators to ogle at the young lord or lady.

Back at the guild, there was a clamor of voices that warned him not to enter. He realized that it was just the other thieves preparing for First Ball. He wondered what Master was doing and if he was meeting with the Olders. He spotted Denalisa, who appeared out of the doorway, followed by Barden. They kissed, clearly to show off for everyone. Denalisa wore a floor-length, high-waisted, red dress that accentuated her belly. Around her neck, she wore a hefty gold necklace in the shape of a smile with small ebony beads. It rested on her swollen belly. Blaze wondered if Barden had found, stolen, or made that ugly piece of jewelry. Barden was dressed in a red tunic that matched Denalisa's dress, with light-brown breeches and shoes that were upturned and pointed with bells on the tip. He jingled as he walked past Blaze.

"Nice shoes, Barden," Blaze snickered. Barden glanced down at his feet.

"They are all the rage up in Venesial, where *my guild* is. The king will be wearing these tonight."

"I feel bad for the king, then," Blaze retorted.

"I assume, based on the way you are dressed, Blaze, that you are not attending First Ball tonight. That is probably a smart decision for you. We wouldn't want you to get lost and end up in a small cave wounded or something for days on end."

Blaze glared at Barden. *What a dandy! I can't believe I ever thought he was someone to look up to, and I doubt he even has a guild.* Blaze glowered at Barden. *Okay, so there's nothing more than what I actually see with Barden. Who else?* Blaze was determined to discover what Hende-Li was talking about. After all, she knew about the Olders being at the guild and the queen of Nashira. His thoughts drifted as he scanned the guild for others who might be part of Hende-Li's warning of undercurrents, when Dellanie suddenly launched her knife by his nose. He felt the cool breeze as it glided just in front of him. He didn't even flinch; instead, he made a face in her direction.

"What was that for?"

"You weren't paying attention." Dellanie had already crossed the room and was retrieving the small wrist dagger from the wall. Blaze watched as she replaced the dagger into the sheath that was tied securely to the underside of her wrist. She tucked it into the long sleeves of her emerald gown that carefully obstructed their hiding place. Blaze then realized that Jewels, Dellanie, and Nightshade were dressed to the hilt for First Ball.

"Apparently you're not going, Blaze. You'd never be able to pull off any disguise," Nightshade mocked. *You too, Nightshade? Go spend your time kissing up to Denalisa and Barden.*

"Yeah, I guess it would be too hard to hide your hands when dancing, huh?" Jewels bowed her head. She was fond of Blaze as a friend and thought the others could be too harsh, especially Nightshade. She tried hard to smooth things over to make everyone like each other. Nightshade took advantage of her kindness and ordered the young thief about.

A commotion erupted when Venom bounded in. Blaze backed away from the girls so as not to be called out yet again. As Venom sauntered around the guild, Blaze noticed that he was dressed in new traveling clothes.

"Are you going somewhere?" Blaze asked Venom.

Venom laughed in his face. "Yeah, I've finally got a real, full-fledged assignment." Blaze's eyes widened. "It is paying well, and I haven't even started yet. Check out these new tailored clothes! I look amazing!" Venom held out his arms and spun slowly to show off his nicely tailored tunic and breeches.

"Woo! Looking good there, Venom!" Nightshade glided up to him and leaned in as though to kiss him, but then recanted the gesture and walked away smugly. Even after her sudden departure, Venom still kept his pose awaiting the kiss. Onlookers laughed, and Venom opened his eyes. He searched the room for Nightshade. She wagged her finger at him and then touched her side. When Venom had finished his little game with Nightshade, he returned his attention back to Blaze.

"You're happy for me, right?" Venom queried.

"You look like a dandy; maybe you should have bells on your toes. But sure. What are you doing for this assignment of yours?"

Venom looked down on his feet, confused. Blaze wasn't making eye contact with him as he talked; instead, he was searching around the main quarters, looking for any sign of anything amiss. Venom followed his eyes until he dismissed the task. "I cannot tell. I have been sworn to utmost secrecy." Venom leaned in to whisper in Blaze's ear. Blaze stopped his search. "I am going on a mission again with Mason." *Mason! He's definitely part of the undercurrent.*

"Where is Mason? I haven't seen him. Is he here?" Blaze sprung upright.

"He's not here yet. I am going with him because I've been deemed overly qualified to start going on missions since the last time I went with him. I fought off all of those rotten hill-people."

Blaze inhaled noisily. *Oh yeah. I remember Venom went with Mason a while ago. It was a week together. I didn't even see Mason when he came back. Why would Mason have given him new clothes?* Blaze narrowed his eyes. *No, Master.*

"But . . . I do have another paid assignment with a couple of other Olders in the guild, which is who I got these clothes from."

Blaze wasn't listening entirely; he was glaring at Ballard's image across from him on Locke's door. Ballard's sly smile seemed to taunt the young thief. Blaze walked past Venom, bumping into him, and grabbed a dagger from the weapons box. He chose a blade that was sturdy and strong and was not his own. Then he stomped over to the door, raised his arm, and stabbed Ballard. Blaze checked the blade to make sure that the dagger was securely in the door. His ear caught muffled voices in Master's office, and he wondered if this was the undercurrents that Hende-Li spoke of. After he stabbed the door, he heard a shuffle of chairs and footsteps. He backed away from the door. Master Locke, seething, swung the door open, banging it against the wall. The guild shook. However, Master Locke looked upon the ensemble, who wore gaping mouths and wide eyes, and nothing seemed out of the ordinary.

Blaze stood to Master Locke's left. He glanced behind the master into his room, which was filled with several Olders and others whom Blaze didn't recognize, though they wore the medallions of Ballardton's advisors, which Blaze knew nothing of. *Undercurrent— it is happening.*

"What is going on out here?" Locke walked out through the door, giving his guests some privacy by closing the door. Venom pointed at the door behind Locke. Locke turned around. A dagger stuck out of Ballard's face. Locke reached up and tried to pull it out of the door, but it would not budge. *Maybe I could do that on my side of the door. It gives a whole new meaning to staring daggers.* Master caressed his chin with wonder. "Whose dagger is this?" Pigeon raised his hand.

"Get it out of the door before it causes a fracture." Pigeon rose.

"Oh, no, Master, it isn't mine. It doesn't belong to the one who pierced the door either. I do know the culprit, if you are inclined to skin my hand for the information." Locke tightened his jaw, annoyed by Pigeon's request.

"Leave it! I don't care. Pigeon, a word." Pigeon shuffled over to Locke, who wrapped his arm around Pigeon's shoulder for privacy and escorted him out of the guild. Blaze looked at Venom.

"I can't believe you got away with stabbing the door! That is amazing. I do kind of miss Ballard's face though. He was like a kind friend." Blaze wanted to throw up at the last comment.

"There are undercurrents going on, Venom. Hende-Li is who she says she is. I believe her."

"Well, then you're an idiot, Blaze."

Blaze stared at Venom, challenging him to fight. The only difference this time was that Blaze had his dagger and training from an
elf; he promised himself that he wouldn't lose, fingers or no fingers.

"Fight me." Blaze's voice was dangerous.

Venom scoffed at Blaze and batted him away. "Why would I
fight you? I'm not even mad at you. I am actually proud of you for
stabbing the door with Master right behind it. I have a meeting to
talk about my mission. See you later." Venom undid his belt and
then retightened it as he walked out of the door opposite where
Locke and Pigeon had exited. Blaze knew he couldn't stay at the
guild. Master Locke would return soon to the main quarters and
ask questions, and Blaze didn't want to have to admit to his deed.
He slithered out the door after Venom.

Blaze didn't mean to follow Venom to the knackerman's yard.
He had no intention of getting involved with Venom's assignment
until he saw Lace. Blaze hid amongst bushes at the end of the
knackerman's property. He had to make sure that Lace didn't do
any harm to Venom—he knew that without his interference, she
was quite capable of sending Venom into the inferno of the oven.
Blaze still itched for a fight, and his new target was Lace. She had
threatened Spider before to entice Venom into compliance. Now
Venom was working with her, probably *for* her, and Blaze couldn't
keep quiet.

Blaze burst out of the bushes. "What does she have on you now,
Venom? Did she threaten Spider?" Venom looked guilty, moving
backwards away from Lace with his hands raised to prove his
innocence.

"There is nothing going on, Blaze. Venom just finally agreed to
work with me."

"Wait! Are you the one who hired Venom?"

"Why would you think that? Besides Venom is able to speak for
himself. Isn't that right, Venom?"

Blaze glared at Venom.

"What do you want him for?"

"A job . . . It's a mission I have. I need some help."

"So . . . you asked . . . *Venom*? That doesn't make sense. What
do you want from him? What are you getting out of this, Lace?
Venom, these are the Olders that you are committed to?"

"Blaze, you are too suspicious. I got him new clothes, as you
know. Venom flaunted them in front of everyone in the guild.
You weren't very supportive of him. And I can't believe you called

Nightshade and me 'Olders.' We are the same age." Blaze didn't remember seeing Lace in the guild. *How does she know that?* Lace had wrapped her arm around Venom. Venom glanced toward her; he nodded in agreement.

"Clothes and what else, Lace? Are you paying him or are you intimidating him and Spider? Don't mess with Spider."

Lace half smiled.

"Oh, I know. I won't mess with Spider, but maybe Snip will. . . ."

"Leave my sister out of this! She hasn't done anything wrong." Blaze looked around for Snip but wasn't in the vacinity.

"Really, Blaze. I haven't done anything with or to Snip, nor Spider. They're both fine. But if you're really interested in what my mission is, I'll be more than happy to let you in on it—for a price. Goddess knows that you are one of us, Blaze . . . or have you forgotten that while you were out hobnobbing with that *Mahdurnian?* Dining with the Princess of Drisana, drinking tea, assimilating with Pixies. Have you forgotten that you were born here? You should be thankful to your blessed mother for letting you stay on Mirias. I'm sure there is a use for you somewhere." Lace walked around Blaze, and the hairs on the back of his neck stood up. Lace reminded him of Jade, a natural comparison since Lace was following Blaze's mother's dark path. Lace wrapped her arms around him, pulled him close, and leaned in. Blaze pulled away. Disgust rose in his throat, but he didn't take his eyes off of her. He moved his hand down to his dagger.

"Lace, get away from me. I'm not going to join you on your mission."

"What mission?" Dellanie appeared behind Blaze, challenging Lace's dominance.

The lionesses were poised to fight. Lace pushed hard against Blaze, teetering him off-balance and into Dellanie.

"Blaze, what are you doing?" Dellanie didn't wait for an answer; she pushed Blaze aside. She launched small daggers from her wrists at Lace. Lace was more adept than Dellanie expected, and she dodged the blades. Dellanie quickly reloaded and sent another barrage against Lace.

"Come on, Venom. We've got to talk." Blaze pulled Venom along until they reached the river's bank, far down away from the guild, and nestled in amongst the reeds. Venom sat down and started removing his boots to stick his oversized feet in the cool water.

"What are you and Lace up to? What is she planning this time? You should know better than to trust her," Blaze whispered. "Is Spider safe?"

"Uh, I'm not sure what you want me to answer first. Yes, Spider is safe. I really have a mission with Lace . . . honestly."

"I don't think you can trust her this time either." Lace had attacked Venom too many times for this new alliance to be legitimate, but he did trust Venom, especially if Spider's life was in danger. Blaze sat down next to Venom in the reed grass. He cut off a cattail with his dagger and began chewing on the cut end. "What about your mission with Mason?"

"It's all good, Blaze. She's—well, we're good. She doesn't jump me anymore or punch me in the stomach. And I am going out again with Mason the next time he comes back," Venom reassured Blaze. "Aren't those plants poisonous?"

"No, it's a cattail, they're good. It's about the only plant I can identify. It has this brown seed head, and if you see that, then you know that it's safe. Mason sometimes makes it into a medicine if he can't buy or find wyssanberry. You know you don't have to work for Lace. She's horrible. Where did she get the money for the new clothes?" Blaze tugged on Venom's tunic.

"It's an assignment for someone else. They are the ones who supplied the clothes I think. I know I don't have to work for Lace, but I know what she wants me to do. It's actually quite simple. I'll be fine." The two boys sat in silence, but Blaze's mind burned, trying to learn what Venom had to do for Lace. *Undercurrents—was this part of it?* Venom splashed his feet in the water, disrupting all the fish. One larger fish surfaced and its tail slapped toward the two boys. They laughed, distracted for a moment. Blaze's mind wandered back to Goldenrod as he looked out across the river. He sighed.

"A coppie for your thoughts. . . ." Blaze smiled from thoughts of love, and his cheeks pinked slightly.

"Oh, they're not worth that much, Venom. But since you asked, I was thinking about Goldie. Remember, you met her in the guild . . ."

"Yeah, that bird sprite came after us. Actually, he raked you pretty good. What about her? Is she your girlfriend? Did you finally make up your mind?"

Blaze blushed. "I really, *really* like her. Not just like her, but *like* like her, if you know what I mean. I can smell the sweet floral scent of her hair, and I love the way her eyes sparkle when she talks or laughs. I don't know, Venom, I have never felt like this before."

"Ooo, Blaze has a girlfriend. Blazey has a girlfriend!"

"Stop, you sound like a Little! And don't call me Blazey." Blaze cuffed his hand at Venom, smiling with embarrassed joy.

"Ha, ha! You're going to date her and her bird! I hope you don't mind a double date." Venom made kissy noises and wrapped his arm around himself. Blaze's face flushed completely.

"His name is Keir. He's okay. No, I'm not dating him. I'm not even dating her. Besides, interspecies romances are gross! What if they changed when you were in the middle? No, I'm sure she feels the same way."

"You're right, I never thought of it. It might be interesting though. So, if not the sprite; how does she feel about being with a thief? You did tell her, right?"

Blaze glanced sideways. "I think she knows. I met her aunt. They were really nice."

Venom laughed with a snort.

"What?"

"Like she's really interested in a kid with no money and no fingers. She's used to being with royalty. And you honestly think that she's interested in you?" Blaze sat silently, going over Venom's words in his mind; they were like his subconscious talking back to him. His self-doubts were real, but to have Venom voice them hurt. He pulled the cattail out of his mouth and threw it on the ground as tears welled, but he blinked them away so as not to embarrass himself anymore in front of Venom. His friend, he knew, would find it to be a sign of weakness.

"Ah, yeah. You know . . . I'll see you later, Venom. Remember, watch out for Lace. She's got a plan, and you always end up on the wrong side of it." Blaze left Venom, who followed his friend with his eyes.

Entering the thieves' guild, Blaze kept his cloak's hood over his head. He didn't want to alert Master that he was back at the guild too early. Blaze didn't know what Pigeon had squealed, so he wasn't taking any chances. He cinched his hood closed, allowing only his eyes to be visible. It reminded him of Shadow. Blaze looked around the guild. Come to think of it, he hadn't seen Shadow in some time. Blaze thought back to his last meeting with him. Did he tell Shadow that he was going to be skewered? Well, that wasn't anything new. He said it all the time. Blaze slinked around the guild. He kept to the perimeter of the common room. It was then that he noticed it.

He crawled into the small alcove under the stairs farthest away from the fires. In the winter it wouldn't have been very warm, but here in the summer he actually found it a cool space for hiding. He didn't recall ever wanting to be this far from the others, even when things had gone south with Ruri, Barden's agemate who ostracized Blaze when he was little. He looked up at the wooden stair support, and there was an image of a pie and a dark, cloaked figure. *Heh*, Blaze surmised, *Gavin and Shadow*. He looked around the bundled cloth that he was sitting on. Some old cloaks—a couple seemed familiar to Blaze.

Blaze used to continually grab Shadow's cloaks. He felt that the little boy was too secretive. He never actually saw the boy's face. He was always clean, but Blaze figured that Shadow must have done everything, even bathe, in that cloak. It was a game, although one of a somewhat bullying nature. Blaze had done everything to try to rip the cloak off of that boy. But Shadow had gotten smart as he had gotten older, and he started wearing multiple cloaks. The ones that Blaze was sitting on now were the ones that Blaze used to hold, dumbfounded, until he threw them back onto Shadow's head.

He felt around to the side toward the wall. His hand slapped against something metal. He pulled it out only to discover a metal pie tray, resisting its heavy weight with his three fingers. He assisted it with his other hand and pulled it onto his lap. Moldy rings stained the tray. *Gavin and his pies*, he thought, shaking his head in disbelief. He examined the tray further, turning it over. On the bottom of the tray, very lightly scratched into the surface, was Adoon's symbol. *Adoon's poison!* Blaze gasped, dropping the tray with a metallic clang on the floor. *This is Borintak's tray*. He had never expected to see the head, eye, and wiggly legs of Adoon's symbol on the actual tray. Blaze thought about it. It must be the trays that he left for the Littles. At that moment, Blaze wanted to run out, grab all the trays, destroy the pies, and check to see if the symbol was present.

A large amount of commotion erupted suddenly in the common room. Blaze popped his head out of the stair nook. Several men entered the guild, carrying several abeetzah rounds. He couldn't imagine why these men were bringing the rounds into the guild. His mouth watered as the spicy garlicky tomato sauce's aroma reached his nose. He tossed the tray to the side and jumped out of the Littles' nest.

"Okay, that should do it! Thirteen abeetzah rounds! I need someone to pay for the rounds." Two men looked at the untrusting eyes present in the room. One of the men held a scroll close to his chest, unsure of what to do. Blaze started forward when Master's door opened. Blaze hesitated and covered his face again with his cloak. Master Locke emerged from his sanctuary. Blaze stepped back.

"Hello, Wooster. Hello, Stayven. It is nice to see you both. Here is the payment for the abeetzah and the beer drum. There's a little something extra in it for you as well. Today is a wonderful day to celebrate. Thank you." Wooster opened the small pouch, nodded his thanks, and retreated out of the side door. Blaze could see the abeetzah now. They were covered in cheese with multiple toppings. If he could read, one even spelled out "Happy Handfasting" in bright red peppers. Some of the other abeetzahs had small pieces of meat topping them. The rounds were a most welcome sight to the gathered thieves, whose main sustenance was watered-down, days-old stew. "Nobody touches anything until our young couple arrives."

"Who got handfasted, Master?" Dellanie said after reading the abeetzah with the words baked in.

"You'll find out soon enough, Dellanie." Locke smiled. He guarded the abeetzah carefully making sure they remained for after the event. Several of the younger thieves kept vigil at the table waiting for the right moment.

"Cups, not yet. You will have to wait." Cups frowned as she licked her lips.

"Master Locke, what is a handfasting? And do you all ways get abeetzah after?" Locke chuckled.

"No, you don't all ways get abeetzah after a handfasting. It is the couple's choice and one they wanted to share. What is a handfasting? Well, do you know what a wedding is?"

"Of course, Cups doesn't know what either is. She is still little." Pigeon approached the table to drool like the Littles. "I personally never saw the need of such things like handfasting or weddings."

Pigeon reached down and attempted to grab a piece of cheese. Locke slapped his hand away. "If you want a child, here take Cups or one of the others. They're all right here, just come and take one."

Locke held his breath. "That's enough, Pigeon." He could see the look on the Littles faces. Dellanie's and Blaze's faces showed their shock as well.

"But seriously, handfasting is better than marriage with a wedding because it is only a short time. Look at yours, Master." Locke shook his head.

"Don't, Pigeon, you don't know anything about it."

"Sure I do. Mason tells it so well. He says, 'you were just about Venom's age when you and Jade were handfasted; then within hours, you caught Jade with Rhatt in your bed. You went right over to the temple and nulled the handfasting.' I'm right, aren't I? Don't deny it, Master. 'Born here,' came about a year later, isn't that right? See I know my guild history."

"Pigeon, you are out of here. You're history is wrong. We will talk about your behavior here later. I will save you a triangle, but you will not carry this attitude today to lessen the events of this couple." Locke pointed toward the exit directing Pigeon out of the guild.

"Don't worry, Master Locke. I'm going, I'm going." Pigeon reached over and grabbed several triangles of the abeetzah before he hustled out of the door. Locke watched after Pigeon as he left, Snip burst through the door calling for Master Locke.

"Master Locke, Master Locke. The carriage has arrived." Locke reached into his pouch and handed a coin to Snip.

"Great news, Snip. Thank you. You did a great job. Now stay for the abeetzah." Snip lit up and jumped up and down excited to be a part of the festivities.

Some of the things that Pigeon had said about Locke's own experience with handfasting was true; even though, he didn't want to hear it so bluntly described. Happily, that was not going to be the case with the couple today as they had been dedicated to each other for many, many years—this just made it official.

"You'll see in a moment. I think I hear them coming now." There were footsteps upstairs on the main floor of the guild. Blaze removed his hood and intently held his breath. There was a bit of murmur from the common room.

"Ha! I know who it is! It must be Mason! He's always looking to hook up with this one or that. He finally did it!"

Master just smiled. Denalisa and Barden entered the quarters, joining Master. They still wore the clothes for First Ball.

"They look just adorable together . . . for always." Denalisa held her hand to her heart in a 'bless their little hearts' fashion. Barden pulled her close from behind, and they turned their eyes toward the top of the stairs.

The upstairs door opened and the couple waited for just a minute before entering the light. As they walked slowly down the stairs, they kept their faces obscured. One had their face buried in their bouquet and the other lifted their tunic to cover all but their eyes. Finally, they reached the landing at the bottom stair, their hands tied together with white ribbons, indicating their commitment to each other and their handfasting.

"Look I'm a bride!" Pip raised his arm with bouquet in hand toward the ceiling surprising the assembled guildmembers, while Dorken dropped his tunic back into position.

"Pip and Dorken! Handfasted at last!"

"That's great! Congratulations, you two!"

"It's about time!" Everyone moved closer to the pair and hurried in to join the celebration. Pip wore a fancy, lacy, turquoise tunic, which he had commissioned just for the day's event, as well as his veil. Dorken wore a tunic that complimented Pip's in color only. They both wore orange breeches in solidarity.

"Thank you so much, everyone! We wanted to share our special day with you all. Please enjoy the abeetzah and help us celebrate! Master Locke, thank you." Master Locke nodded and he held back the Littles until Pip and Dorken where ready.

"Congratulations to you both! Your handfasting is definitely reason to celebrate! Well, Dorken, you and Pip should start." Pip had taken his first step off the stairs, and he felt faint. Dorken caught and kissed him. Cheering erupted in the guild house. This was truly a momentous day. A handfasting hadn't occurred in the guild in Blaze's memory. Pip looked around and started to worry.

"Master Locke, I don't see the root beer drum. Did Wooster, Stayven, and the others bring it?" Master placed his hand on Pip's shoulder.

"Yes, Pip. It's here. Don't worry. It's all taken care of. Congratulations, Pip and Dorken." Master Locke tapped Pip's shoulder reassuringly. Dorken began picking up slices of the abeetzah rounds and passing them out to the assembled members.

"Master Locke, who ate the first piece? That was supposed to be for Dorken and me?" Pip observed with hands on his hips.

Locke bowed his head. "Pigeon."

"I'll have to have a word with him. He just ruined my whole day! You couldn't have stopped him, Master? Shameful." Pip fanned himself with his bouquet and whispered to Dorken.

"Nothing's ruined and there can't be anything wrong about today," Dorken soothed leaning into Pip resting his head against his forehead.

After everyone was served, Dorken and Pip ate the official first bite, signaling that it was okay to feast. Once the food was consumed, the drum was opened and poured into small cups made from tree bark and then was passed around.

"Pip," Dorken started. "I feel that I have known you since we were just a little bit older than Cups here." Pip chuckled and covered his mouth. "I remember the moment you came walking in through the door. You were covered in paint since you were living under the duke's manor house and they had just painted it, which is how they found you. Master, not Master Locke, but Master Needum, was an exceptional reader of people and put us together to look out for each other. Here we are, years later, still together. I love who you are, what you are, and how you are.

"I wouldn't change anything—except maybe how many times we got in trouble over the centuries. But even that, Pip, was okay because we have had each other. I love you. Now that we are handfasted and have Cerenth's blessing, I know that I could never live without you. I love you, Pip, and nothing will ever change that. Handfasting is only a temporary arrangement, a trial if you will, to begin our love. However . . ." With those words, Dorken bent down on one knee. He held open his hand, revealing a ring. "Pip of Ballardton, I want to make this last forever so I believe a marriage would be sensible. I would like to make you my wife to have and to hold forever and ever. I know that we aren't bonded, but that could change in time, and having this life as our own choice is more important to me than anything in the world, Pip. Will you marry me for life?" Pip started crying.

The onlookers held their breath; it looked to many like Pip hadn't been prepared for this and that Dorken completely took him by surprise. With tears stopping Pip's words and catching in his throat, Pip made a high-pitched 'e' sound.

"Yes, Dorken, Yes! I thought we had to wait a year by the rules of handfasting! I have always loved you too! Yes!" Pip dropped to his knees, throwing himself onto Dorken and passionately kissing him. Everyone was clapping, cheering, and whistling; even Blaze took part.

"Oh," Pip began after standing back up and trying to quiet the crowd, "next time, we'll have cake too! A really big cake! With our names on it. This abeetzah had 'Happy Handfasting' and the new cake will say 'Married—Pip and Dorken' right across the top of it! Oh, and it'll have flowers all over it! You know the ones: like they have in the window at Two Realms Inn! Mm, that'd be delicious!"

The Olders started talking all at once, chattering away with the ideas of such a royal affair.

"Ooh, abeetzah and cake! We'll be here for that!"

"Congratulations, Pip! Dorken! Now that's really something to celebrate!"

"Wow!"

"Huzzah!"

"I don't think I've ever been so happy!" Pip raised his hands in the air excitedly. Dorken raised his in the air, catching Pip's hands and then lowering them down between them.

"Isn't that what you said at the handfasting, Pip?"

"Yes, but now I say it because I am doubly blessed just to be handfasted and soon to be married to you, Dorken."

"Pip. Dorken." Master Locke approached the happy couple that was hugging each other and smiling ear to ear. Pip rested his head on Dorken's shoulder and Dorken kissed Pip's head. "I have a gift. Actually, it's from Mason. He apologizes that he couldn't be here today, but he has paid to renovate the side room for you both. You can make all the design decisions, and I'll try and find a new place for the storage once Denalisa and Barden return to their, uhm, guild. The two of you can use the room for as long as you wish." Pip started to squeal again and ran up to Locke, kissing him on both cheeks while hugging him. Dorken also ran up and hugged Locke. Locke's face reddened. "You're welcome. I also have something else, but I'll give it to you later." Locke whispered the last line so only Pip and Dorken could hear.

"Okay, Master Locke. Is it something naughty?"

Locke blushed, reddening with the visual image that Pip invoked. Pip and Dorken returned to the dining table.

"Everyone eat up. There is more here. Master, can we put this in a stasis pouch for another day? We'd hate to have it go to waste. It's such a special treat." Master nodded.

Blaze went back to the little nook with a full tummy. The comfortable little nook and the sweet sounds of conversation lulled Blaze to sleep.

"

CHAPTER 18

MASON

Good morning, everyone! I'm back from my mission!" Mason greeted the guild.

"Hey, Mason! Welcome back! It's been years. How goes the love life?" Pigeon blurted out from his chair near the fire.

"Oh, it's okay. I met a mer-girl. . . . She was so beautiful and enticing. We were truly in love. But then I met her dad and he said, 'No daughter of mine is going to handfast with a land dweller,' blah, blah, blah. I was sent away from her. Then, I met a girl . . ."

"Mason, you and your love life! Why don't you try being more like Pip and Dorken?" Pigeon chuckled.

"I see what you mean, Pigeon, but one day I'll surprise you all, and I'll walk in and announce my handfasting day! Is Locke in the office?"

"Nah, he was going to talk to the mayor. Something is afoot, but of course I don't know what's going on."

"Yeah, in and out, in and out, the joys of being master of the guild. So glad that I didn't get *that* mission; it's not worth all the trouble. I'd never do it."

"Mason, is that you?" Locke poked his head out from behind his door. "Come on in. Pigeon, I need you to run this across town, please." Locke handed a scroll to Pigeon, who looked at the scroll with interest. "No reading! Besides, it's from the mayor, and it's spelled shut."

"S-H-U-T. Shut. That's how it's spelled," Mason said to Pigeon, who grimaced at Mason's joke. Mason grinned with glee while Locke hung his head at the pun, although his laugh lines showed his enjoyment.

"Come on in, Mason. I was just unloading from my visit with the mayor. There's a lot going on. I hope you won't mind going out again so soon?" Mason followed Locke through the door into Locke's office. He agreed to the mission without knowing what it would entail.

Blaze entered the guild later that evening. He had just eaten his full at Two Realms Inn, so he returned much later than he had originally expected. He knew that the others would be pack-piled in slumber and he'd have to fight through the pack to find his own space. He stealthily opened the door and shimmied inside, making barely a sound. His eyes adjusted to the darkness as the fire was barely flickering. He grabbed the fire poker and stirred the fire back to life. The small embers pulsed with energy. He grabbed some kindling and tossed it onto the embers. The embers swallowed the kindling and then they thirsted for more. Blaze added more kindling. When the fire awoke, Blaze added a larger log, and then, toward the back and leaning on the first log, he added an even larger log to feed the hungry blaze. The fire illuminated the room when he turned away from the fireplace.

Dark eyes studied the young thief. They stared out from the shadow and Blaze, now accustomed to the light, greeted those eyes.

"Mason! I didn't know you were coming back." Mason smiled, crinkling the edges of his eyes. "You missed Pip and Dorken's hand-fasting. We had abeetzah! Next time they're going to have cake with words on it and everything."

"Eventually, we all come back. I know I missed the handfasting. I saw them earlier and congratulated them." Blaze sat down at Mason's feet. He happily waited for a story of his adventure. Mason was a storyteller, and even though Blaze was sure that some of Mason's stories were tall tales, especially ones that involved Locke, he still enjoyed the telling. Mason's stories kept the days and winters bearable. He always made Locke look extraordinary during their missions together, but there was always some humor thrown in that peppered the taste of the tale. "I have been waiting for you."

"For me? Why? What did I do now?" Blaze crossed his arms across his chest and a mix of emotions crossed his face, from annoyance to curiosity.

"Blazey, why do you think that you did something wrong? I am getting ready to head out on another mission . . ."

"Yeah, so? You always go on missions!"

"If you let me finish, I'll tell you the part that is different." Blaze nodded, annoyance showing on his face. "Okay, so there is this mission that I am going on, and I want someone to go with me."

"Oh, really? So why are you talking to me and not Venom?"

"Because I want you to go with me." Blaze frowned.

"Did Venom say 'no,' so that's why you are asking me? He has been waiting for you to take him when you came back."

Mason smiled amusedly. "I already took Venom, and I haven't spoken to him at all since I've returned. I'm taking someone else this time."

"Maybe you should take Dellanie, Nightshade, or . . . Pigeon?"

"Pigeon? Why would I take Pigeon? He's too old now. Dellanie and maybe Nightshade will be getting their own missions soon, I surmise. No, I want you to go with me."

"Me? Why?" For a moment, Blaze thought he realized what this was all about. "Oh no! I see what's going on here. You're sending me away again. You can't do that!"

"What? Blaze, your horses are galloping away with you. You are getting off topic. I am not sending you away. I don't have that kind of power. This is an actual mission, Blazey." *Is it undercurrents?*

"Don't call me 'Blazey,' Mason. I'm not a Little anymore, so stop treating me like one."

"I forgot. I know that you don't want me calling you that. And I'm not trying to, Blazey—er, Blaze."

"I don't want anyone ever calling me Blazey again."

Mason's eyes were wide. He wondered what had gotten up in Blaze's craw. Knowing that Goldenrod would be leaving at the end of the Festival his heart sunk at the idea that he would be gone for any part of their time together. It had been such a small window of time, but she had made such a huge impact on him that to be separated would be like dying.

"Sorry, Mason, I can't go."

"Excuse me, Blaze? It wasn't really a request, but rather an order."

"An order?" Blaze's eyes widened. *Undercurrents. This is it.* "Are you *ordering* me on this mission for another reason, Mason?"

"Yes, if I must, Blaze. What do you mean for another reason? It's a training mission. That's it nothing more. It'll be good for you. This one fits your skill set."

"I didn't know I had a skill set." Blaze startled Mason with the remark.

"You do, but why are you arguing with me? I thought you'd jump at this chance. It pays well. You wouldn't have to worry about scrounging for measly coppies or selecting spelled pouches any-more after this. It'll be a boost for you. Blaze, I don't underst—"

"You don't have to understand, Mason. I'm just not going." Blaze turned his back on Mason and began preparing himself for refuge inside the pack pile of his age mates.

"Stop this right now, Blaze."

"I'm getting ready for bed."

"Well . . . yeah, I can see that, but that is not what I want you to stop. Although it would be easier to talk to you if you were look-ing at me and not moving between people." Mason's eyes followed Blaze around the quarters, sometimes straining to see the lad as he found the smallest of openings. "I don't think you'll fit there."

"Stop telling me what to do. You're not Master and you're *defi-nitely* not Rhatt or Jade. I don't have to listen to you."

"Really? Is that how you want to play this, Blaze?"

Blaze looked up from his newest opening, searching to catch Mason's eyes just over a small Little called Stunk. Blaze moved away, finally smelling the reason why the girl had earned that name. He rounded back out through the pile, defeated that he couldn't find a reasonably sized space. He placed his blanket roll on the floor and laid on top of it. "Blaze, it'll be worth it. I can't say what it pays at this moment. There are eyes on us." Mason caught the firelight in Pigeon's, Lace's, and Dellanie's eyes. He was sure there were more listening that just kept their eyes shut too tight for sleep. Lids closed quickly at Mason's words, and fake snoring quickly filled the room.

"We'll talk in the morning, Mason." Blaze lifted his body and covered himself with his lightweight blanket, turning away from Mason. "That is, if you can find me," he muttered.

Mason found Blaze the next day at the market fairly quickly. He was surprised to see him with a noble girl, talking as though they had known each other for years and economic differences were invisible. Mason drew a detailed drawing of her to ask Locke who she was later.

Blaze pulled Goldenrod around the town, showing her every nook and cranny of Ballardton. He took her on a tour up the road that led to the temples. After identifying each temple building, Blaze continued the tour by following an offshoot trail that led to an opening to the ruins of Ballard's manor.

"This used to be where the great wizard Ballard lived, Goldie. He rose Ballardton up from mere dirt with the strength of his magic, and he erected this great manor! The manor has since fallen, and it is now a dungeon. No one goes in there because it is full of all sorts of monsters. It's really dangerous." Goldenrod leaned forward, but all she saw were the ruins of architecture and a stone wall that was covered by an overgrowth of weeds and vines.

"That's the dungeon that my little cousin, Aldric, talks about. He said that he couldn't wait to get here, so that he can go in. I think he's been a few times so far this trip." Blaze snorted an exasperated sigh. "Oh, don't worry about Aldric. He says he used to go all the time when he was a little kid and never got hurt. Uncle Delrik isn't too happy that he goes down in there, though, based on his facial reactions," Goldenrod reassured. "I guess we shouldn't either. I wouldn't want to make my uncle mad at me, too."

"Yeah, you're right. You wouldn't want that." Blaze tugged on her arm, pulling her back down the road. Halfway down the slope, Goldenrod stopped and looked behind her.

"Do you think we're being followed?"

Mason slunk down in his hiding spot, surprised that the girl had caught sight of him.

"I thought I saw a hawk back there," Goldenrod pondered with worrisome embarrassment. "I really hope Keir isn't following me." Blaze scanned the treetops, searching for something that could easily be hidden within the forest growth. Mason sighed with relief.

"Nah, it's just us. Come on! Have you tried abeetzah rounds yet?"

Mason continued tracking the pair, taking a shortcut off of the road and stopping just before the market. Mason noted Blaze's genuine smile, which was unlike any that Mason had seen in a long time. They stopped at the pieman's stall first, then headed to Wooster's street to get a shared slice of an abeetzah round. Blaze and Goldenrod ghosted the tourneys, sneaking in right under the constables' noses. They watched the mages perform magical tricks, such as lighting a torch from a hundred paces facing backwards. Cheers abounded as the winner was declared, but Blaze and Goldenrod mocked the winner's skill.

From the tourney grounds, the two ran down Kings Highway toward the big oak tree. Mason trailed behind with stealth. Goldenrod pulled Blaze to a halt and leaned on him, panting. He instinctively put his arm around her, holding her close. Mason gained the lead on the two before he slunk into the brush near the tree. Walking now, Blaze wrapped his arm around Goldenrod, and she reached up, holding on to his hand.

"I really hope Keir didn't follow me. I want my aunt and uncle to trust me. I've learned so much that I don't even need him to translate for me any longer." She leaned her head on his shoulder. "I feel so safe with you." Blaze blushed. He again glanced around for Keir.

"Why don't we forget about the stupid Burd? Are you having a good time, Goldie?" Goldenrod stopped and looked into Blaze's eyes. She smiled at his awkward grin.

"How could I not? I got to see so much today. Ballardton is amazing, but I don't think it would be quite so amazing if I was with anyone else." Goldenrod moved closer to him. He laughed nervously. He felt the world dissolve away, and he moved his arms to accept her into a hug.

Seemingly out of nowhere, Snip and Spider appeared, screaming and running at them. Blaze spun around, catching Snip, but Spider pulled Blaze off of her. Goldenrod laughed wholeheartedly as Blaze tried to catch one or the other. The children were definitely able to outsmart Blaze by running haphazardly in either direction.

"Snip! Spider! Stop this! Just . . . go find Venom or something!" Blaze yelled, frustrated by the pair. Goldenrod sauntered up next to Blaze, took his hand in hers, and leaned her chin on his shoulder.

"I think they're adorable." Goldenrod smiled amusedly at Snip and Spider. Blaze glanced sideways at Snip.

"Believe me, they're not." He returned his attention back to Goldenrod.

"Come on, let's go over to that big tree."

Blaze hesitated.

"Maybe we shouldn't, Goldie. There is an elf who often sleeps in the tree. His name is 'Marn and he's often drunk." Goldenrod beamed.

"You know Telmarn? I met him in Drisana. He's really kind. He refused to come with us. Something about he couldn't come here." While Goldenrod was talking, Snip was behind her, mimicking her stance and mocking her. Blaze stared daggers at his little sister, who enjoyed making him angry. Then, without warning, Spider dramatically embraced Snip who air-kissed Spider the way that only children who still think the opposite gender is yucky do. Blaze's eyes widened and when Goldenrod noticed his expression, he prevented her from turning around.

"I think the oak tree would be a great place to go." He grabbed her arm and escorted her over to the big oak tree. Goldenrod glanced behind her shoulder and caught sight of the two children. She laughed outright. "Don't laugh at them." He yelled back at Snip and Spider, "Go find Venom! Now!" The children scampered off, giggling hysterically while making kissy sounds in the air.

Blaze leaned his back against the tree. Goldenrod did the same immediately next to him. She then turned her body towards him, looking him straight in his eyes. She raised her hand to rub his cheek. He smiled. He turned towards her.

"Blaze . . ."

"Mm?"

" . . . You know I like you." Blaze nodded. "I mean *like* like you." She had words in Mahdurnian that would describe it clearer with more distinct phrases.

He smiled sheepishly, feeling the rise of an awkward moment. She moved a little closer to him, their bodies nearly touching. She started slowly leaning in to kiss him. He didn't back away. She kissed him on his closed mouth. He pulled his head away from her. He could taste her and feel the softness of her subtle, wet lips on his. She followed him and they kissed again. Blaze moved his hands to pull her closer. They relished the moment. When they had finished, Blaze wrapped his arm around her fully. His stood up a bit straighter and all that mattered to him in this world was this girl and that she thought enough of him to kiss him.

Mason nearly revealed himself, but he was amazed at Blaze's interaction with Goldenrod. He wore confidence and self-assurance like a cloak of maturity. This girl could be of some valuable interest to Locke. Finally, Blaze walked a sore-footed Goldenrod back to the Two Realms Inn. They held hands and looked into each other's eyes. They asked each other to leave first: a childish game for young love. It took the intervention from the Drisanian princess to move the teenagers apart. Princess Eloine wished the young thief a good night, and he just stood there, staring after them with his hand raised in a superficial wave of thoughts and desire.

"Blaze. There you are! I finally found you. You've been a hard one to catch today." Mason took the moment to coerce Blaze back to joining him in the mission, interrupting the teen's emotions.

"Huh? Oh, hi, Mason." It took Blaze a second to realize the reason for Mason's arrival. "Oh no! I'm not going on a mission—*not now!*" Mason placed his hand on Blaze's shoulder.

"I promise that I will not tell Locke about our conversations or about the girl. I promise that it will be swift; then you can get back to the, eh, important things in life." Blaze raised his eyebrows at Mason, wondering what Mason knew. "Besides, wouldn't you like to buy something nice for your girlfriend?"

Girlfriend? The thought resurfaced again, but it still seemed almost foreign to Blaze. *I really like, like her. So maybe it'd be nice to get her something.* He looked around. *That's a nice rock.* He bent down to pick it up, wiping it on his tunic. Mason started to laugh. "You can't just give the girl you kiss a rock off the ground."

"Why not? It's kind of nice." Blaze rolled the stone in his hand until he lost his grasp and it rolled away bouncing to the safety of a bush. *Wait, how did Mason know I kissed her?*

"Ah, young love! The days when the simplest things make the most sense, like a dirty old rock. That is not what girls want, Blaze."

Blaze stared at Mason. *What do girls want? Oh, I know: a dagger or a wrist strap, both of which cost coin. Where would I get the coin from?*

Blaze looked up with renewed interest in Mason and his mission, and he grinned eagerly.

"What's the mission, Mason, and how much does it pay?"

"Well . . . since you asked Blaze . . ."

"You kind of made me ask, Mason."

"Ah, I guess I did. It's a simple one, but it pays a full pouch of ebons. Give or take."

Why? Why would it pay so much? Blaze wondered, but Mason continued, answering his questions for him. "It involves going into Cadmaria, dropping off a scroll, and then returning back to Ballardton. See? Simple."

"Cadmaria?" Blaze stumbled on the word as it caught in his throat.

"Yes, Cadmaria. With your pouch full, you'll have to have it spelled. After all, everyone was awake last night so they know you are heading out on a mission with a substantial purse to be had. There is nothing worse than losing the pouch just after getting it," Mason warned.

"Oh, I'll probably lose it anyway, but there is something I need, so . . ." Blaze wanted to get something to give to Goldenrod so she wouldn't forget him. Something that a girl would want.

"So is that a yes?"

Blaze sighed heavily and exaggeratedly. "Yes. Also when you say 'simple,' do you mean fighting? Venom said that you and he went on a mission and you both fought hill-people."

"We only fought hill-people, Blaze, because Venom made them aware of our location. We probably won't see any of them or anything else of any importance to be worried about. We need to become shadows for this mission—not seen or remembered. We will become just a blank face following the rules of the land and we won't—do you hear me?—we won't pull any weapons on anyone or go against their established laws."

"So . . . we're going to deliver some stupid scroll and that's it? It's not fair, Venom got to fight."

"You only want a fighting mission? Go sign up with the mercs or the army."

"I think those are probably the better ones, right? Ruri used to say that," Blaze explained.

"Who cares about Ruri? He's long gone, and good riddance. He wasn't all that he thought he was. Fighting missions are the most dangerous."

"With danger there's money. Look at the dungeon."

"No, there isn't. A lot of the fighting missions are only because of mistakes, and mistakes don't pay. So please focus. There is only one mission, and this is it. Do you want it or not?" Blaze had never seen Mason so angry, at least not at him. Mason always had a soft-spoken voice with a hint of a laugh at the end. Blaze looked back out toward the direction of Two Realms Inn, exhaled air, then turned back to Mason.

"Okay, I accept the mission, Mason, as long as we are back before Festival ends."

"No doubt. I suspect we'll be back before the end of the week, and you'll have time with the girl."

"The girl's name is Goldie, and she is a noble in Drisana. And she likes me." Blaze said the end of the sentence with childish glee and a dopey grin that made Mason laugh.

"Do you like her?"

"Maybe. . . a little." Mason caught Blaze in a bear hug. Blaze struggled slightly away and punched Mason gently in the arm.

"I have to go, Goldie." Blaze held her in front of him with their heads bowed and touching. Goldenrod didn't want him to go."I promise it won't be long—no more than a week." She embraced him. The warmth of her body touching his was a welcome new part to their relationship. She was soft and her hair covered his nose. He inhaled the aroma of freshly ground, dried wildflowers with hints of Pyrrinian oils that perfumed her hair. *Shampoo from Two Realms Inn.* This is the safety and comfort he had wanted—no, *needed*—his whole life. *I don't want to go; I never want this moment to end.* Goldenrod pulled away. Tears welled in her eyes.

"What's wrong?" He gently lifted her chin so their eyes met.

"Well, I'm leaving soon Blaze, and I don't want to leave you." He pulled her close, reassuringly."I was wondering, would you ever . . .?" Goldenrod stammered, afraid of Blaze's response.

"What? What is it?"The whole world had disappeared, and they were the only ones left.

There was no nobility, no guild house, and no trying to survive—there were only the two.

"I was . . . was wondering . . . if you'd ever . . . maybe, you'd want to . . . come to Mahdurna, where I am from?"

He looked at her, his mouth agape. The question was simple and honest.

"Never mind, it was stupid. Why would you want to come to Mahdurna? After all, it's not like here . . . at all." Blaze reached up and put his finger to her mouth. She stopped talking, and she waited for him to answer.

"I'd like that very much, Goldie. You could show me what a— how do you say it?" He searched his thoughts while his lips tried to turn into Mahdurnian words, but they failed him. "I don't know what it was called, but you could show it all to me." She smiled at him. She had never felt this way about anyone before. Blaze was the complete opposite of everyone she had ever dated but when it came down to it, he was her perfect. She looked around, suddenly aware that Keir was nearby probably watching the whole scene. A light breeze fluttered by. *Was that Keir?*

"Okay, so after you come back, we'll go to Mahdurna." Out of the corner of his eye, he noticed Mason, who had been waiting and standing nearby all along. His face reddened, and he agreed to go with her.

"I have to leave now, Goldie. I've kept Mason waiting too long." Goldenrod glanced at Mason, who waved to her. She held Blaze's hand. As he turned to leave, she held on, waiting for the last moment to let him go, letting their fingers slip past each other until he was gone.

"Isn't she great, Mason?"

Mason smiled knowingly at the young lover.

"Yep, she's great, Blaze. But are you going to moon over her the whole while? We'll be back before she leaves. I spoke to her aunt, Princess Eloine, who assures that they will still be at Two Realms Inn by the time we return. They will be visiting with the Timerian nobles, as she was once fostered with the queen and duchess as children."

"Why are people fostered, Mason? I never understood that." Mason nodded. It was a good topic to distract Blaze while they walked toward Cadmaria. Mason was happy to not have to hear all about the girl, which seemed to be a repetitious onslaught of, "Isn't she great?" Mason cleared his throat and started.

"People are fostered for many different reasons, Blaze. First and foremost, the nobles are fostered to make an alliance between kingdoms and a promise of a betrothal. Think about it; let's just say you were noble-born . . ."

"I'm not, I was born here." Blaze crossed his arms, stuck in a constant critique of his birthright. Mason glanced sideways avoiding Blaze's glare.

"I know. I was there that day. I was one of the first to hold you. You were so small and you were just wrapped in a sheet. Jade

handed you to me and then you peed right on my . . ." Mason
blushed and glanced at Blaze, who obviously wasn't impressed of
being reminded that he was once a tiny baby with bodily functions. "This is just hypothetically speaking. Let's just pretend you
were nobly born and didn't pee where you did."

"Why do you always bring that up? I was a baby, and babies pee.
Just the other day, the Little called Straw peed right on Master
Locke's door. He actually hit Lord Ballard's feet, and that image is
about equal with my nose!" Blaze laughed so hard that he couldn't
stop. Tears streamed down his face as he remembered the scene.
After glancing back at Mason's straight face, Blaze summoned his
control. "Now we always let Straw go ahead of us."

Mason closed his eyes, suppressing a full-on fit of laughter
himself.

"Okay . . . I'm sorry that I brought up that you peed on me when
you were a baby."

"Mason! You did it again!"

A rustling in the brush caused Mason to hush Blaze's voice while
he took careful steps toward the sound. Blaze followed, blade
already drawn. Mason put out his hand to stop Blaze's footsteps.
He reached the brush and two gray voles scurried out around his
feet. Mason exhaled a sigh of relief, and Blaze was amused by
Mason's reaction to a couple of rodents, which were commonplace
in the guild.

"Don't look so smug, Blaze. You never know what you might
run into. You should always be aware of your surroundings." Mason
started walking again, and Blaze caught up with him.

"But Mason, we are on King's Highway. There wouldn't be any
monsters or anything out here."

"Okay, that may be true about the monsters, but there could
always be hill-people lurking, or highwaymen, or thieves."

Blaze stared dumbfounded at Mason.

"Thieves! Really, Mason? Oh, no! That would be horrible! I'd
hate to run into some *thieves*." Blaze over dramatized his mocked
fear.

"They might intercept the delivery. You have to be wary of all
people that you come across." Blaze looked at the parchment scroll
that was hidden in his satchel. *Why would someone care about this*

parchment? It's useless. Reading Blaze's body language, Mason realized the boy's thoughts.

"It is worth more than a king's ransom." Blaze stared at his satchel long and hard. It was hard for him to believe that words would be worthwhile. *More than a king's ransom? They're just stupid words. How could they be worth that much? Would that be a gold piece? Or would it be worth a dragon coin?*

"Come on, Blaze. We have to get going. I'd like to get to the border before the evening breaks. I no longer want to talk about the scroll. It is imperative that we keep its existence a secret," Mason whispered in Blaze's ear. Blaze nodded in agreement and understanding.

Blaze and Mason continued on in silence, but the silence was awkward and could tip someone off to their mission, as silent companions traveling together were unusual on the road. Mason decided to take up the conversation again where they had left off prior to the voles. "What were we talking about, Blaze? Do you remember?"

Blaze thought for a minute but his memory eluded him. He was noticing the road and how they chose an offshoot of King's Highway. They had continued through the woods into an area that opened up into a clearing. Blaze had an overwhelming feeling of being there before. He started to look around with fearful anticipation.

"Oh, I remember, Blaze! We were talking about fostering!" Mason's cheery interruption made Blaze jump.

"Shhh, Mason. This looks like the place." Blaze searched the area for any markings that were familiar. "The clearing . . . this clearing was once full of devlins, Mason." Blaze remembered Amoria. Her face still haunted his dreams, especially in the dark of the winter when his belly growled and his pouch was empty. Amoria was probably a devlin by now, he figured, and a new queen had risen to walk aimlessly in search of her next successor.

"When? How do you know that devlins were here?" Mason was confused. *Were these strange behaviors what made him unsuccessful?* Mason wondered. Blaze crouched down to examine the flora. He searched in nearly every area of the clearing—but what was he looking for? Mason couldn't tell.

"On my turn-year when I disappeared. There were devlins, Mason, and a queen too." Blaze ran back to Mason trying to convince him of something that was never told.

"A queen with devlins? A devlin queen, Blaze? That's not true. Devlins travel alone in the night. Maybe you didn't see what you think you saw." Mason was giving him the look, the look he received when the adults didn't understand him. The look that says, "You're unpredictable—we can't trust you." It was a look that he had hoped never to see from Mason. He had seen it many times from Locke and many times from the other thieves. His heart fell. Blaze had wanted to tell Mason about the devlins, but now he just kept silent and glared. Blaze saw a look of disgust, but, it was a look of confusion, an adult trying to figure out a puzzle that was never-ending. A puzzle that could be solved if you just stared at it long enough.

Blaze started forward again without a word to Mason. The forest opened to a trench that had been carved out of the land. As they trekked on, the furrow deepened. The sides of the furrow were topped with slick, obsidian banks that would be difficult to climb. Mason ran along behind Blaze. The woodland foliage began to thicken underfoot; creeping vines, moss, and ferns caught his feet with every step. Hearing Mason's scuttle behind him, Blaze quickened his step.

He tripped when he stepped into a hidden depression. Mason caught up to him.

"Are you okay?"

"What is that up there?" Blaze pointed to the bank. Mason nodded.

"That is the residue of a slugslime trail. We are actually in the track right now."

"Will we see a slugslime?" Blaze asked.

Mason chuckled. "Don't worry, this track has been here for a very long time. You can tell because of all of the foliage inside of it. Besides, I've taken this way to Cadmaria many times, and I have yet to see a single one. You may want to keep an eye on the sky, though. As we enter Cadmaria, we will see dragons."

Blaze's eyes sparkled. He had never seen a dragon before. He knew there were dragons deep inside the dungeon and that Dellanie had gotten in far enough to steal their treasure and their scales, but maybe now he could get a dragon scale of his own. *I'd take it and exchange it for a dragon coin. Or I could give it to Goldie as a gift! I bet no one has ever given her a dragon scale before. Yep, it's decided. I'm going to get her a scale.*

"Don't go thinking that you'll be able to get rich from a scale," Mason said, reading Blaze's mind. "Mostly the dragons we'll see are silvers, and they are as common as voles and raskulls that live in the wildwoods, Blaze— everywhere. But be wary of these commoners. They are vicious, and once they smell blood, they attack without care, sometimes eating each other." Mason pulled out a map from his satchel and studied it. "Cadmaria isn't that far now. We'll be there in the morning. We should start to make camp soon, maybe just up ahead. It looks like there is a small grove of trees coming up." Mason rolled up the scroll and returned it to his bag. It wouldn't be too much longer until Blaze could see Goldenrod again.

Setting up camp wasn't that hard. Mason did the majority of the work and sent Blaze searching for dead wood on the ground. There seemed to be a lot of fallen wood, so he didn't have to scrounge very hard. After returning with the wood, Mason showed Blaze how to start a fire from nothing. It took some time, but after several attempts, Blaze finally got it.

"It would be easier if we had a mage with us, Blaze. One of the first spells learned by the mages is light a candle spell. It also works with lighting a fire." Blaze knew that mages took many shortcuts in life. They were soft and didn't know the truth of living. He was glad he was not like them.

The warmth of the fire was familiar and was a soft comfort in the wilderness. The shiny banks helped to lighten the area with a red, shimmering hue. Blaze held his palms open, feeling the heat warm his hands. A soft but cool wind tugged and pushed against his back. The fire strained to stay lit, flickering all the while. Mason set a pot of water on top of the fire and placed two potatoes into the embers. It would be a simple dinner, but a dinner, nonetheless.

"While we are waiting for the food to be cooked, I want to share more information about the task at hand." Blaze shimmied forward, leaning in to hear every word. *Finally, we are getting to the good stuff,* Blaze thought with excitement. "So first off, where is the item that I gave you?"

Blaze looked up, blinking blankly at Mason. Mason's eyes widened, but a swift smirk crossed Blaze's face. "It's here." Blaze patted his side. "I have it safely hidden like you told me. I'm not simple, Mason."

Mason relaxed. "I know. Okay, but no more jokes about its whereabouts. Deal?"

"Yeah."

"Okay. We are heading to the Pierced Slugslime. It's a tavern in central Cadmaria. We are going to find a woman with a red headscarf. She is our contact. We'll order two drinks at the bar, and she will ask us an unusual question."

"What's the question?"

"I don't know."

"Then how will we know? Is there only one woman in all of Cadmaria wearing a red headscarf?"

"Of course not. Believe me, we'll just know. Oh, and don't have a tell on your face when you are asked the question. Just keep looking grumpy, like usual."

What? I don't always look grumpy. Do I?

As if reading Blaze's every thought, Mason responded appropriately. "We can't always see our own faces, but you have been looking angrier lately—except when you are with the noblewoman."

Blaze's face slid into a dopey half smile. *Goldie.*

"Try not to interrupt again. This is extremely important; our lives depend on the success of this mission." Mason paused and looked at Blaze seriously. Blaze sat upright, straighter than he ever had before. "This is either a success or a fail, and I'm not in the habit of failing at my missions, Blaze. There's no coin in that. Now, she'll ask us a question and we'll invite her to join us. You will be between the two of us since you're carrying the parchment, and then you'll use the skill known as sleight of hand. Don't look at me like that—I know you know sleight of hand. Finally, she'll leave, but she'll pass the parchment on and so on. Then we'll leave the tavern. Any questions?"

"Who will she pass it on to? I thought it was *extremely important*. What if it gets in the wrong hands?" Blaze whispered, making sure the trees could not hear him.

"It's of no concern to us who she passes it on to or if it falls into the *wrong* hands. We aren't here to partake in their politics. It is important, but that's not our mission. The guild will receive payment for services rendered—that means that we did our job. When we return, we will be compensated." Mason grabbed a thick, long stick that he had been poking the fire with and rolled a potato out of the embers. Mason produced two potatoes, which were

once plump and had now taken on a wrinkly skin as their interiors
withered as they cooled. "Careful, it's very hot." Mason reached into
his satchel that had been tucked just behind him and pulled out a
full skin of birch beer. He passed the skin to Blaze. Blaze took a
swig, then returned it to Mason. Blaze unhitched his eating knife
from his belt and stabbed the potato, which emitted a loud hissing
sound. Mason grabbed his potato with a gloved hand and retired to
the bedding that he had set out.

The evening was clear, and the moons danced across the night
sky. Blaze couldn't see much from within the slugslime trench, but
he enjoyed the smells of the new growth and the burning embers
of what fire still smoldered in front of him. He ate the potato well
after it had cooled. Eventually he lay on his bedding, but dozed on
and off throughout the night anticipating the next day.

CHAPTER 19

PIERCED SLUGSLIME

THE MORNING BROUGHT THE SUN, a breakfast of cured, dried meat, and the packing up of the camp. It felt like it took years to Blaze because he was so eager to carry on. When they started walking again, Blaze was surprised at how much the woods looked similar to Timeria. He kept stride with Mason, but every so often, his pace would falter due to his curiosity. Blaze kept his eyes to the sky, waiting and hoping to see the Silvers. He was as fearful about dragons as he was excited.

Blaze remembered how the storyteller Skelly would mystically appear at festival times to talk about the Great Mage, Ballard. Intertwined within those tales were images of dragons flying freely above Ballardton. Inside the tales, Ballard controlled the dragons and kept them from causing harm to any Timerian. Ballard had cast a country-wide safety spell, which forbade the dragons from openly flying in Timeria. It had lasted centuries, keeping Timeria safe. Other places were not as fortunate as Timeria. Nashira, the nocturnal elvin kingdom, lived within the destructive path of these great dragons. There, rogue dragons were forever on the prowl.

Cadmaria also suffered much under the tyranny of the dragons. Silver dragons were bestial and vicious. No one was safe from the Silvers. Although Silvers tended to flock, they had no loyalty to anyone aside their hunger lust. With his eyes skyward, Blaze was not as careful as he had been before their arrival into Cadmaria. Crossing the border from the wildwood into Cadmaria was a definite shift from woodlands to farmland. Blaze surmised that they were following the main road now. Fences kept cattle and sheep penned in and trespassers out.

After walking for what Blaze thought was hours, the two travelers arrived at their destination. Central Cadmaria was a bit busier than Ballardton. There were actual buildings for their marketplaces, each with their own sign telling the name of their wares. Blaze stopped at a sign with a great big pig painted on it. The sign was made of splintered wood. He called out to Mason, who had walked slightly ahead of him.

"Mason, can you come over here?" Mason rejoined Blaze, who whispered, "how come these signs don't have letters?"

Mason laughed outright. "It's true, they don't. There are many in Cadmaria that cannot read, so it is unnecessary to add the words."

Blaze slowly nodded. "What do you think the pig means?"

Mason glanced over to Blaze and then to the sign. "Blaze, think about it. What do you think it means?"

"Um, I don't know . . . Maybe a butcher?"

"Yes, very good. See if you can figure out the next one." The game continued on, with Blaze figuring out the silversmith, the cooper, the clerics, and the apothecary. Then he stared up at a sign that had been recently painted and was made of wood, just like most of the signs in Cadmaria. The background was a light blue with a slugslime drawn in the middle. The slugslime was painted the exact color of mucus, but the most interesting detail was the arrow sticking out of the slugslime, precisely striking its eye. He looked around for Mason, but Mason must have snuck into the apothecary three shops down.

Blaze stood there, waiting for Mason to reappear. As he waited, two men walked by and they, too, stared at the sign. The first man made a gesture toward the sign, which was acknowledged by the second man.

"Can you believe it? They pierced an arrow through the slugslime's eye. That'll never kill a slugslime. They know nothing about how to pierce a slugslime. Right, Shale?"

The second man laughed. "Yeah, but it would sure make it angry! It'll be spraying all of its ewz outwards from sheer anger," Shale retorted shaking his body to emulate a slugslime.

"Not everyone knows this, but the real way to kill a slugslime is to pierce it through the small dark spot on the top of its head. If you miss that spot, you'll have one mad slugslime on your hands." The first man pointed to a spot on his head near his hairline. "Oh yeah. Shall we go in to the Pierced Slugslime Tavern for a drink, Shale?"

"I thought you only cared about signs, but the ale here is the best in all of Cadmaria, despite its unfortunate name," Shale replied.

"It's only the best because this is where we are right now."

"You better believe it, Zaffron. You better believe it." Zaffron wrapped his arm around his friend's shoulders, and the two danced into the Pierced Slugslime. Blaze watched after them, but then returned his attention back to the sign scrutinizing it for new meaning. Mason soon emerged from the apothecary, carrying a muslin bundle.

"This is one of the best places to get wyrmwort. It'll stop any burn in seconds; okay, maybe more like minutes. You have to crush it down with a mortar and pestle and then add boiled water to make a paste. It works amazingly well. I just had to get it when I saw it in the window. I'm sorry I didn't tell you where I was going." Mason secured his bundle in his satchel. Blaze pointed at the sign. "Yep, that's it. Let's go in. You, first."

As he walked into the Pierced Slugslime, Blaze was amazed to see how dark it was. The curtains on the bar front brought light to only the front tables, which was in stark contrast with the rest of the tavern. Stopping in the middle of the room, Blaze closed his eyes to become accustomed to the darkness. His hesitation caused patrons to yell as they tried to reach the bar, and Mason ran smack dab right into Blaze's back. Blaze opened his eyes and turned to see who ran into him while Mason gestured for him to move forward, even though Mason himself was still squinting. The room was a blend of brown tones. Blaze's eyes caught sight of Zaffron and Shale, who it sounded like were engaged in speculation about the longest length of a slugslime to have ever been captured. They gestured with their hands, each time pulling them further apart. Once his eyes had adjusted, Blaze guided Mason to the bar. It was similar to the one at Lords and Ladies, which was not surprising since the inn was owned and operated by Cadmarians. They also enjoyed the Cadmarian aesthetic of metalized objects. This bar was a metalized wood top with a blackened metal front. To Blaze, it came off as cold and distant, but it seemed that most of the patrons were pleased with the aesthetic, as was Mason.

Mason enjoyed traveling. He loved to go from place to place and was pleased that his master allowed him to visit places all over the world under the guise of missions. These missions were like having a secret that only he knew, especially when he was in a situation where there were plenty of other people around that were unaware. Today was one of those days. Blaze carried the scroll securely. Instead of carrying it in his satchel as Blaze would have preferred, Mason had insisted on wrapping it closely to Blaze's chest like under-padding for armor, though Blaze wore no armor. There was a string that Blaze had tucked inside his sleeve that could release the scroll. It would fall neatly to his lap, to be given privately to the red scarf lady who had yet to make herself known.

"What'll you have, handsome?" A bar wench approached Mason. Her nearly bare breasts blossomed out from her bodice, creating a shelf-like appearance. Mason glanced into her cleavage and then glanced at her stern and worn face.

"What do you recommend, my love?"

"So, handsome, I'd recommend the Spicy Slugslime Milk. It contains a locally made rum with a jigger of syrup, spices from Pyrrin, and milk, all shaken and put in one of our Pierced Slugslime shaker glasses. It really is a way to remember your trip to Cadmaria and is a keepsake for all."

"Great, that sounds grand. We'll have two. One for me and one for my companion here."

The wench eyed Blaze curiously. She raised an eyebrow.

"Actually, I have a special signature drink for this young one. Don't worry; it's similar to the Spicy Slugslime Milk, but it isn't quite as spicy as the original. Pyrrin spices can be too strong for young pallets."

"I've had Pyrrin spices before. They're good. My friend, Hende-Li is the best cook . . ." Blaze stopped, noticing the disapproving look on the woman's face. "Thank you, I'll have the one for children." He bowed his head, attempting to lower his enthusiasm and calm his expression.

The wench worked diligently at the bar, her back toward Blaze and Mason as she prepared the drinks. She turned back towards the two travelers, smiling and catching Mason's eye, then violently shook the Spicy Slugslime Milk. All the while, her bosom shook up and down. Mason grinned with delight. Blaze caught Mason's arm.

"What's up, Blaze?" Blaze gave Mason a disapproving look."Oh, don't worry about that. It's just flirting. It's harmless. She wants more coin, so she is trying to make me interested in her. I'll pay her my standard amount, and not a coppie more."

Blaze nodded, relinquishing his grasp.

"Do you see the woman?" Blaze whispered. His heart raced as he waited for the moment of exchange. He had rescanned the room. Zaffron and Shale were toasting each other with ale, laughing away the outside world. A couple in a far corner snuggled together, whispering as they kissed. Blaze thought back to his kiss with Goldenrod. It was nothing like this couple's kissing, but it had made the world stop. He longed to return to her.

The bar wench walked in front of his view of the couple. He watched her return from the icebox with chilled milk in a frosty pitcher. A young boy scurried around the room, navigating through chairs and tables and dodging the bar wench as though he had done it his whole life. *Must be the proprietor's son*, Blaze thought. *I still don't see the woman with the red headscarf. She must be here somewhere.* Blaze's thoughts were his own, at least he thought.

"Remember what I said about your tell, Blaze. Fix your expression. I can read your thoughts just by looking at you. Good. Okay, just enjoy your drink. It's here." Blaze leaned forward and sniffed the less spicy version of the Spicy Slugslime Milk. It was served in a stemmed coupe with a cinnamon stick perched inside like a decorative straw, giving Blaze the sense of drinking a very rich, fancy drink. It was unlike anything he had ever had. The smell of the spices and rum created a sense of relaxation. He had no idea how a drink could do that, though he was sure these were not Pyrrin spices but rather some takes on the original. The aromas had a distinct flowery sickliness to them. He said nothing to either the wench or Mason. Milk was a privilege and one that Master Locke tried to provide at the guild. Specks of spice peppered the milk rum drink as he brought it to his lips. He sipped it. It was stronger than he had expected; he was sure it contained more alcohol than Mason's much larger glass. At first sight, Blaze had been disappointed that Mason had more of the drink, but after tasting the cocktail, he was glad his was so much smaller; he didn't want any more than the one sip because it burned his esophagus.

Blaze scanned the room again. Several people had entered: three men with turbans and two women with headscarves, but none that were red. Blaze sipped on his drink, and after every sip, he reminded himself that it was horrible and he wasn't going to drink any more. With every additional sip, Blaze felt his face flush, and he found himself dreamily amused by his drink. Playing with the cinnamon stick, Blaze twirled the contents of the cocktail, creating a small whirlpool that seemed to separate the milk from the rum. He enjoyed the activity, but he was feeling tired. His eyes closed and his head bobbed, shocking him back awake. He held his head up against the heel of his palm, lazily relaxing into the effects of the drink.

"Excuse me, young sir, but do you know the way to King's Highway?"

Blaze shook himself out of the dreamy stupor and looked up at the woman standing in front of him. The woman was roughly Mason's height and wore a sari with blues, oranges, and reds. Her wimple was a solid red. It was wrapped intricately over her head and around her face and was tucked under her chin. She also wore a face veil, which covered all but her eyes. Her eyes were dark brown, enhanced by the outline of long, thick eyelashes. Since she had yet to receive an answer, she tried again. Blaze stared at her, blinking blindly like she had just asked him to shave a Lupin on the full moons. He was actually thinking about the answer to her question, which was an odd question because he didn't think that Cadmaria had a King's Highway like they do in Timeria. *Oh!* Suddenly, his mind caught up to the conversation. *She means our King's Highway. She's the one we are here to see.* He held up a single gloved finger, indicating his need to wait. He tugged on Mason's tunic, but Mason just waved him off. He tugged again.

"What is it, Blaze?" It was then that he saw her. He sat upright, giving her his undivided attention.

"Sir, can't you tell she's married? Just look at all that fabric?" The bar wench spoke loudly, trying to attract Mason's attention. She then returned to her duties, annoyed by the loss of a hopeful marriage proposal.

"Oh, it is good to see you. Did you ask my companion a question?" Mason leaned in over Blaze to listen carefully to her question.

"Excuse me, but do you know the way to the King's Highway?" The woman's voice was sultry with a touch of a Cadmarian accent.

"Yes, my lady, I'd be happy to show you. Would you care for a drink?"

"Excuse me, barmaid, may I have a tropical slugslime?"

The bar wench nodded, glaring at Mason as she walked away.

"Perhaps we can all go to the table and discuss the quickest route." Mason waited for the red-scarf woman's drink to be served. He carried it to the table, following her. Blaze had wanted to discard his drink but then remembered the plan, which included everyone bringing a drink to the table. Looking into his drink, he thought, *Yuck! This is probably what a slugslime really tastes like.*

Walking over to the table, Mason spread the map out. The map concealed the table like a tablecloth. The red-scarf lady sat with her ankles crossed and her legs slightly angled to the right. Blaze sat next to her, awaiting the moment of exchange. She moved her veil to drink and gently sipped the cocktail. Blaze watched her, though he didn't mean to stare. She didn't make any movements that weren't planned or calculated. She was refined in every way possible. Even though he was unable to see her whole face, there was a familiarity about her. She glanced up at him. He darted his eyes away. *She reminds me of Princess Eloine. Clearly she isn't Goldie's aunt, but it's how she is carrying herself. Does she realize that she's sitting next to two thieves?* He lifted his drink and took a full mouth gulp of the wretched concoction. Once it was in his mouth, he wished it gone, but the only thing he could do was swallow. He made a disgusted expression, which caused the lady to suppress a giggle. Mason tapped him to get him to settle down but it was too late. He coughed until the alcohol had burnt off of his tongue.

During this time, Blaze noticed a move toward sleight of hand. Mason glanced at him, waiting to see if he noticed the cue. He did. His hand turned slightly as he pulled the string to release the parchment. He grabbed the scroll and passed it to the lady who was also just as skilled at sleight of hand. Where she put the scroll, Blaze couldn't tell. He surmised it was neatly tucked in her sleeve. She grabbed her drink and threw it into Mason's face.

"How dare you? I'll never leave my husband!"

Mason's mouth was agape. He looked around the tavern, and his face reddened with embarrassment. The bar wench smirked. Blaze's eyes followed the red-scarf woman, who dashed into the kitchen and out of sight. The mission was complete, but Blaze figured it wasn't the way Mason expected it to turn out. Slowly, the bar wench approached their table, carrying a cleaning towel. She tossed it at Mason's face.

"You could have had a real woman; all you had to do was ask. Stupid." She adjusted her bodice, raising her breasts higher in the garment, spun on her heels, and flounced away. Many of the patrons were looking, but none seemed interested enough to do anything about Mason's predicament. A man at the bar raised a glass to Mason and another walked close to the table, carrying a drink. He set the drink down on the table. Blaze glanced into it and was repulsed by the bubbling green sludge. The man stood there, waiting for Mason to drink it.

"It'll help you forget that incident and that loose tahtar."

Mason smiled at the man.

"Thank you so much, good sir. However, I regret that our son here will be unable to forget his mother's actions. It would be unwise of me to leave in such a stupor as a Green Soother would cause." The man nodded his agreement, grabbed the drink, and slapped Mason on the back. Blaze thought he caught sight of the man tearing up.

"You be a good son to your dad. Do you hear me, son?" Blaze nodded quickly as to not upset the man. "That's a good boy. You take care." He nearly lifted Mason out of his chair, spilling the Green Soother, and hugged him. "Yeah, you take care of your boy, too."

"I will. His mother is a scoundrel."

Blaze smiled, knowing the truth. The man returned to the bar.

Leaving the tavern was easier than Blaze had thought it would be. Mason had to wipe down the map before he rolled it back up. They had waited until there were hardly any patrons in the Pierced Slugslime before slipping out into the late afternoon light. Mason had placed an ebon on the table for the bar wench. Blaze had a burning question, but held his tongue until he and Mason were alone. It was time to get out of Cadmaria and back to Goldenrod.

"Blaze, I'm very proud of you. You did really well today. I'm sure you are going to get more missions from my recommendations to Master."

"Really, Mason? I didn't really do anything. It's not like I even *had* to."

"Yes, Blaze, you did. You followed the mission perfectly, and that is what a mission is all about."

Blaze stared at his feet. "But when you went out with Venom, you got to fight. It wasn't a stupid mission like bringing a scroll with stupid words on it to someone at a pub."

Mason let out a full belly laugh. "Blaze, first off, every mission is different. I believe we have already had this conversation earlier. We really shouldn't talk openly about this here." Mason lowered his voice. "As I told you before, the only reason we had to fight was because Venom was too noisy, and hill-people that dwell out in the wildwood were alerted that we were there. It is the only reason why we had to fight. You were stealthier than Venom was—I don't think that boy could ever be quiet even for a minute."

Blaze looked around at Cadmaria. They were nearing the center of the capital. The buildings were closer together here. There were people on either side of them, and they pushed their way past, even knocking into the young Timerian. Blaze felt the urge to rub his ear, but he wasn't sure why. *Well, at least I fit in here.* His ears were perfectly round from the Cadmarian Ear Cutter—rounder even than most Cadmarians. He looked up at Mason, a sinking feeling in his stomach.

Blaze had known Mason since he was born. Mason had brown, tousled hair, a slight goatee that he trimmed close to his full face, which usually held a smile that lit his whole countenance. He was more of a father figure than anyone else at the guild, and Blaze's love for Mason ran deep. When Blaze had any trouble, it was Mason who would come to his aid. For the most part, Blaze listened to Mason.

As they trudged through the capital, the beat of a drumming cadence erupted, deafening the onlookers. A cart with a man walking behind it who was strapped by a tether at his waist led a procession of horses, constables, soldiers, and townsfolk that enveloped Blaze and Mason into their fold. Between horse hoofs, the cart's speed, and the beat of the cadence, the man was mostly being dragged along behind. His tunic fell around his hips, allowing his bare chest and bloodied back from an earlier thrashing to be visible. His hands were tied and his ankles chained. Following the cart, Cadmarian constables wore hoods of misty gray and carried axes.

"All must bear witness! No one is allowed to leave the city! All must bear witness!" A bellman who stood in the cart rang out the

alert. He repeated the announcement. Mason acknowledged the
bellman with a slight bow while maintaining a neutral expression.
Blaze took a deep breath and tried to appear as calm and unaffected
as Mason.

"Can we go? You promised I'd get back within the week." Blaze
leaned into Mason, whispering his quiet plea.

"You heard that, right?" Mason whispered back."We have to
stay and watch the execution."

Mason followed quietly alongside the road, trying desperately
to remain indifferent to the celebration. Blaze took his lead from
Mason, keeping his head down and glancing sideways. *What could
that man have possibly done that would account for this?* Blaze wondered to himself. A Timerian execution was a very rare occurrence
and one that had to be for offences against the crown. The only
person Blaze could possibly think worthy of that 'honor' would be
the thief who stole the prince and replaced him with a changeling,
but their identity was still a mystery, even to the king and queen
themselves. The procession stopped at the center of a square. There
was a stone dais that had steps leading up to stocks. The stocks
were unveiled when the cart carrying the accused stopped in front
of the platform. A priest stepped forward. The man pulled away
from his bonds, jingling the chains.

"No, no, no! Please, Your Eminence! I ask for your forgiveness!"
The prisoner fell to his knees, genuflecting, hoping to appeal to
the priest's mercy. Blaze watched in horror. He looked around at
the audience of spectators, expecting a similar response. However,
many were smiling with gleeful anticipation: entertainment at its
best.

BOOM! The drum rang out again. BOOM! This time it was a
single strike on the bass drum that marked the time of the man's
imprisonment. BOOM! Blaze's heart waited for the next note.
There was an unnaturally long rest between the beats. BOOM! The
drum vibrated. Then the constables released the man from the cart
and led him up the stairs to face the priest. The drummer banged
the drum again, but this time the beat quickened. Blaze imagined
that it was the man's heartbeat increasing as he was shoved at the
priest's feet.

Suddenly, the drumming ceased. Silence blanketed the capitol.
Everyone waited with bated breath to hear what the priest was
going to say, but it was the jingling of the chains that interrupted

the silence first as the man shifted his weight back and forth. The priest raised his arms and the crowd gasped.

"I present to you the accused, Cathal of Tibor. He is accused of publicly aligning with a Vassyric Order of Knights. These knights have been associated with the God Vassyr in name only and have been corrupted by the dark gods of Mirias. Therefore, the Vassyric Knights have become enemies of the state and have been driven out of Cadmaria due to their crimes against our country, our livelihood, and all of humanity. These knights have been found guilty of multiple inexcusable acts of child endangerment, including, but not limited to, sacrifice, trafficking, molestation, and indoctrination; slaughtering of Cadmarian leaders including our own dear King Runyon, who fell heroically on these knights' swords whilst protecting his people. Our temporal ruler, High Priest Septimus, will canonize King Runyon in the near future. It is with the high priest's decree that we accuse Cathal of Tibor to be sentenced to a single day in the stocks unless he renounces his loyalty to these traitorous knights. How does the accused plead today? Innocent or guilty?" The constables pulled Cathal to his knees and held his head to meet the priest's gaze. A woman screamed and wailed in the street.

"Please somebody, save my son! Cathal, renounce your allegiance to these knights. He is not one of them, Your Eminence, I promise you that!" The priest stared long and hard at the woman before returning his gaze back onto Cathal.

"How do you plead?"

"I am guilt-free. I cannot renounce my loyalty. Gods save us all!"

The priest smirked, raising his lips in a snarl.

"Fine. Place him in the stocks. I will ask you again, Cathal. We are not without sympathy for our enemies." As soon as his hands were free, Cathal fought against the constables as they transferred him to the wooden structures. Cathal's mother keened as she watched the abuse. Mason leaned against a tree looking uninterested in the activities. Blaze tried to keep a bland expression, fighting against his disgust at the trumped-up charges and brutality. He could see public humiliation in his own future based on how Constable Sterling always treated him.

"What are we going to do Mason?" Blaze whispered, without turning his head. Mason stood up, grabbed his satchel, and ushered Blaze away. They walked to an inn, which stood opposite the square. Mason approached the innkeeper.

"Good day, sir, so much excitement today." The innkeeper had a pointy little nose that housed a small pair of wire-rimmed glasses, over which he peered to see Mason. Blaze took an instant dislike to the man.

"Yes, we'd like a room."

The innkeeper eyed up Mason and then Blaze. "Do you want only one bed?"

Mason shook his head. "No, two beds are preferred. This is my son."

The man looked disappointed as he reached behind him to grab a key. "He sure is a fine one—your son: young, strong, and handsome with perfectly round ears. He could fetch a nice price if you are interested in getting a few extra coins for the night. If you're interested, I could comp you the room too." The man peered at Blaze from head to toe and smacked his lips. Blaze felt embarrassed, humiliated, and disgusted. Never before had he been propositioned. He swallowed hard, glared at the innkeeper, and stepped behind Mason.

"Thank you, but no. We will have nothing to do with that; although, we do thank you for the offer." Blaze was aghast. *How could Mason say that?* He was surprised that Mason didn't just jump over the small counter and punch the man squarely in the face like he himself wanted to do. After paying the man for the room, Mason tried to calm Blaze down with a hand gesture. "It's okay. We'll talk about it later," he whispered.

"You're not from around here, are you?" the innkeeper pried. Mason smiled back at him.

"Oh, we're from Cadmaria, but near the border of Timeria. Stupid Timerians with their crazy ears." Mason scoffed.

"Pointed ears are a delicacy here, you know. We do sell Cadmarian Ear Cutters if you're interested in capturing any Timerians. We have them in different sizes, from infant to adult. Just send their ears back here and we'll pay you well for them. The longer the point, the more you'll make." Blaze felt sick to his stomach, between this innkeeper and the injustice outside.

Mason gave a put-on laugh. "Oh, we don't see many Timerians, but I'll think about it. Now about the room, are we all set?"

"Oh, yes, my fine sir. You'll be in Room Twenty-two. It is on the front of the building, second floor—you'll get a great view of the action outside. Tomorrow will certainly be exciting. Oh, and if you change your mind . . . just ask for Fennian. Sleep well."

Arriving in the room, Blaze said nothing. He looked around; the room was much smaller than those in Lords and Ladies. The walls were a drab yellow and a stale smell of urine struck his nose, as if the linens hadn't been changed between several guests. Grime coated the single window, making the room darker than day would suggest. Blaze opened the window, and a dust devil swirled into the room, coating everything with another layer. Mason sat down in an oversized chair that hinted of luxury, though the tear in the back was a perfect home for mice. Along the edges of the room were mouse droppings, and Blaze was sure bugs infested the mattresses.

"I can't believe you suggested that I'd be interested or that you'd want to sell me! What are we doing here anyway? Can't we just go home?" Blaze turned angrily on Mason.

"Of course not, Blaze. I never suggested that I'd sell you at all. As you heard from the bellman, we cannot leave the city limits. If we try, we most definitely will be noticed and that could land us both up on that dais with the knight. Now listen and listen hard; this will help you on any mission you ever take. You must become one with the place. Be seen and yet not seen. Fit into whatever role is needed to get the mission completed. Right now, we are Cadmarians and we cannot change that, or we will be exposed. We must adhere to their laws and their beliefs for now. Since we were part of the lot of spectators even by accident, we must follow through with this. That is why we are staying." Blaze shut the window quickly and a puff of dirt rose into his face making him sneeze. He coughed it away.

"What are we going to do about that down there? It's wrong! The man is going to die because he is with the Vassyric Knights! Vassyric Knights are good and just. That priest was lying. Why did everyone believe him? I think they're all happy that he's going to die." Blaze kept glancing out the window. A single thought crossed his mind. *Undercurrents.* He wanted to ask Mason, but instead he rubbed his sleeve in a circle, cleaning the window to see the young man on the dais. He watched as passersby threw fruit at Cathal. Children mocked him and threw stones that hit his face causing instant bruises. "He might not even make the night. Why is there a covering above the stocks, Mason?"

Mason walked over to the window. "That covering will conceal him from the Silvers. Tomorrow, if he survives, he'll be strapped to that table over on the side and he'll watch as the Silvers lunge down to eat his flesh. It is a horrifying way to die, but it is ideal for the Cadmarians. It keeps all of their people fearful and law abiding. Lies become truths in order to make sense of crazy. Unfortunately, we have to watch it like Cadmarians—completely unfazed by whatever happens. Do you understand—no emotion? You need to be in control of your emotions. This is a normal occurrence here. It is even celebrated."

Mason turned back and went to lock the door, but he was surprised to find that there was no lock cylinder in the door. He had unlocked the door upon their arrival, but he now rethought it. *I guess I didn't and it is just for show. Why?* He glanced at Blaze, who had grabbed a stool and was intently watching the stocks. *Oh, I know why! Nope, Fennian, not tonight—not ever.*

"Good morning, Blaze." Blaze awoke stiffly. He had fallen asleep against the window, sitting on the stool. He glanced at the beds, which were still made from the day before. Mason sat in the overstuffed chair, pushed up to the door, holding his dagger tightly in his hand. The door had opened during the evening, but Fennian had been unable to get past Mason. He had reached in to see what was blocking the way only to reach out and touch Mason's hair. Mason sliced Fennian's forearm with a swift and able blade. His injury deflected any further attraction to Room Twenty-Two.

"I think I need to use the loo, Mason. Where is it?"

"It's outside, right behind the inn. You are not using it, Blaze."

"But, Mason . . ."

Mason knew the teen's distress, but he couldn't be sure that Fennian wouldn't attack Blaze when he was unattended. "We are going to leave. We'll head back to the tavern for breakfast and you can use the loo there. I think it is safer."

Blaze was impatient. The less Spicy Slugslime Milk, with the fake Pyrrin spices, was finally finding its way home and Blaze knew he wouldn't be able to walk that far to the tavern.

"Safer? How old do you think I am, Mason? I have to go to the loo—now. I can handle myself. Isn't that why I'm on this mission with you? Or are you just following Master's orders to get me away from the guild?" Blaze's stomach gurgled, and he could feel a pain in his side. "I have had worse moments than a fight with that weasely little innkeeper."

"He'll probably have help, Blaze."

"Pshaw! Don't worry, I'll be right back. My dagger's in my boot." Blaze pushed Mason and the chair out of the way exiting out the door. He ran toward the loo, only to be confronted near the rubbish bins that stood near the back exit of the inn by two burly men and the unctuous innkeeper. His stomach ached, but he fought against any reaction. He retrieved his dagger.

"Oh, he's a pretty one, Fennian. He's mine." The first burly man hurled forward, but Blaze quickly moved, allowing for the man to stumble by his own force and inertia. The second man lunged, armed with a spear. His hands worked the spear shaft with ease and control. Blaze ducked and blocked against it, his small dagger long enough to stop the close-range encounter. Blaze tucked his dagger into his belt and grabbed the spear shaft. He had practiced this art many times over the years with Dellanie, though she used crossbow bolts. Blaze thought this was much easier. He held onto the shaft and used the man's overt size to knock him into his partner rendering both useless.

Blaze turned toward his final opponent, pointing the spear at Fennian. With fierce gritting teeth, he charged forward, growling. Fennian screamed, begging for Blaze's forgiveness; his glasses fell to the ground. The spear's point was close to the innkeeper's throat.

The Cadmarian didn't dare move, but Blaze noticed his thugs were regaining their footing.

"Call them off or you're going to die today."

Fennian believed the boy to truly mean it. He nodded his head in agreement. "Gon and Syph, go away. I don't need you right now." Gon and Syph stopped in their tracks. They backed off because they were fully aware that Fennian would die if they didn't. One thing was quite clear: the teenager was well trained.

"No! You're going to tell them to leave me and everyone else alone and that you'll never do this again! Do it! Tell them now!" The spear tip inched closer, and Fennian realized that Blaze meant business.

"Okay, okay. Gon and Syph, we're going to leave him alone."

"And . . ." Blaze encouraged.

"And we're never going to do this again . . . to anyone." Blaze's stomach pain intensified and as he held his side, grimacing, Fennian realized that this was the perfect time to retreat. Blaze ran to the loos, which were set back against the treelined border of the inn's property.

"Are you all right? It took you quite a while to come back. I was getting worried." Blaze carried the spear as a trophy of his encounter.

"It was just the less Spicy Slugslime Milk. I'm fine."

Mason noticed the spear and pointed at it. Blaze shrugged.

"I just picked it up somewhere." Mason accepted Blaze's answer. The young thief sighed with relief because he didn't want to explain everything that had happened on the way to the loo. He'd never live that one down, just like peeing when he was a baby. *Ugh, why do adults have to be so annoying by remembering everything?* He tossed the spear on the bed. "Are we going? Also, did we give the scroll to the right person? How do we know? She was so authentic when she threw that drink into your face." Mason smiled. *Good, boy, you're back thinking about the mission.*

"We are going in just a few. Yes, how many Cadmarian's would ask about a Timerian road—it was a nod to our guild. The drink thrown in my face . . . Well, that was a new one, but it was a good way to end the gathering and divert suspicion." Mason grabbed Blaze's spear, thrust it into his satchel, and tossed the satchel to Blaze, who caught it. "Let's go. I don't think we will be able to avoid the proceedings outside. We should get a pretty good spot that will allow us to leave swiftly if we leave now."

"What about breakfast?" Blaze grinned at Mason.

Mason tossed him a roll from his bag. "We don't have time to go anywhere now. You took too long in the loo." Blaze looked up at the ceiling, annoyed by Mason's comment.

"You're not going to let me forget this, are you?" Mason's grin spoke volumes, and the teenager slumped behind Mason as they exited the room.

CHAPTER 20

SCALES

OUTSIDE, A CROWD had already begun to gather. The drummer had been joined by a piper, and the two played requests from the crowd, who threw coppies onto the platform. With each turn, the piper would bend down and pick up the coppies, and then drop them into a bucket. The echo of the coppies tossed into the steel bucket indicated that they had just started, and were hoping to fill the whole bucket before the priest arrived. Standing next to the performers in the stocks was Cathal of Tibor, looking weary and dehydrated. He raised his head and his face was swollen and cut with black and blue welts. His wrists were bloodied from attempts to escape the stocks. The man looked defeated. Blaze looked around the square again.

He found the familiar faces of smirking entertainment seekers. He noticed the righteous lot who taunted Cathal for his crime against Cadmaria. They shouted death threats and obscenities at the young man. He also saw Cathal's mother. She was calm, as she cared for other members of her village and her priestess. Tears welled in her eyes, but those around her comforted her. They prayed, but Blaze knew not to whom they called on for favor, or whether they were already asking for the man's safe departure from this life into the next from Goddess Hala.

Robed figures wandered in and out of the crowds. Their white gowns were reminiscent of those worn by Priestess Elanit back in

Ballardton. They seemed to find approval within the spectators' arena. Blaze followed them with his eyes.

"Hello, young man. Are you looking for a good deal today? How would you like to buy, for a small fee, a piece of the three Demesnes: the Realm of Light, Eldon's Kingdom, and the Realm of Darkness? Who do you follow?" A wandering vendor approached Blaze rather aggressively. He picked up a small bottle with a liquid. "This, my fine fellow, could be yours. It was once a favor given to King Runyon by the Princess of Light herself. It is worth a small fortune, my young sir; but for you, a single ebon."

Blaze doubted its authenticity. "So . . . you think that this little glass bottle that you can buy at the tavern with ale in it, was once given to the king by Goddess Rhiun? Really? I'll bet that it has some of that water over there that is dripping off the roof."

"Well, it's not for a doubter like you. Good day, sir." The vendor stomped off, heading toward Cathal's family. Blaze looked around the square. There were nearly thirty-five robed figures and one stood close to him. He felt uncomfortable and told Mason, but Mason hushed him, telling him to watch. Blaze could see the priest from the day before waiting at the bottom of the steps to the dais. The musicians noticed also, and quickly retreated with their loot and instruments. The priest caught the drummer by the arm, instructing him on his duties. The drummer nodded as he gave the bucket to the piper, who took off through the crowd.

Cathal didn't see the priest approach from behind the stocks. Blaze watched. His heart raced and he wanted to flee. Mason placed a hand on his shoulder, squeezed him reassuringly, and whispered, "It's going to be okay." Blaze could smell the incense that was newly set by each of the hooded priests. The stench burned his eyes, nose, and throat. He coughed, ridding himself of the intrusive smoke. As he watched Cathal struggle to free himself, Blaze unexpectedly felt enraged by the young man, but he couldn't understand why. The crowd started to yell and curse at Cathal. The priest raised his arms as he moved in front of the knight. The audience hushed, waiting for the priest's words. Blaze could tell that magic was at play.

"Yesterday, Cathal of Tibor, you were accused of treason for aligning yourself with the Vassyric Knights. After a day and night in the stocks, how do you plead today? Guilty or innocent? Renounce your allegiance and live another day." The smoke circled over the heads of the crowd. The priest repeated his words. "Renounce your faithful commitment to the Vassyric order. Renounce your knighthood or be strapped to the table!"

"Strap him down! Strap him down!" The crowd chanted, raising their fists in unison.

After several minutes, the priest settled the audience. The smoke puffed out in gray billows, fanned by the priests.

"Please let him speak. Cathal of Tibor, how do you plead?" Cathal shook his head. The smoking incense affected him and he blinked blankly at the priest. His mother approached the dais. "You are his mother, are you not?" She nodded that she was. "Do you wish to say something to your son? You may speak freely." The smoke sank like a pool of morning fog, draping over Cathal's mother.

"Strap him down!" She began the chant, and the crowd erupted, joining her. Once again, the priest settled the audience.

"Speak now, Cathal. What say you?" The young man raised his eyes skyward and moved his lips. Suddenly, a strong wind moved across the square, sending the smoke away from Cathal. He blinked and regained his strength. "We cannot hear you! How do you plead?" Cathal turned his head to meet the priest's eyes.

"If I were to die today, it would be by my own hand. My lord Vassyr does not lead us astray. By Vassyr's sword, I plead that I am a true and faithful guardian of Vassyr's virtue, honor, and fortitude. I shall never renounce my commitment to my duties as a Vassyric Knight. Kill me, but you do so with all of the Realm of Light watching and knowing that the Darkness comes from within. I am and will always be Sir Cathal of Tibor, Vassyric Knight to his royal highness, King Runyan, my liege. For my whole life, I have been sworn to protect Cadmaria—today is not unlike any other. My life belongs to the Vassyric Order. I have done no wrong. I have served Cadmaria and Lord Vassyr well. My blood is on your hands. Gods save Cadmaria!"

"Done! To the table, then!" The priest turned dramatically as the smoke returned to the dais. The spectators took up their chant again.

"Strap him down! Strap him down! Strap him down!" Blaze watched as Cathal's mother threw a rock at Cathal hitting him in the head. Stones took to the air as the constables transferred Cathal from the stocks to the forged metal disc. The top had blistered from immense heat. Leather straps and chains fastened Cathal's body to the table. Once secure, the priest loomed over Cathal's face and stared down at the young knight.

"Your treachery has caused these actions, Cathal of Tibor. Your blood is on your own hands; mine are clean. You cannot turn against your duty as a Cadmarian without paying a price. This is the price of treason against Cadmaria." The priest addressed the vocal crowd. "Cadmaria will rise to power! Cadmaria will be the hub of the world! We will smite any who oppose us! Long live Cadmaria!" The priest poured a sticky orange liquid on to Cathal. The man writhed, pulling away from the tethers, ripping open his wrists and gouging his feet raw. The priest turned to his right nodding to the constables.

"Release the Silvers!"

The smoke covered the spectators making them virtually invisible to the arriving Silvers. The priest walked off the pedestal with large confident steps and a grin across his face.

In the sky with their mouths drooling from hunger, the Silvers swooped. The aroma of the sticky goo enticed their senses, causing the Silvers to hunt for only the sweet lure. Three silvery arrows flew toward the square, and their stomachs growled for the food offered, creating a thunderous roar. Blaze had never seen a dragon in person, and he was surprised by their emaciated look. Imprisoned since their last feeding, they were free and starving and getting closer with every passing second. The drummer pounded his drum with an anticipating rushing beat. The Silvers were above them now. People screamed running for cover, but the Silvers didn't see them through the smoke. They swooped down on to the square getting a closer look at their prey.

With bad eyesight and a poor sense of smell, the Silvers attacked. The drummer ran for safety. Talons scraped the table and tore into Cathal's flesh. A Silver landed with its forelegs on the table, sniffed against Cathal, and then began ripping gobs of flesh from his stomach. Cathal screamed in pain. With Cathal watching the giant beast, the Silver pulled out his intestines, shaking its head to break the tubing. Blood, flesh, and stomach bile drenched the crowd. Blaze watched in dumbfounded horror. Cathal gurgled his last breath. The stench of death was becoming unbearable, and Blaze raised his face mask to cover his mouth and nose.

"Hala, guide him," Mason whispered. Another Silver flew over the crowd, diving through the air, grazing the table, ripping apart

Cathal's torso and pulling off his feet, which were still bound to the table. It tossed most of the lower body into its mouth with one gulp. The Silvers pulled at Cathal's body, fighting over what was left of the knight. Two Silvers perched above, nibbling on the man's upper body; they began a tug of war over the remaining bits. Cathal's head detached in the struggle and rolled into the square, nearly at Blaze's feet. The knight's eyes stared straight ahead, his horrified expression frozen in death.

Blaze looked up at Mason, only to catch movement from his peripheral vision. The Silver had its eyes on the severed head. Blaze drew his dagger as he leapt out of the Silver's path. The dragon turned its massive head to get a good look at Blaze and bared its teeth. Then it charged. Blaze circled around the dragon, moving faster than it could follow. Mason had never seen Blaze move so fast. The dragon growled as it turned to look for the young Timerian.

"Blaze!" Mason screamed, his heart in his throat. Blaze ran again at the Silver with his dagger aimed at the beast. The dagger bounced off of the Silver's scales and it turned back to attack Blaze, but another Silver intervened biting the first. Fire engulfed the first dragon and Blaze slid under the dais. Mason ran to Blaze's side, pulling him away from the onslaught of dragon fighting dragon and away from the square. Blaze and Mason ran, dodging in and around the frenzied crowd until they found themselves back at the inn.

Without hesitation, they entered the inn, breathless. They watched the square from the lobby foyer. The hooded priests with the incense had mostly dispersed. People who had run in search of safety and were injured or trampled by the mob were now scurrying away from the Silver battle. The last Silver soared over the dais, falling into the other two, chomping its great jaws into another Silver's flesh. The three Silvers fought for their lives and the meager morsels that once were Cathal.

"What were you thinking?" Mason grabbed Blaze, turning him around. "You almost got yourself killed. You can't get involved in the middle of that kind of a situation. Ugh! You're just like Locke . . . crazy!"

"I'm not like him at all! Don't compare me to him!"

Mason hugged Blaze, who pulled away. He looked out of the window. The battle was coming to an end. Two silvers lay dead while the other one ate their flesh. Dragon parts and human flesh littered the square. The winning dragon consumed the others, looking like a carrion bird. The battle was done. The last Silver raised its head, chewing on a final, stringy muscle. It moved the muscle down its long throat, biting at the air until it consumed the last bit. Then the dragon took to the sky. It circled the square before flying off, in the direction opposite of the way it had entered. With the fleeing dragons, the attack had ceased, and the city returned to a semblance of normalcy.

The streets sparkled with the reflection of Silver scales left behind in the onslaught. In the spot where he had narrowly escaped the dragons' attack, he could still see Cathal's head on the ground, close to where it had fallen not more than half an hour ago. Watching the streets, a constable walked through the muck, kicking pieces of flesh—he cared little about to whom the pieces belonged. He strolled over to Cathal's head, removed a bag from his pouch, picked the head up by the hair, and dropped it into the bag. The constable slung the bag over his shoulder and hummed to himself as he journeyed on to the high priest's tower on the far edge of the capitol.

"Do you want to talk about this, Blaze?" Mason gestured to the remnants on the ground. Mason had become accustomed to this type of injustice from multiple missions. He had become complacent and numb to the horrors, but he could see it clearly in Blaze's eyes. Trying to be brave still, Blaze swallowed back his tears and wiped them away with a clean part of his cloak, shaking his head that he did not. Mason smiled. Feeling the need to heal the pain of his charge, Mason grinned and excitedly changed the subject. "You know that was your first dragon you've ever seen. You should take a scale home. Maybe for Goldie, or to show off to Dellanie." Blaze sighed and thought about Mason's suggestion. *I'm going to get one so I never forget.*

"Yeah, Mason. I'm going to get a scale. Wait here," Blaze instructed Mason, without looking at his mentor. Mason didn't abide by Blaze's instructions and followed him. *It's surprisingly quiet,* Blaze thought. *The quiet after the storm.* He grabbed a scale, rubbed it on his tunic, and placed it in his pouch for safekeeping. Odors of sulfur and death hit his nose as he walked silently around the square. He glanced at the table. The remnants of Cathal's feet and ankle were still bound to it. He felt the urge to vomit, remembering the attack he had witnessed. "*It'll be okay,*" Mason had reassured him before Cathal's sentencing.

"You said it was going to be okay. He wasn't okay. I feel like I knew him."

"You did not. We only know him by his conviction to his order."

"But he's dead now. Killed by the people he swore to protect... why?" Tears welled in Blaze's eyes. "Why do people have to die?" Mason squinted, unsure of the direction that this whole conversation was headed.

"It's the natural order of things. It is the way of Eldon's Kingdom. All creatures are born, and all creatures die. It is as it has always been and it is as it is supposed to be."

"It doesn't make it any easier. I've always followed my God, King Eldon, but these deaths were needless."

"These deaths were not the work of Eldon, Blaze. There is a darker magic and violence here." Blaze felt a more personal connection to Cathal's death, though he was unaware of it until he vocalized it.

"But, Mason, did Rhatt die similarly? I have a blurred vision of his death. I think he was pulled apart like Cathal." Mason didn't know for sure. He wasn't there at Rhatt's death. Blaze had returned to the guild telling everyone that Rhatt had been skewered. What had bothered Mason most was that Blaze had distanced himself from Rhatt's death as if his father had been discarded like a broken tool.

"Blaze, I don't know. You and Jade told us that Rhatt had died. There was never any body. We hope that there might have been a mistake, and Rhatt is still alive."

"No, Rhatt is very much dead, Mason," a female voice spoke. It was cruel and cold and could belong only to Jade, who wore the robes of the hooded priests that had lit the incense. Neither of the thieves knew where she came from, but her approach was startling, and they turned and faced her. Mason pushed Blaze behind him protectively. Mason could feel Blaze shake at Jade's sudden appearance. *Had she been watching us? How long?* It was a thought shared by both Mason and Blaze. "Rhatt's power was given graciously to our Goddess; his sacrifice does not allow him to return to this life or any other. His soul will forever belong to my Goddess. He was a fool—gave himself up for . . . nothing." She glanced at Blaze on the final word. Her words held a twinge of a mocking laugh, and they struck Blaze to his core.

"If that's true, Jade . . ." Mason began.

"*Priestess* Jade of the Temple of Good," Jade corrected, outstretching her arms for effect.

"If that's true, *Jade*, Rhatt saved the one person who mattered the most to him." Mason leaned forward threateningly. "By giving himself up for Blaze, he saved himself from your Goddess. The Goddess Hala knows."

"Yes, I am a priestess." Jade ignored everything that Mason said.

"No one cares. You're still aligned with the Dark Queen."

"The Goddess herself, Queen Mykondra, has touched me, and with her touch, I have increased my power. My devotion has not gone without notice." Jade thought back, pausing on her own memories of her youth. Her thirst for power had moved her actions ever since that day.

Jade glanced at Blaze, who peered around Mason, wondering why the conversation had stalled. Jade jovially reacted to his appearance, speaking to him as though he was a pet. "Any magic or sprite powers yet? Is Mason taking you out for a walk . . . maybe to see the big city? The whole execution of the traitor was thrilling, don't you think Blazey?" Jade circled around Mason, who spun on his heel, following her with his dagger ready. Jade was unpredictable and not to be trusted. "Mason, by Her blessed eyes, he is my son!"

"You're not worthy of being called his mother, Jade."

Jade grinned, unimpressed. "I gave birth to him. You were there, Mason. You can verify it. Blaze is my son, and you can't stop me from speaking with him. That is all I want—to speak to my darling boy." Mason averted his eyes. It was true. He was there the day Blaze was born to Jade. The horrible truth was that it was all true. Every word. Blaze was born to Jade, and there was nothing he could do to stop Jade from talking to Blaze. There was always something that nagged at him about the events. Mason had never forgotten, and in order to get to sleep at night, he would recount that day every evening trying to figure out the discrepancy. Unfortunately, the discrepancies were like a puzzle tugging on his subconscious mind trying to find the the pieces that were missing, even though, the puzzle seemed whole; perhaps it was more of a desire that Blaze wasn't born to that wicked, uncaring, power-hungry whore. But he was, and there was nothing that Mason could do to change that.

"All right, you can speak to him, but if you hurt him in any way, I'll hurt you."

"Oh, please, Mason. Pshaw!" Jade snickered with a haughty smirk. Blaze took a deep breath, controlling his emotions as he moved cautiously toward his mother, his posture revealing no respect for the woman. Walking around Mason, he could feel fear rising up in his body, shaking his legs as he anticipated her attack. *What will it be this time that she takes from me?* He watched his feet as he walked closer, managing the courage and knowing that Mason was behind him to protect him. He slowly raised his head when he reached her. She could see the fear in his eyes and the slight tremble of his body. It gave her power and she relished it.

"So, you're officially a Cadmarian now?" He asked in just above a whisper.

"You knew that. I have been since Tima was born."

"Snip! Her name is Snip! As long as she is with me, her name is her own and not yours to have. What do you want from me?" Jade cackled and he flinched at the sharp noise. Her voice resonated through the square.

"Your life! Your soul! I gave it and now I want it. It belongs to my Goddess. I marked it as thus and now I'm ready to take it."

Upon hearing her words, Blaze laughed, and his fear left him. "That is the stupidest thing I've ever heard! How long have you been practicing that?" The absurdity of her words gave Blaze resolve and strength that he never knew he possessed. He took a deep breath and then he spoke.

"So, how do you want to go about taking it, Jade? I guess you could start with my arm that you nearly severed off; or we could start with my other arm that you have torn out of its socket many times; or maybe we could start with just going to the temple and placing me on the altar, which I vaguely remember. Or, better yet, why doesn't your goddess just strike me right here, right now?" Blaze extended his arms, waiting for Mykondra to smite him.

Jade glared at his mockery. "You're a simple fool. My Lady will take you when she is ready. All of those times I marked you, and I will do so again."

"No, Jade. I have finally understood who . . . no, what . . . you are, and both Snip and me, we don't want anything to do with you ever again. You can go and follow your beloved Goddess for all we care, just leave Snip and me out of it. Let us live our lives away from you."

Jade was breathing hard. If she hadn't been in her robes, she would have run him through. His disrespect was enough to send her over the edge. *Does he think he is better than me? No, he's mine and so is Tima. They were the ones that I chose to manipulate and to control as I please.*

"Now you listen here, you little dirty scallywag. I gave you life, which means, and let me spell it out for you: you owe me! You owe me all of your power. I will never let you be better than me. Know your place, boy! You are a dunderheaded simpleton and you will do as you are told." Blaze stood up straighter with his head tipped back defiantly.

"I am not simple and I have outgrown the need for you, Jade. I will follow my own path, whether that means that I stay at the guild forever like Pigeon or head off on missions every week like Mason, or, I don't know, maybe there is another path that I can't see yet. But I do know, Jade, that you are not on any of them. And as for your Goddess, let her come. King Eldon will protect me." Blaze turned away from Jade and began to saunter off, but she caught his arm, digging in her nails, making it bleed, and marking him again. Blaze glanced at her hand, and then he matched her gaze. Her smile faded, and she released his arm temporarily. His face pale from the encounter, his eyes wide, and sweat wetting his brow, he looked toward Mason. *I can't believe I did that.* He wanted to throw up, and the snatching of his arm had sent terror down his spine.

"Wait! You have something that doesn't belong to you." Blaze turned back toward Jade, unable to conceive of what he had that she would want. Jade sneered at him with a malevolent gaze. "I want you to hand it over." Blaze instinctively patted himself down. What was he carrying? There was nothing of any importance that Jade could possibly want. He wore his tunic, breeches, cloak and belt, attached to the belt was his pouch, his eating knife. He wasn't carrying his satchel any longer since the mission was complete; Mason held on to it. He did have his boots that concealed his dagger.

"I don't have anything, Jade. I don't know what you're talking about."

"Oh, I am sure you know. Give it back now!" Jade took a step back, looked around, and signaled an alert to a mounted constable. "They stole the scales! They stole the scales!"

"What? No, I didn't. What are you saying? It was on the ground." Blaze fumbled. Mason sprang into action; Jade didn't hurt the boy physically, other than some nail marks, but to be thrown in a Cadmarian dungeon would be a true death sentence.

I didn't know you couldn't take any scales from Cadmaria, even Silver scales; they're hardly worth anything, Mason thought as he grabbed Blaze's arm, nearly pulling it out of its socket.

"Come on, Blaze! We have to leave the capitol immediately. There's no telling what actions she's launched." Blaze hurried alongside Mason. He looked back at Jade. She mouthed the words, "I'm coming back for you." Then she ran a single finger across her throat, leering widely. Blaze stumbled. He regained his footing and looked to Mason for direction.

"We have to separate. They can't get both of us. I know you're fast, Blaze. I'll meet you back in the woods where we made camp. Don't worry, we'll both make it out of here. Not so boring a mission any longer, huh?"

"Mason, okay, but what about the scale that I picked up?"

"Keep it. It's not really about the scale, but it'll be a reminder of this day! Now run! I'll go in this direction. Be prepared to fight." Mason arced away from Blaze and turned back toward the mounted rider. He spooked the horse, making it rear up. For a moment, the rider lost sight of both culprits, but Mason jumped around, gathering the rider's attention. The rider blew a whistle that alerted everyone around him.

Blaze didn't waste his time. He sprinted away from the square, running past the apothecary and through a crowd of shoppers. At the end of the street, another mounted constable blocked the way. Blaze changed his direction and followed a herd of teenagers, who pushed him away and into the street. He fell into the dirt. The teenagers pointed and shouted to the constable. "He's one of them! Get him!"

They picked up stones from the ground and threw them at Blaze. Blaze tried to dodge the rocks, covering his face with his arm, but he was hit in the chest and shoulder. The horse loped toward Blaze. The constable drew his sword, altering his weight and throwing off his horse's gait. Blaze glanced up at the constable and rocks or not, he ran back toward the square. He sprinted for the dais and slid underneath it. The whistle blew again.

From his hiding spot, he could see people rallying against him and Mason. The scurry of the mob worried Blaze. Legs of all sorts crossed in different directions. Then the group of teenagers ran past the dais.

"He's a rat in a hole. We'll catch him."

Blaze breathed in deeply. It was now or never. He had to get to the camp. He had to get back to the safety of the slugslime furrow. *A plan*, he needed a plan before he proceeded, but his mind was empty. He hit himself in the head, hoping for any clear thoughts. His heart raced. He'd have to just go through and react to whatever came his way, but he'd start off by being the rat that he had always been.

Blaze slipped out from under the platform, staying low to the ground, hiding behind any structure between him and smallest groups of swarming Cadmarians. Crouching down, he sprinted across the square to a whitewashed house. His way was clear and his movements alerted no one. Walking quickly and with purpose, he made his way to the back of the house. Clotheslines zigzagged across the yard. A servant exited the house, carrying a large basket of clothes; seeing Blaze, she screamed, dropped her load and ran back inside.

There was no time now. A cloak longer than his own lay on the ground. He snatched it and pulled it over himself. Leaving the yard, he walked hurriedly back toward the apothecary. He knew no other way. He looked around and took his walking cue from those around him. He quickened his pace and tightly held his hood. Horse's hooves stomped next to him in the street. He glanced out from under the hood just enough to see the constable's shiny boot in a stirrup and quickly turned away. The whistle wailed again. Blaze turned, running away, but the breeze tore off his hood. The cloak wafted stiffly behind him.

"There he is!"

"Get him!" His feet moved without thought while he unfastened the cloak, which flew out out behind him. Hooves clapped in rhythmic beats, galloping toward him.

"Stop, thief!" the constable yelled out to him. It might as well have been his name, he had been called it so frequently in his life. He slipped between buildings where the horse could not follow. The constable took up his pursuit, waiting for the young thief to emerge from the alleyways. Blaze tried to blend in with a group of Cadmarian women, but they catwailed and hit Blaze with their bundles. Blaze turned around while protecting his head.

"My Gods! Children these days are such perverts! Oh, Constable! This boy!"

The constable released the horse into a controlled gallop. Upon seeing the boy, he swung his sword at the boy's head. Blaze ducked under the sword and slid under the horse's belly, avoiding the hooves. The horse fell with heft to the ground. The constable struggled to move out from under the horse's weight. The sword had chinked away, skipping like a rock on water. Blaze ran to the sword, picked it up, and turned toward the fallen constable standing above him. Holding the grand sword with two hands, he thrashed at the air, demonstrating his knowledge of swordplay.

"Easy now, boy. Nobody needs to get hurt. You can get away. Go on; I'll not tell." Blaze could see the constable reaching behind him. He swung at the air again threateningly. The constable stopped reaching.

"Your life is over and it will be for naught. Goddess Hala will never accept you." Blaze inched forward; his footwork was precise and strong.

"Please, I pray you, spare me. I have twins at home—just born." Blaze glared at the constable, spat, and spun around, carrying the robust sword erect as he hurried down the road. The constable sighed, bowing his head in defeat as he knew the punishment for letting a thief go in public would be his death sentence. As he retreated, Blaze kept his path hidden, ditching the sword in an open pickle barrel.

Once he was out of the capitol and into the farmlands, he slowed his pace, following the foot traffic of the peasants. He nodded a good day as he passed. In the sky, Silvers flew without care or even interest for those on the ground. The sweet aroma of a cooling pie hovered in the air and Blaze's stomach acknowledged his hunger, but he kept moving. The furrow was nearby and he hoped that Mason would already be there with potatoes roasting in the fire.

After locating their camp, Blaze made a fire and waited. He knew Mason would be okay; he was always okay. He returned from every mission unscathed. Today would be the same. Gathering larger limbs and pulling down some unattached widowmaker branches that hung down from trees, Blaze focused his energy into making a lean-to. He found some berries that he recognized from the market and he placed those on a rock near the fire. He wished Mason was there because he was unsure of what he needed to do to the berries, if anything. Cooking and recognizing wild food were not skills that he had ever wanted or looked into, but his stomach was starting to ache from not eating. Blaze took some of the rocks from the fire and placed them into water that was contained in a hollowed-out log that he had fashioned with his dagger. The rocks heated the water to a boil. Once boiled, Blaze removed the rocks with two sticks, singeing his gloves a bit. Then he put the water aside to cool assuring that it was safe to drink. While he waited, he ate the berries, but his stomach thirsted for Hende-Li's stew. The evening had come fast and the memory of the day's events seemed like forever ago. Tired, Blaze sat near the fire. Using his dagger, he whittled a stick to a point which kept his focus and worry at bay. He glanced over at the lean-to. He could close it up to conceal himself as he let the fire dwindle, but in the meantime, he'd stay awake in vigil for Mason's return.

After some time, Blaze's eyes grew heavy and his head bobbed with bouts of sleep. The fire had grown low to burning red embers. Images of Jade raking her finger over her throat and the sound of her voice kept replaying in his dreamy mind. *"I'm coming back for you."* Her words, perverse in sound and in tone, always ended with a demonic laugh that scared Blaze awake. He couldn't wait any longer: he stumbled to the lean-to and sat on the leaves that were his bed for the night. He moved a thick, heavy branch in front of him, hiding his existence to the world. A cool summer wind whistled through the branches, but it soon lulled him asleep, wrapped warmly in his cloak.

Footsteps outside of the lean-to startled him awake. Frozen in fear, he held his breath. The footsteps tramped around his camp until they settled into silence. He could see a shadow through the large limb that was the lean-to's door. The person was out there, waiting and listening. Based on the footsteps, he knew it had to be a single man; at least he didn't have to worry about having to fight a crowd. He could pretend that he was still asleep or that the lean-to was empty, but he thought that might be a stretch. There was no way around it; he had to leave the lean-to to escape.

He quietly pushed on the branches behind him, but they were wedged against the structure and a large boulder. With force, he started to push a branch sideways, but the whole lean-to rustled loudly. He pulled out his dagger. He peered through the leaves and could see the hood of a cloak. Slowly, he moved the large branch that was the barrier between him and the stranger.

"Why don't you just come on out, Blaze?" Mason called over his shoulder.

Blaze sighed, relieved, and held his chest to calm his heart. As Blaze emerged from the lean-to, he noticed that Mason was barely moving. He was sitting in front of the firepit, gently holding on to his side.

"I didn't know it was you, Mason. You scared me a bit. I've been here awhile. I got here pretty quickly. I just had to outrun the constable. Did you run into some trouble, or did you go shopping?" There had been no doubt in Blaze's mind that Mason wouldn't come back. His reaction, while subdued, was what Mason had hoped it would be. Mason had done some first aid to himself, which seemed to hold while he made it back to camp. He didn't want to alert Blaze to his injury, so he kept it secret, trying to overcompensate by doing more than he should.

Mason chuckled. "No, I didn't go shopping. You did a good job setting up camp, Blaze. I actually didn't know where you were at first, and then I heard the branches scraping against the rock. Do you know what kind of berries these are?" Blaze sat next to Mason at the fire. He shook his head. "They're elderberries. They're a tasty fruit, but they're also very seedy, so don't make a pie." Mason's eyes twinkled. There was a memory there, but Blaze didn't ask.

Mason went forging for more elderberries in the forest while Blaze kept watch by the fire. Mason returned with his pouch filled with the berries. It was enough to tide them over until they could catch some meat or scrounge for different fruits of the forest. Something was off with Mason, but Blaze couldn't exactly figure it out. They were taking too long to return back to Timeria and Blaze wondered if Jade was still on their trail. He didn't press Mason to leave, but his patience was wearing thin. Mason had tried to catch a rabbit but it escaped so he fed them the food he had brought with him. The meal consisted of jerky with a handful of elderberries on the side.

After eating, Mason informed Blaze that they were going to head back toward Timeria. It would be no more than a day or two. He mentioned that he had to stop by to see someone who lived just on this side of the Timerian border.

Blaze never quizzed Mason on why he had been late, and Mason never offered any information either. Together, they decided that leaving Cadmaria would be the best choice. Blaze was looking forward to seeing Goldenrod again, as they had already been in Cadmaria longer than expected.

Disassembling the camp was much easier than making it, Blaze thought. However, there was a lot to do to bring everything back to the way that it had been before they had arrived. Blaze was entranced as he snuffed out the fire with sand. The fire snuck around the sand, bursting back to life, until Blaze finished dumping the rest of the sand into the fire pit. Mason watched him as he studied the fire. *Things to do and you're watching the fire go out.* Mason was short on patience. He fought against the pain in his left side as he began to tear into the lean-to. The structure was strongly built, and he only managed to remove the door and half-heartedly cut into a small part of the frame. Exhausted, Mason kicked the frame, and then he left it alone, falling into a sitting position onto the ground. Blaze could see that Mason's breathing was labored and that he favored one side.

"Mason, are you all right?" It was surprising to see his mentor in distress. Mason lifted up his tunic to reveal that his first aid was all for naught. A blood-soaked patch with white paste oozed over a gash covering his left side. Blood clotted around the edges of the wound but the center of the impact was raw, wet, and a deep fire red.

"I'll be fine, Blaze. I tried to care for it in hopes that it wasn't quite as deep as I had thought. I probably should have alerted you to the injury when I first came into the camp. Can you pass me the water skin and my satchel? I have some stuff in there." Blaze did as he was told. Mason spread out a handkerchief and then set down several items that Blaze recognized from Mason's medical kit. Mason first grabbed a bottle of soap, cleaning the wound and rinsing it with the tepid water from the skin. He held his breath and tears ran down his face involuntarily while he writhed in pain. After waiting a few minutes, Mason involved Blaze in the activity.

"It's a little late for me to do this as the healing has already begun, but I don't think it will stay closed on its own. I need you." Blaze stood up, ready to do whatever Mason needed. "Okay, do you know how to thread a needle?" Blaze nodded. Mason handed a bottle of alcohol to Blaze. "Wash your hands with this, use it all up. Then don't touch anything else. We'll let your hands air-dry. I need everything to be as clean as possible." Mason handed Blaze the bottle, who turned away from Mason before removing his gloves and pouring the liquid over his hands.

"I learned this from Master Sito, the tailor at Ceretheena Castle. He always needed help mending some of the staffers' uniforms and it was a weekly duty." Blaze worked at threading the small needle with the sinew thread. He had wanted to use his mouth to get a thinner end, but he thought better of it, knowing where the needle and thread were headed.

Mason smiled. "Great, so you know how to sew. Blaze, I'm going to hold the laceration closed, but first I need you to tell me if I need to trim any of the jagged edges."

"I don't see any jagged edges, it looks smooth like this had been made by a very sharp knife."

"Great, Blaze. Thank you. I don't need to fix the edges then. Okay, are you ready to sew the wound closed?" Blaze leaned over Mason and froze.

"Uh, Mason, what kind of stitches? I know a running stitch, a blanket stitch, and an invisible stitch that you use to close a seam together. I've used the last one on some of the pillows in the red sitting room in Ceretheena."

Mason chuckled.

"They're not that kind of stitches. They're really more like a series of knots that hold the skin closed." Mason picked up the needle, piercing his skin as he demonstrated the procedure to Blaze. His pain level increased, but his very matter-of-fact demeanor made it easy for him to complete the task, and he had Blaze's help when needed. "The stitches are made by first making a suture knot at the beginning of the cut. Here, I'll show you. You want to go into the skin so you are perpendicular to the top of the skin, and you don't want to go too far away from the wound, but you also want to make sure that you can close the skin together. Make sure that when you are stitching, that top layer doesn't turn under, either. Now, take the pliers, and using the long end of the sinew thread that is attached to the needle, you are going to wrap it around twice, and then grab the short end and pull that end through. This will create a square knot." Blaze carefully followed Mason's instructions. The sewing of skin was different from material, but he took care not to do any of the things that Mason warned against. As he focused his concentration, he was surprised to see that his hands shook on their own. It made him nervous that he was going to do all the wrong things.

"Mason, my hands are shaking just a little," he said, in the calmest voice that he could muster.

Mason nodded. "It's okay. Mine did too when I first learned how to do this. You're doing a great job." Mason didn't really know how Blaze was doing. He didn't dare move to get a better angle. "Now take the pliers again and wrap once around with the long end pulling the short end through, and then repeat that one final time. You've just made a secure end. I want you to make that running stitch that you know, but you are going to go back and forth, connecting skin every length of your thumbnail. Then, you are going to secure the end like you did to start. Have you done that?" Mason's voice was showing his exhaustion and pain. Blaze took a moment to answer as he was slowly working on securing the knot.

"Yes, Mason. I did, just now." Blaze felt the need to relax his muscles. His back hurt from leaning over Mason and he was sweating from his nerves. Mason sighed swallowing as he did.

"Great, Blaze. Now, cut the thread. You'll need to do about six to seven of these little running stitch sutures across the whole wound. By the end of this, Blaze, you'll be able to sew up any straight wound with ease. I should have taught this to you years ago, but you never seemed to stay in one place long enough." Mason thoughtfully fell into the regret that all parents feel when they are overdue in teaching their children an important life skill. "I'm sorry that I have to make you do this now. Are you ready to continue? I'll try to move to a different position. This way I can help keep the skin together and guide you as you work. There is a cloth that you can use to wipe off the blood as you sew. Okay? Start by working along the skin."

Blaze worked diligently. The task was difficult with limited mobility of his fingers, but with some patience, he was able to stitch up Mason's wound. For once, he felt proud of what he had done. This would be something that he could use when he was on his own missions, as mishaps were a part of the job.

After he finished, Blaze found another bottle of alcohol, and he washed up with that. He wrapped all of his tools, bottles, and cloths in the big handkerchief and returned them to Mason's satchel. "I'm proud of you, Blazey, that was remarkable. In my medical kit, I need the wyssanberry. Take out a small sprig from its container."

Blaze had seen wyssanberry many times in his life. To him, it had a taste of rotting dirt and the smell of dirty bugs, but its healing properties were enough to overcome all that. He found several differently sized vials in the medical kit. He opened the first one, which emitted an odor of fragrant roses. Another one was rubbing alcohol, and a third was a thick mustard cream that he had never seen before. He opened some others until he discovered the overbearing smell of dirty bugs secreting out of a wide-mouthed vial. He poured out a single sprig of the wyssanberry; in his hands, the wyssanberry wilted and turned to a dark slimy goop. He licked it. *Ick, it tastes so bad, this has to be it.* He handed Mason the vial.

"Do you want this one that's in my hand?"

Mason looked over and noticed the wyssanberry goop. His eyes widened and he slapped his forehead."Oh, Gods, Blaze! I forgot that the wyssanberry always does that when you touch it. A whole sprig, too? Oh, that's a small fortune dead in your hand. I'm sorry, I didn't think. Here just give me the vial and I'll take some berries off myself." Mason opened the vial, carefully pulled out a sprig and pulled off three berries. He tossed the berries into his mouth and chewed them while he returned the remaining stem back into the vial. Mason let out a sigh of relief. The wyssanberry was helping already and after consuming it, the berry would help heal the wound from the inside. Mason loved wyssanberry and all it was capable of to heal the wounded and the sick."Goddess Wyssa, miracles of miracles, you have given us this berry that heals and protects all. May your wyssanberry provide the healing necessary for this poor and ungrateful soul. I thank you for your generous gift, my Lady." He looked to the sky. He thanked Blaze, too, and then he settled into sleep, careful not to open any of the stitches.

Mason awoke well into the day feeling rested and better. He looked around at the camp only to find that Blaze had returned the forest back to what it had been prior to their stay. Now it would be hard to tell that someone had camped there for days. Blaze swept away the last of his footprints with a long pine branch. A wave of dust flew over Mason, and he coughed it away, garnering Blaze's attention.

"Oh, good. You're up. Are you feeling better, Mason?" The older thief nodded as he rose to his feet, grunting with pain."I think we should get going before it gets dark. Do you think you can travel?

I got this for you." Blaze handed Mason a long stick that he had stripped of bark, making it smooth and usable for walking. Mason realized that Blaze must have been working on it for quite some time.

"Thank you, Blaze. You're going to have a great tale to tell Venom about your mission when we get back. That was very thoughtful of you. There are a few times that I remember when Rhatt had similar good instincts; you are just like him. You have all of his good characteristics." Blaze grinned with glee at being compared to his father. Mason took the stick. Blaze draped the two satchels over his body, allowing Mason to be free of anything cumbersome. Mason looked up and noticed the sun's location. "I know it's late, Blaze, but I did promise you that we'd be home soon. We'll keep moving even at night. After the furrow, we should be able to reach the Timerian border. We'll make camp there, and then in the morning we can make our way back to Ballardton." Mason did a final check of the camp, and the two began their journey back to Timeria.

Dusk had settled down on the land. Mason had grown tired and was walking more slowly. Blaze realized that even though they hadn't been walking very far, there was no way that Mason was going to make it all the way to the Timerian border.

"Mason, maybe we should stop now."

"No, no, we'll keep going, Blaze. I made you a promise."

"It's okay. You didn't expect to get skewered."

Mason chuckled and shook his head. "You're right, I didn't. You know, let me have my medical kit again. I'll eat some more berries and then we can make it farther along. Okay?" Blaze walked back to Mason, opened the medical kit, and pulled out the wyssanberry vial. Mason took it, opened the vial, and took two more berries off the sprig. "Thank you. You can place it back in the kit." The berry juice filled his mouth, fulfilling the thirst that Mason felt. Leaning on his walking stick, Mason felt his side. It was warm, but cool in comparison to what it had been before Blaze stitched it up.

Mason thought that he should probably check it again. He looked at Blaze and met the boy's eyes. They were pleading for him to hurry along, so Mason didn't say anything and kept moving.

After walking a while longer, Blaze turned back to Mason. "I think I need to rest, Mason. Is that okay?" Blaze knew that Mason was struggling to maintain his stamina. "Do you need a drink? I filled the skin up before we left." Blaze led Mason to a rock off the path before giving him the skin. Mason drank loudly until Blaze silenced him, catching sight of a herd of deer running and jumping down the path toward Cadmaria. They twisted and turned in their trek. Blaze sprang out onto the main path, staying close to the edge. Their behavior intrigued him and he had never seen so many deer in one place. After the herd had passed, pheasants, grouse, and quail took to the sky, squawking in panic. Each animal cried in terror and rang out an alert. The haunting sounds of the elk rang out through the wood. Fear of the unknown noises and panicked, crazed animals froze Blaze where he stood. The trees were too far away and he wished for a hole to hide in. *What was everything running from?*

More creatures ran by, crashing through the underbrush, their eyes wild with fear as they ran, it seemed, for their lives. Rabbits, squirrels, gnashers, and wolves ran together. They encircled him, ignoring him. Squeals and cries of fear called out over the furrow. All creatures were afraid of what was coming. Blaze smelt the sulfuric stench of fire and stepped back into the safety of the woods, wondering what caused the fury. A pair of devlins, like the ones he had met previously, had taken to the trees to increase their speed. A bunch of dragons circled over something just north of Blaze and Mason's position. *Ah, it's the Silvers. That's what they're all running from. Hm, maybe I should make another lean-to.* A sizzling, bubbling noise of momentum, along with the sounds of an immense weight slogged closer.

Blaze stood watching both the sky and the land. He was unaware of what was coming at him, but noticed the Silver dragons alerting others of the presence on the ground. The noise halted. The Silvers kept their positions in the sky until something attacked them from the land. It impaled the Silvers. The dragons screeched out a warning, lighting the darkening sky with fire, fleeing for their lives. Silver scales fell from the sky like small razors as the sole surviving dragon beat the air above him, following the same path as the land-bound animals. Blaze protected his head with his arms as scales tumbled from the sky, all while a forceful wind emerged, knocking Blaze off his feet. Blaze scrambled up and dashed back, terrified, toward Mason, who sat slumped, asleep.

"Mason! Mason! Wake up!" Blaze rushed to him and helped him to his feet.

"Come on! I don't know what's coming, but it's big and can injure dragons from the ground."

Mason hustled to his feet, and the two thieves ran. Mason tripped and Blaze caught him, looping Mason's arm over his shoulders.

"What do you think it is? Hill-people, maybe?"

"I don't know, but it took out the Silvers."

"Silvers? Were they circling?"

"Yes, how did you know?" Mason pulled away from Blaze.

"It's a slugslime! Run for your life, Blaze! Go!"

"I'm not leaving you, Mason."

"You are if I say you are, and I'm saying you are. Go! Run!" The slogging beast drew closer. Blaze pulled Mason along. "Let go! Don't argue, Blaze. Run! There is no time!"

"I'm not leaving without you!" Blaze held on to Mason, who stumbled over tree limbs and flora that would soon be melted into nothingness. An acrid, bitter, and sour smell rose from behind them.

"You will! It's coming." Blaze saw a way out. He'd get Mason to a higher spot and the two of them would wait for it to pass.

"We just need to get out of the furrow over the glassy edge." Blaze ran to the left, dragging Mason by his tunic up through the furrow.

"It won't work, Blaze, they're as big as the furrow. That's what made this. It's a slugslime! What more do I have to say? Run! Run away!" Mason pushed Blaze away, but as he did, he stretched open the stitches and cried out in pain. Blaze turned back to help Mason, who batted him away again. "Just get out of here, Blaze! Be more like Jade and less like Locke, will you? Leave!" There was no way that Mason could go any farther. He had fallen to his knees and was holding his side. Blaze leaned in to help him and Mason swatted him away again.

"I'm not leaving you, Mason. If we don't go back together, no one goes back. Isn't that what a mission is about?" Mason struggled back up to his feet. Blaze almost felt Mason's pain himself. There was no doubt, and Blaze's heart hurt to know, that Mason wouldn't be able to outrun the slugslime. They had to get to the highest ground possible. He glanced around the area. In front of them was a tree—not high enough. To their left, the land dipped into a hollow. To their right, Blaze could see a mound of land—not enough to call a hill, but a lump on the surface. He knew that was the place that he would leave Mason—hurt and in pain, but alive. "Nobody gets forgotten, Mason." Blaze grabbed Mason by the arm, wrapped Mason's arm around himself, and mostly dragged the older thief to the highest spot. By the time they reached the top, Mason was by far overworked and exhausted. His breathing was heavy and shallow. A thought crossed Blaze's mind, and Mason started protesting again between breaths.

"It's not safe, Blaze," he wheezed."You need to leave. That's an order. Go! Run! Nowhere is safe from a slugslime." Blaze nodded, remembering Mason's assurance of his speed. He placed his arm on Mason's shoulder to silently acknowledge the farewell."I'm standing to fight, Blaze," Mason said. Blaze met Mason's gaze. There was determination in Mason's eyes as well as the horrific pain he was enduring. *I know what to do*, Blaze thought. *Act without thinking.*

"Fine, Mason! I'll leave! I'll go." Blaze appeared to be surprisingly angry and he held his hand on Mason's shoulder. He moved close to Mason's ear, whispering."Goodbye, Mason." Blaze's words tickled Mason's ear and broke his heart. The boy dropped Mason's satchel, leaving all of the healing supplies with him, but kept his own. He grabbed the walking stick, testing to see its reach. He checked on his dagger in his boot as he fled without Mason.

Mason knew what was coming. The slugslime would be his final moment. He'd be absorbed by it and no one would know. Mason wished for Locke. They had never battled a slugslime before; the closest they had gotten was seeing one at a lake, drinking until it was full. They had run as far away as they could. Blaze should be farther away by now. Mason had basically raised Blaze, when he was home. He thought about everything he had done wrong. It was never enough, but hopefully enough to get him on a fair path. *Fare well, Blazey! I will give my regards to Hala. I'm coming home.* Tears ran down his face as he struggled to find any remaining strength.

Blaze held tightly to the walking stick. It would make a nice weapon. He knew how to kill a slugslime, even if he had never met one, based entirely on the banter of two old sots. If it was as large as the furrow, then the spot on the top of its head couldn't be too hard to miss, after all. Now he just needed to divert it, to get it to follow him in a different direction, away from Mason. It was foolish and he knew it, but it was worth the chance. *Act without thinking*: words that came to the forefront of his mind, reminding him that his father was always with him. He heard the slugslime dragging itself closer and closer. At last, it came into view. It was smaller than the furrow, but still grandiose in scale, inching along with a body over eighteen feet in length, and close to six and a half feet tall. Blaze was sure it could pick itself up off the ground, as was depicted in the Pierced Slugslime Tavern sign.

It had eight protruding tentacles that pointed toward the earth just below its mouth, sticking out like fingers. A large mantle covered its head, down to the middle of its back. Its tail dragged along behind the mantle. On top of its head, it had two retractable tentacles with eye spots that were only for deception. Along either side of its mantle were protruding, barnacle-shaped eyes that moved independently of one another. The creature had a single foot that moved muscularly, aided by a thick mucus acid, called ewz, that ate through its surroundings. It had three red-brown lines painted along the top of its pale, gray-green body and tail, with a series of irregular circles on its head that artistically decorated the beast. Filaments soaked in ewz saturated its whole body. When provoked it shook out its ewz in all directions. It was the ewz, Blaze realized, that had attacked the Silvers.

Blaze carried the walking stick, aimed to fight. He knew he had to be quick and he had to be prepared, but that was as far as his plan had formed. The slugslime focused its eyes on Blaze, opened its mouth, and roared out a squeal of delight and anticipated attack. It shifted its position by a mere foot, aiming itself toward Blaze. Blaze thought he was ready, and as he waited for the slugslime to reach him, he rethought his tactic. Although the walking stick would allow him to be far away from the slugslime, he knew that it would not cut the creature down. It wouldn't do any real damage. Based on the speed of the slugslime, Blaze had time to quickly hatch a new plan. He reached into his satchel pulling out the short top of the spear shaft with its metal tip that he had taken from one of Finnian's goons. His reach would be nearly double his arm's length. He knew he needed to get above the creature, but how?

In the slugslime's path, there were tree limbs scattered with their root balls pulled out and limbs drooped down, torn from trees but never fully severed or resting on crutches within. It stopped in its tracks. Blaze watched as it detected a fawn that had been separated from its mother and waited, hidden in the grass under a branch, for her return. The fawn bawled a loud "baa," sensing the danger that was forthcoming, and it tried to scramble to its hooves. Its attempt was futile. The slugslime raised its head, opening its mouth while arching its back to attack the small, feeble animal. With a fluid movement, the slugslime engulfed the fawn whole, silencing its distressed cries, and then returned to its trail of destruction. Blaze picked up a stick and threw it at the slugslime. Its eyes focused back on the Timerian and it picked up speed, which amazed Blaze, given its size. Blaze started to run, guiding it away from Mason's location.

"Blaze, run! Get out of there!"

Blaze looked back to see Mason holding rocks in his looped tunic and throwing them toward the slugslime. The slugslime hissed and slowly turned, undulating an ewz track behind it.

"Mason, stop, I can handle this!" Blaze's words fell on deaf ears as Mason only heard the rushing of his blood. Blaze was angered by Mason's actions. He looked down, formulating a new plan that would, hopefully, confuse the slugslime. He reached into his satchel, remembering that he had a coil of sinew cording and prayed that he remembered the knots that Venom insisted on teaching him. Blaze lashed the walking stick and the spear shaft together. He began the connection with a clover knot on the walking stick, and then he added the shaft next to the stick while keeping the tip clear of the end of the stick. Working approximately halfway down the spear shaft, Blaze wrapped the cording, tightening a half-knot and then repeating on the other side. He worked until he had about eight knots on either side. He pushed them into each other locking them into position. He made one final clover knot, securing the cording for good and cut the length. Quickly, he wet his finger and rubbed spittle onto the cording, hoping that it would tighten as it dried. Blaze pulled on both poles and they held securely.

Blaze looked back toward Mason and the slugslime. The two were close together. Mason limped, holding his side, wincing from pain as the slugslime moved in to strike. Blaze took to his heels. Before long, he was near enough to the slugslime to throw the spear. He knew he had to be careful and precise as he drew back. He yelled as he released the spear, launching it as close to the slug-slime's head as possible. The spear skittered off of the slugslime like a pebble skipping on the water; however, Blaze's luck had turned in his favor, and the slugslime turned its eye toward Blaze, allowing the spear to cut it. The slugslime rose up onto the heel of its foot and stood at eight feet tall. It squealed in agony and then changed directions so quickly that it slammed back onto the ground to pursue Blaze. Blaze checked to see if Mason was safe. He was.

A green fluorescent gel bled from the slugslime's left eye, and the creature was coming for him. Blaze had wanted to try to retrieve the spear, but there was no way he could avoid a direct attack if he did. Ewz began to drip from the slugslime's body, and Blaze wondered what that meant, exactly. He couldn't think about it. Stopping to think would be his downfall. As Rhatt had said, "Act without thinking, Blazey." Rhatt's voice ran like a broken record as it kept circling back to those four words. Everything else in his head was silenced—he simply moved because he had to.

The slugslime rose on its heel again. This time, it jumped at the young Timerian, rocking the area. Blaze stumbled and quickly regained his footing. He could hear the slide of its body as it landed in a pool of ewz. The ewz splashed up. He felt a burning in the back of his leg. He cuffed it away. The ewz started to eat at his glove. He pulled it off and dropped it on the ground. Blaze pulled out his dagger and started to climb a tree. If he could just get higher than the tallest part of the slugslime, he'd be safe. He replaced his dagger in his boot.

Without challenge, Blaze scaled the tree. He climbed until he felt the tree sway and the branches start to tremble and break under his weight. The slugslime followed. It reached up to pull him out of the tree; in response, Blaze slunk down, holding the thickest part of the limb and hoping that it wouldn't be able to touch him from this height. The beast used its lower tentacles to pull up on the tree, garnering strength to lift itself higher. Blaze could see its injured eye, which was immobilized; green gel leaked from the eye down its side, neutralizing the ewz wherever the crystalized blood touched. The slugslime reached with its lower tentacles, swatting at the branches just above its face, but Blaze was too high up and the tree would not break under the slugslime's weight.

Blaze breathed a sigh of relief, until the slugslime started banging itself against the base of the tree. The tree held fast its position, but trembled at every quake. Branches cracked and dislodged, showering them down on top of the slugslime. Angered, the slugslime slid down off the tree. Ewz pooled below it, creating a recessed hole. Too many hits and the tree would fall. Blaze could see his next move. He noticed a limb that was severed from the tree, but hooked on another branch. It was in close proximity to the vulnerable spot on the slugslime's head.

Blaze began to climb down. He made his way, carefully, to the top of the stuck limb, and as he did, the slugslime shook its body, flinging ewz out in all directions. Luckily for Blaze, the tree's bark and leaves spared him from the acidy goop. Blaze stopped in the tree. The moons were starting to rise and purple hues were darkening the forest. Blaze realized that he needed an extra layer of protection, and he removed a cloth from his satchel, covering his mouth and tying the cloth behind his head. He pulled up his hood. He sat on the limb looking down to check on the slugslime. It was a big glob of mucus at the base of the tree. It seemed unnatural in its frozen position. Blaze took to his feet, swinging, climbing, and jumping in, through, and around the tree. All his training over the years, competing at the tourneys, even with a broken arm, were spent preparing for this mission and this particular battle, he realized. He reached the branch. He glanced down at the slugslime: it hadn't moved at all. It was still regaining its ewz and the setting sun danced over its body, alerting Blaze that it would soon be moving again. *It seems to take it longer to recharge with every additional attack. Hm.*

Pulling up on the widowmaker branch, Blaze freed it. It was longer than he had thought, so he snapped it with his foot to make it a usable length. He laid the broken half across two joints to keep his actions concealed from the slugslime. From his boot, he grabbed his dagger and began chipping into the snapped end. He worked quickly and diligently, hollowing out a long, empty space. On either side of the log, he made an x that he intended to use to bind everything together. He opened his satchel once more and removed the sinew twine. He looked at the length, hoping that he had enough to accomplish this feat. He tucked his dagger's pommel into the branch's edge, and then, using a shear lashing, he secured the blade into its home. Blaze kissed his blade, praying, "My dear King Eldon, may this dagger stay true, and may I survive this day." Blaze raised his makeshift spear, pushing and pulling it in the air. He felt not a twinge or even a wiggle of movement.

He looked down at the slugslime. It was gone. He looked for its trail, but he saw none. *Could it have gone after Mason?* He started to spring from one tree to the next, careful not to fall or drop his weapon. There was neither hide nor hair nor ewz that he could find. He spotted Mason, who was waving his hands in the air. Blaze waved back, but Mason didn't stop waving. Blaze glanced behind himself. The slugslime was on its heel again, dripping ewz out of every pore. The stench of rotting waste filled his nostrils. Mason turned away, covering his face with his hands.

Blaze knew he only had seconds to react. He jumped out of the tree, still holding onto his make-shift spear, and tumbled down behind a large root ball. Mason had turned back to see Blaze's actions. He gasped, witnessing a disaster that he knew was coming. Ewz sprayed off of the monster's body, hitting trees, brush, small animals, and birds. The slugslime knew its prey was in that hole. It slithered along over the root ball and hole, burying the teen, dissolving his body into an acidy unrecognizable mush.

Oh my Gods, he's gone! Tears flowed from Mason's eyes. He sank down and banged the ground in unbelievable grief and pain. Blaze was like a son, and he cared for him more than anyone. His side bled, and he let it. The tears were only for Blaze. In his mind, he could see the last moment over and over. With the loss of Blaze, Mason felt deep sorrow and regret for taking the teen on this trek. *All the lad ever wanted was to be just like his father. That wouldn't have been so bad, would it? Why did we always persist? I have the poor boy's blood on my hands. Not on Locke's hands. Mine. Mine.*

CHAPTER 21

moment

MASON EXPERIENCED THAT HORRIBLE MOMENT when you want to share something with the person who is no longer with you. The one who you know has been given away to death, but you need to tell them this secret that you have been harboring their whole life. Mason's tears spoke his unspoken words. *There was something amiss about your birth. Something that just wasn't right about it.* Mason closed his eyes and the pain reverted him back to the moment when Blaze entered the guild and everyone's hearts, except maybe Jade's. He was sure, for one sweet tiny moment, even Jade had a soft spot for Blaze, in the most vulnerable state that Mason had ever seen her in, and it all started with the surprised entrance of a Cadmarian woman at the guild, who announced that Jade was ready to give birth.

* * *

The Cadmarian woman arrived at the guild holding a bedpan and a small clothes tub. She said nothing when the door was opened, even as she pushed past Mason. She looked around the common room. She turned up her nose in disgust. Putting down her tub and the bedpan, she busily commenced her work. She found a broom and started sweeping. Mason tried to stop her.

"Excuse me. What are you doing here?"

The woman pushed the handle of the broom into his chest and waved her hands in the air. Mason tossed the broom to the side.

She glanced up at him, gesturing for him to start sweeping. She grabbed her tub and went to fill it.

"The baby. The baby is coming," she said, with a heavy Cadmarian accent, as she hurriedly carried the tub into the center of the main quarters of the guild.

"Are you pregnant?" Mason glanced down at the woman's abdomen. *No, no sign of a bump there.* "What baby?" He stood in front of her attempting to get her to talk to him.

"The baby. Mistress Jade's baby. It comes soon. We must prepare for arrival. Hurry, sweep floor to make clean space for baby. I get clean cloths." The Cadmarian woman flew out the door running toward the camp field.

Mason called after her. "How do you know this?"

The woman was not interested in answering any questions. Mason sighed and decided that if a baby was coming to the guild, he could sweep a little. Once he started, he found that he enjoyed seeing the results—a clean floor. Pip and Dorken, who were forever together, entered the guild, disregarded Mason, and went straight to sit at the table. They had cards, and immediately started to play a game.

"So supposedly Jade's baby is coming today." Mason shrugged at the two men.

"Yeah, so?" Dorken retorted pulling a card out of the stack. "What have you got, Pip?" As if the words finally reached Pip's ears, he responded with a squeal of delight and twisted in his chair to face Mason.

"Is it really true? Jade's baby is coming today? Oh, is it a boy or a girl? Oh, the gender doesn't really matter. You only need to know so as to know how to wipe the baby's bottom. Other than that, the baby could be genderless. Can we all promise to treat the baby as just a baby? Ooh, they'll be the littlest Little. That's so adorable!"

"Babies come when they want. There are no exceptions." Mason listened to Dorken. He was right; Mason couldn't deny that in all of his years, no matter how ready the mother was, the baby waited until they were ready. Dorken lit up a smoking weed stick. "You're wasting your time sweeping, Mason. The guild house is like a magnet for dirt, dust, and other unwanted things." The Cadmarian woman slammed open the door carrying clean dry bleached cloths. Noticing that Dorken was smoking, she shooed him from the guild house only to return without the weed stick.

"Are you a midwife?"

The woman waved Mason away while she was placing the cloths in various places around the guild. One in the tub of water, one hanging from the mantle of the fireplace, another on the hearth. She examined Mason's hands and then with confidence she draped one over his shoulder.

"You should ask Jade. I only know that the baby comes today."

Dorken scoffed. The woman placed a cloth between Pip and Dorken, who moved it out of the way of their game. She gently slapped their hands for touching the cloth. "It's for the baby. No touch it."

"Why don't you just put everything in Jade's room? It'll be easier to birth a Little in that room with a bed than in here with all of our stuff." Dorken approached the door and opened it. "It isn't even locked. That's strange. It's always locked."

The woman quickly removed all the cloths from where she had so diligently spread them out. She went in and out of Jade's room repeatedly until she returned for the tub, which she placed on the hearth of the fire. Mason approached the woman again.

"Can you please tell me how you know Jade's baby is coming today?"

The woman placed her hands on her hips. "I know these things. Also, she knows. She sent messenger to me. It is a lovely autumn day for a birth, too." The woman turned back to her task.

"Do you have the knife ready to heat to red for the cord?"

"No no, in Cadmaria we use water. It is good. Do not worry about women's work, young man. I have prayed to the Goddess for safety measures."

Mason let her handle her task and let her be. He sat down with Pip and Dorken, joining in the game. He stewed about the process of the midwife's care, and thought that if need be, the baby and Jade could be brought to the healers. *Well, if the baby is coming, maybe a healer should come . . .* Mason's thoughts were cut off as the door burst open falling off its hinges.

Jade leaned in the doorway. Her skirts balled in front of her. She leaned forward, moaning in pain. The woman ran to her and led Jade to her bed; the door to Jade's room swung shut, but never fully clicked closed. A muffled cry, and then sounds of scurrying came from the room. Mason walked closer to the door; he strained to listen as Jade mumbled instructions. Suddenly, Jade screamed a loud, fierce cry. Mason jumped. In between her cries he heard Jade's voice.

"Make . . . look . . . enough . . . right . . . yes . . . that." As he started to push open the door, full infant cries echoed through the guild. The unique newborn "la" cry signified that the baby had indeed been born.

Pip jumped with joy, and Dorken met Mason at the door. The midwife swung open the door and carried the wrapped infant into the main quarters to wash off its birth. Mason oversaw the woman and watched, unable to assist, while she placed the baby in the warming tub of water on the hearth without checking to feel the temperature. The baby stretched out its arms and startled, causing it to cry harder. Mason could see the baby was a boy. Once satisfactorily cleaned, the midwife swaddled the baby in another cloth. She held the baby to her shoulder, rubbing his back to calm him. He had hair that was black as the night and stood up in all directions.

"Where is she?" Rhatt rushed into the guild house carrying a crumpled parchment clasped in his hand, a harried expression open on his face. He saw the midwife. His expression of worry changed immediately to surprised joy. "Is that my baby?" His expression calmed as he reached out to take his newborn. "Is it a boy or a girl? Oh, please be a boy."

"He's a boy."

Rhatt lifted him up and straightened his arms to look at his baby's tiny face. The baby's head drooped, and Rhatt changed how he held him. He held the baby's head with care as though he had held twenty thousand babies in his life. He moved to a chair and sat down with his son.

"I've never seen anything more beautiful in all of my life. My son . . ."

Mason held his breath looking over at the slugslime. It hadn't moved at all. He had heard that slugslime took time to digest their prey. For the moment, he knew he was safe. He would have to get out of the area. He picked himself up, holding his side. Tears fell as he remembered Rhatt holding his small treasure with pride and glorious joy, naming him Blaze because he was going to set Mirias ablaze.

And I've sent him to you, Rhatt. One mission. I pleaded with Locke. Just let him go with me. I know he can do it . . . Oh, I was so wrong . . . Mason's anguish and agony outweighed his pain.

CHAPTER 22

REBIRTH

THE SLUGSLIME ventured forward. It searched in and around
the root ball hole for what it could not find and so desperately
wanted to devour, its antennae reaching out again to feel for
what it couldn't see with its eyes in their orbital sockets. Just as
the slugslime had slithered over the hole, Blaze sneaked out and
rounded behind the slugslime, carrying his long-handled dagger.
He hid near the trunk, concealed by the dirt and the roots at the
bottom of the fallen tree. He breathed hard and wondered how
to attack next. His heart pounded in his chest and he could hear
the rush of his own blood. *That was close. I have to be more careful
next time. Okay, Blazey, ready* . . . He drew in a large breath and ran
around to the left side of the slugslime, knowing this could be the
last strike that he would ever make.

Unseen, Blaze attacked. He pierced the slugslime's other eye,
cutting it deep, spewing its green bloody gel all over him. The gel
was harmless, but stuck like the burrs of a burdock plant to his skin
and clothes.

The slugslime wailed and thrashed back and forth, its sight
impaired by the attack. Blaze climbed another tree, hoping to
catch sight of its spot of weakness on its head. The monster shook,
releasing more of its own blood, rather than the ewz it had desired.
Blaze climbed faster and higher. He was momentarily back at the
tourneys, running up the pole, beating his opponents—beating
Aldric—to win the day. Then he was at the top of the tree. He let

go and stood balanced on the tree branch. He adjusted his mask as it slipped higher up his nose.

He gripped the log and kissed the dagger one more time before inverting it toward the slugslime. He waited for what felt like a millennium for the slugslime to ripple forward, slowly, on its foot. It finally made its way below Blaze, who stood stoically, ready for the final attack. Blaze saw his mark. The spot was nearly a perfect circle and it had a slightly darker tinge of brown. *There!*

Blaze jumped up, using his whole weight to increase the force of his thrust and waiting until the final moment to release his hold on his dagger spear, guiding the shaft to its target. As the blade found its mark, he hurled his body away as far as he could. He somersaulted as he fell, and then managed to spring back up onto his feet, surprising himself. The dagger spear continued on its flight into the slugslime's head, which erupted the bubbling green bloody ooze like a volcano. The creature fell with a solid thud.

Looking towards the sky, Mason let out a wail of anguish, looking for answers where there were none. On his knees, he leaned forward and rested his head on his hands, praying. His head pounded from sobbing. He lifted his upper body and sat on his feet. Tears stained his face, and his eyes were bloodshot from crying. He shook his head, trying to erase the past events. *How can I go back without Blaze? What do I tell Locke?* His head swayed back and forth as he tried to answer these questions. There was only one. Once he thought it, it was clearly the right choice. *I won't go back.* He garnered strength and resolve. He wiped away the tears from his eyes, smearing his face with dirt and mud. His brow furrowed to a determined glare. Mason grabbed his satchel and rummaged through it.

Inside, he found a small leather pouch. He held it carefully in his hands as he lifted it out of the satchel. He tossed the satchel aside. He pulled on the pouch's ties. He reached in and pulled out a wad of muslin. Holding it with the tips of his fingers, he tossed the pouch toward the satchel. He carefully lowered the muslin into the palm of his left hand, unwrapping it with his right to unveil a minute vial of a silver powder. *The hoof of a winged equisprite from the Tessan Mountains. I won it in a game of Live or Die. I've always carried it with the hopes of never using it, but now would be the time.* Mason pulled on a string that snapped the wax seal. He pinched

BLAZE

the cork and it gave way. *To kill a hawk, you feed it a poisoned rat. To kill a slugslime, you feed it a poisoned . . .*

He raised the vial, toasting death with the slugslime as he gazed in its direction. Luminessa had entered the sky and was casting light over the area. Mason could see the slugslime, but was there something more above in a tree? A cloaked figure silhouetted in the crest between day and evening jumped out of the tree. *Blaze!* Mason saw everything clearly as Blaze thrust his spear down into the monster while dashing sideways to avoid the ewz and the creature's outer body. Mason dropped the vial at his feet, spilling the contents on the ground. "Blaze!" he called, his eyes wide and his heart erupting with joy. He couldn't believe his eyes! Blaze was alive! He limped hurriedly across the gulley, struggling with his side, to reach Blaze.

When Mason arrived, he could see the slugslime's lifeless body. He raised his eyebrows in surprise. "By the Gods and Goddesses, Blaze. You killed the thing." Blaze turned his head.

"Yeah, but my dagger's in there." Blaze sighed, pointing at the slugslime's belly.

"Well, then it's gone. You can't just climb inside of it to get it."

"That's a great idea, Mason. Thanks!" Blaze grinned. He climbed carefully up the slugslime's back, walking on the green gel toward the slugslime's head where the spear stood erect. Blaze pulled on it carefully, trying to dislodge it. Finally it released, and Blaze flew backwards onto his bum, sliding down the slugslime's blood-covered mantle. He grabbed onto the right eye until he was safe. Burns and marks from the ewz covered his body, and his tunic was tattered, but he didn't care. He looked at Mason. Mason hugged Blaze as though it was the last embrace he'd ever feel.

"You're still bleeding," Blaze pointed out.

"So are you," Mason said flatly, with a twinge of a smile in his eye. Blaze looked at his arms, body, legs, and bare hand; it was the first time he had noticed the wounds. They festered and upon inspection he became more aware of them, but he didn't really care. The rush of killing the slugslime was intoxicating and invigorating. He was bouncing up and down, excited.

"Calm down, Blaze. You will need the healer as well."

Blaze tried to do as he was told by breathing in deeply, but it didn't calm his excitement. On the backside of his hand, he noticed a hole burned by the acid. Curiosity allowed him to examine the wound. He wiped the blood away with his other hand. *I wonder if it'll scar,* he thought. Looking back at Mason, he smiled sheepishly.

"I'm fine, Mason, you worry too much. You might want to use one of your vials to collect the green slugslime blood; it makes the acid useless." Mason nodded slowly, realizing that Blaze had learned more about slugslime than anyone at the guild. He wondered if others knew this information.

"Interesting." Mason raised a curved finger to his lips in thought.

"Mason," Blaze started, "are you ready to go? I feel like I could run straight to Ballardton right now."

Mason felt his side, realizing the intense pain of the pulled stitches and the stress to the wound as if it was the first encounter again. "We can go, but I'm going to have to suffer through, Blaze. I think this is already infected. We can go to the healer in Timeria just over the border. I know her well." Blaze nodded, shaking his head and releasing green goop onto Mason. "Oh, that is so gross. We're going to find you a place to clean up and use some of the burn ointment on all of those welts; you're absolutely covered."

"What about the vial?"

Mason retrieved an empty vial and Blaze made his way back to the slugslime and filled it.

"Great, now we can go—the sooner the better. I think I've have had enough of Cadmaria for a while," Blaze admitted, while slapping his hands on his thighs.

Mason placed the glowing green vial in the medical kit, careful not to let it touch the other vials. Mason looked at Blaze; he wanted to get out of the woods before the boy started to glow in the dark from the slugslime's blood.

By the time Mason and Blaze had reached the healer's cottage, Mason had become delirious with fever. The infection was spreading into his blood, causing a blood line to appear on his skin. It snaked along, heading toward Mason's heart. Mason had eaten roots that would help to prevent any further spread of the infection, but only temporarily. Blaze helped Mason to the door. An olive-skinned woman opened it. As soon as she saw Mason, she ushered Blaze through and into a side room where Blaze laid Mason down on a table.

"What happened and what in Gods' names is all over you?"

Blaze blushed."Nothing special. Mason took a blade to his side. It was stitched, but the stitches came out."

"Stupid, stupid, Mason. What were you thinking, you lunkhead? Always turning up at my door with one wound or another." She stared at Blaze pointedly."I'm waiting for the rest of the story. I'll need to know more before I can help him and you, so go on … and …"

"Oh, and I'm Blaze." Blaze held out his gloved hand. The woman laughed. She picked up a basket, which contained a blanket and several vials similar to Mason's.

"I meant, what is all over you? What happened to your hand?" Blaze quieted down. It was obvious that she could tell that his fingers were missing since he was still only wearing one glove. The healer looked at the boy who suddenly seemed melancholy. She smiled with amusement."We don't have time for you to be sensitive, lad. Sorry, I'm not good with names."

"I lost my fingers years ago."

"Ha! I don't care about that. What is that green stuff?"

"It's slugslime blood." Her head spiraled around toward Blaze.

"Slugslime? Their blood is blue—not this glowing, green, jellied goop that is all over you. Now tell me the truth."

The healer was working on Mason and Blaze didn't want to distract her.

"I'm waiting, lad."

"I know you said it wasn't slugslime blood, but it is because … I killed one." She stopped her healing and raised her head to look into Blaze's eyes. He didn't turn away. He was confident in what he had done, proud even. A smile rose to her lips.

"Ha! I know you're lying. There is no way to kill a slugslime! Any weapon just bounces off of their skin."

"Yes, there is. You have to find its weak spot which is on the top of its head."

"You sound like you are an authority on slugslime," she said sarcastically."Did you hire Mason to go find you one just so you could hunt it?"

Blaze furrowed his brow. *This healer's crazy.*"No, why would I do that?"

Mason roused awake, his side nearly closed and his fever gone."Why would you do what, Blaze?" Blaze described the situation to Mason, who laughed and confirmed the truth of Blaze's story.

"But everyone knows that slugslime blood is blue and that's definitely a glowing green. Besides, I don't think you can kill a slugslime."

Mason nodded proudly. "Yep, he sure did. I didn't see him until it was over. I thought he had died. Thank Cerenth he didn't. Instead, the slugslime was dead and that green goop is its blood. Its body is just over the border in Cadmaria. It has medicinal properties as well, Vestia. You might want to collect some."

"Well, don't you go anywhere, lad. I am going to grab some of that stuff. You'll have to tell me more about the properties and if you think they have value. I'll grab some of it right off of him. He has enough for a vial or two, maybe more." Vestia finished her healing and went in for a kiss, but Mason pulled away shaking his head. Vestia grabbed two vials and a tiny, bowled spoon. She began collecting the slugslime goop off of Blaze's clothes and skin. Blaze felt uncomfortable, but he allowed her to continue until she had filled the first vial. Then he pulled away and grabbed her hand stopping her invasion.

"Vestia, you can take it from his clothes." Mason called from his spot on the lounger. "Do you have any that he can change into? You can keep the slugslime blood in exchange for the healings and clothing. What do you say?" Vestia returned to Mason's side and he leaned into her. She blushed. "Oh, and you remember, Blaze. He was the young one you healed at the guild so many turn-years ago—the boy who was stuck in the vault." Recognition crossed over her face.

"Well, I cannot believe that! This lad is that skinny little boy back then? Let me see you. I think I have some tunics and breeches that you could go through. They're in a trunk in that room. You can change there, too. Be careful taking those off, lad. I need all the slugslime blood that they will yield. I'll need to test it." She reached up and wiped some of the green gel out of his hair. She licked it. "Hm, it tastes okay. Doesn't really taste like anything. What do you think, Mason?" Vestia fed some to Mason. "I cannot believe that is the same boy."

Blaze walked into a different room, happy to be away from Vestia and whatever she and Mason were doing. He carefully removed his tunic and breeches. Standing nearly naked, Blaze opened the trunk. She wasn't lying about having an array of clothing. He sifted through and found one tunic that was red-brown with a brocade ribbon down the front and along the collar. It was a bit big, but it was good enough for now. He found breeches that were dark gray, which was the closest to matching the tunic. In the trunk, there were gloves and belts. He stole these as well. He felt better—he felt complete. Without the glove, he might as well be nude.

"Are you done in there, Blaze?" Mason yelled from the other room.

"Yes, Mason. I'll be right out."

"It's okay, laddie, you can take your time. We're in no rush." Vestia giggled and Mason got up to check on Blaze.

"I have to. I'm responsible for him." Vestia protested, trying to regain Mason's attention. "Will you heal his wounds?"

"Only, my dear Mason, if you promise to return and stay for three days."

Mason thought about it; then he sighed. "Yes, Vestia. I will, I promise." Vestia rose with renewed energy.

"The lad, what's his name?"

"Blaze."

"Oh, that's right. I forgot. That's an odd name. Did he earn it?"

"No, it's just his name."

"Blaze lad, come along, dear." Blaze's eyes widened and he looked with trepidation at the door. "I'll start your healing now. I probably should have done it between changing from your old clothes into the new ones because then I can see where I need to heal. I'll do my best as you are." Vestia led Blaze to the table where she had healed Mason, but she gave Blaze a chair to sit in. He stood up.

"They'll heal on their own. I'm fine."

Vestia slit her eyes. "I know you're from Ballardton because I've healed you before. I imagine you've been healed by the clerics there."

"Maybe, why?"

She placed her hand on her hip annoyed. "Have you been to the healers there? It's a simple question and I expect a simple answer."

"Yes."

"I can always tell. You lads and lasses don't ever want to be healed. I am sorry for what you may have endured. I won't hurt you. Now, sit." Mason nodded for Blaze to oblige. Vestia had a soothing way about her. She excused Mason, giving Blaze privacy knowing how hard things were for the foundlings of Ballardton where Iolanthe's temple scorned their existence. Vestia was careful not to offend him.

She asked him to remove his gloves and he did hesitantly. She reminded him that he hadn't been wearing a glove when he arrived.

Vestia held his hand in hers, turning it to catch the light. It was the first time someone had held his hand skin to skin. She examined his hand, running her fingers over his stumps. *Hmm, these were done with a precision tool and these were done with a dagger that had a rolled edge on its blade. Poor lad, nothing I can do to help with his fingers, that would have had to been done at the time of the loss. I assume he was at the clerics for these. Reprehensible.* There were scrapes and scars across his hand. The acid burn on the back was deep, and seriously infected. It would take quite some time to close it with healing and prayers to Iolanthe. Then she examined his other hand. It too was in a similar state with the stubs and scratches.

"Your hands are very soft, Blaze. I assume you never take off the gloves. The scratches will heal. You fared much better than I would have thought, coming face to face with a slugslime." Vestia returned back to the deep acid-bulleted hole. It would need to be cleaned before she healed it. She reached over to a side table drawer and pulled out a glass pipette. She filled it with distilled salt water, which she worked around and under Blaze's skin and hand. After she had filled up his entire hand with the water, she pressed against the fluid, removing it through the opening. She caught it all in a small bowl; the fluid was a cloudy, red-tinted color with green ewz mixed in. Vestia lifted his hand to her eyes, peering into the concave hole. Confident that she had removed all of the infection, it was time to close the wound. Vestia gently placed his hand on the table. She gathered up the bowl.

"Don't move. I'll be right back."

Blaze didn't move. He could see Vestia with her head in a closet. He could hear her mumbling to herself, but it never was enough to reach his ears clearly. Vestia resurfaced in front of Blaze with two books: one herbal and one a prayer book to Iolanthe. He dragged his hands across the table. Vestia caught his wrists. "Don't move. I have to check to see if there is a slugslime prayer." Vestia skimmed through the book. "No not this one, that's for the dead. Hm, this might work—you're not close to death, but it does pray for the living, which fits." Once again, she took his hand in her own. She began the prayer:

"Oh, dear gracious Goddess Iolanthe, to whom I devote myself and my work, I pray that you oversee the healing of this son of Mirias. His battle had been a difficult one leading us now into your care. A slugslime wound that we pray will never, um, I'll leave that part out. I'll start that line again. A slugslime wound that we pray will be *healed* in your name. Oh, Goddess hear our prayer as we send him off to Goddess H . . . uh, let me change that, as we send him off into the world. Oh, hear our prayer." She hovered her right hand over his. "You know, we might have to change these prayers. Update them."

He could feel the wound in his skin. It warmed with the active healing. He pulled away, but she held fast. The wound felt larger than his hand, taking his entire focus. His skin felt like it was crawling, bubbling. He imagined it with boils. He pulled it toward him. She held fast, his hand afire as the cells regenerated. Finally, she released her grip, and his hand sprang back to him, the feeling of movement gone. It was calm. He stared at it, knowing that he had been healed. "Blaze, here is a cooling cream that will help settle those nerve endings that still remember the injury. This is not something that is recommended in Ballardton, but I find it helps not only the body part, but the soul. Oh, and Blaze, when you get injured again, please do not poke at the wound. It gets infected."

Mason and Blaze said their farewells to Vestia, who reminded them to come back if they ever needed healing again.

She was eager to begin the journey to the capitol to expose the properties of the slugslime blood. Of course, that was after she harvested everything she could from the dead slugslime near the border. "I expect you to return Mason to fulfill your promise."

"Yes, Vestia, I said that I would." She kissed Mason.

"And Blaze, it was nice to see you again. If you ever need me, I am here. Don't go to the local abbey—come here instead." Blaze nodded. They waved their farewells and the two thieves were off, healed and ready to go home.

Mason and Blaze walked into the guild, right past Venom, Nightshade, and Lace, who conspired by the door, trying to be inconspicuous. They looked up and pointed.

Blaze stood up a bit straighter and taller. He knew they were dying to find out what they did on their mission and how they fared. Mason greeted Dorken and Pip before knocking on Master's door.

"Come in." Mason and Blaze sauntered into Master's room. As usual, Master sat behind his desk. He got up and greeted Mason with a hug and shook hands with Blaze, who felt distrust for the genuine greeting. "How was the mission? It took a bit longer than expected." Mason sat down first, then Locke, and finally Blaze.

"No, it was fine. Blaze did a great job. He followed the instructions to the letter. I would highly recommend Blaze for future missions. I don't think he needs to be accompanied either, Master. Was the payment received?"

"Yes, Mason, always direct when it comes to the coin." Master reached down and pulled out a chest. He opened it and held up a gold coin. "Blaze, the client was very pleased with your performance and respect. They felt that they could trust you both. Here's your payment." Locke slid the coin across the desk to Blaze. Blaze stared at it, then looked up at Master, and then back at the coin. Mason smiled.

"Go ahead, Blaze, pick it up. You deserve it. You worked hard."

"Um, it's a gold piece." Both Mason and Locke confirmed that it was indeed a gold piece. Blaze slid it off the table into the palm of his other hand. "Is it really mine?"

"Yep, you earned it." Blaze fiddled with it and Mason and Locke exchanged glances. "Is everything okay, Blaze?"

"Oh yeah, it's fine. I've just never held a gold coin that was mine before. This is my first one."

Mason furrowed his brow. "Is that true? Locke, didn't Blaze make a salary at Ceretheena?" Locke hushed Mason.

Blaze looked up accusingly at Master. "Did I? You never mentioned anything about that. What is a celery—it must have something to do with coins?" Mason chuckled. "Or, whatever Mason said."

"A salary. It's a payment you receive when you work for someone. And yes, you did get a salary, but not equal to a gold piece, Mason. I put it in the safe for when you decided to leave, Blaze. I can put this with it if you want." Blaze twirled it in his hand, then he dropped it in his pouch.

"I'm really angry at you. What else have you kept that was actually mine? And about this coin; I'll keep it."

"Let me explain about your payment, Blaze." Master glanced at Mason. "I've never kept anything else. I have always been fair with you."

"Just shut it Master! I don't want to hear it. I'm done."

"Wait, Blaze! I held onto it so that you would have something to bring with you when you leave, but since you were successful on this mission, I could give it to you now. I'll go get it." Locke started to get up, but Blaze stopped him.

"Forget it, Master. I didn't realize that it was there, so there is no loss."

Master sat back down. "Are you sure, Blaze?" Blaze nodded.

His anger didn't subside, but he was ready to go show off the gold piece in his hand to his age mates. "Okay, anyway, do you want to tell me anything about your mission, Blaze? This is called the debrief. You explain the events and if anything or anyone struck you as unusual."

"Hm. We went to the tavern. The red scarf woman was nice, but she threw her drink into Mason's face. The bar wench was mad at Mason, too. That was about it for the mission itself."

Mason was stunned; Blaze had only mentioned the actual mission and not the other events that had happened after the mission was over.

"And . . . and we saw Jade. That's it. Can I go now?" Blaze was eager to leave. He knew that Mason would talk about Cathal, Jade, the innkeep, and the slugslime. All except for the Vassyric Knight were unimportant. "Oh, one last thing: was the red scarf woman a noble?"

Locke and Mason both shrugged. "We're not sure what or who she was. She could easily have been an actor. We don't know exactly who the client is on some of these missions. Okay?"

"Okay." Blaze exited the room. Mason was nearly on pins and needles trying to control his excitement about the other events that had unfolded.

✦

Exiting Master's room, Blaze pulled out his gold coin. It was a risk he wanted to take. He hoped to make the others, especially Venom, jealous. But Venom, Nightshade, and Lace had all disappeared into the hustle of Ballardton. Pigeon, however, took notice. He edged closer to Blaze.

"That's a nice shiny piece of gold, Blaze."

Blaze smiled proudly.

"Yep, it sure is, Pigeon."

"Where did you get one that pretty?"

"From my mission. I just got back." Pigeon walked around Blaze.

"What did you have to do on your mission to get such a pretty coin?" Blaze eyed Pigeon.

"I'm not supposed to tell you. I know you've gone on missions before, Pigeon; you know this." Pigeon stared at the coin.

"You know, I have a way that you could double that. Do you want in? It's a sure thing, Blaze." Blaze glanced suspiciously at Pigeon as he returned the coin to his pouch. He wrapped his fingers around the bottom of the pouch making sure that he held onto the coin.

"Pigeon, I know all about your sure things. I'm sure I want no part of them. Ask someone else; maybe you can get a Little to fall for it. The rest of us know what you are trying to do. The sure thing is that you will surely take the coin. So, no." Blaze smiled, confident that the coin was safe in his own keeping.

"Eh, you don't know what you're missing." Pigeon waved Blaze away, annoyed. Blaze shrugged, happy to have seen through Pigeon. "I could give you information about that pretty little thing that flew in here one day speaking Mahdurnian."

Goldie!

"What about her? Tell me, Pigeon!" Blaze grabbed Pigeon by his collar. Pigeon smirked lazily.

"You know us pigeons, we hear things when the others don't think we can hear." Pigeon returned to his bench, hoping to lure Blaze into his clutches.

"What about her? What's happened?" Blaze ran at Pigeon, dagger drawn. "What do you know? Tell me everything." Blaze glared. Pigeon could see his own reflection in Blaze's dagger. The dagger's edge had rolled and its point was blunt. Pigeon smiled.

"Your dagger is useless. You've damaged the blade and tip. You can't harm me. It looks like I have the advantage here." Blaze examined the blade. It was true—the blade was ruined, but it could still be fixed. After all, he did have a gold coin. "Unless, you want to make a trade. I give you information and you give me some coins."

"Coppies."

"Oh, this information will talk with a gold."

Blaze glanced up at Pigeon. "No, I'm not giving up my gold for anything." Blaze pulled away from Pigeon, who shrugged.

"Hey, that's up to you, Blaze. I guess she cares more for you than you do her. She left calling out for you." Blaze stalled at the door. *Do I give up my gold for Goldie?*

"Left? Several ebons, Pigeon. That's a good trade for the information." Pigeon held out his hand. "Here." Blaze placed six ebons, all that he had, into Pigeon's greedy hand.

"She was kidnapped."

"Again?"

"All of Ballardton is searching for her. The bird that attacked us was strung up like a chicken on a spit. It's quite hurt. They're not even sure if it'll wake up."

"Who do they think did this?"

"They don't know, but I do."

"Who, Pigeon? Who?" Blaze hung on every word.

"Oh, I think I told you six ebons of information already. You can get more information if you want to give up a gold. Isn't she worth it?"

"Ah! You are so infuriating, Pigeon! You never get to the point. You always want more."

Pigeon smiled arrogantly.

"I'm not giving you a coppie more. I'll find out who on my own."

"You're making a mistake, Blaze. You could already have cost her her life." Blaze turned away from Pigeon as he thought about the situation. *Do I give him the coin? If I do, he could tell me nothing at all, but then again, he did tell me for the ebons. What do I do?* Blaze turned back to Pigeon.

"No, she's not dead and I know it."

"How did you know that she wasn't? Did you already know all this information? Who told you?"

"You just told me, Pigeon. Thank you for saving me a gold." Blaze left the guild ready to find out anything, but he didn't know where to even start searching.

"Find her! Or it'll be all of our heads!" Sterling frantically screamed at his company. Blaze knew most of them but only some by name. His body tightened with fear.

Constables Sterling and Avery darted by him.

"Where did they find the bird-sprite?"

"It was strung up in a tree near here. Injured would be an understatement for its condition," said Sterling.

"I thought it was more sensitive these days to call sprites the same way everyone calls other people. You know—he, she, they. "It" is a word that may make sprites feel badly about being sprites."

"Then *it* shouldn't have been born a sprite. *It's* the curse that *it* will carry for the rest of *its* days and those days seem to be numbered."

Avery shook his head at Sterling's choice of words and tirade. Blaze kept his distance, following Sterling straight to the tree. Avery stood sentry as Sterling investigated the spot of the attack. A puddle of blood stained the trampled grass. *Burd must be close to death*, Blaze surmised. He felt his heart sink and his stomach fluttered just thinking about what if . . . he must have been run through taking the blade for Goldenrod, as any protector would.

People from across Ballardton had come to gawk and follow the constables, as Blaze had. These people were too caught up in the excitement of the chase and the incident to worry about the young thief. Blaze backed off, listening to the town's gossip.

"I can't believe this has happened!"

"Never before in all my years! A royal guest goes missing—poof! Just like that!"

"I think they should check the rivers and the wells; oh yeah, they should definitely check that one well near the north-east side of town. It's so murky. A body could absolutely be hidden in there."

"Most definitely!"

"Well, I overheard Chief Constable Tommik say something about one of those young boys from that guild. You know the one near Her temple. He may have something to do with this."

"Yes, apparently she's been with that boy for some time. It was only a matter of time before this kind of thing happened. Those children should be rounded up and shot on sight. What are they doing to help out Ballardton? They just make it diseased."

Blaze gazed down forlornly.

"I know! All they do is steal, steal, steal. My friend—her husband is one of the piemen—is always having trouble with those guttersnipes. Her husband has a plan to eliminate them one by one. *He* is helping our constables and Ballardton." Blaze grit his teeth. *Borintak, she's talking about Borintak. How could she even think that?*

"Oh, come on now. That's no way to talk about children. We need to find them good homes so they don't have to live on the street." *Finally.*

"Really? Do *you* want to take them in?"

"Well . . . no, but I don't have the room for children. I would if I could."

"You would if you could! Then why haven't you? Don't go talking about something you know nothing about. Those children are wickedly evil. I bet they all go to Her temple, too. Evil."

Blaze held his tongue, tightening the muscles in his jaw, and glared in their direction.

"Oh, Captain Sterling! Is there any word on the young noble? This is just horrible!" A middle-aged woman waved to get Sterling's attention. He straightened his belt, pulling it higher on his hips, and then sauntered over to her.

"Hullo, it's so good to see you again. We have some leads that we are following."

"What is the name of the boy that she was seeing? Have you apprehended him with your strong muscles?" The woman boosted Sterling's ego, egging him on to tell her more about the investigation. Blaze was interested too, but he covered his face with his hood, worried that Sterling would grab him if he spotted him.

"Sure, would you like to feel them? Boom!" He held up his arm, flexing his muscles, which were unimpressive. She rubbed his muscle and oohed and aahed over his strength.

"Sterling, what about the investigation? Do you know who did it?"

"We're pretty sure that it was the boyfriend. We just sent someone over to get him—we are saying it is to just ask him some questions." Sterling laughed.

"Oh? What kind of questions?"

Avery walked over to refocus his captain back on his job task. "None of which Captain Sterling can speak of, lady. Sorry for the inconvenience."

Avery caught sight of Blaze's face under the cloak. He slid behind the lady and grabbed Blaze by the arm. "Excuse me, but I think we need to talk." Blaze pulled away. "You don't want to make a scene, Blaze. Do you?" Avery whispered. Blaze shook his head. *Not with this crowd. If they knew who I am, they might stone me to death.*

Sterling glanced around the woman. Upon seeing Blaze, Sterling rushed forward.

"That's him—Blaze! He's the boyfriend!" Avery and Blaze sighed. Sterling pulled off Blaze's hood. "See! It figures that he would be here. That's pretty sneaky, but that's what we would expect of a thief!"

Blaze looked around at the townsfolk; his eyes were wide, fearing their reactions. He watched their expressions change to anger. They started to scream at him. He glanced over at Sterling and saw a glimmer of amusement and pleasure in his face.

"You're just like them, Sterling. You're just like those Cadmarians. They don't care who dies." Sterling, enraged, backhanded Blaze across his face. The flirtatious woman covered her mouth gleaming with delight at Sterling's take-charge display.

"You shut your mouth! You're coming with us. I'll hold him, Avery. You go tell Chief Constable Tommik that I have our suspect." Sterling manhandled Blaze, pulling him away from Avery's grasp.

"Hey! I know you. You stole from my stand in the market, spooked my horse over on King's Highway *and* now you've killed that beautiful girl! I once even saw him climbing the wall outside of Lords and Ladies. By the time, I got the constable he was gone! Get him, Sterling! I hope you die in that vault!" A man yelled at Blaze. The other townspeople restarted their tirade. Constable Avery raised his hands trying to calm the angry crowd, which was quickly escalating.

"Sterling! I need some help here!" Sterling looked back at Avery and the angry mob, who began to chant."

"Vault! Vault! Vault! Vault!"

"I have my hands full with this flotsam here." Sterling turned Blaze toward the crowd, which immediately quieted their voices. "Here . . . Stop! Everyone just stop! We will get the information from him. I guarantee you that. This boy has evaded the constables for the last time." Blaze struggled to get away from Sterling, but the man held him with a secure grip.

Avery stepped forward. "Captain Sterling, I do believe that he is innocent until proven guilty. We are not in Bevisson or Cadmaria. Our chief constable will decide his immediate fate, but as of right now, he is just going to speak to this youth. I know we Timerians are better than both Bevisson and Cadmaria, isn't that so, Endale?" Avery called out the man who had recognized Blaze. Endale pursed his lips and glanced away. "Since when do the good people of Ballardton, no, Timeria, have no desire for a child who has seen his own share of strife to receive justice and be able to defend himself? When do we wish a child to go into the vault? Good day, folks. There will be no more gatherings like this, as per Chief Constable Tommik's immediate order."

The crowd began to disperse and the woman who had tried to explain that the children just needed good homes mouthed the words, "I'm sorry" to Blaze. He didn't respond to her, but he wiggled to free himself from Sterling's tightened grasp without luck. Avery approached Blaze and Sterling.

"Let go of him. He can't talk if you squeeze the life out of him. I'll escort the boy back to the constabulary, Sterling." Avery reached out for Blaze's arm, but Sterling pulled Blaze closer to him.

"I've got him, Avery. I can keep him at bay; besides I outrank you." Avery smiled thoughtfully at Sterling.

"I have no doubt that you can, but I don't see him giving us a fight, Sterling. I'll take him back and you're correct, Captain, prison transfer is far below a city captain's duties?"

"Well, you are right Avery, that is true. However, this whole investigation is important enough for me to handle it. Anyways, you're too soft, Avery. You're too willing to take his side because he is a child. I spit on that." Sterling spat a large amount of mucus on the ground.

"We have yet to hear his side and he won't talk because he's angry and scared. This will not help the young noble at all." Avery was calm and collected, choosing his words with care. "Therefore, may I please escort Blaze to the constabulary?"

Sterling squawked, but eventually he had no argument to counter Avery's, especially with so many people watching. Sterling nodded, but kept his grasp on Blaze's arm, bruising the skin. Avery faced Sterling, staring defiantly into his eyes. Sterling pushed closer to Avery. There was a battle brewing, Blaze could see it. Avery stepped into the fray, and he didn't falter. "Let go of him, Captain." His words were cool and calm in a sea of ire.

"All right, Avery, its above my position as captain anyways. Here, you take the scum! We'll make him pay for his crime against our king—against Timeria! Everyone, look here!" Sterling grabbed the ensembled townsfolk's attention. "This is Blaze. He's a thief here in Ballardton, and he killed the young noble girl from Drisana!" The dispersing mob watched with fear and fury aimed at Blaze. Sterling grabbed Blaze from Avery and spun him around so everyone could gawk at him. Avery closed his eyes. Abashed, he knew Sterling had just written the youth's death sentence.

Avery stepped in front of Blaze. "He's just a child! He is trying to survive like all of us. Do not heed Sterling's words. He is just a child." Avery tore Blaze away from Sterling like a schoolboy retrieving his favorite toy from a bully. "He's just a child."

Blaze didn't know how to react to any of this. He was in the clutches of Sterling, who had just destroyed his whole life in one sentence. He was scarred, and no matter how Avery spun it, the townsfolk knew what he was. The blinking sign of "thief" that once floated above him, graciously gifted by visiting pixies, was still very visible to all that looked upon him. He could never outrun this scar.

Blaze's escort to the constabulary was without incident. Avery was swift in his removal from the area as he noticed the mob was rebuilding itself with Sterling enabling them to act. Fear that a visiting noble could be taken so easily and so violently, as evidenced by the near slaying of the sprite, struck the townsfolk. They realized that they didn't stand a chance against the criminals that lurked amongst them especially now that they had a name and a face. If it could easily happen to a tourist, then it could easily happen to a local. The mob was escalating, and Blaze was the center of their thoughts and comments.

Avery led Blaze down some stairs to a lower level of the constabulary. There was a hallway with a series of rooms off of it, but all Blaze could see were closed doors. The hallways and doors were painted the same drab grey that decorated the upstairs. *I guess the constables don't like color,* Blaze mused, realizing at the same time just how horrid a situation he was in. At the end of the hall, one of the doors was open and Avery guided the boy into the room and sat him at a table in front of Chief Constable Tommik. "Chief Constable, I believe you know Blaze." Avery left the room to stand sentry, shutting the door behind him.

"I do indeed know you, Blaze." Blaze turned halfway in his chair and didn't look at Tommik. "I have known you your whole life, and this is what you do on the crest of adulthood? Look at me when I am talking to you, Blaze."

"Why? You and Sterling and Avery and everyone have already made up your minds. I heard Sterling talking. 'We're going to let him think that we just want to talk.' It's a lie. It's always a lie in Ballardton."

Tommik laughed. "Serious as always. Blaze, do you remember the day you brought this to me?" Tommik reached into his pouch and pulled out a green plastic man with moveable arms and legs. Blaze narrowed his eyes but was surprised to see Tommik holding and playing with the little man. He smiled slightly and turned back toward the table. Tommik handed the little man to Blaze.

"I do. You keep it on the shelf above your desk upstairs."

"You gave it to me the first day I started on the job here."

"Did I? I think Mason brought it back for me. He was on a mission somewhere out west. I think it was near Drisana actually." Tommik smiled.

"I looked into it. It is actually from Mahdurna, believe it or not."

"I was a Little, which makes you stupid." Blaze tossed it back to Tommik.

"No, it was a kind gesture. You gave me everything that you had including a little piece of string. It was from that moment that I vowed that I would do everything I could to protect the children of Ballardton. This has become a symbol of my commitment."

"Well, you should throw it out. It isn't working." Tommik moved the legs on the green man and made it sit in the middle of the table. Blaze picked it up. He straightened the legs out. "You let Sterling put me in the vault."

"I know. You weren't supposed to be in there. I didn't think any-one was in there. Nobody was ever supposed to be in there."

"You never apologized."

Tommik wiggled in his chair. He swallowed hard. "You're right, but if I apologize now, you wouldn't accept it. Would you?" Blaze narrowed his eyes.

"Probably not, but you could still say it."

"I'm deeply sorry that you were wrongfully locked up in the vault."

"Dismantle it."

"I can't. I don't have the authority."

"Who does?"

"The king."

"I'll ask him."

"I'm waiting for that. It would be a grand day for sure. Hold on." Tommik walked to the door and opened it. He stuck his head through the door and whispered to Avery. Tommik returned to the table. "Okay, so tell me about you and the noble girl."

"There's nothing to tell."

"I heard you and her are dating."

"I don't know."

"You don't know if you are dating?"

"We kissed once."

"That sounds like dating."

"One kiss doesn't make it a date. I never really went anywhere with her." Blaze blushed, suppressing a pursed smile.

"Okay, so how did you meet her?"

"She was in the market."

"Yes, go on."

"She was in the market, and she didn't know which pieman to go to. If you want to protect the children of Ballardton, you should get rid of Borintak."

Tommik looked surprised. "What does Borintak have to do with children?"

"He poisons his pies." Tommik laughed.

"Now, I know that's not true. I ate one of his pies just this morning. They have more fruit in them than Nerapi's, although Nerapi's pies have a flakier crust. If they could just get together, they'd . . ." The door swung open. Avery entered with a tray of goodies including pies, a root beer skin, tea, and some biscuits with an assortment of jellies. He placed them down in front of Tommik and Blaze. Blaze scanned the sweets. His eyes fell on the pies. He felt the urge to grab one but pulled back. Tommik grabbed a couple of biscuits and poured himself some tea.

"Help yourself," he offered, after shoving a whole biscuit in his mouth. Again, Blaze reached out for the pie, and then thought better of it.

"These are Borintak's pies, right?"

"Ah, yes, I guess they are. They were fresh this morning."

"No, I don't want anything."

"I thought you were hungry. I know I was hungry. Okay, eat or don't. It's up to you. So, you were saying." Tommik leaned back in the chair munching on a pie.

"I saved her from going to Borintak."

"But his pies are good."

"Sometimes you don't see things that are happening right before your eyes. You don't want to see it so you look away, Constable. Borintak kills Littles."

"You know we have a case that's open. Maybe you can shed some light on it for us. It's a boy who was found dead up on the hill near the dungeon. We figured he was killed by something from it. Did you know him? We had a portrait painted of him to get some leads. I'll send someone to get it."

Tommik banged the table three times. Blaze looked at Tommik like he was crazy. The sweets and the tray excitedly jumped with every hit.

"Yes, Chief Constable." Avery opened the door with his dagger drawn.

"Ah, good, Avery. No need for the dagger right now. Can you get me the portrait of the boy on the hill?" Avery scurried out of the room, returning just as quick with a wallet-sized portrait. The portrait was of a boy with mousy brown hair, darker skin, and brown eyes that were smiling. Blaze recognized the image immediately.

"That's Gavin. He was at the guild. You left out the pie filling; it was always on his face or his tunic. He ate pies from Borintak's stand. Was Shadow with him?"

"No, but I know Shadow. Haven't seen him in a while now that you mention it. So, Gavin was his name. Funny, now that you mention it, he did have a tray next to him. We couldn't figure out what killed him, though. When he was found, Rollo thought he was just sleeping until he tried to rouse him. That was when he knew the boy . . . Gavin, was dead. Rollo wrapped the boy in his cloak and carried him back here, cradling him in his arms. We all felt the boy's loss. It was horrible. Together we collected coin and gave it to Lady Marnie's temple for his send off to Goddess Hala. May Marnie protect his soul!"

"How long ago was that?" Blaze was surprised that Tommik was telling him about Gavin's fate.

"Oh, a number of years now; about the time that the duke and duchess returned. It seems like just yesterday." Tommik teared up as he looked at the portrait again. He banged the table, just once this time. Rollo entered. Blaze surmised that the number of times he banged the table indicated who he was calling.

"Yes, Tommik. What do you need? Avery told me you asked for the portrait."

"I know his name. It's Gavin. We can tell Marnie's temple to pray for him with his name.

Poor lad. Also, ask Borintak about him. He may have seen him at his stand."

"Will do." Tommik handed the miniature portrait to Rollo who, nearly silently, voiced "Gavin" so that he could remember when he wrote the boy's name on the back of the portrait. Rollo left.

"Okay, now we really need to talk about the noble girl. Let's talk about the last time you saw her."

"I had a mission. I left. I came back and I found out she was missing. I saw the constables running, and I followed them like everybody else. Now I'm here." Tommik shook his head and slurped at his tea.

"I love your use of details, Blaze. Maybe you need to get some tips on how to tell a good story from that storyteller." Blaze didn't want to tell every little detail to Tommik. It was pointless. He didn't need to know. "So . . . let's take it back a little. Tell me if I'm wrong. You went on a mission?"

"Yes." *I said that. This will be annoying.*

"What kind of a mission did you go on? Did it involve the girl in any way, shape, or form?"

"No, why would she need to go on a mission? I went for the guild." *Okay, don't tell him anymore about it. It's over and it's done.*

"Um, okay. Have you been on a lot of missions for your guild?" Tommik was fishing for information; not only about Blaze, but also about the guild's activities.

"What does that have to do with finding Goldie?" Tommik cleared his throat and sat up straighter in his chair.

"So then you said you left, right?"

Blaze tightened his jaw and made a fist. "Yes, I left; that was the last time I saw Goldie. She was safe and she was fine. She was with her aunt, the Drisanian Princess."

"And the bird?"

"I think so. He hides well. He's tiny, so probably. He usually sits here on her shoulder. He's annoying." *Stupid Burd got himself skewered. I didn't see that coming.* Blaze chuckled to himself.

"Okay, so then what happened?"

"Nothing. I left. Like I said, end of story." Tommik shifted in his chair. He took a moment finishing his tea. He slammed the cup back down onto the table.

"Come on, boy! Work with me. There must be something. Anything you can tell me about what happened." Blaze inhaled. There was nothing. He had been busy fighting a stinking slugslime, for Gods' sakes. In Tommik's eyes, there was a pleading desire. *I only know what Pigeon told me and I can't say that. It wouldn't be right.*

Honor amongst thieves, isn't that right? I learned that when I ousted
Ruri way back when.

"That's it, Chief Constable Tommik. Here, take your little man
back. I'm done. Let me go." Tommik stood up. Blaze followed him
across the room with his eyes.

"You want to go?"

"Yes."

"Then tell me what I need to know; the girl's life depends on it."

"You're a liar, Chief Constable. You told me that you wanted to
protect the children of Ballardton. You even told me about Gavin.
We weren't friends. We weren't even enemies. He was just another
faceless child at the guild who just happened to eat pies all the
time. Borintak killed him. I'd stake my life on it. But I don't know
anything about Goldenrod except that her hair smells sweet and,
for some reason Gods only know, she talks to me. To me. A peasant.
A thief. A nobody." Blaze leaned on the table, yelling at Tommik
for his stupidity. Tommik stood there, speechless.

"I only protect children, Blaze. You're not a child; I can see that
now. Sterling was right. You can go, but don't go too far. We are
watching you." Tommik opened the door. Blaze glared at him as he
walked out. In the hallway, Blaze bolted as fast as he could out the
constabulary. *Someone knows something and I'm going to find out who.*

CHAPTER 23

LIARS AND THIEVES

ENOM WAITED for Blaze, circling like a caged animal. He had already walked a path in the dirt when he saw Blaze slip out, a hood covering his face. He ran, catching up to Blaze. "Where are you going?"

"Anywhere. Maybe to the river's bank. I can think there." Venom nodded and the two boys circled around through town to the murky fountain. The air was familiar; not refreshing, but familiar. Blaze glanced into the fountain. He couldn't see anything through the sludge. *Maybe, just maybe, she could be in there.* He pulled out his dagger and gently raked it along through the water, hoping and yet not hoping that he would hit her. There was nothing that big to indicate her presence there. He exhaled a sigh of relief. Venom watched in horrified silence.

"Come on. I'll clean my blade in the river." Venom nodded. After another half an hour, the two friends reached their spot. Blaze lay down on the bank with his head toward the water. He cleaned his blade. The water washed away the impurities of the fountain. His hands were clean. He sat up.

What's going on? Venom wondered amazed at how sure and confident Blaze suddenly seemed. "How did your mission go?"

Blaze shrugged. Silence stayed between them. Venom stared motionless down at his feet as though he would lose them if he didn't watch. Blaze looked out into the trees across from them. He ran through his head everything that he knew, but nothing seemed out of the ordinary. *Venom, Nightshade, and Lace were conspiring near the door. When I came out, they were gone. Why Lace? Did Venom go on his assignment?* There was no doubt; Blaze would have to confront Venom. He'd have to be careful, or he'd spook him.

"My mission was boring. Sorry it took me so long to answer. This whole situation with the constabulary is maddening."

Venom nodded in agreement. "I saw Sterling grab your arm. It was rather bold of him. He really hates you."

"He does, I know. They're all liars, Venom, all of them: Sterling, Tommik, and Master. Did you know that Master kept some coin that I had earned when I worked for Ceretheena?"

Venom was startled. "I wonder if he does that to everyone or just to you?"

"I'll bet he does it to everyone, but I just caught him at it. He's a liar. I'm just glad, Venom, that I can trust you. I think you're probably the only person I can trust around here." Blaze wrapped his arm around Venom's shoulders. Venom patted Blaze's gloved hand.

"Yeah."

"Hey, I forgot to ask. How did that thing you did with . . . who was it with . . . go?"

Venom smiled proudly.

"It went well. It was a lot easier than I thought." Blaze removed his arm and inched closer to Venom showing interest in every word. "It was with Lace and Nightshade. We talked about it, remember?"

"Oh, yeah. I remember. So, are you done now?" Venom thought about it.

"Well, it's complicated." Blaze raised his eyebrows. "I don't know. It keeps changing. You were right about Lace. It's not really Nightshade. She's just following Lace around, you know." Blaze understood. Looking up at the sky, Venom leaned back on his hands. "Nightshade and me, well, you know, we go way back. Back to the moment, Spider and I arrived in Ballardton. We were exhausted. I had carried Spider most of the way on my back. We just kept walking. We got lost on North Road, which starts in Bevisson. On our way, we almost ended up joining with the hill-people. Spider liked them. I didn't, but they did give us a warm meal one night and a place to sleep. I ended up falling from exhaustion near the clerics. I dropped Spider too. I'm not happy about it still. I don't forget stuff, Blaze, but you know that.

"So this girl just appears that day. She helps us up and leads us to the guild house. It seems almost fantastical now, but that's how I remember it. The girl, as you know, was Nightshade. We immediately hit it off. She says that I shouldn't bring Spider in—that they don't like Littles—so I find a place for him to live. The caves where he still is; that's where I brought him. You know how safe it is; no one has ever bothered him. Then I came down to the guild. I met you, Aldric, and Dellanie. I also met Jewels. I just met everyone, and I got to eat the soup. So that's why I kind of go along with Nightshade. If it weren't for her, I wouldn't be here."

Blaze furrowed his brow. It wasn't exactly the way he remembered Venom's arrival going, but this wasn't completely about the truth. It was about Venom's truth and how he saw it. How he wanted it. Blaze just listened and let Venom go on.

"Yeah, I know she's important to you."

Venom nodded.

"So, Lace has been leading her and me around, you see. We didn't want to do it, but you know Lace, she has wicked tendencies. Did you know that her dad is the knackerman?" Blaze shook his head. "He is. She told me the other day. She made me do it, Blaze. I didn't want to, but she was going to hurt Spider, so I had to. You understand, right? It's just like when you told me that you were going to live on a fiefdom with those people. I went to get Spider and we were ready to go with you, but instead you left without us. Spider was heartbroken and I was deeply upset. I thought you were my friend, Blaze. You're like my brother, too, so you can see why I got so upset about what happened when you came back. But what I didn't tell you was that Lace had seen you walking down from where your camp was and she told me that you were back. She reminded me that you left us behind. You can't do that—not to Spider and me. Not to me. It just brought all those feelings back. I jumped you and made sure you hit your head. She was whispering from behind a building to cut you, to stab you, and then she told me to take a trophy. She told me to take your finger. But I was so caught up in the moment, I took two. You asked me that day you came back, who'd buy fingers? It was Lace. She bought your fingers from me."

Blaze was shocked, reeling from this news. He wanted to vomit. Every emotion and feeling from that day rushed back to him. It had been so hard going back to the guild, but he had known he had to. It was the only place he knew and after losing the staffers, it was home. Venom was still his friend, everyone at the guild—still family in the end. There was a learning curve with having to relearn how to hold things. He had felt that way twice in his life: once for each hand. Blaze felt butterflies fluttering in his stomach and he felt dizzy. He lay back down on the ground. The world had a new look to it. It spun around on itself with Blaze at the epicenter. He covered his face, trying to recover. He had to—for Goldenrod.

"So, Venom. You still haven't told me what she wanted you to do on this job of hers."

"Yeah, I know. I haven't gotten there yet." Venom turned on his side to face Blaze, resting his head on his hand. "So, you can see how happy I was when you came back and we went back to the way we were before you left. I'm just really glad that you weren't at a fiefdom after all. It made everything less disturbing. I think that's it." *Gods help me.*

"Venom, what about Spider? How did she threaten him?" Blaze uncovered his face looking up at the treetops that seemed higher than they had been before the world started spinning.

"Oh boy, did she ever! Everything is for Spider. I'd die for him. She told me that if I didn't do this, she'd go up to the cave and slice Spider up into little pieces and then she'd tell the constables that I did it. If anybody knows me, they'd know that I'd never do anything to Spider. But I couldn't let her hurt him, so I had to do it. I didn't realize how serious it was until she ran that bird-sprite through inside and out. She then had Nightshade tie it to a tree and leave it for the carrions to finish the job."

Blaze closed his eyes. Spider's face came to the forefront of his mind. He could see the innocence of childhood in those huge blue eyes with his black mop of hair and a smile that could melt the ice during thirteenth month. The horrible thought of Spider not being a part of the world anymore cut Blaze to his core.

"But what about Goldie?"

"Well, that's where I don't know. I don't want to make any trouble, but Lace keeps telling me that I need to do what must be done." Blaze shot up and turned to face Venom, but Venom lay on the ground nonchalantly. "I don't want to hurt anyone else. I know I hurt you, Blaze, but it would be awful to hurt your girlfriend. I didn't, Blaze. I walked out of there. Then I heard about you being taken to the constabulary and I had to go see if they let you out. They did, so everything is okay. Right?"

Blaze hunkered down to be even with Venom's eyes. "No, Venom, Goldie is still missing and who knows what Lace plans to do with her."

Venom looked uncomfortable fidgeting with a piece of grass that he picked unknowingly. He twisted it in between his fingers tying the blade of grass into a loose knot. *How do I tell Blaze this? Deep Breath.* "I know, Blaze. She's going to slit her throat and then leave her on the hill near the dungeon like she got caught up in it." Upon hearing Venom's words, Blaze felt a rush of pain in his heart and belly and his face lost all color. Tears welled up in his eyes and fell down his cheeks.

"When? Or has it already happened?" Hurt, betrayal, and loss all fell on Blaze's face while he awaited the answers to his questions. Venom was surprised by Blaze's reaction, which was much calmer than expected.

"It hasn't happened, yet. Lace needed to prepare. I think she is trying to get Nightshade to do it, so her hands were clean. Lace first thought about putting the Mahdurian in the knackerman's fire. I talked her out of it. I couldn't let that happen." Blaze shook his head, "no."

"But you could let her throat be sliced? Venom, do you feel responsible for Goldenrod's death? She doesn't deserve this." Blaze was on his feet now. Tears blurred his vision, but he needed to hold them back. Venom had to see the wrong in this.

"Of course not, Blaze. That's why I waited for you. That's why I told you all of this. I know that if she dies, we'll never have any more festivals and nobody will come here. We'll all starve because there'll be nothing here. No coin in the summer, just like the winter. I don't want that. I didn't want to be a part of any of this, but you know. . . Spider." This time tears fell down Venom's cheeks. He rubbed his eyes and sobbed. Blaze's expression was stern and set. Venom looked up at him.

"Where, Venom?" He grabbed Venom, who went in for a reassuring hug, but Blaze grabbed him by his tunic and pulled him to his feet.

"Uh, Blaze, you're hurting me." Venom felt choked and emotionally injured.

"Where is she?" Blaze pulled Venom closer as he raised his arm to punch the older boy.

"Wait! Let me think." Venom held the side of his head. He glanced back at Blaze, who crossed his arms, waiting for Venom's answer. The summer coin was what allowed him to live throughout the year and support Spider. He couldn't let it all go. If he was incarcerated for Blaze's girlfriend's death, then who'd take care of Spider? He feared Lace's wrath if she found out who told. There would have to be contingencies that would keep Venom safe and, most importantly, Spider.

"Okay, Blaze. I'll tell you where she is, but you have to keep me out of this. I don't want to be a cause of there being no more festivals and I really don't want anyone to think that me or Spider were a part of this. Also, if you can, Blaze, try to help Nightshade out of this too."

"No, Nightshade doesn't get my mercy. She's forever following around Lace, and toying with people." Blaze shook his head refusing to let Nightshade off the hook.

"Please, we were both manipulated to join Lace. Please? Do you agree to these terms?" Venom held on to Blaze pleadingly as he started to sob. Reluctantly, Blaze agreed. Venom inhaled and spoke clearly and resigning to his part of the scheme. "She's in a small outbuilding near the edge of the town. Nobody uses the building, but it gets hot in there." Blaze couldn't identify the building in his mind.

"Which side of town? Toward the capital or toward the big oak?"

"It's toward the big oak." Blaze sprinted up King's Highway. He dodged many horses and carts that were leaving Ballardton; the festival was now complete, and news of Goldenrod's disappearance still lingered. *I'm going to find her!*

Blaze found the small outbuilding after some searching. He scaled the wall and landed on the roof, where he was able to confirm that Goldenrod was in there through a small rodent hole near a hanging branch. The door was bolted shut. He leaned down to peer through the hole. Goldenrod slumped in a chair with her wrists and ankles tied. Her mouth was gagged. Her neck was encircled with a noose. He couldn't see much else. He found a spot across from the outbuilding and waited for Nightshade and Lace to return and open the door.

After some time, his dedication paid off and both girls arrived. Lace was fully armed, but Nightshade had only her dagger. It was obvious to Blaze that Lace didn't fully trust Nightshade, keeping her in a more passive role. Lace held the key and unlocked the door. Blaze sneaked closer, hoping that he could get close enough to enter with Nightshade. But she noticed a presence and prepared for a fight.

Swiftly, Nightshade slammed the door behind Lace. With dagger in hand, Nightshade turned to make her stand against Blaze, whom she had seen only as a cloaked figure. Blaze ran toward her. She held the blade to stab expecting him to complete his path. He stopped just short of her and laughed at the absurdity of her intent. Her face reddened with embarrassment and she lunged at him. He sidestepped and she stumbled. Blaze quickly got behind her and the door. He banged on the door with hopes that it would bring Lace outside. Nightshade regained her footing and ran back toward Blaze. She caught his cloak on the tip of her dagger, uncovering his face.

"Blaze!" She gasped, but continued her attack nonetheless.

Blaze spun around her effortlessly anticipating her moves similarly to those of the slugslime. He kept clear of her blade, trying to regain his spot. He knew that if he could catch her at the right moment, he could knock her off balance and take control of the fight. She struggled against him. He was no longer the small weakling that she believed him to be. He was strong, smart, and extremely quick. As soon as she had found her target, he was gone from that spot.

Nightshade started slashing at the air, trying to hit any part of him. She felt her steel cut into his flesh, but he still moved away. Figuring out that he was trying to get behind her, she backed into the side of the building. Blaze tossed his hood and cowl at her; she slashed at it, screaming with her eyes closed. The fabric tumbled to the ground in rags at her feet. He took to the roof again. She opened her eyes and waited, breathing heavily, knowing that he was there, but unable to locate him.

He dropped down beside her, disarming her and kicking the dagger away. She began a new attack, punching, scratching, and kicking at him. He grabbed her hands, trying to catch her off-guard once more. As she pulled away from his grip, she tried to kick him. He caught her leg mid-swing, knocking her off balance to fall hard on the ground. She gasped and collapsed in pain. He picked her up and carried her into the woods. He knew he had to be quick and make sure she didn't cry out to Lace. He retrieved his cloak from where it had landed and he finished shredding it quickly into strips of fabric. She was only half awake, allowing him to restrain her easily. He connected the strips to each other and then wrapped them around Nightshade tightly enough that, he hoped, they would hold, at least until he could get Goldenrod out of Lace's grasp. Angry, frustrated tears wet her reddened face.

"Blaze . . . I didn't mean for it to get to this point. You know how Lace can be. It's not my fault. Please . . . let me go." She reached for his dagger, but he moved his body away from her. *I just hope I've tied these tight enough that she can't wiggle free.* Blaze grabbed Nightshade's face, but she refused to look at him. She squirmed, twisting her body in strange contortions, trying to free herself.

"Nightshade, I know this is all Lace. I won't lead the constables to you or tell them you and Venom were involved, but I will hold this over you. Get out of your ties, one way or another, and I'll see you back at the guild. One day, you will repay me." He released her face, breathed in deeply and picked up her dagger and headed back to help Goldenrod.

Next, Blaze stalked the outbuilding. He waited until he could hear something inside. A scuffle or anything would suffice, but all he heard was deafening silence. He scaled the wall and peered in, looking to find any signs of life. Goldenrod was moving, but she didn't seem to be conscious of her surroundings. She neither cried nor talked. Her hair snaked across her face, sticking like spaghetti to a wall.

Lace paced around Goldenrod, tapping a knife against her palm. Nightshade's disappearance must have made her nervous. Blaze ran back to Nightshade and grabbed her cloak, hood and the keys from her belt. Nightshade protested.

Blaze was surprised that Lace hadn't locked the outbuilding. She must have been waiting for Nightshade to do the deed so that Lace's hands would be clean. He hoped that she wouldn't realize that Nightshade's clothes had changed. He kept his head bowed. He had watched Nightshade enough over the years to know her movements.

"Finally! Where were you? It doesn't matter. Give me your dagger. It's time."

Goldenrod started to writhe in the chair; muffled screaming echoed inside the tiny shed. Blaze moved closer to Lace, keeping his head down until he was right beside her. He grabbed for his dagger. With a single move, Blaze held Lace in a chokehold with his dagger, ready to attack. Lace glanced behind her to see Blaze. She started to laugh.

"Stop! Stop laughing!"

Lace did not stop. Her laughter was ringing in his ears. He attempted to carry Lace out of the building, but she entangled her feet with his, knocking him off balance. He lost his grip on her and she turned to face him. With blades drawn, both Blaze and Lace were ready. Blaze pulled off Nightshade's cloak, flinging it at Lace. Without waiting for Lace to recover, Blaze swiftly unbound Goldenrod's ligatures.

"Goldie, run!"

She bounded for the door, opening it to her freedom. Venom caught her, followed by several constables and clerics.

"It's okay. I'm on your side now," Venom whispered to her as he guided her the rest of the way until she was safe in a constable's arms. Then he charged back toward the outbuilding, but Captain Rollo caught his tunic preventing him from entering.

Blaze and Lace were fully engaged in hand-to-hand combat. They circled around, keeping a safe distance from one another. Lace's sword had a farther reach, giving her the advantage. She lunged at Blaze slicing at his torso. Blaze blocked her next attacks with his blade. He twisted his dagger around the longer blade, catching the dagger's pommel against a weak spot in the sword's blade. The sword fractured flinging its tip uselessly to the floor. Blaze made his move and slashed at Lace's arm, but he missed, as she saw the strike coming and blocked it with the remainder of the sword. Then, she dropped the sword and flung wrist daggers at him, which he dodged easily from years of practice with Dellanie. The daggers thudded into the wall. While she recovered from her astonishment, he darted forward. He backed her into a corner readying his foray. Hatred raged inside of him. All that she had done to him, Venom, Spider, and now Goldenrod screamed for revenge. She scratched at his tunic with nails fit for a cat. She scraped him, but he didn't stop. Lace was disarmed. She pulled out her boot dagger shaking as she pointed it toward him. But he had faced worse opponents, and he was not going to let her get away.

"You're done," he snarled. Lace stabbed at Blaze, but he kept coming. She struck again. There was no feeling of pain or fear; there was only fury and it turned him into a killing machine. She raised her blade up to attack; he blocked it, sending it flying to the side. Lace was defenseless, and, at last, she fell to the floor wailing for his mercy.

"P-please Blaze, spare me. I-I didn't know she was important to you." Blaze was prepared to kill. He raised his dagger, poised to silence her forever.

"Blaze! Stop, please. Blaze!" pleaded Goldenrod.

He turned and looked back at her. She was standing in the door of the shed again, her face pale. Blaze stopped, his arm in mid swing. Lace nodded in agreement, then tried to crawl away in Blaze's moment of distraction.

"We must forgive her. She doesn't know what harm she causes. She needs . . . I don't know the word . . . mind help. All life is important—even hers."

Blaze followed through on the swing, inverting his dagger, and rendering Lace unconscious. He looked at Goldenrod, panting, and wondered why she had returned to this place. He bled from the scratches Lace had given him. She ran to him. He raised a hand, halting her footsteps even though all he wanted to do was to hold her.

"Don't. I can't. She is beyond help. There is an absolute evil here with her, Goldie. Lace nearly took your life. How can you possibly want to save hers?"

She moved closer to him. A large contusion was visible on her forehead. He rubbed her head, moving aside blond tendrils of hair. She cringed at the touch but didn't pull away. She leaned into him and he kissed her temple. Open, shiny wounds circled her wrists, showing where she had pulled against her restraints. He ran his hand over her wrists, looking at her sadly. She wrapped her arms around him and rested her head on his shoulder. She was warm next to him. He could smell the sweet perfume under the musty smell of the outbuilding. She was his and he was hers.

"Because, Blaze, we are all part of this world. Each one of us is worthwhile, from the biggest creature down to the tiniest insect. God . . . er . . . Gods made them all. They are all valued because they all have life. I will not allow Lace to be killed. She can be saved. We shouldn't hate so much. We just need to forgive each other for our past mistakes and judgements." She pulled him to her and held him closer. He closed his eyes, sinking into the smells of her and her undying love. *Forgiveness. Mahdurnian thinking,* Blaze contemplated. *It's completely strange, but she has soothed the fury that I felt before.*". . . And killing is wrong."

He scoffed a bit at her last statement.

The constables rushed the outbuilding. Rollo grabbed Blaze and held him with his arms behind his back. Avery restrained Lace and carried her out of the tiny building to arrest her. Goldenrod stared daggers at Rollo, and she tried to grab Blaze away.

"I have to, Lady Goldenrod. The cleric is coming to assist you—you don't look well. It is abundantly clear who is at fault here, but until someone else verifies it officially with a higher rank, I must do my job."

"If you can see that he is innocent, then why can't you let him go?"

A crowd had gathered and Blaze glanced around for Venom. He kept his head down. Goldenrod ran up to Blaze, reaching for his hand. He closed his eyes; it was futile."I don't care if you think you have to. Blaze saved me from her. Let him go . . . please," Goldenrod begged, pulling Rollo's arms away from Blaze, trying to release him.

"Goldie, don't. He has to. I know that and I'm not happy about it. You are hurt." Blaze spoke to his feet, but his words hit their mark loud and clear. Cleric Lania approached and gently pulled on Goldenrod's arm. Reluctantly, Goldenrod allowed Lania to lead her off, all the while turning to look back at Blaze. He knew that when this was all over Goldenrod would return to her country, Tommik would return to his desk, and Sterling would keep hunting him until his head was mounted on Sterling's wall. The townspeople of Ballardton would know him as the thief that kidnapped the noblewoman and almost ruined the Festival. He could see some of them staring from a distance even now, as he walked, bound by Captain Rollo's restraints. He could hear their cries and ridicule. Of course, Master was nowhere to be seen. Blaze glanced up without moving his head.

Sterling approached."I'll take him the rest of the way, Rollo. I'll make sure he gets back to the constabulary in one piece." Sterling smirked wickedly, looking down his nose at Blaze with his hands on his hips. Rollo raised his eyebrows.

"Sterling, I am more than capable of escorting this young hero to Tommik. I don't need you punishing him further. I know what you are capable of and you will no longer abase him or any other whom you have been entrusted to protect. Avery told me of your unethical practices the other day and I am finally standing up to it. Tommik will be receiving my report, which will be sent to the capital. You will no longer be able to act the king at the constabulary."

Blaze looked up at Rollo, scoffing at his sentiment. To Blaze, he whispered, "I am truly going to make changes here. I promise you." *Right, so you're going to carry the banner of the little green man on the shelf.*

"Eventually everyone becomes complacent, Captain," Blaze said. For the rest of the journey, Blaze kept silent. Rollo didn't press him further as he turned Blaze's last statement over in his mind.

"Rollo! Remove these restraints from the boy. He is not at fault."

Blaze lifted his chin defiantly as Tommik ran down the stairs of the constabulary. Rollo untied the tethers. "You proved me right, boy. I knew that you couldn't leave her to suffer and that you knew who had done this. We just had to follow you. Protecting the children of Ballardton—that's my job. Thank you for your help. Lace is going to be dealt with appropriately. The young clerics are helping to heal her now. You are free to go." Rollo bowed to Blaze, giving him the respect he felt the boy deserved, and Blaze bowed back awkwardly.

"Oh, Rollo, stop that. Let's head over to see the suspect," said Tommik. For the small amount of respect that he showed, the constable earned some of Blaze's admiration. Blaze watched after them. He thought that his time with Goldenrod was now over. His story, he knew, wouldn't make it onto Mason's lips during winter; not that he really cared. He sniffed his tunic. Aside from his own sweat and the dust and mildew from the building, he could smell her sweet perfume. He took immense pleasure in it.

Blaze dilly-dallied as he walked through town. He was surprised that there were few travelers on the road. A soft end-of-summer breeze ran over him and he inhaled more deeply. Autumn was in the air. That meant his birth day was coming soon. It wasn't a special turn-year and it didn't matter. He would be the only one that remembered it. He'd had a very long year, which culminated with him standing up to Jade, fighting a slugslime, and saving a damsel in distress. *Yeah, that is so story-worthy.* He was actually proud of himself, for once in his life. Nothing could ruin this day. Venom bounded up to Blaze as he walked through the center of Ballardton heading down King's Highway.

"Are you okay?"

Blaze chuckled. "Well, let's see. I've done some amazing things lately and I can't even describe them. No one seems to care. Ven—" Blaze began. Venom wrapped his arm around his shoulders, listening. "When it mattered the most, you stepped up and did the right thing. I'm proud of you for that." Venom stood up a little straighter with a bit of pride.

"Yeah, I did. But you do know how Lace is. . . ."

Blaze admitted that he did.

"Oh, thanks for getting Nightshade out of there, too. I told Nightshade she should head north to Barden's guild or something before Lace gives her up." Blaze hadn't considered that.

"What about you, Venom? Are you going to leave? She'll definitely give you up."

Venom smiled.

"Nah, I saw the constables coming while you entered the outbuilding in Nightshade's cloak. Nice touch, by the way. They had been tracking you. I climbed up on the roof, watching everything through a hole in the shingles. I watched the whole fight and when I could see that Goldenrod needed to be pulled out; that's when I went in. The constables took her from me, and then she started insisting that she had to go back in to help you. She is something else, that girl—strong willed."

Blaze stared off dreamily.

"Yeah, she is. I won't see her again, and maybe I should leave, too, because of what Sterling did." Venom pushed his body into Blaze playfully knocking Blaze off course.

"You know you'll never leave here. Remember, you were *born here*—and what did Sterling do anyways?"

Blaze clenched his jaw and the anger showed on his face. "Don't worry, I remember that I was *born here*." Embarrassment crossed his face. "Sterling called me out in front of all of the townsfolk. Called me a thief even." Blaze bit his lip.

"Wow! Nothing could be further from the truth! How dare he!" Venom feigned his disgust. "Come on, Blaze, you've been called worse." Venom pulled Blaze by the arm, forcing him to stop near the tournament grounds. "Just wait, will you?"

"Why? What's wrong? I just want to go back to the guild. I stink and I just need to bathe and bandage up these scratches and where Nightshade got me. Okay?" Venom still held him. He gazed up the road toward the camps, released Blaze's arm, and pointed. Blaze squinted to see. Hende-Li ran with her colorful scarves billowing behind her like wings on a pixie. Spider and Snip ran just behind her at her heels.

"She's here for you." Venom whispered.

Blaze took off in a run. When he met Hende-Li, they embraced in a hug and danced in the middle of the street like they were both back at her tent, without any cares in the world.

"My Little Brother, I am so proud of you! Your brother, who is a bit of an untrusting soul, sent Spider to fetch me. I must hear everything that has happened since we last saw each other." She placed her hand on his shoulder, noticing the small wound from Nightshade's blade. She didn't say a word to him about it. "Come, you must come to the tent. A full meal will make everything right that may feel upside down right now. I have slow-roasted a pheasant just like my dear Odyson does back in Pyrrin. It's fabulous. It is one of my favorites."

"Well, if it's one of your favorites, Big Sis, then I have to try it." Blaze beamed. "Can we all go, even Venom?"

Venom joined the group hesitantly.

"Of course, he can, but if he ever takes my earrings again, I swear, there won't be any food for him." Hende-Li gave Venom the side eye. He raised his hands in front of him protectively and resigned to her rules. Spider stomped up to his brother and stepped on his foot hard.

"You don't do that to my friends, Venom! I wish I was a horse because then I'd know it would really hurt you." Hende-Li put her hand on Spider's shoulder. She knelt down to see him face to face.

"Little Brother, such anger for one so young. Venom was doing what he felt was right. And I know forgiveness, but I don't forget." Spider pursed his lips and crossed his arms, agreeing with everything that Hende-Li said. They both shot a glance at Venom. "Now, my brothers and my sis, let's go back to the tent and celebrate Blaze's heroism." Together, the five of them walked holding hands up the road back to Hende Li's camp.

✦

Blaze woke to another day of Pyrrin incense and perfume. He couldn't imagine anything more perfect than the days that had passed. By day three, Blaze was alone with Hende-Li, she had offered for him to stay as long as he wished. Hende-Li walked up to him when she noticed that he was awake.

"Here, Little Brother, let me check those wounds. The paste should be helping those little healers inside of you to do their jobs and fix you up quickly. Turn so I can see those scratches first." Blaze did as he was told. She removed the bandages from Blaze's chest where Lace had scratched him. "Mm, hmm. Looking better already. I think you can clean that paste up yourself, if you're so inclined. Don't go getting it all over my bed linens," she teased as he sat up. "Now, this dagger wound might take a bit longer as it didn't have any torn edges and it was a bit deep. I cannot believe you wanted to sew that up yourself. Why someone would want to sew up themselves is beyond me."

She pulled off the bandage. Her minute, perfect stitches pulled the skin together. Hende-Li's medical skill was well beyond any in Ballardton. She was pleased with the stage of healing and she prayed over it as she had done since he arrived at the tent. Then she set a new bandage and sent him to go wash up. As he left the tent, his leaving rattled the wind chime that was set up to announce the coming and going of visitors.

As Hende-Li sat alone in the tent, the wind chime rattled again. "What did you forget this time, Little Brother, soap?" She hurried to the back of the tent and grabbed the soap to bring back to him. When she returned to the entrance, however, she was surprised to see the noblewoman standing in the doorway.

"Please excuse the condition, my Lady. I had not expected visitors of your distinction." Hende-Li bowed as she hurried around the tent picking up this and that. As Blaze returned to the tent, he deliberately rattled the wind chime, as it had become a bit of a game. He had anticipated her calling out to him; instead, he only heard hushed voices deeper inside the tent itself.

"Big Sis, is all well?"

His eyes widened when he saw her. She was standing, as were her aunt and Hende-Li. He ran to her and embraced her more tightly than he had ever held anything in his life. Goldenrod hugged him back.

"What are you doing here?"

She smiled, her eyes twinkling. "I found Venom, and he told me where you were. Aunt Eloine insisted that we come." He turned to face the princess, bowing in perfect staffer fashion. Goldenrod held on to him, grabbing his arm lovingly.

"I am sorry for my disrespect, Your Highness."

Eloine approached him and gave him a hug. "You are hurt," she said. "Here, allow me."

Blaze felt the skin mending at her will, lipids and platelets working cooperatively to heal the openings as skin bound to rejuvenated skin and muscle to muscle. After mere moments, the wound was healed by her touch, and the stitches were nothing more than thread on top of his healed skin. Hende-Li could sense the princess' healing and she approached Blaze. She removed the bandage to discover the strings of thread. She brushed them off of his skin.

"All fixed, Little Brother. Couldn't have done it better myself," Hende-Li teased, in awe of the princess' ability. "But I don't believe the two of you came to my tent to do this charity work, now did you?"

"Yes, you are correct, Lady Hende-Li. I am most appreciative of your hospitality." The princess turned to face Blaze.

"Prince Delrik, our entire kingdom, and I are indebted to you for the bravery and courage that you showed in our most desperate hour, when Goldenrod was lost to us. Please accept this small token of our appreciation with this pouch, these clothes, and these boots. If you ever need anything, please do not hesitate to ask, Blaze. Thank you again." Eloine hugged him and he felt like a rag doll. She placed the pouch in his hand. Then she retrieved a bundle of clothes wrapped and tied with silken ribbon. "I do hope you like forest brown. Goldenrod picked it out, probably to match your eyes." Eloine backed away to speak with Goldenrod. Blaze stood, dumbfounded. Hende-Li crossed the room to attend to him.

"You look like a fish who has been removed from the ocean. Go get changed. Show her your appreciation." Blaze returned to the small tent that Hendi-Li used as a washroom. It had the privacy she desired. Scarves decorated it, as did similar decor from her tent. It must be a Pyrrin thing, Blaze assumed—not that he didn't enjoy the privacy himself. He removed his breeches and replaced them with the ones from the ribbon-bound pack. They were folded and Blaze immediately recognized the stitching. There on the hem was Tailor Sito's stitchery signature: a green moon and a blue lake, representing the Spring District and Ceretheena. The fabric was soft and breathable, but suitable for the upcoming autumn. He unfolded the tunic, the same mark. The forest brown was a strange weave that was a mix of brown and green threads. Blaze could see the making of the material at the loom. The sights and smells of Tailor Sito's room were visible in the fabric. It seemed only yesterday that he had been there, but his memory had set aside those days until today.

Blaze put on the tunic. He couldn't believe the custom fit as it snaked around his skin. He ran his hands over it. He looked to the mirror that hung askew in the washroom. Gloves had fallen to the ground and he picked them up. Tailor Sito's stitchery marked the gloves at the heel of the hand. He tore off his own and replaced them, the leather soft as doeskin. His fingers flew into them, making him feel that the gloves were too big. After a beat, however, the gloves closed around his hands matching them to his fit. *Magic.* It made his heart jump excitedly. He readjusted the mirror and then backed up as far as he could without falling through the side of the tent. He could see most of himself. His head was cut off, but he was visible from his torso to his knees. He raised one side of his mouth in a sly grin.

As Blaze approached Hende-Li's tent, he sneaked up without disturbing the wind chimes and grabbed Goldenrod's hands. She was startled until she realized it was him, and she held fast onto him.

She had wanted to kiss him, to thank him for saving her. However, she felt she had to refrain from her normal reactions as she was still just a guest of the Drisanian royals. It was true that Prince Delrik's first wife, Alys, was Goldenrod's paternal aunt which allowed her to receive so many open doors, but none of them were more important than the one that she had traveled from Mahdurna for: to find her own mother, who had disappeared abruptly while she and her brother were at school one day. Her heart raced and she felt her face flush as she thought to tell Blaze the information that had driven her to come and see him one last time. Holding his hand, seeing how he was suddenly so much more than the boy who had helped her at the market or the thief that he was born to, her heart melted.

Hende-Li had approached them both; she handed Blaze a dark green ribbon to contain his hair, and then leaned in to whisper in Goldenrod's ear. Goldenrod nodded, and agreed to follow

Hende-Li out of the tent to the spot where she and Blaze had danced.

"Goldie, it is such an honor to meet you and your beautiful aunt. Please sit for a moment. Do you prefer Mahdurnian? I know it would be easier for you." Hende-Li switched to Mahdurnian. "Goldenrod, you are lucky to find this one. He, like my dear sweet Odyson, is one of a kind. Blaze is one that you can count on. There aren't many men in this world that you can say that about." Hende-Li switched back and forth between languages as she spoke. Goldenrod smiled, looking down at her feet.

"But you are going to leave him now, aren't you? I can tell by your body language. I'd hate to see him hurt again. But you must do what you must do."

Goldenrod looked back at Blaze. Hende-Li was good at reading people, and Goldenrod sighed reluctantly, knowing that this was the time.

She spoke in Mahdurnian. "Thank you. We are going back to Drisana today. I don't want to leave him, but I know his life is here and I could never expect him to live in Mahdurna. I have a crazy neighbor . . ." Goldenrod's voice trailed off. Hende-Li hugged her.

"Little Sis, it is always best to tell him. Tell him what is here in your heart without allowing your head to edit the words. Be selective in how you handle this, though; emotions are hard . . . for everyone." Hende-Li gestured to Blaze to join them.

"Is everything all right?" Blaze queried, seeing that Goldenrod looked forlorn. Hende-Li assured him that everything was.

"I must say that your Goldenrod is the pick of the garden. She is as pretty as you have described, and then some. Beauty is found on the inside instead of the out—though both seem to be beautiful, in my opinion."

Goldenrod blushed from Hende-Li's words. To Blaze, Hende-Li whispered, "Love her as you know her, Little Brother. I'll give you both your privacy."

Hende-Li returned to the princess and they started to leave the campsite with the promise of a quick tour.

"I will be out front waiting for you, Goldenrod. Blaze, thank you again," Eloine remarked as she left, before bumping into the wind chime.

Blaze glanced at Goldenrod. He took her hands into his own. He sighed.

"You're leaving."

Goldenrod gasped and covered her mouth with her hand. Then she looked away and a tear fell from her eye. He gently cupped her cheek and moved her face to meet his. "I can tell. I knew it was a matter of time. Nobody ever stays forever."

He kissed her hands and she fell forward, leaning into him.

"Blaze . . . ," she said, the words choking in her throat. "Blaze, I want to stay . . ."

"But you can't." His heart sank but he couldn't let her feel bad about it. "Besides, you have to leave and I can't follow you to Drisana; that would be crazy." He glanced at her, waiting for a reaction, hopeful that she would disagree. Her silence was answer enough. Words caught in his throat, and he suddenly realized that he couldn't manage the easy, dismissive attitude that he had planned on presenting when this time came.

"I promise, we will see each other again." She enveloped him in a hug. For one fleeting moment, they were together. As she had done previously, Goldenrod initiated the kiss. He kissed her back, but his eyes shot open when he felt her tongue in his mouth. He pulled away at first, and then allowed her intrusion, moving closer to her body. Finally, she pulled away from him and whispered in his ear, "I want you. I have since the first time I saw you, but I have to go. I have to find my mother." Tears welled in her eyes, and he tried to wipe them away. "I will be back for the Festival next year. Will you look for me?" She kissed him again. "I love you and I always will." She turned from him, and as she ran out of Hende-Li's shelter, she was sobbing.

He waved after her, never moving.

"I love you, too."

CHAPTER 24

HORSES AND LITTLES

HURRY UP! We'll miss them. We need to run." Spider desperately sprinted ahead of Blaze, stopping every so often to encourage Blaze to move faster. Blaze was a reluctant participant in this race. A few years had passed and his heart still hurt. He hoped that Hende-Li would return, but his heart sank as he recalled that Odyson had insisted that she stay in Pyrrin for some sort of celebration. He knew it was going to be a long, lonely festival. He had learned that none of the townsfolk would bother him if he was dressed in more upscale clothes. He used the majority of the coin from his reward from the Drisanian Princess for such, and to groom his hair so that it looked much as it had in his staffer days. These small changes made him seem more than just the thief that Sterling had called him out to be.

"Ugh, what's the hurry, Spider? The markets aren't going anywhere. I just want to go back to the big oak. She might come this year."

Exasperated, Spider circled back to Blaze. Blaze misunderstood Spider's return and thought Spider was giving him permission to return to the oak.

"No, wait, Blaze! I want to show him to you! Please!" Spider pulled on Blaze's arm.

"It's just a horse, Spider. It's not going anywhere until after the auction. Horses are either sold at auction or sent to the knacker . . ."

Spider stopped pulling and looked up at Blaze with the most endearing look of despair he'd ever seen. With a sigh to signal his exasperation with Spider, Blaze said he'd continue, and see the stupid horse. If the comment was heard, Spider didn't respond; instead, he smiled and pulled Blaze the rest of the way to the stand.

"There, there he is! Can you see him? He's all black, and look how he shines in the sun! He's beautiful!"

Blaze looked at the horse merchant's stands. There were some decent horses there, and the best were placed up front to entice buyers, but none were black and shimmering.

"I just love him. Don't you love him?"

"I don't even see him! Spider, where are you looking? I see some chestnuts, a sorrel, a dappled gray, but I don't see a . . . oh!"

Snip stood next to a weather-beaten black horse. She brushed its mane with her hand and spoke softly to it. Blaze clenched his teeth, disturbed by the Littles' choice. *Oh, no! They've both fallen for this flea-bitten nag!* Blaze knew exactly where this horse was headed. If the merchant could sugar coat a sale to a buyer or blind them, then maybe the horse wouldn't end up at the knackers, but it would be a long shot. Blaze shook his head at the two children who were petting and pawing over the run-down steed.

"Who's a good boy?"

"You are. Yes, you are."

Snip made kissing noises at the horse. Flies attacked its eyes and an everlasting stream of goo fell out of them. His coat was dull and fleas flew off of it and crawled onto the adoring children.

Blaze looked at the horse with more clarity as he examined the nag with a shopper's eye, stepping back for a better view. *Maybe there is something of value here.* It wasn't that old, but it had been so badly abused that the best place for it might be the knackers, just to put it out of its misery. It made him sad that this horse would end up there, especially given the loving response from both Spider and Snip. But none of that was up to him.

"That's a mighty fine horse, right there."

Blaze scoffed. The children shook their head in agreement with the merchant who approached Blaze from behind. "I've had a lot of interest in that one. He's one of my finest stock." Blaze said nothing. "Not a day over two years, that one. Do you like him?"

The seller picked up Snip and placed her near the poor horse's neck. Spider excitedly tried to climb up until the seller placed him behind Snip. Spider hugged Snip and Snip hugged the horse. The horse breathed hard and repositioned his footing to allow for the slight gain in weight. The seller wiped his head with worry, but continued on about the horse's supremacy.

"Wait, let me stop you right there. I am not buying this or any horse."

The seller furrowed his brow, snatched the two children off of the horse, and confronted Blaze.

"Then what are you doing here? Leave my stall before I call the constables! And stay away from my horses!"

Blaze grabbed Snip and Spider by their collars and guided them roughly away. The two children cried, reaching out for the horse. Blaze jumped in front of them; he couldn't believe the way they were acting.

"Snip, since when did you care about . . . anything, let alone a horse? And Spider, you act like this every year. Get over it. It is going to the knackers—end of story. I'm sorry, but it's true." Blaze stormed off, heading back toward the tree. The two children stood motionless, mouths aghast, tears falling from their eyes.

"Do you really think she's coming back?" Venom climbed up into the big oak and settled on the platform that Blaze had become accustomed to dwelling on. "You're not going to make any coin sitting here."

"Uh-huh. I am staying here. I don't care about any coin. She said she was coming back, Venom. I have never felt this way. I feel like I've been sucker punched, and I'll never be okay again." Venom wrapped his arm around Blaze.

"Love; it just stabs you, right about here." Venom touched the place where Nightshade had stabbed him. The two boys chuckled. "I know. It's hard, but . . . ah, never mind."

"What? No, tell me." Blaze wriggled free of Venom's grasp. "What?"

"Well, it's just . . . um, well, we all think . . ."

"By Eldon! Just spit it out for Gods' sakes!"

"None of us thinks she's coming back."

Blaze stared down at the ground. Venom's words were a confirmation of his own self-doubts. His wealth, or lack of it, was a factor—he should have known. He did, but he couldn't let his heart succumb to what his head already knew.

"I can see your point, Venom, but I need to wait for her. It's like the Gods and Goddesses put us together for a reason. It couldn't be all for nothing."

Venom looked at Blaze pityingly. "Like you're that important to the Gods and Goddesses, Blaze. You're just a small little thief from a tiny guild. You're no more than a speck. For Eldon's sake, no one cares, Blaze. You need to stop thinking this way and start living your pathetic little life. I'm sorry, but it has to be said, Blaze. It just does. That's all. There is no real happiness—just what we fool ourselves into believing."

Blaze said nothing. *Born here. Born to the guild, born to a short life splattered with violence, starvation, and death. Born here. But I don't want to die here.*

"You're right, Venom. They don't care, but I am the one who cares about them. I always have. Eldon's protection has brought me to this spot in my life. Sitting here, waiting for a girl, who I may or may not ever see again. But what I had with her, even for a short while, has been enough to fill me with this longing for her. Can't you see that? Can't any of you see that? Gods help me. It's my life, and I don't have to do anything that you or Master or anyone tells me. I will follow Eldon always. That is a fact that I know is true. How can you deny me any piece of happiness? I would never deny your happiness with Nightshade, if that was what you desired. Friends keep each other's secrets and help them achieve their desires. Venom, are you really my friend?"

"Of course, I am. I've always defended you. Not everyone likes you, Blaze. It might be because of how you tell everyone that they're going to get skewered. Nobody wants to hear that. It's like a Littles' game that you play. Grow up, Blaze. There is a great wide ocean out there that is up for exploring. I want to see that ocean and ride the waves of adventure. Nightshade isn't for me. I haven't seen her since she left. By Her marks, the only girl for me is the wayward sea. I was just playing. The most important people in the world are . . . well, first and foremost: my mom. I know she's out there. We just got separated. Spider is second, and thirdly, believe it or not . . . is you, Blaze. I'd do anything for the three of you."

They sat in silence. Blaze looked out through the trees. Another coach approached. He didn't know how to respond to Venom. The coach turned to follow the road, avoiding the massive tree's trunk. *The Drisanian seal!* The royal coach of Drisana: the same one that had carried Aldric away from the guild. It was here right in front of him. He had waited so long. He froze. He rubbed his eyes, making sure it wasn't just his mind playing tricks. Goldenrod was here. *I cannot wait to hold her again.* He leapt to his feet.

"Where are you going, Blaze?"

"She's here. She's here, Venom. See, Gods know. She's here," Blaze yelled excitedly as he descended from the tree. He jumped out into the highway. He waved to catch the driver's attention.

"Wait! Wait! Please." The coach suddenly came to a halt. The driver looked back at the teenager in the road.

"Are you hurt?"

Blaze didn't answer the driver. Instead, he stood looking at the door with the royal crest staring back at him. The door shook, and with a great deal of force, swung open.

"Blaze! It's you!" Aldric sprang out of the coach, knocking Blaze over.

"Aldric, get off me!" The bright blond-haired boy picked himself up and offered a hand to Blaze. Blaze didn't accept it.

"Look, Silwyn! Eloine! It's Blaze!"

Over the years, Blaze had seen Aldric running about. The boy had gained a little height, more muscle, a healthy glow, and a little round tummy. He hugged Blaze, who pushed him away. Aldric didn't care and he came back in for another hug, grinning at the old game. Princess Eloine of Drisana emerged from the coach followed by Silwyn, who was now fostered to the Drisanian royal family. On seeing Eloine, Blaze bowed. He felt that he couldn't look at the Drisanian princess; he didn't feel worthy, even though their last words had been about how thankful she and Drisana were for his heroism. Her beauty was breathtaking, and he again felt small and insignificant in stature and societal position, but her welcoming expression soothed some of his awkwardness.

"Calm down, Aldric. Get back in the coach. It is good to see you again, Blaze," Princess Eloine greeted him. "Is there anything the matter? I hope everything is well. We still cannot thank you enough for getting Goldenrod back to us." Eloine's voice was soothing and calming.

Blaze glanced inside the carriage, hoping that *she* was there, just hiding behind something. Unfortunately, Goldenrod was nowhere to be found.

"Are you looking for Goldenrod?" Aldric blurted out loudly, causing Silwyn to cover his ears. Blaze glanced away, not wanting to admit it. "She's not here, Blaze! She's looking for her mum. Didn't she tell you that was how she found all of us? Her mum— my aunt—just left her, her brother, and her dad, who's my mum's brother." Eloine glanced back at Aldric. "Okay, I won't say anything more." Aldric slunk down on the bench. Silwyn made a silly face and the two boys instantly laughed.

"Do you need a ride into town, Blaze?" Eloine offered.

He shook his head.

"Please come in, ride with us."

Blaze thought a moment, then climbed into the coach. He sat next to the still-giggling preteens. Across from him, Eloine sat with her twins, Teagan and Tierney. They leaned into their mother. Blaze tried not to look at them because when his eye caught Teagan's, she pouted, and when he caught Tierney's eye, the boy hid his face sheepishly behind Eloine. Trying not to upset them, he focused on the inside of the coach.

The interior walls were painted a deep burgundy, with a tiny repeating pattern of the golden royal crest. The velvet seats were overly plush and surprisingly comfortable. The gentle rocking of the coach was calming. There was a gentle breeze that drifted in and out of the windows, but Blaze couldn't figure out where exactly it was coming from. The boys next to him pushed up against him.

"Are you really looking for Goldie?" Princess Eloine suddenly asked, her voice gentle. Blaze looked down at his feet.

"Ah, maybe." Blaze finally spoke; his voice was small and almost inaudible.

Eloine smiled softly.

"That is what I thought, Blaze. Goldenrod, as Aldric said, has been searching for her mother for some time now. "I honestly do not know when she will be returning to Ballardton. She was quite dispirited over her ordeal. However, I am sure that she will return after she learns more about her mother's whereabouts. Keir will be escorting her to Kamiria when she is ready to return to Drisana."

"Keir's alive? Is Goldie still in Drisana?" Blaze asked, unable to suppress the hope in his voice. "She said that she was coming back this year."

"No, I am sorry, she's back in Mahdurna. She had wanted to see her father, and she will return to Drisana for holiday. Yes, Keir is alive and he still recovering; sometimes, even sprites have a long road ahead of them in the healing process." Eloine took Blaze's hands and through her touch, she channeled her magic to him helping to calm his disappointment. The warm sensation ran up his arms, and he felt his shoulders relax. He glanced at Eloine's young son and then back to Aldric, who smiled broadly when he noticed Blaze's attention. He released his hands from the princess', and the tension returned to his shoulders.

"I see. She's never coming back, is she?" He banged on the side of the coach to get the driver's attention. "Stop! Stop this thing! I want to get out."

Blaze kept banging the inside of the coach, then the roof, hoping to get the driver's attention. As every moment passed, Blaze felt the coach closing in on him. His heart raced and he knew the princess, Aldric, the elf, and the two Littles could hear it just as loudly as he felt it.

"Sit down, Blaze. There is a pull cord," Aldric tried to tell Blaze, who wasn't listening to his former comrade. Aldric tugged on the pull cord, alerting the driver to halt the ride.

"If you are looking for Goldenrod, Blaze, would you come back with us after Festival? You are always welcome in Drisana," Eloine suggested firmly, trying to settle the teenager as she attempted to guide him to a seat. Blaze wasn't coherent in his frenzied state. *I need to get out of this thing.*

"Sit down!" Princess Eloine scolded in her best mom voice.

The horses stopped, and the driver leapt down off his seat to check on the princess. The carriage driver emerged hurriedly from the side of the carriage and yanked open the door.

"What is all of the commotion? Are you all right, Your Highness? Are the children ill?" Blaze tumbled out and took off at his fastest speed. "What is wrong with that boy?"

"Nothing, Kapian. I am sure he was just upset about something that he learned."

Blaze continued sprinting toward the guild house. He rounded the corner and passed the fountain down the side road. The knacker was burning his stock today. The smells irritated Blaze's eyes and nose. He caught sight of the knackerman, leading a donkey-driven cart that held a large animal. The animal was covered by a tarp, but Blaze could see a black tail flowing out from underneath. His mind raced with fear that it might be Spider and Snip's horse. He ran up to the knackerman.

"What is it, boy?"

"Is it . . ."

"Dead? Quite. I just got it from the horse seller. They wanted it out of the marketplace as soon as possible. Bad for business." The knackerman spit chewing tobacco onto the ground. Blaze stepped over the slug of black slime and rounded to the back of the cart. Flies circled the dead animal. He grabbed a portion of the canvas tarp. "Boy, what're you doing back there? I ain't got no time for this. The fire is a-blazing, and I got some work to do!" The small donkey led the cart, which jerked every time the poor creature caught the scent of death. Blaze flipped the tarp over. The tail spilt over the side of the cart and Blaze was relieved to discover that it wasn't Spider's horse. Instead, it was one of the prime horses that had lined the edge of the market.

"Sorry, knackerman. I thought it was somebody I knew. You can bring it to the furnace now."

"Hey, boy! You going to come back and fix that tarp? The flies are a horrendous horde today. Hot, too! And we don't take care of no horse-sprites, boy! Boy!" The knackerman slouched and shook his head, exasperated with the young thief.

"Venom! Venom!" Blaze ran into the guild and down the stairs. "Has anyone seen Venom?"

"No, why?"

"What's the emergency?"

"Do the two of you have a date?"

"Yeah, something like that. Venom! Has anyone seen Venom?"

"Stop your yelling, Blaze. Venom isn't here." Dellanie surprised Blaze by coming up behind him. "You're going to raise the dead and Goddess Hala won't be happy."

"Dellanie, have you seen Venom? I really need to talk to him. It's important. It's about Spider."

"Spider is so cute. He has the largest eyes. He doesn't look anything like Venom. Is he okay?" Dellanie started removing her weapons, which were discreetly hidden under her clothes. She began with her wrist blades.

"Yeah, he's okay. I just need to talk to Venom about something."

"I saw Venom talking to a woman at the horse stall."

"Talking or taking?"

"Definitely talking. There was something magical about that woman, even *you* would've been able to tell that you couldn't take her pouch."

Blaze made a face. Dellanie finished removing her armaments and slid them carefully into a long leather case. She dropped a flap over the blades, rolled them into a bundle, and tied it shut. She tucked it into the middle of her belongings.

There was one blade that she had left out; a dagger with cheap scales on the tang and her name engraved on the blade. She tossed it into the weapon's chest. Blaze had never thought of offering up a dummy knife to the chest. He always added his boot dagger and hoped that no one would take it. Luckily, no one had yet. He prayed every time he tossed it in the chest that it would be safe. Dellanie noticed Blaze's stunned look; she curled her lip into a sly half-smile.

"That one," she pointed at the chest, "is one that I purchased for an ebon, and I got a couple of duplicates at the bladesmith's. It wouldn't cut through broth even on a good day, but it's good for the chest…" She eyed Blaze. ". . .since I've lost a really nice one a while back."

Blaze laughed at the cleverness of Dellanie's replacement and knowing that he did indeed steal her dagger from the chest. Dellanie raised her eyebrows, wondering if Blaze was in a playful mood, or his typical truculent one. He held onto his smile as he considered Dellanie's genius.

"Yes, 'queen of all she sees!'" *Playful.* It had been some time since they had played this game. However, Dellanie didn't have time to play it today, especially not in front of everyone.

"Did you hear what I said about Venom's whereabouts?"

He stared at her for a moment, surprised that she didn't join in their game. Shrugging, he nodded that he had heard her.

He left the guild with renewed purpose.

Blaze found Venom at the market stand. He was holding a bag in his hand. He readjusted the bag and threw it over his shoulder. The bag draped over Venom's shoulder with a ball-shaped bundle bulging out from inside.

"What's in the bag? Is it a dead cat?" Blaze asked as he approached Venom. Venom twirled it back in front of him, easily holding it aloft by the top of the bag.

"Nah, I don't have warts." Venom stuck his hand in the bag and pulled out sugar cubes. "They're for Spider's horse."

"Oh, you know about the horse. Did you buy it?"

"Ceri said that the vendor will only sell it at auction."

"Who's Ceri?"

"She's Spider's friend. She's really nice. Hey, where's your royal caravan? I thought you'd be with the girl. Or did the bird sprite scare you away?"

"She's not here. I'm done waiting. I guess she's not coming back. Sorry that I got mad at you. I just didn't want to hear it, but you were right."

Venom patted Blaze's shoulder. "It's all for the best anyway."

"Come on, Spider and Snip are with Ceri, petting the horse."

The two boys chased each other through the market, in and out of stands, picking up fruit and pouches along the way. Eventually, they ran around the corner to the permanent stands. The taller horses still stood at the front, but in the place of the one that Blaze had seen at the knackers, there was a palomino mare. Venom led Blaze to the children, who were sitting and eating in front of their favorite horse. A woman sat with her legs crossed, handing the children jellied bread. Snip and Spider were deeply engaged in conversation as the older boys approached.

Venom interruped. "Ceri, I'd like you to meet Blaze. He's like . . . I mean, he's my brother, too."

"No, he's not, Slugslime Face! He's my brother!" Snip stood to defend herself.

Venom pointed at Snip. "I can't believe *you* are calling *me* Slugslime Face. You still have green snotty hair. I think *you* have slugslime on your face." Ceri raised her hands to settle the two children.

"It is very nice to meet you, Blaze. I have heard many things about you." Blaze turned away, fearful of the stories she may have heard. He reached for the horse and rubbed its side. Blaze could feel its ribs and felt a kinship with the poor thing. With his eyes on the horse, Blaze mused aloud to those around him.

"How much do you think it'll cost to save him?"

Ceri glanced around Snip to stare at Blaze's back. "I'm not sure, but the vendor mentioned something about some silvers, which would be the most he'd expect. I want all of you to know that this horse is not a horse, but a horse-sprite, or an equisprite."

Blaze turned and glanced at Ceri. All of them were stunned. It was hard to conceive that the weather-beaten black horse was actually an equisprite. *But there was something that drew the two Littles to pinpoint it out of the lot here.*

"Sometimes, they get stuck in one form and cannot return. We can bring him home to the hidden valley, east of Brynmoor. His people would be able shift him back to his other form."

Blaze stood up slamming his fist into his hand, determined. "We need to find enough coin to get this horse . . . uh, equisprite. And we'll bring him home. Let's leave the guild and find a higher purpose. Who's with me?"

Spider rose with enthusiasm.

"Yay!" Snip joined Spider in his celebration.

"I'm in." Venom admitted.

As Blaze became more familiar with Ceri, he realized that Dellanie was right when she said that Ceri was magical.

Blaze was cautious with her. He was annoyed by her open familiarity with the Twins of Light and how she spoke as though they were companions rather than Gods. He took caution, too, when he shouted Eldon's name.

Blaze and Venom collected their combined wealth and still came up with less than a single silver between them. Blaze considered retrieving his gold and other coins that he had tucked away within Master's vault. Ceri did not contribute, as she suggested that this should be their combined effort.

There was time for Blaze to watch Ceri. With the children keeping vigil day and night with the horse, Blaze noticed that she talked to him, and that the horse acted differently when Ceri was near.

Venom, forever the skeptic, had followed Ceri when she left to pray to the Twins, but he always lost track of the woman.

Today was the day. Blaze secured the last buckle on his newly acquired black leather tunic. He was ready. The armor was soft as a newborn lamb and fit like a second layer of skin. He tested it for its flexibility while breathing in the sweet aroma of the leather. It had a strong coat of fence under the boiled leather breastplate, which would protect him during the journey.

The journey—the mission—was to bring the equisprite home. Blaze smiled with thoughtful glee. The excitement of the unknown rose happily inside of him and his heart jumped with exuberance. Nothing could take away this feeling.

He slapped his lap as he rose from a chair. He grabbed his belt and wrapped it securely over his armor. A short-sword rested neatly on his right hip. He reached for the small, dual-edged sword of his childhood. He admired it.

The blade was forged by fire. The fuller snaked up the center of the blade making it lightweight. The pattern of damascus rippled throughout the blade. The edge was flawless aside from one small roll, which he picked at, attempting to pull the metal true. The hilt was much too small for his adolescent hand. However, the pommel's size didn't bother him. He twirled it through his fingers to elegantly switch from forward grip to ice pick grip before sliding it into his bootstrap.

He picked up his kit and placed it in his pouch. He admired himself in a mirror, and the image staring back at him was someone new. Confidence, clarity of who he was shone through the reflection strange to his own eyes. His eyes—he met them—stared curiously back at him. Hazel eyes that knew him—every mistake, every thought, every deed. Maybe they knew what was to come, Blaze pondered with a sense of urgency, but he pulled away from the thought, leaving his reflection within the silver-toned frame.

Leaving Two Realms Inn was easy and he could move freely about in these new clothes. People nodded their greetings as he passed with newfound authority of self. He discovered that he liked greeting people and noticing their responses. As he walked down King's Highway, he continued acknowledging those on the road. He had a new interest in people. The interest was no longer focused on their pouches, but rather on their job or position. He realized that their clothes established that identity, just as his new leather armor established him as more of an adventurer than a common thief.

He found himself at the guild house. The sun set from radiant oranges and reds into pinks and purples. The small, whitewashed building forever remained the same. There would always be someone to stir the pot, someone to serve the watered-down soup, someone to tend the fire, someone to best, and someone to pick on. It didn't have to be him. He had risen beyond his white clapboard birthplace to become more than what his parents had sought.

Eldon would protect him as he lived on the sword's edge of balance between light and dark.

A Little scurried past him. Blaze caught him by the hood, pulling him to a stop. Pleading gray eyes stared up at Blaze, and the Little cupped his hands expectedly. Blaze smiled; the struggle was real for all time. Blaze opened his pouch and removed two items. He dropped the coppie in the Little's hands as he knelt to talk to the boy. Blaze held out the second item.

"Here, take it. It's my kit. It has served me well and it'll unlock your future." The Little stared, wide-eyed, at Blaze for a moment, then snatched it out of his hands, running down the street to the back of the guild house. Blaze waved after him, but the wave was not to the Little.

"Bye, Rhatt. Bye, Dad."

"Oh! There you are, Blaze!" Blaze turned to find Venom, Snip, Spider and the equisprite standing together. "Let's go. We have to meet up with Ceri by the old tree," Venom finished.

Spider moved closer to Blaze and grabbed his hand gently. He glanced up at the taller boy and began to pull the young adventurer along.

"We have to get going," Spider encouraged. "It's time to go."

Blaze glanced back at the building as it slowly receded into his past. He smiled turning back to Spider.

"Okay, Spider. Let's take him on his journey home!"

ACKNOWLEDGEMENTS

This is the place that I tend to overlook because I just want to get into the story and my ADD won't let me read a single word more. But don't fret, dear Reader, if that is your intent. I don't mind if you continue on and choose the prologue first or head right into Part 1. The book in your hand is the one that I have always been distracted with. The one that if there was a book such as this, I may just have been able to read it without having to re-read the same line twenty times to just get the sentence to make sense in my head. When reading becomes difficult or boring, take a break. I am with you, dear Reader, and I understand. Together we will embark into the World of Mirias. I have written this book by parceling it out in parts allowing you a momentary escape. I am not above acknowledging that reading is sometimes a chore, but my wish for you, dear Reader, is that Blaze captures your imagination as he did mine. Therefore, my first acknowledgement is to you. Thank you for taking your time to walk with Blaze.

I would like to thank my husband, John, and my children, Francie, Will, and Patrick, for their understanding, love, and encouragement as I decided to reignite this journey. I love you always. Thank you also for supporting me with my crazy ideas that are more of a stream of consciousness, stories, or even solutions to problems.

Next, I would like to thank my "sissy", L. A., this would never have been possible without your constant companionship and your love of magic, elves, dragons, and all things fantasy. Your joy of reading has been so fierce, and you openly shared these worlds through your lips to my ears all with the hope I would love books just as much as you. I couldn't imagine not having the childhood that our parents allowed us to enjoy without you.

It has taken me some time to find all of my sisters but find you I did. Thank you for all the fun times and serious talks over the years and the many years to come. Thank you to Tina Eggert, Diana Frankforter, Stacey Hobbs, and B. B. Russell. To Tina and B. B., thank you for helping to make the story grow. To Diana and Stacey, thanks for the first reads.

To Leonora Henderson, the real Hende-Li, my Big Sis, my first editor, and my most enthusiastic fan. I couldn't have done it without your undying support, knowledge, and encouragement. Your words have always spoken to me. I hope you enjoy Hende-Li and find yourself within her. You have always been an inspiration for me. You are the most amazing teacher, builder, and person that I have ever known. I am thankful for you and Frank every day.

To my cover artist, Thomas Drew (thomasdrew@gmail.com): your art has captured the essence of Mirias and of Blaze. I know that your art will draw my dear readers in and my words will keep them captivated. You are an incredibly gifted artist, an amazing person, and an absolute friend with a fantastic caring family, who we all adore.

I couldn't have published this novel, without the continued support from these amazing people who recognized the need for Blaze to exist in our world, at this moment: my amazing publisher, Dede Cummings of Green Writer's Press, Steve Eisner of WWC, Ben Tanzer, Marilyn Atlas, Charita Cole Brown, Ken Sherman, Judith Krummeck, Peggy Moran, Amber Griffith, and Trish Lewis.

To my fellow WWC Authors, who I have watched grow and blossom before my eyes as we individually birth these beautiful works into existence: Samantha Howlett, Barbara Newman, Nancie Laird Young, Sue Roulusonis, Elise Von Holten, Jane VanVooren Rogers, and my dear kindred spirit, Beth.

To both of my GWP Editors, Emma Irving and Sarah Ellis thank you. To Emma, my unwavering appreciation to you for helping to improve Blaze in all ways and for seeing it for what it is, as you have helped to shape it into the dark polished novel that I had always envisioned. You pushed me beyond what I thought were my limits and I am forever indebted to you for helping to make this story more engaging, prevalent in today's world, and one that I believe will last the test of time. To Sarah, thank you for your understanding and education of tying words to the world and finding a way to keep my dear readers in the World of Mirias. To

Ferne Johansson, my GWP proofreader, thank you for fine tuning every word and helping to cherry-pick different adjectives to rightly identify the meaning that I had intended and for allowing me time to make any adjustments. To Jackson and Dede, for the timeless layout and your ability to see my vision and make it a reality through your talents. I am above enamored by your choices.

To Rich Avery for your world view and making sure that Pip and Dorken were relevant and not stereotypes. For allowing me also to reach out one last time to discuss Pip's and Dorken's identity in their own handfasting. I thank you for your friendship and for our enjoyable conversations.

For my beta readers and supporters, I cannot thank you enough for investing your time in reading the early version of Blaze or the finished version, or any in between. Thank you, Tim Ringgold, Eric Michael Schrader, Alex Morsanutto, Patrick James Lynch, Dr. James D. Weston, Dr. Michael Lorenzo, Paulette Trowers-Lawrence, Charlotte Natwick, Carolee and Gary Kaylor, Elaine Polsfut, Jamie Young, Meagan Murray, Kristin Hill, Lois Frankforter, Becky Schweitzer, Cindy Goldberg, Ashley Smith, Michaela Salvo, Avery Frankforter, Liliana Russell, Conley Russell, Evan Craig, June and Pamela Lape, Heike Karsch, Jill Fattig, Pat Perkins, Sandy Rabinowitz, Darrell Dublin, Antonio Liguori, Gina Shumilla, Mary Malin, Carolyne Sakonchick, Jim Bulger and the rest of my Calcagni family.

To my HTA family, I will always love you for allowing me to expand my creativity into the classroom and in our school. Thank you also for listening to me as I droned on about my book.

To my wonderful bleeding community, thank you for your support especially Connecticut Hemophilia Society. I would be lost without you all. Thank you for welcoming us warmly.

To Nolan Russell, my young publicist, keep up the good work! It's time to assemble the Knights of Mirias into action!

To Chris Calamita for encouraging me to continue writing and asking for more while we worked. Thank you also for showing me your cartooning and how to draw dragons. To Marshayla Vereen and Sarah Kennedy who happily read parts of the first chapter asking me follow-up questions and wanting to know more. All three of you, have inspired me to continue writing this book. You have always been exceptional people.

To all my students, past, present, and future: thank you for showing me the good in others and how you can achieve your dreams despite any and all challenges.

To all those who kindly listened as I excitedly rambled on about *my book*.

To my *Knights of Mirias*, who are helping to spread the word about the birth of this work encouraging others to join the guild. **If you wish to join the *Knights of Mirias*, head over to my author page on social media or send an email to: worldofmirias@outlook.com.**

Finally, to anyone that I may have accidentally forgotten to mention because, like Winnie-the-Pooh, "I am of little brain" sometimes and am easily distracted, so please don't think it was intentional if I left you off this lengthy list.

Thank you for Joining the Guild!

CPSIA information can be obtained
at www.ICGtesting.com
Printed in the USA
BVHW072150120921
616612BV00002B/10